Carousel Seas

Carousel Seas

Sharon Lee

A Baen Books Original

Baen Publishing Enterprises
P.O. Box 1403
Riverdale, NY 10471
www.baen.com

ISBN: 978-1-4767-3696-9

Cover art by Eric Williams

First printing, January 2015

Distributed by Simon & Schuster
1230 Avenue of the Americas
New York, NY 10020

Library of Congress Cataloging-in-Publication Data

Lee, Sharon, 1952–
  Carousel seas / Sharon Lee.
      pages ; cm. — (Archers beach ; 3)
Summary: "Archers Beach, Maine, in the Changing Land, the last and least of the Six Worlds, where magic works, sometimes, and the Guardian husbands the vitality of the land and everyone on it—earth spirit and plain human alike. Kate Archer, Guardian and carousel-keeper, has been busy making some changes of her own, notably beginning a romantic relationship with Borgan, the Guardian of the Gulf of Maine, Kate's opposite number. But now a former sea goddess sets up housekeeping in the Gulf. She's determined to challenge Borgan's authority—and doesn't care if she endangers Kate and everything she holds precious" — Provided by publisher.
  ISBN 978-1-4767-3696-9 (pbk.)
  I. Title.
  PS3562.E3629C34 2015
  813'.54—dc23
                                    2014038691

10 9 8 7 6 5 4 3 2 1

Pages by Joy Freeman (www.pagesbyjoy.com)
Printed in the United States of America

Many, many thanks to:

Meg Davis, for writing
"Captain Jack and the Mermaid"

Steve Jackson, for being a good sport

Mike Barker, for beta reading par excellence

Archers Beach, Maine, is a fictional town, though it owes portions of its history, coast line, and geography to the communities of Old Orchard Beach, Ocean Park, Kinney Shores, Camp Ellis, and to the Rachel Carson National Wildlife Refuge.

The Chance Menagerie Carousel at Palace Playland in Old Orchard Beach occupies roughly the spot where one would find the Fantasy Menagerie Merry-go-Round in Fun Country at Archers Beach.

The cure for anything is salt water:
sweat, tears or the sea.

—Isak Dinesen

It is not the strongest of the species that survives,
nor the most intelligent, but the one
most responsive to change.

—Charles Darwin

In the Changing Land, a stranger . . .

By ways unseen, she came to the sea.

There, she paused, caught by the murmur of the surf, to over-look the undulating surface, and the drowning reflections of stars.

She had been afraid, but now she was content, with the damp breeze caressing her cheeks, and the whisper of moving water in her ears. Her head felt bright and empty, like a room made ready for a tardy guest.

She breathed in, tasting salt; and sighed, tasting desire.

It was good, the sea.

Yet, for all that it was *a* sea, and good, it was not *her* sea; so much she knew. It was very nearly everything she knew, now that she was free . . .

Free.

She considered the thought, and so recalled a dreary, long expanse of fog: imprisonment.

An imprisonment that had ended without warning; the ties that bound her exploding; ejecting her into a maelstrom of cha-otic forces. She had narrowly escaped dissolution, snatching up what power she might before a sizzling bolt singed her hand, awakening her to danger.

She ran, then; ran for her life.

Ran.

Until instinct brought her to the sea.

Which was not, so said her heart, *her* sea.

No, she thought, gazing out over the breakers, and the white mists rising from their lacy skirts to the stars; this was no sea... no sea...

This was no sea...

...such as she...knew.

She knew...the ways of the sea. Of *a* sea. She knew the silken caress of water against naked skin; the sweet rocking of the waves; the exuberant crash of breakers. The sea...*belonged* to her, and she to it. Neither could thrive without the other.

And, yet...this was *not* her sea.

That certainty burned in the bright empty space of her mind. She felt the truth of it in her soul, even as she longed to step into the waves, to immerse herself, and become one with the waters. Surely...surely even a stranger sea would shelter her?

She stepped forward, until the frothing edges of spent breakers twined 'round her ankles like crystal chains. From... somewhere—perhaps the past?—she heard a keening, and felt a shiver of fear.

But that, she knew, was nonsense. *She* need never fear a sea.

She waded further out, bending to stroke the silken backs of swells.

Power petaled over her skin, soft and damp, smelling slightly of mud. She straightened, the energy she had stolen stirred watchfully at the base of her spine.

From the rolling waters before her rose a woman, yellow-haired, and pale of skin.

"My name is Daphne," she said, and her voice was as fair and as strange as her seeming. "The sea brought your scent to my sister and me. We would make common cause with you."

Common cause? she thought. A seductive swell stroked her waist; she yearned toward it, aching; lost for a moment...

...which would not do. She was at risk here, with her bright, empty head, and her meager supply of power. Sternly, she forced herself to regard the yellow-haired woman, who stood motionless among the moving water. Fair face, and fair words, and the woman *wanted* something from her. There was a slender safety in being needed. Best, then, to learn more.

"What is your cause?" she asked the yellow-haired woman.

Her own voice was high and lilting, like bird song. She smiled to hear it.

Before her, Daphne also smiled, showing the pointed teeth of a goblin.

"Our dominion has been torn from us by a usurper. We would have it back."

Goblins were not trustworthy; she knew that. And yet this tale of having lost dominion . . . resonated. And she knew, though she did not know how—*very well* she knew in what manner to deal with a usurper.

"I am interested," she said, and again the goblin smiled.

"My sister and I offer you safe passage, and our protection, while we explore these matters further," she said.

The sea sealed the promise; she felt it in the busy current, and bowed.

"It is done."

She clasped the white, webbed hand of the goblin Daphne. Her own was long and tan and free of webbing.

The odor of mud grew stronger as Daphne manipulated her magic, binding them together.

"We go now," said the goblin, and drew her beneath the welcoming waves.

CHAPTER ONE

I put my palms flat against the unicorn's gilded saddle, and stepped Sideways. This was the tricky part—well. And not burning down the carousel in the process.

The unicorn, in Side-Sight, was a void, a blankness, nothing but a carved wooden animal, with neither wit nor soul about it.

Exactly what you'd expect, right?

Right. Except if you happen to be looking with wizard's eyes at the Fantasy Menagerie Carousel in Archers Beach, Maine. *Then*, what you'd expect to see in Side-Sight would be two things:

One: a binding spell enclosing the entire animal, woven with interlocking cords of forgetfulness, immobility, and sleep.

Two: the faint red gleam of a soul, ensorcelled and unaware, barely visible between the binding cords.

The fact that this wasn't what there was to be seen by those with the ability to see such things...

...was very, *very* bad.

Which was why I was standing on the carousel at midnight-oh-six with my hands on the unicorn's back, raising just the tiniest, rosiest smidge of power, pinching it off, and placing it into the hollow wooden body.

I withdrew my will, and watched as the mite of power settled into its new home.

5

"Does that," I asked aloud, though without stepping out of Side-Sight, "look convincing to you?"

"You're doing fine, Katie," Mr. Ignat' said from his lean against the utility pole. Let it be said that Mr. Ignat'—the Ozali Belignatious, formally—is my grandfather. He's also my spellcraft tutor. Which means he can run circles around me, magically speaking, and by rights ought to have been the one doing the detail work, except...

...well...it's complicated.

See, until very recently—by which I mean a little under twenty-four hours ago—five of the twenty-four animals and one chariot that comprise the company of the Fantasy Menagerie Carousel had been...prisons. Prisons for people from other Worlds—criminals so badass their own people had given them over to the council of beings called the Wise—sort of an inter-World court of last resort. Who had, in their—dubious, in my view—wisdom bound those criminals into the carousel in the hope—*even more* dubious—that the natural forces at work in the Changing Land would do...something...possibly beneficial to them.

Oh. This place here, that we like to call the Real World? The citizens of the other Worlds call it the Changing Land, when they call it anything at all; the last and the least of the Six Worlds.

So, a little less than twenty-four hours ago, all five of the prisons had been breached, all five of the prisoners unbound, awakened—and freed. After which—and very naturally—they'd run off.

Except the two who were dead; they had just...evaporated.

I'd like to say that nothing about this rather comprehensive mess was my fault, but unfortunately, the only truthful thing I can say is that *not all of it* was my fault.

I'm Kate Archer, Guardian of the Land of Archers Beach, carousel-keeper, and Ozali-in-training. And, no, I'm not making *any* of this up.

"All right, then," I said to Mr. Ignat'. "Onward to step two."

This was the easy part: a simple matter of reweaving the shredded bindings. I had the binding spell down cold, having watched my grandmother weave it every Season and end-of-Season since I was even shorter than I am now. In fact, I'd put the previous set of bindings in place at the beginning of this current summer Season, Gran having been busy elsewhere, and that...was the reason that *I* had to place the decoys. My magical signature was all over the bindings—as it should be. If anyone—no, let me be specific—if any of the Wise happened by and looked with Ozali eyes at the carousel, they would therefore and correctly see my signature everywhere.

That might, according to Mr. Ignat', buy us some time. And there was a chance—granted, a *very small* chance—that whoever was doing the looking would be fooled into thinking the prisons were still occupied by prisoners.

The reason *that* was important is that the . . . let's say, the *major architect* of the jailbreak had been after the liberation of one, specific prisoner. One, specific, *wrongly imprisoned* prisoner. Having recovered that prisoner, his sovereignty, his life, and the life of his recovered lover stood at forfeit, the moment it was discovered that all the prisoners were free.

So, I was covering for a jailbreaker. Say my sense of justice was offended by the imprisonment of an innocent. Hell, say that I was tired of minding a jail, a job I hadn't signed up for—and I was pretty sure Gran hadn't, either. The Wise had just sort of . . . decided that we had volunteered.

The Wise being what they are, it's really better not to protest these little whims of theirs.

Now, it's true that I had no idea why the remaining four individuals bound to the carousel had been imprisoned—and at this point, I didn't care to know. The carousel was dangerous enough, being as it also was the official Gate between Worlds, without the added danger of pissed-off magic-using criminals escaping to ravage the countryside.

I *am* the Guardian of Archers Beach; I take my duty to the land—belatedly, I admit—seriously.

If the Wise wanted a prison, they could damn' well build their own, out 'tween-Worlds someplace.

The bindings were in place. In Side-Sight, the unicorn looked precisely as it ought.

More or less.

"Well done, Katie!" Mr. Ignat' called. "Only four more to go!"

"Piece o'cake!" I said with a heaping tablespoon of false bravado.

Then I walked down the curve of the carousel, to the next empty prison.

CHAPTER TWO

**Monday, June 26
Low Tide 6:16 A.M. EDT
Sunrise 5:02 A.M.**

The hallway was familiar; comforting as only places known from childhood can be. Once, the ceiling had arched far above my head; the walls had been wide enough for myself and Jaron to walk side by side. Now, I walked with head bent, the gold and amber tiles warm beneath my soles; my wings stroking the walls.

For all of that, I walked swiftly, anticipation lengthening my stride. Jaron would be waiting for me in our rooms. Of course he would—had we not bound ourselves, heart, soul, and body, by and before the land and the people of Varoth? We were one in everything—save politics. In that thin realm alone, there existed a difference—for I was Prince Superior, Regent of the Land of Air and Sunshine, while Jaron was Companion and Consort.

The door to our rooms was before me, the tilework gleaming in the subtle light.

The tiles formed an image of a minali tree, indigo flowers nestling in such abundance against soft yellow leaves that the supple white trunks bent beneath the joyous weight of them.

I moved my fingers, calling the door's key from the ether to my hand. I slid it home, turned it, heard the mechanism work...

The door swung open—

Into chaos.

Hangings had been torn from the walls; furniture upended,

books thrown down from the shelves with respect for neither pages nor binding.

Heart in throat, I thrust myself into the ether, crossing the ruined parlor in a single step, coming into our bedroom, where all was orderly, the seductive scent of losterberry yet floating in the air, and a table laid with wine and such delicacies as might please them to share, and in the deep chair next to the table, waiting for him, was...

Not Jaron.

Ambassador Finaskai rose and bowed, wings spread, as if he counted himself my equal.

"My Prince," he said. "I have gifts for you."

He swept up one of the covers on the table, and there, terribly displayed with flowers and sprigs of new plants, as if they were some toothsome delicacy, a feather, a lock of hair, and a small cup of golden liquid that could only be blood.

Horror gripped me—I knew the feather, the curl, the blood. How should I not?

"We have him safe," Ambassador Finaskai said. "Is that so, my liege?"

It was so; I would have known it, had they killed him. I *should have* known it, when they hurt him... but that was for later.

"And you wish him to remain safe," the ambassador continued. "You will rule as my colleagues have long suggested."

Rage roared through me—

—and I woke, gasping, sitting straight up in bed, which, had I been taller, would have earned me a stern meeting with the bulkhead.

Because I was on *Gray Lady*, Borgan's tidy Tancook Schooner, and the man himself was right beside me, breathing deep and even, clearly very much asleep.

Me, I had a feeling that Prince Aesgyr's rage had kind of burned the sleep out of me for the foreseeable future.

I shivered, trying to work the dream—no, *the memory*—out from the front of my head to the back, where I stockpiled the other terrible and desperate events of my life. Not that the memory that had woken me had been mine, exactly...

"Kate?"

I sighed.

"I didn't mean to wake you," I said. "Go back to sleep. I'm going up on deck."

"Bound to be cold up there, this time of the mornin'," Borgan said, reasonably enough. "Snuggle down into the warm and tell me about it, why not?"

"Because you've got to get up in a couple hours to fish, and growing boys need their sleep."

His laugh rumbled in his chest, and I smiled in spite of myself. "I'm thinking I reached my growth a few years back."

"We'd best hope so," I agreed.

"So what woke you? Bad dream?"

"Bad memory—and it didn't even have the grace to be my own." I shook my head. "Borgan, you don't want to hear this."

"Now, that's where you're wrong. I do want to hear it. Snuggle down here and tell me. That's the Varothi's memory plaguing you?"

Obviously, he wasn't going to just go quietly back to sleep, damn the man. I slid back down under the covers and settled my head on his shoulder with a satisfied sigh. Borgan has very satisfying shoulders.

He shifted a fraction, and put his arm 'round my waist.

"So, then..." he prompted.

So, then.

I sighed again, and nestled my cheek against his skin, trying to figure where to start. He already knew that I'd shared *jikinap*—that's magic, to you—with the Varothi prince who had engineered the jailbreak at the carousel. The prince being the wily sort, it seemed as if he had arranged for the sharing of power specifically so he could get my insider's knowledge of the prisoners and the World Gate. That I would also be left richer—if that's what it was—by some bits of his knowledge, skill, and memories hadn't seemed to bother him at all. That neither one of us would, by virtue of the sharing, be able thereafter to give the other the sound trouncing we both clearly deserved, had apparently been perfectly acceptable to him.

That I would immediately report his transgression to the Wise—well, he had my number there, as five bound, empty animals, and Mr. Ignat', could testify.

"I dreamed," I said slowly... "I *remembered* the event—when Prince Aesgyr's consort was taken from him, and the terms of his continued existence—unharmed—were spelled out." I sighed, remembering the Prince's horror, his anger, and his despair...

"He wasn't pleased."

"Guess not. Fixed it, though, didn't he?"

"I don't... think so. I think he's *fixing* it, which is why he took Jaron to Daknowyth, instead of back home to the Land of Air and Sunshine. Something's afoot, but he's not out of the woods yet."

"Took a big risk, then... a couple big risks."

"Maybe not so big," I yawned. "At least Mr. Ignat's happy."

"Old gentleman never did have any fondness for the Wise."

"Well, who could? Hyperpowerful Ozali whose thought processes are just a little idiosyncratic? That sound trustworthy to you?"

Borgan's laugh rumbled in my right ear.

"Not too fond of them yourself, seems like."

"You?"

"I just keep my head down, is all."

I snorted lightly, feeling my eyelids drifting down.

"Best you nap a bit," Borgan murmured, and I felt a tingle, like salt spray over my skin.

"You putting a well-wish on me?" I asked him, sleepily suspicious.

"Would I do that?" I felt his chin nestle against my hair.

"Yes," I said.

And slipped away into a deep and dreamless sleep.

I don't know how such a big man can move so quietly. Or maybe it was the sleep-tight spell that let me snooze right through him getting up and out. Borgan's a fisherman; fishing Mary Vois' boat for her, by agreement. The boat had been Mary and Hum's sole livelihood, all the years of their marriage. Hum'd died almost three years ago, and Borgan's taking over the fishing of Mary's boat for her is, so I gather, some sort of balancing on the part of the sea. Borgan being the Guardian of the Gulf of Maine, like I'm the Guardian of Archers Beach, any such promises the sea might've made would be his to keep.

Well.

I stretched in my nest of blankets, and threw them back, swinging my feet out and down to meet the cool deck.

Time to get doing.

Borgan had left coffee in a mug in the galley for me—still nice and hot with just a smidge of sea magic wrapped 'round to keep it that way.

What he hadn't done, as I discovered when I hit above decks, was leave the dinghy for me to use.

Gray Lady being at her mooring, some distance away from the dock, this presented an interesting problem.

Or did it?

I leaned my elbows on the rail, and looked out over the stretch of sun-spangled water between me and the dock, wondering if I dared.

See, one of the things I'd gotten in the exchange of power with Prince Aesgyr had been the ability to go from *here* to *there* without going in between. Sort of like having your own personal tesseract.

I'd used this new skill three times, more or less by accident. Using magic by accident, as Mr. Ignat' will be pleased to explain *at length,* is—short form—stupid. Magic use and spellcraft are all about control. Just like there's more to firing a gun than pointing it, closing your eyes, and pulling the trigger. You need to have a target, and you need to have the skill and the control to hit the target. Otherwise, you'll hurt or kill some innocent bystander, which will—trust me on this—make you feel like shit.

So, all the best arguments were for getting a handle on this new skill. And practice, as Mr. Ignat' also said, makes perfect.

I considered the placid waters of the Gulf of Maine once more; eying the distance from *Gray Lady*'s deck to the dock.

I should, I thought, be able to do it. If I flubbed, I'd get wet, and be forced to display my less-than-elegant breaststroke to an unsuspecting world. An embarrassing outcome, but by no means life-threatening.

All righty, then.

I straightened, centered myself, brushed metaphorical fingertips over the power coiled at the base of my spine...

And willed myself to the dock.

Nothing happened.

I frowned. Before me, the sea glittered in the sunshine, and the dock—was gone.

I looked down at the weathered boards on which I stood. I turned to look across the water to *Gray Lady,* dancing a little jig at her mooring, like she was laughing at me.

Well, let her laugh, I thought, and looked down again.

"That," I said to nothing more than the air and sunshine, "was slick."

I bounced then, once; skipped to the end of the dock, and jumped down to the sand. Smiling, I turned north, heading up the beach toward Dube Street, and the old house overlooking the dunes.

CHAPTER THREE

Monday, June 26

The *Journal-Tribune* was on the porch when I got home.

I'd had a pleasant walk up the sunny, already-warming-up-nicely beach. The Fourth of July was just a week and a day in the future, and the Beach was starting to fill up with tourists and summer people. Despite the fact that it was well before nine o'clock, people were playing in the surf, while little kids with buckets and shovels and starfish molds were hard at work on architectural sand projects. A pod of teenage boys engaged in a running game of Frisbee broke around me, the disc arcing above my head—"'Scuse us!" one boy called over his shoulder as they thundered down the beach toward the Pier.

I even spied one hearty couple drawing a bocce court in the sand.

Who could doubt that summer had finally arrived?

It wasn't until I was climbing the steps to the porch that it occurred to me to wonder why I hadn't wished myself all the way home, instead of just across the water to the dock.

"Kate," I said, bending over to pick up the *Journal-Trib*, "you lack vision."

Or maybe not; it *had* been a nice walk, and I was feeling mellow and at peace with the universe.

Until I flipped the paper over so I could see what was above the fold.

CAMP ELLIS TO EVICT DUMMY CATS...was the headline— and a shocking one, too. The Dummy Cats—so called because the colony was headquartered in the remains of a former railroad shed that had served the Dummy Railroad—were a Camp Ellis institution. The colony had been established at least fifty years ago, and had been stable for almost that long. The cats earned their keep by holding down the rat population—always a problem in a working harbor—and the whole town pitched in to keep them fed, and housed, and inoculated.

They were warp and woof of the town, as much as any other resident. There was no reason to evict them, unless the town councilors had unilaterally lost their minds.

But it appeared that the councilors hadn't lost their minds. According to the *Journal-Trib*, a new resident—a summer person by the name of Talbot—had taken the cats in dislike. They were unsanitary, he claimed, and unsightly; they scared his wife, hissed at his kids, and were very probably bringing down the value of his summer residence.

He said this and more, loudly, to the townies, who, mostly, ignored him.

Then, he took his grievance to the town council.

In my opinion, the town councilors should've told the nice man from Away to eat his hat, but, in Maine as elsewhere, money talks. In this case, money was talking via big city lawyers who were threatening to bankrupt the town with legal fees unless the cats were destroyed—Option One—or moved—Option Two.

The councilors buckled. To their credit, I guess, they took Option Two.

"So," said a raspy, cheerful voice behind and below me, "still looking for news of a friend?"

I pivoted in place and shook the paper lightly at Peggy Marr, who was renting the basement studio for the Season. Peggy managed the midway; she's almost exactly as short as I am; plump, and fiercely competent. She has a sense of humor that I understand and a soft, gooey interior to balance the tough Jersey-girl exterior. Her fashion sense is...interesting. This morning, for instance, she was wearing pink sneakers to match her pink hair, black jeans, and a black T-shirt with the following message written out in glittery pink cursive: THE TRUTH WILL SET YOU FREE, BUT FIRST, IT WILL PISS YOU OFF. —GLORIA STEINEM.

In case it's not clear, I like Peggy a lot.

"Good morning, Jersey. Cup of coffee?"

"That'd be swell," she said, climbing the stairs. "Seriously, Kate—bad news?"

I handed her the paper and turned to deal with the door.

"Bad enough. Some guy from Away's all offended by the Dummy Cats."

The door opened easily, which it had been doing ever since I let Borgan in. I kind of missed the way it used to stick tight; the flat-footed kick required to get it unstuck had been . . . cathartic.

"Be a couple," I told Peggy over my shoulder, as I turned right, toward the kitchen.

"No hurry."

She leaned against the wall, frowning down at the paper. I got the coffee out of the fridge, started the water running in the sink, and slotted a paper filter into the cone.

Peggy sighed, and took the newspaper into the living room, adding it to the pile of guidebooks and maps on the coffee table.

"This is the kind of guy who gives the rest of us from Away a bad rep," she commented. "Now I know why you folks say it that way."

Peggy being from Away herself, she'd caught the nuance quick. I poured water into the reservoir, set the pot on the plate and hit the *on* switch.

"There's Away and Away," I told her. "The people who come up to Maine because it's empty and unspoiled and like moving back twenty years in time, and who then start agitating for things to be like they are in Baltimore, or New York, or Philly—they're the worst kind. The rest of you"—I gave her a grin—"can't help having been born disadvantaged."

Peggy laughed.

"How'd it go with the cell phone company?" I asked, opening the cupboard to get down two mugs. Peggy's cell phone had been the victim of a tragic accident just recently, and I hadn't seen her since, my own life having taken a turn for the hectic.

"They're sending a replacement, free of charge," she said. "The insurance covered it."

I turned to look at her. "You had insurance on your cell phone?"

"The warranty was still in and the insurance came with," she told me. "You can stop looking at my second head now."

"Sorry," I said. "You want a bagel?" I frowned, counting backward from my last visit to Beach Bagels. "Hang on; I might not be able to make good on that."

I opened the fridge. It was looking kind of white and bare inside. Right. Time for a trip to the grocery store. Good thing today was my day off.

"How 'bout we trade out bagels for scrambled eggs and toast?"

"You don't have to feed me at all."

I straightened enough to look at her over the half door.

"Look me in the eye and tell me you ate breakfast, or that you have any plans at all to eat lunch."

"I'll probably have a smoothie for lunch," she said earnestly. "If there isn't a crowd."

To fill her free time in between managing the midway, Peggy also runs The Last Mango, feeding the world, one smoothie at a time.

"Hey!" she said suddenly. "I forgot you wouldn't know—Felsic's crew really did take care of the stand—you'd never know there'd been a fire."

She hadn't told me, but it wasn't a surprise. Peggy was dating a *trenvay*—Felsic, that was—and practically the whole crew working the midway were *trenvay*. Repairing a wooden booth wouldn't put them in a sweat. The machinery, though...

"I'm down one juicer," Peggy said, as I extracted eggs, cheese, and milk from the fridge, backed out and shut the door with a nudge of the hip.

"That's going to be dicey, with the Fourth coming right up, but the factory says they'll express one, and it should be here in plenty of time."

I started cracking eggs into a bowl. Peggy opened the fridge, and got out cream and what remained of my last loaf of bread.

She poured coffee and cream, and brought the mug with the sunflower painted on it over to the counter where I was working.

"Thanks."

"It's an honor to assist an artist," she told me. "I'll take care of the toast, too."

The muted clang of a buoy bell wafted across the kitchen. I looked up, frowning.

"What the hell?"

"Doorbell," Peggy said, already crossing the kitchen. "I'll get it."

Doorbell? Tupelo House's doorbell was a ragged belling, like hounds giving tongue at the sight of quarry after a long chase. Having once been quarry, and heard the hounds belling behind me, I'd never really bonded with the doorbell.

...which now sounded like a buoy bell.

And why, I asked myself, whipping eggs with a little more vigor than was probably necessary, *does the doorbell sound like a buoy bell now, Kate?*

I sighed, gently.

Because Borgan—who had been forcefully apprised of my feelings in re the bell—had probably fixed it for me. Honestly, welcome a man into the house and right away he starts messing with tradition.

"Kate?" Peggy called from the door. "It's Henry Emerson."

"Henry!" I called. "C'mon in! I'm just about to scramble some eggs. Am I adding some for you?"

"Thank you," Henry said. "I just had breakfast. A cup of coffee would be welcome. I apologize for intruding, but I have the letter here, and time is an issue."

Hell, yes, time was an issue. I'd forgotten about the letter—well, no. I hadn't forgotten about it; the press of other matters had just shoved it to the back of my mind.

"You're not intruding," I said, pouring whipped eggs into the frying pan. "Jersey, get the nice man a cup of coffee. And, hey—take a look at that letter, will you? If it's not a conflict of interest, I'd like your opinion."

Peggy cleared the table and made a new pot of coffee while I read the letter.

"Seems to cover all the points," I said to Henry, and "Thanks," to Peggy. "States the case clearly. I say give it to Jess, and let's start getting signatures." I became aware of the quality of the silence from across the room, and turned my head to look at Peggy, who was standing hipshot against the sink, arms folded over her chest.

"Not?" I suggested.

She sighed.

"I don't bear any particular fondness for Arbitrary and Cruel, but they are my employer, so I gotta be careful, here," she said, slowly. "I don't think I'm telling any secrets if I say that corporate culture firmly embraces the 'most profit for least effort, expense, and upkeep' model of doing business."

"Right. Which is why we're being careful to show them how there's money in it for them by keeping the park open past Labor Day."

"...how *maybe*, if the committee's right that there's a market, there might be some unquantifiable amount of money in it for them, a couple years down the road." Peggy shook her head. "In Arbitrary and Cruel Land, that's tantamount to asking for a loan. Or a raise." She shook her head, came back to the table, and picked up her mug.

"I don't think that letter will make any difference to Management's plans," she said, and drank coffee with the air of a woman who has, perhaps, said too much.

I looked to Henry, who was being patient and poker-faced, because Henry's a lawyer and that's what lawyers do.

"Can't hurt to float the balloon?" I offered. "Worst they can do is say no, like Peggy says."

Henry nodded. "I agree. The final decision, of course, rests with the committee."

That was true enough; I wasn't a decision-maker on this, just a volunteer selected by our chair, Jess Robald, to make sure the letter covered the points identified by the committee.

"It's a good idea, trying to grow the Season," Peggy said suddenly. "Twelve weeks is...really short."

"Used to be longer," I told her, "though I don't think we were ever a twelve-month destination. When my grandmother's back in town, I'll have you over and she can explain how it used to be, back in the good old days."

Peggy grinned. "I'd like that."

"It's a date, then." I looked to Henry. "You want me to take that to Jess? I need to go down to the carousel this morning, and check in with Vassily."

"That would be very helpful, Kate, thank you," Henry said. He put the letter in the center of the table, drank off what was left of his coffee and rose.

"Thank you for the charming company—and for the coffee, which was delicious."

"Or at least better than Bob's," I said, giving him a grin. "Thanks, Henry. Stop by anytime."

"I may avail myself of that." He turned, then turned back, one eyebrow quirking.

"Do you expect your grandmother home soon?"

Henry is Gran's lawyer—and mine—this by way of saying that his question was reasonable on both a professional and personal basis. To the best of his knowledge, Gran had been out of town for a good nine months. Since Henry's also one of those mundane folk who can see the *trenvay* for what they are, and not only hears, but contributes to the making of, fey music at the big Midsummer Eve party, he also knows that Gran is a dryad. And that a dryad *can't* leave town, unless she wants to kill herself and her tree.

The full story of where she was at present, and where she'd been before was complicated, so I opted for the next best answer that would ease an old friend's worry.

"I hope to see her soon," I said, "but I don't have a date."

There was a longish silence while Henry studied my face, his normally soft blue eyes ice-sharp.

I must've looked convincing, because he nodded and sort of smiled.

"I'm looking forward to seeing her again," he said. "Bonny's an old friend." He turned to Peggy.

"Ms. Marr, it's been a pleasure. I hope we'll meet again during the summer."

Peggy smiled. "I'm happy to have met you, Mr. Emerson."

I got up and showed him to the door, thanking him again. Then I watched him walk, carefully, down the steps, gray head slightly bent.

Henry, I thought, with a sudden clarity that made my chest ache. *Henry's getting old.*

I watched him safely to the end of the block before I went back inside, and shut the door.

CHAPTER FOUR

Monday, June 26
High Tide 12:36 P.M. EDT

It was too early for Vassily to be at the carousel, so, after I left Peggy at the Mango, I walked across Fountain Circle to Fun Country, down Baxter Avenue, across the service alley, and deep into Kiddie Ride Land. There I found Jess Robald, not, as I had expected, with her head inside Tom Thumb's temperamental engine, but sitting on the operator's stool, coffee cup propped on the control panel. Her head was bent over a newspaper.

"Morning, Jess," I called, bracing a foot against the lowest rung of the guardrail, and crossing my elbows on the top.

"Hey, Kate! Pretty one, ain't it?"

Jess grinned like she was actually glad to see me—which she probably was, Jess being the kind of person who manages to combine thinking the best of people with being a realist. She got up from her perch on the stool and came over to the rail, folding the paper into thirds as she walked.

"You see the Trib?" she asked, shaking the paper at me. "Moving a buncha wild cats is front page news?"

"They're townies," I said. "How'd you like it if one of the summer people decided carnies were bringing down his property values and petitioned the town manager to have us moved out?"

"Manager couldn't be on the phone to the bus company fast enough, I'm thinkin'," she said with a half grin. "But, c'mon

Kate—what's the fuss? Councilors say they're gonna set 'em up nice in the country—barn, mice, birds, plenty of sunshine and good farm air..."

I sighed. "The Dummy Cats are an established feral cat colony. Camp Ellis is their home. Relocate them, no matter how nice the location, or how far away, and half'll try to find their way back to the Camp. Some'll make it; some'll die. In the meantime, while the cats are away, the rats are going to throw themselves one hell of a party."

"There's that." Jess frowned thoughtfully, and crossed her arms on the top rail. "Best to leave the workin' system in place."

"That's it," I agreed, and pulled the folded letter out of my back pocket.

"Henry Emerson asked me to bring this down to you. I looked it over, like I said I would, and I asked Peggy, over at the midway, to take a look, too. I think it's a good letter that addresses all the points the committee talked about."

Jess cocked a sapient eye. "What's Peggy Marr, who works direct for Management, think?"

"That Management won't be persuaded," I said promptly. "But we've gotta try, Jess."

"Hell, yeah, we gotta try. Though I'll tell you what, Kate—I think we *need* to have the park with us, if we wanna stretch the Season out from twelve weeks. People won't just come for the ocean, 'specially once the weather turns."

"We've got other options," I said, slowly. "There's the new art gallery..."

Jess shifted, and I held my hand up, forestalling whatever she'd been about to say.

"No reason there can't be more destination stores—*like* the art gallery. If we can offer unique shopping, that might tempt the Leaf Peepers to stop at the Beach on their way up-country or down. That means all the stores, plus the motels, and restaurants would have to be on board with staying open longer on spec, but most of them have town roots."

Jess gave me an odd look. "You really think we can pull this off," she said.

I raised my eyebrows. "Don't you?"

Jess took a breath, and let it out on a nod.

"Yeah. Yeah, I do."

"I thought so."

I straightened up from my lean on the rail and used my chin to point at the folded letter in her hand.

"Take a look; see what you think. If it's good, then let's start getting signatures. The sooner we hear back from Management in New Jersey, the sooner we'll know exactly what we've gotta do to make this thing work."

Jess laughed. "Keep talking like that, and I'll step down and make you committee chair."

"No, ma'am!" I said with a grin. "You're the motivator; I'm minion material." I raised a hand. "See you later, Jess. You need me to take a shift persuading signatures out of people, let me know."

"I'll be taking you up on that," Jess said, raising her hand in turn. "Thanks, Kate."

The storm gate was open when I got back to the vicinity of the carousel, and delicious smells were emanating from Tony Lee's Chinese Kitchen. I sniffed appreciatively, but sternly turned my steps toward the carousel. Business before pleasure. Or egg rolls.

A tall, slender figure was at the operator's station, standing straight and easy. Vassily the greenie, that was; I recognized the hoodie, if not the stance. "Greenie" is what we call the summer temp workers the Chamber of Commerce imports from Ukraine and Russia and Poland and other countries. It comes off of "green help," and isn't quite accurate, because we get a fair number of greenies who come back to us, Season after Season.

Vassily, though; he was a true greenie from Ukraine working his first Season at Archers Beach. He is, or had been, morose, and tense from carrying the baggage of a bad past and a recent tragedy. He's devout—at least, he believes in heaven, hell, and angels, which counts as devout with me. And he'd also been touched by Prince Aesgyr, whom he believed to be an angel. Believing that, he'd opened his soul, so the prince could use him as a living gateway into the Changing Land, and have the use of Vassily's body here, if he chose.

In exchange for this, Prince Aesgyr, in his role as angel from heaven, had promised to redeem Vassily's soul, and give him a free pass to heaven when he died.

I'm not an expert on souls or redemption; I have no idea if Prince Aesgyr can come anywhere close to making good on his promises. Though, thinking about it, if any Ozali I'd ever met could, it would be Aesgyr. In any event, I suspected the point was moot, Prince Aesgyr having gotten what he came for. At the very least, though, he had given Vassily...peace. I'd seen it in his eyes yesterday when I'd come in for my shift, and I could see it right now, just looking at his back.

"Morning, Vassily," I said. "How's it going?"

He turned. He *smiled*.

It was the smile of a man with no stain on his soul, and no doubt of his future.

I took a careful breath. That smile made my chest hurt—quiet, deep-rooted joy isn't something you see, up close and personal, every day. Or even every year.

"It is going well, Kate Archer, thanking you. And for you?"

"I'm good, thanks. The new lock working okay?"

"The new lock is very excellent, and I see nothing funny or suspicious when I come to open up." He smiled again. "Nancy already has asked me these questions."

I heaved a deep, theatrical sigh, and turned my hands palm up.

"I'm gonna make Nancy manager, and retire to Florida."

Vassily tipped his head slightly to one side, apparently giving this statement serious consideration.

"I think you will not like Florida?" he said slowly. "You will be away from those things that give you meaning. This beautiful carousel. And Anna. And *this place*." He moved his hands, forming an oblate against the air, possibly intending to encompass all of Archers Beach. Which was more correct than he knew.

It occurred to me to wonder, then, if Vassily'd gotten a dash of knowledge from Prince Aesgyr, too. That worried me for a second, since Vassily obviously fell into the subgroup of those mundane people who can see, and do not fear, the wyrd. It was only a second's worry, though; done was, after all, done. Nothing I could do about it one way or the other.

What bothered me a lot more than the state of Vassily's soul was Prince Aesgyr's long-term plans. All very well to release a being wrongly imprisoned, be he lover or passing stranger. And all honor to him, for granting Vassily that smile of tender peace.

But he *had* to be planning to punish those who had conspired against him. And if he was planning on involving the Changing Land in any part of that—

Okay, *now* my stomach hurt.

"You are not any more good?" Vassily asked.

"A little less than. That's what happens when you think too much."

"Yes," he said wisely. "But you will not go to Florida."

"You got that. Too many bugs, too much sun, not enough snow. I like it fine right here."

I hesitated, because it was a stupid thing to ask, then decided I could afford to be stupid today.

"Do you have everything you need?" I asked Vassily. "You're getting your pay?"

"I need nothing. Samuil receives my pay, to keep it safe on account."

Oh, really? I thought.

"That's nice of him. When will Samuil give you your money?"

"When we are come home," Vassily assured me serenely. "After the agency has its fee."

"Sounds good," I said, which wasn't exactly the most truthful sentence I'd ever spoken. "Well, if you're all set, I'll be getting on with my day."

"Yes," he said. "It is a beautiful day."

"It is," I agreed, and left him.

Two minutes later, I was sitting at the table in Tony Lee's back kitchen, coffee and egg roll to hand, keeping out of Anna's way while she monitored the various foodstuffs in process.

Apparently satisfied with progress, she joined me at the table with her mug.

"What's bothering you, Kate?" she asked.

I laughed.

"Am I that obvious?"

Anna smiled and sipped. "Only to those who love you."

I shook my head. Anna is the nicest person I know—not the sappy kind of nice that's all sweet words and no backbone. Knowing Anna, you just want to *do better*, so you'll be worthy of her faith in you.

"I was just talking to Vassily," I said, breaking open my egg roll. "Asked if everything was going good for him, if he was getting paid..."

"Ah," Anna said softly.

I looked up from my plate and waited.

Anna sipped, her eyes focused somewhere between me and Ukraine, then she sighed and looked at me straight.

"Vassily told you that his pay was being saved for him by the team agent..." She frowned.

"Samuil," I supplied, and she nodded her thanks.

"Yes. Samuil is holding everyone's wages, and Vassily will receive his money when he gets home, after the agency fee has been paid."

"You sound like you've heard this story before," I said. Tony Lee's fed all the Fun Country greenies, and Anna knew each one by name, knew the names of their hometowns, and their siblings. Knew what they cared about, dreamed about, and what scared them. People talk to Anna, that's all. They can't help themselves.

"I have heard this story," she agreed, "and it's troubled me in the past. I talked with Katrina about it. She told me that they're not cheated, and she praised Samuil's diligence in taking care of them, and making certain that their contracts aren't breached." She paused.

"I thought that Katrina might be—getting special treatment, so I talked to Sergei, too. He tells essentially the same story."

Anna produced a smile.

"Katrina has been with the program for the last five years; she told me that this year she is Samuil's assistant. There's increased responsibility, but also an increase in her rate of pay. She's very pleased."

"So you're saying that it's a cultural thing," I said slowly. "That as long as the...arrangements are within bounds, what's to complain?"

"That seems to be it," Anna agreed. "Does Vassily feel otherwise?"

"Vassily seems to feel that Samuil will safeguard his interests and his money, and that he'll get paid when he gets home." I made owl eyes at her. "After the agency gets its fee."

She laughed.

"I think that the agency's fee might get smaller every consecutive year, but that's speculation," she said. "What I do know—what we've both seen—is that they tend to be hungry when they get to us."

"They do," I agreed, thinking of Vassily adding enough sugar to his coffee to make rock candy. "Well. I guess I won't meddle, then."

Anna nodded, and got up to check her cooking. I finished my egg roll and the last of my coffee.

"You need anything in town or around?" I asked, as I stood up and deposited plate and cup in the trash can. "Today's my errand and grocery day."

Anna threw me a smile over her shoulder.

"That's very kind, Kate, but I don't think we need anything right now."

"Right, then," I said, moving toward the back door. "I'll see you tomorrow."

"Take care—and give my love to Andre. You two are going to be so good for each other."

I turned to look at her, but she had her back to me, her attention on egg rolls.

News travels fast in a small town.

I slipped out into the service alley, closing the door behind me and making sure the latch caught.

Fountain Circle was crazy with people, the circle drive itself packed with pedestrians. Summer cops on bikes wove around and between the happy vacationers, and the air rang with talk and laughter.

I smiled in spite of the racket and the press of bodies. It was a good crowd. If arrivals kept up at this rate, we'd be standing room only by the Fourth.

My cell phone vibrated vigorously in the pocket of my jeans. I dodged a family group—mom, dad, and three kids from about fourteen down to rides-on-dad's-shoulder.

"Hello?"

"Kate," Borgan's voice sounded in my ear. I'm embarrassed to say how much pleasure it gave me to hear him.

"Hey, there, Andre—Anna sends her love."

"That's a gift worth having," he said comfortably. "Tell her I'll treasure it."

"I would, but she's up to her elbows in egg rolls and I'm wading through the gridlock in Fountain Circle."

"Tell 'er myself, then, next time I'm by. You free for dinner tonight? We never did get to the Italian place up on Route 1. Way the town's filling up, I'm thinking this evening's our last best chance 'til fall."

I smiled.

"It sounds great. This time," I promised, "I'll remember."

"I'd appreciate it, though you forgetting turned out all right."

"*All right?*" I demanded, since my forgetting our previous date to dine at the Italian place on Route 1 had led directly to the first time Borgan and I had made love.

"Well, what I mean to say is, it was nice."

"Nice! I'll show you *nice*."

"I'll look forward to that," he said, and I heard the laugh in his voice. "I'll pick you up at six, Kate."

"See you then," I said, smiling like an idiot, even after we'd hung up.

CHAPTER FIVE

**Monday, June 26
Low Tide 6:17 P.M. EDT
Sunset 8:27 P.M.**

"That . . . was delicious."

I put my fork down on the plate that had only moments before held a substantial slice of tiramisu. Borgan and I had opted to share dessert—an enlightened decision, considering what had already gone before.

I leaned back in my chair, picked up my cup and had an appreciative sip of really excellent coffee.

"Rest of the meal was nice, too," Borgan offered, with a half-smile.

I eyed him.

"I'm beginning to think that when you say *nice*, you actually mean . . . oh—supercalifragilisticexpialidocious."

Borgan tipped his head as if considering.

"Gotta admit it, Kate, *nice* is a lot less of a mouthful."

"Oh, agreed! But it's a little . . . tepid. An amateur might think you were less than enthusiastic, take her veal saltimbocca and retire, weeping, from the field."

"Hadn't thought of it that way," he allowed, raising his cup to his lips. He drank, and sighed in a satisfied way as he put the cup back in the saucer.

"Being a Mainer, I've got certain traditions to uphold," he pointed out.

"True enough." I finished my coffee, and echoed Borgan's satisfied sigh. That was some *nice* coffee.

"Maybe," I said, meeting his eyes firmly, "we could meet in the middle."

"I'm open to suggestions."

Borgan looked exceptionally fine tonight, in a black shirt with mother of pearl buttons. His braid, hanging casually over his shoulder, looked subtly different; I couldn't decide if he had added another bead or shell to those already woven in, or if he'd oiled the heavy length, or...

"See, now, *nice* seems better'n just nothing," he said, and I shook my head, ruefully.

"Got caught up in the scenery. How about *wonderful*, or *terrific*, or even—*great*?"

"I can try 'em on and see how they fit," Borgan said equitably, and then turned his head to smile at our waiter, who had just arrived to ask us if we needed anything else. Assured that we were in fine fettle, he gave Borgan the check and cleared away the dessert plate, forks, and coffee cups.

"This was a good choice," I said, while Borgan pulled a credit card out of his wallet. "We'll have to come back again, after the Season's over and we can move on the roads again." I hesitated, then added, hearing the note of defiance in my own voice. "My treat."

Borgan looked up from the check folder.

"That'd be...great," he said, and smiled.

Borgan has a red GMC pickup truck with leather seats to die for. I settled happily into the passenger's side, and pulled the seat belt snug.

The fact that Borgan not only owns a truck, but drives it, apparently when and where he pleases, was almost as strange as the fact of Gran's sojourn in the Land of the Flowers, leaving her tree rooted, as it were, in the Wood on Heath Hill. See, *trenvay* are tied to certain pieces of land, or rocks, thickets, or stretches of swampland. Some of the older, and thereby stronger, can leave their own place and wander around town. Gran, for instance, set up housekeeping in Tupelo House on Dube Street. Borgan being the Guardian of the Gulf of Maine, he can apparently range up and down the coast far enough that he found a truck useful.

And I guess, really, it's not all that strange. After all, I left Archers Beach—walked away from my oath and my duty and all the family I had left—and lived for years in the dry lands, employed as a software engineer.

The only thing was that I'd been dying at a pretty good clip, without Archers Beach to sustain me.

"So," Borgan said, snapping his seat belt, "like to go for a ride?"

"That sounds so . . . normal."

"That mean no?"

"It means yes."

"All right, then. Where'd you like to go?"

Well, there was a pesky question, wasn't it? I considered Portland, but I wasn't craving a city. A small ride in the extended twilight, that was what I wanted. Something with a pleasant aspect, that wouldn't take all night. I had plans for a good percentage of all night.

Nice, was it?

"You want to go down Camp Ellis?" I asked. "That's a pretty ride."

"So it is." He started the truck and slipped it into gear. "Give you a chance to stick your nose into the cat business, too."

I laughed.

"I'd be honest and tell you that I'd forgotten about the cats, but I know you wouldn't believe me."

"Might try it; I could surprise you."

He turned right onto Route 1 out of Anjon's parking lot, the truck gathering speed effortlessly.

"Are there"—I said, rolling down the window so I could smell the complicated odors of the salt marsh we were passing through—"are there any other Guardians of the Land, up or down the coast?"

It had never occurred to me to ask the question before, and I sort of wondered why it occurred to me now— Oh. The cats. If Camp Ellis had a Guardian . . .

"Well, now," Borgan said. "There's some. Not so many now as had been, and never were a lot. Off the top of my head: Stonington, Roque Bluffs, Cutler, Barrington"—he threw me a half-amused look—"that's in Nova Scotia. Had been a woman at Surfside, but her folk didn't understand it." He stopped, suddenly, as if he hadn't exactly meant to mention the Guardian of Surfside.

"What happened?" I asked, assuring myself that I just wanted to know, and that I wasn't jealous.

"What happened..." He sighed. "They sent her away, is what happened, by reason that she was crazy. That's what her father said, and signed the papers to put her into a hospital in Portland. When she came home, she might as well have been dead. Married a man her father picked out, had his baby, then...she faded." He shook his head. "Wasn't a drop of harm in that girl, an' her father could never say the same."

He guided the truck 'round a curve, then threw me a half grin.

"Happens Camp Ellis has a Guardian. I'll make sure to introduce you."

"I'd like that," I said, truthfully. Borgan was the only other Guardian I'd met, and his service was different in key ways from my own. "What's her name, the Camp Ellis Guardian?"

"Melusina Cosette Dufour," he said promptly. "But everybody calls her Frenchy."

The public landing parking lot in Camp Ellis was about half full of cars. Borgan pulled into a spot overlooking the little spit of beach and the boats moored in the Saco River. The last, long rays of sunlight kissed it all: gilded the water, turned the sand to gold, and the working boats into the barges and barques of kings. Wood Island Light was precision-cut from shadow, standing tall and black against the rosy sky.

Borgan turned off the truck, and I sighed in simple contentment.

"Did you miss this, when you were out in the dry lands?" he asked.

"I did, at first, all the time," I said slowly, watching the wavelets brush gently against the little beach. "Then, it was like...it was like I convinced myself it wasn't—it had never been—real. Just some place I'd made up out of my head, and it would be stupid to cry myself sick every damn' night because I was missing a place that didn't even exist."

"That's some powerful spellwork," Borgan said, after a moment.

"Powerful stupidity, more like," I corrected. Something moved in the corner of my eye. I turned my head and saw that the door of the red shack to our left had opened, and a stick figure in jeans, flannel shirt and a gimme hat was limping in our direction.

"Looks like the lot man wants his fee," I said.

Borgan turned his head, then popped the door and got out.

"Evenin', Frenchy!" he called.

"Don't you 'Evenin', Frenchy' me, you son of a hake! Where the hell you been?"

I opened my door and jumped to the ground, shutting it firmly before I walked around the back of the truck.

"Been about," Borgan was saying. "Piece o'business took me outta the way for a bit."

"*Piece o'business*," Frenchy repeated. "And what kind of—"

I walked into her line of sight about then, and she stopped her scold to give me a long look out of peat-brown eyes before she returned her attention to Borgan.

"I can see that kind of business might've kept you, all right."

"Be polite," Borgan told her, and stretched out his hand. I took it, and let myself be pulled closer to his side.

"Kate, this is Frenchy, Camp Ellis Guardian. Frenchy, this is Bonny Pepperidge's girl, Kate Archer, Guardian of Archers Beach."

"Pleased to meet you," I said, which was more true than not. Frenchy didn't bother to return the sentiment.

"Archer of Archers, are you?"

"That's it," I agreed, there being no sense to denying it.

"And you're pleased to meet me for why?"

"Because, not counting Borgan, I've never met another Guardian."

She gave a sharp crack of laughter, and smacked Borgan on the arm.

"I like that—*not countin' Borgan*! Oughta happen to you more often."

"Time enough, and I'm pretty sure Kate'll cut me down to size," he answered equitably.

"'Bout time you met your match." Frenchy turned back to me. "So, now you met another Guardian, what d'ya think?"

"I think it's a good thing you started whittling Borgan before I got to him."

That earned me another crack of laughter, then she pushed her gimme hat back up on her head, showing a short, curly profusion of brown hair. I frowned. The sense I had from her was that she was old—her face was gaunt, tanned to leather by wind and sun. I reached for the land to sharpen my senses—and touched something that was...land. It responded to my touch, tardily; I heard a slight fizzing inside my head, as if I'd hit a radio station hovering on the edge of my reception area.

I withdrew my touch, carefully and respectfully—no snatching—
and produced a small bow for the Guardian on whose land I stood.

"Sorry. Habit."

"Don't I know it?" Frenchy said cheerfully. "Used to be I'd get
over to the Pool now and then, to share news with John Lester.
Had the damndest time mindin' my manners. Nature's nature,
is what it is."

The Pool in local parlance is Biddeford Pool, across the river
and east, toward Wood Island Light. So there was another...

"Been gone some amount of time, now, John," Frenchy continued. "And nobody rose up to take his service." She shook her
head, a shadow passing over her worn face. "Still miss 'im. Quite
the man, wasn't he, Cap'n Borgan?"

"John was a fine man and a good Guardian," Borgan said.
"Did just as he ought."

Frenchy turned back to me.

"So, you got specific questions? I'll let you know that I doubt
it—Bonny Pepperidge wouldn't let you outta her sight 'less you
knew how to go on."

"Mostly," I said carefully. "Mostly, I wanted to meet another
Guardian—and now I've done that, *and* met you. If I do come
up with questions—which I'm likely to do because I'm new at
this—it's good to know there's someone I can ask." I grinned.
"Gran's a stickler, but she's not a Guardian."

"Lady o'the Wood; that's damn' close, but I take your point.
Sure, I'll be on standby. Got a cell?"

I did, though I was faintly surprised to find that she did.
We exchanged numbers, and then I said, "Do you mind talking
about the cats?"

Frenchy laughed shortly.

"Why not? Everybody else is talkin' about the cats, like they
just fell down from the moon or somethin'. You'd think a smart
fella from Away'd know enough to leave what works alone, but,
no; there's none o'what you call common sense at home. Trouble
is, while there's some of us who'd partake of a little civil disobe-
dience, there's others of us who want the cats gone, and agree
with Mr. Talbot about how they're a nuisance and a sanitation
issue, though we take care of 'em proper, and all of 'em have
their shots and their records and we get 'em fixed soon's it's safe."

She shrugged, and jerked her head at me.

"You wanna see 'em? C'mon with me."

I looked at Borgan.

"You and Frenchy go on," he said. "I'll just sit over there by the operator's shack and take the parking toll, if anybody comes in."

"Might be one or two yet," Frenchy said, glancing at the sky. "'Preciate it. We won't leave you long."

Frenchy's pace was strong, but not fast; it was easy to keep up with her while we walked toward what was left of the old Dummy Railroad terminal.

"Been talkin' to the cats, naturally," she said. "Most want to stay—well, sure they do; the Camp's their home. Some have relatives in Ocean Park...Saco...down to your own Beach, and they're receptive to the idea of moving where they're more welcome. So, there could be a compromise made. Trouble is, Mr. Talbot's not a man to stint his principles—makes compromise a mite difficult. Joe and Walter—fishing men, they are—might be making some headway in educating him about the rats and the mice and suchlike vermin they might not have down Away in Phillydelfa."

"I think they have rats in Philadelphia," I said, stepping over a length of old rail. "In fact, I'm sure of it."

"Did seem to make sense that there would be, it being a seaport."

She slanted a glance rich with mischief toward me. I raised an eyebrow, and she added, entirely straight-faced, "So I'm told."

"That's pretty good," I said.

"All's it wants is practice. Right 'round on the landside's where it's open. Got some protection from the sea winds, and privacy for their comin' and goin'."

We came around the shed, and paused just short of entering. I sniffed, smelling fur and cedar and brine. It was dim, and I half-reached for the land, remembered my manners at the last second, and brought my hand up, palm cupped.

The power coiled at the base of my spine wakened briefly, and a globe of light formed on my waiting palm, illuminating the murky inside with a soft yellow glow.

"Nice trick," Frenchy said.

"Thanks. I'd hate to have to tell you how long it took me to learn it."

Inside the shed, green and amber eyes caught the light and

reflected it back to me. I could make out maybe ten cats on various levels created by beams, corner shelves, and platforms—somebody had been busy making sure the place was habitable; on the floor were bowls of dry food and other bowls, full of water.

"Is this all of them?" I asked.

"*All* runs to twenty-three," Frenchy said. "Not everybody uses the place; they'll kind of shift in and out as it pleases 'em. They're *cats*, after all. No time cards or sign-out sheets for them."

"They're feral?"

"Some are—there's about eight, nine that don't tolerate people, and barely tolerate other cats. You'll maybe catch sight of their shadows somewhere out on the town, or down the dock. The rest are pretty mellow; they've got no fear of human people—no respect, either," she added, and it seemed like she was making a point to one of the cats inside the shed. "Four of 'em like people, fools that they are. Can prolly place them through the animal shelter, but that still leaves a nineteen-cat problem." She moved a bony shoulder in a half shrug. "Back o'the envelope, call it a fifteen-cat problem, taken as a given that those with connections elsewhere'll move on."

I nodded while I considered the cats inside the shed and they considered me. They were gray cats, mostly, some showing white feet or markings, more short-haired cats in the sample than long. I didn't see any kittens; all of the cats present at the moment were mature enough to take care of themselves.

A shadow moved in the side of my eye, and I turned my head to the right.

The murk parted before him like savannah grass before a lion; a plushy black with a long, plumed tail and a white smudge along the right side of his face, from nose tip to the outer edge of a bright amber eye. He stalked up to me, then paused, staring into my face. His was flat-nosed and broad, his ears notched with past valor.

I looked back at him, carefully not moving.

This appeared to satisfy his sense of propriety. He continued forward, leaned in to weave 'round my ankles once, and went on, out into the old train yard, about business of his own.

"You must be somethin'," Frenchy said, and her voice actually was a little hushed, as if she'd just witnessed an event of no small moment.

"King Cat?" I asked, trying for flippant.

"Near enough. The fishing men call him Old Mister, and even they do what he says."

"Well, then I'm glad I passed muster."

Frenchy gave me a funny look, her eyes squinched together, then said, "Yeah," in a not particularly convinced tone.

I grinned and put my light out, reabsorbing the tiny bit of power.

"I'd best get back to Borgan," I said. "You don't know what kind of mischief he'll get into if he's bored."

Frenchy laughed.

"You're gonna do that man all kinds of good," she said, and led the way back across the yard.

CHAPTER SIX

Monday, June 26
Nautical Twilight 9:49 P.M. EDT

We carried our wine glasses out onto the summer parlor, and stood at the front rail looking over the dunes and the beach and the sea.

The tide had turned and was coming back in, but there was still a lot of sand laid bare, and a fair number of people scattered across it—mostly walking, a good number with their dogs, now that the daily curfew was done. From up the beach, toward Surfside, came the *snap-snap-POP* of cracklers going off.

"Early," Borgan murmured.

"Got to get in shape for the Fourth," I pointed out, though I wasn't a fan of amateur pyrotechnics, myself.

"There's that."

I sipped my wine, eyes on the sweet swell of the waves behind the perambulating figures.

"Pretty night," I said, eventually.

"Is," he said easily. "Take your glass back inside?"

I handed him the empty.

"Thanks."

I heard him move behind me, light-footed, and curled my fingers over the rail, eyes half-slitted, a deep contentment filling me.

It wasn't all that long ago that the view from my apartment window had been of a parking lot and cars parked around a central "garden" that was nothing more or less than artfully arranged boulders and multicolored gravel.

Away is a different country, and they do some very strange things there.

Behind me, a board creaked gently—which he must've done on purpose, so as not to startle me—and then I felt him at my back, big and warm and solid.

"Why *Gray Lady*?" I asked,

"Little bit of long sight. Had a notion a lady was gonna come outta the fog and shake me up some."

"Yeah? How'd that work out for you?"

"It's been nice so far."

I laughed.

"What I meant was—why do you live on *Gray Lady*?"

"Well, after all my time and trouble fixing her up from what Uncle Veleg'd left, I had to do *some*thing with her, and I promised the family I wouldn't sell 'er. Besides, I like living on the sea."

"But you could live *in* the sea," I pressed, not certain where I was going with this, except now that I thought about it, most *trenvay* lived among, or on, or with their particular piece of land, rock, or swamp. Granted, a Guardian wasn't ... exactly ... *trenvay*, but—

"Or, *under* the water. Like a mermaid ... or a seal ..."

"You don't live in the land, do you?"

"Could I?" I asked, momentarily diverted, then I realized what he'd done. Never argue with a *trenvay—or* a Guardian.

"Your gran lives in a tree," he pointed out.

"That's because Gran's a dryad. It's what they do. Besides, mostly she lives here."

"And why's that?"

Damned if I knew the answer to that one. Gran had lived in Tupelo House during all my memory. I'd never thought to ask her why, even though I knew her nature.

"Gran does what she does," I said to Borgan. "She has her reasons, and woe to any fool who asks her for them."

He laughed. "There's that. Takes a steel backbone to deal with Bonny. Well, then, speaking for myself ..."

He paused, the pause stretching out until I was afraid I'd been something far worse than impertinent. Panic clawed at my throat, which was stupid, and I knew it, but ...

"Speaking for myself," he said again, very quietly. "The Gulf o'Maine's my service and my support. I'm her Guardian, but that's a knife cuts both ways. I swore to protect her, and guard her from harm; but, too, it's up to me, to hold her from *doing* harm. Understand some things're just nature; there's no cruelty, or intention, behind 'em. But other things—there's more behind 'em than nature. There's malice, sometimes, because the land hurts her, and she wants to strike back. That's where I reach in an' guard her from hurting herself.

"If I...mingled with the sea, let her wash through my spirit, and surrendered all of me to be part of her—I'd fail my oath, and my Guardianship wouldn't be anything other than wrack and whim."

I felt his hands on my shoulders, warm and comforting, yet somehow conveying the information that he wasn't quite as calm as his voice would have me believe. Slowly, in case it was the wrong thing to do, I leaned back into his chest. The pressure of his fingers increased, and I knew, at least, that it had been *a* right thing to do.

"The Gulf o'Maine, now," Borgan said, still talking as low as if we were hunting tigers. "The Gulf o'Maine's one of the richest and peacefullest pieces of water in all this world. There's a lot of angry ocean out there. A *lot* of angry ocean. Add that into the weather shifting—no malice there, just nature. Science, like they say. Science or malice, though, landfolk are gonna die.

"If I can keep the Gulf alive; if I can keep her peaceful and... *disposed toward* the land...we're gonna need the Gulf o'Maine, all the damn' world of us..."

He snorted, then, maybe a laugh.

"So, long story short, that's why I live on *Gray Lady*, and not with a mermaid under the sea."

No, my evil genius piped up. *Instead he started a relationship with a land woman—a* Land Guardian—*in hope that'll count as another point toward the Gulf's peacefulness toward landfolk.*

I didn't say it; I do know better than my evil genius. Mostly. This, apparently, was one of the less mostly times. My chest cramped a little, thinking it was the Guardian he wanted, not Kate Archer. I took a breath, to ease it, reminded myself that Kate Archer and the Guardian were pretty well inseparable, and leaned my head back until it rested over his heart.

We stood that way for a minute or two before Borgan took his hands away from my shoulders and wrapped his arms around my waist.

"Penny for your thoughts," he said, still soft.

Well. It was lucky for me that I had a second level of thought running under the half-hurt.

"I was thinking that your approach makes sense, Captain, but I'm wondering—how far does familiarity go? When Prince Aesgyr and I shared power, all sorts of conditions snapped into place—including us not being able to hurt each other. Which I'm starting to think might include more than just sympathy for the devil. If, for instance, he comes out of Varoth—*or* Daknowyth—and parks an army right here on the Beach, how much is his influence worth? Is my nature stronger than our . . . bond?"

"That worries you, does it—the sharing?"

"Not the sharing," I corrected. "The *results* of the sharing. In my case, will it be force enough to turn me from my service . . ."

". . . and in my case, will it be enough to hold the Gulf from anger?" His arms tightened and I felt him sigh. "No way to know that, is there?"

This is getting 'way too serious, Kate. You had plans for this evening, remember?

. . . but if I was only his science project, then I wasn't certain my plans were a good idea. I didn't exactly know what I wanted from this new and still fragile relationship, but I was pretty sure I wanted *some*thing. Something . . . ongoing, and . . . steadfast.

I'm not all that good at even straightforward relationships. I didn't think I could begin to handle one in which boy's commitment to his duty drove his wooing of girl . . .

I took a breath, pushed thinking to the back of my mind, and turned around inside the circle of his arms.

When my breasts were pressing into his chest, I put my arms around his waist, and looked up into wary and quizzical black eyes.

"And you say *I* worry too much."

The corner of his mouth twitched. "I try not to let it keep me awake at night."

"That's no good. I *particularly* want you awake tonight."

"Maybe you can give me another reason, then."

"That sounds like a challenge," I said, lifting my hand and running my fingers around his braid. It was heavy and warm and *satisfying* in a way I'm not sure I can even begin to describe.

"How about we play a game?" I said.

"What kind of a game?"

"I'll do something, and you'll tell me whether it's nice, great, wonderful, or terrific."

"Those're my only choices?"

"I don't want to confuse you."

"Fair enough."

My fingers tightened on his braid.

"Ready?"

"Yes, ma'am."

I pulled firmly, and he bent his head in response, while I came up on my toes—and captured his mouth with mine when he came into range.

Some time that I refuse to quantify in minutes or years later, I leaned back, knowing that he wouldn't drop me; watching his face.

"So," I managed, my voice shaking, "which is it?"

He looked thoughtful. "I'm going to kiss your ear."

"No side trips! Make your choice, sir."

"Well, the part where you yanked on my hair, I wouldn't call that *nice*, necessarily. The kiss, that was...you sure about the ear?"

About the only thing I was sure of was that I wanted to kiss him again—ears not being entirely out of the equation—not to mention other things...

"The kiss, that *was* nice," he said, and before I could whip up even a little bit of bogus outrage, he did kiss my ear...and other things...and sometime...later...we went inside and up to the bed.

Sometime *much* later, sated, peaceful, and just about to tip over the edge into sleep, I felt his lips against my ear again, and his voice so soft it seemed like my own thought.

"*Supercalifragilisticexpialidocious.*"

The goblins had offered her every courtesy, welcoming her into the cavern wherein they dwelt, rough fare though it was. Some effort had been made to make the stones more pleasing—sea grass rugs had been lain, and kelp curtains hung, to separate one area from another. There were treasures displayed, to her eye meager, though surely the best that goblins might have.

She had been given food, and drink, and a shelf lined with sea grass upon which to recline. They had observed the courtesies— neither Daphne nor her sister, Olida, asked for her name, her station, or her affiliation. They treated her, subtly, as one of a higher order, yet comported themselves with such dignity as even goblins might attain.

Olida, at least, bore wounds of a recent nature, and hers was the voice most raised in the listing of wrongs set against them by this other, this *Borgan*, who had seduced the sea away from them.

There was some trickery within the narrative, of which she took no offense. They were, after all, goblins; trickery was their nature. Still, this wresting—she thought it not a recent thing, no matter the pains Daphne took to tell the tale wide in certain portions, nor Olida, to obscure the precise course of events.

She had already deduced that this stranger sea was not bound to these, save as a sea is bound to all its creatures. This sea's love—*that* lay elsewhere. Perhaps it lay with the creature *Borgan*, perhaps not. Wherever its present location, whatever its current object, she had decided before the goblins' tale was half done that the love of this sea would very soon be *hers*.

The character of this sea pleased her; there was a calmness in its currents; a certainty of its power; a deliberation, and a pleasing order, in its movements.

Yes, this sea *would be* hers. The goblins were negligible; they would either yield, or they would die. The *Borgan*—*there* might lie a challenge, if only half of Olida's charges were true. The sea itself... that would require subtlety, and sureness, and power. She might manage it—she *would* manage it, but first...

She must reacquire her name, her history, and the full sum of her powers.

From the goblins, she had hidden the extent of her disabilities. The same deep knowledge from which she drew her understanding of goblins counseled her to keep any injury secret from them.

It was the presence of this deep knowledge that gave her hope of a speedy reunion with herself. In the meantime, she listened carefully to the goblins, and put what questions seemed good. Eventually, she allowed it to be seen that she was weary, and somewhat weak in her limbs.

This was, perhaps, a little dangerous, goblins being what they were.

However, she *was* weary, and a little weak; but the goblins needed her, or what they thought she was. In her judgment, they knew as little as she did about what she truly was, but they had made certain shrewd guesses and come to believe that she could be of use to them.

Something stirred in her breast at that thought—outrage, that *she* might be *of use* to goblins!

Ah! How she yearned to learn the truth of herself, and to know whether that hauteur was earned... or a pose.

But Daphne had asked her something—yes: What was her counsel to them regarding a method of attack?

"Sisters," she said, smiling softly, wearily, at them from her recline. "I have heard much to amaze me, and my heart bleeds from your wounds. I wish to counsel you wisely and well. In order to do so, I must think upon all you have told me. If there might be some secluded grotto where my meditations might go forth, undisturbed?"

The goblins exchanged a glance. They were bewildered, perhaps; she did not think they were plotting against her. She had value to them; having given them nothing yet save the courtesy of listening to them.

"There is," Olida said, "a room that might serve, sister. It's further back, and behind these rooms. We'll be here, and will protect you."

"It's not," Daphne said, warningly, "well-appointed—only a grotto, sister."

"All I need is peace and a space in which to float. This grotto sounds as if it will serve well. Might I be guided there?"

It was Olida who showed her the way, and who left her alone, to rest and to meditate.

She spun, surveying the space, and acknowledged that Daphne had spoken truly—it was not well-appointed, being only a small stone cubby, where the currents ran lazy and sweet.

It would do.

She reclined among the waters, her black hair floating gracefully about her. She closed her eyes, and slipped willfully into sleep.

CHAPTER SEVEN

Tuesday, July 4
Low Tide 6:22 P.M. EDT
Sunset 8:26 P.M.

The Fourth of July is the centerpiece of the Season. People had started hitting town in earnest Thursday night, but the real announcement that the celebrations had begun was the triumphant—not to say noisy—arrival of the motorcycles, precisely at noon on Friday, June 30.

The annual motorcycle cavalcade wasn't a town PR stunt, though maybe it should have been. It's the result of a concerted and considerable effort on the part of motorcycle clubs statewide, not to mention those from places Away, like Massachusetts, Detroit, New Hampshire, Baltimore...as well as numerous indie riders.

It's a big show, and a big noise—kind of a foretaste of the formal fireworks on the Fourth—and most people have fun. There are those from other parts of Away who flinch when they see Saracen colors or an Iron Horsemen patch, but, really, you're more likely to have trouble from an unaffiliated kid on his first ride drinking too many beers and deciding to take on the bar than you are from an experienced rider from one of the clubs.

That as was, the bikes arrived at the crack of noon, just as Jess and I were leaving Marilyn's office, having delivered the letter, signed by every owner-operator in Fun Country, with the exception of the log flume's Doris Vannerhoff, who we hadn't expected to sign, anyway.

Marilyn had also done what we'd expected; she read the letter, then told us that the park's open hours and Season length were Management decisions. She promised to fax the letter to Management right away, thanked us for our time, and, if she didn't actually tell us to leave, she did look pointedly at the door.

Usually, you can hear the bikes coming in from 'way down Pine Point, growling and roaring up Route 9, the sound rolling toward town like a thunderstorm coming across the ocean.

Jess and I having been in Marilyn's office, we'd missed the slow reveal, and stepped out onto the midway just as the lead bikes hit the center of town and swept up the long hill of Archer Avenue, toward Route 5.

"Summer's here!" Jess screamed into my ear, and I gave her a thumbs-up before she headed off down Baxter Avenue to reclaim Tom Thumb from one of Donny Atkins' on-loan greenies.

Well, long story short, the town started to fill up, like the people had heard the motorcycles' roar all the way up to Quebec, out to Chicago, and down to the hills of West Virginia—had heard it and come running to Archers Beach, to merge with and be part of the big noise.

By the time the day itself rolled 'round, the noise was a constant underlying roar, drowning out the sound of the sea, muting the racket of the rides and the games, and even the auditory mayhem spilling out from Ka-Pow! Every square inch of sidewalk on Archer Avenue from Fun Country all the way up to Wishes Art Gallery was filled with people. Fountain Circle had 'em stacked three deep, and there were lines waiting at all the rides, and most of the restaurants.

You work a seasonal job in a seasonal town, you don't want to complain about the place filling up with people, but the sheer number of them was the reason that Borgan and I had decided to watch the firework display from the deck of *Gray Lady*.

Even there, though, we didn't completely outwit the crowds; as night came on, and well before the 10:15 posted start time, big boats and little boats began to nose into Kinney Harbor, jockeying for the best position, setting down anchor while folks settled into deck chairs, their voices carrying over the water as they drank their wine or their beer and waited for it to be time.

Borgan made dinner, which we ate up on deck, watching the boats come in and the slow appearance of stars in the darkening sky.

"That was wonderful," I said, helping him carry the plates below.

"Glad you liked it. Was afraid you'd be offended."

I frowned at his back. "Why would I be offended?"

"Well, it being fish."

"I like fish," I said, handing him my load of plates. "Did you think I didn't?"

"Now, it's like this," he said, turning 'round and leaning a hip against the counter. "Back aways I knew a man—lobsterman, he was. And one day his little daughter come to meet us at the dock, and she says to him, 'Daddy, why don't we ever eat lobster?'

"Now, he straightened right up like she'd smacked him, and he raps out, 'Because we can afford meat!'"

I laughed.

"That'll've been *quite* some time ago—lobster's a luxury food now, even in some parts of Maine."

"Well, he was old family lobster; likely his ideas had been formed by his daddy."

"There's that."

We washed up, comfortably. After the galley was shipshape again, he got down his two wine glasses, while I dealt with the bottle.

The cork came out with a satisfying pop, and I looked a question to Borgan.

"Might as well take the whole bottle up. That way, we won't have to move from the comfy seats if we want another glass."

"Is that efficient, or lazy?"

"Efficient," he said promptly, and I laughed again.

He took one step forward, carrying the glasses, frowned slightly, and turned back to open the cabinet and take out a coffee mug decorated with an image of Bug Light.

"Company?"

"Could be. Now I've gotta figure out who gets the mug."

If company was coming, she/he/they/it hadn't arrived while we were below. More watercraft had, though.

"If my legs were longer, I could walk across the harbor on the bows of boats."

Borgan looked out over the accumulated company.

"Is getting a little thick, isn't it? I'd hate to have to try that walk myself, but I take your meaning. Wine?"

"Please."

He poured and we settled side by side into deck chairs. Idly, I wondered where our visitor would sit, when or if they arrived. If *Gray Lady* carried a third chair he wasn't being in any hurry to bring it out.

I raised my glass, "To the land and the sea," I offered.

Next to me, he raised his glass in answer.

"Stronger together than apart."

We drank. I sighed...

...and a high, fretful voice reached us clearly across the water.

"How much *longer*, Grandpa? I wanna see the fireworks!"

"Should only be another couple minutes, Eddie. Now, remember what I told you about keeping your voice down, because sound carries over the water, and we don't want to bother our neighbors."

"But our neighbors aren't here!"

"Sure they are," said a second high voice that seemed older than the first child's voice. Possibly a sister. "Everybody around us on their boats, they're our neighbors, because we're near each other."

Depending on how old she was, that was either a good or a darn good parsing. It probably wouldn't satisfy her little brother, though.

I sipped my wine, listening to other, lower voiced conversations, and watching the stars. It was good and dark by now, and I was starting to enter into Eddie's feelings. When *were* they going to start the show?

It was just about then that I heard a faint plash, as if someone had thrown a beer bottle into the water. I turned my head toward the stern.

"That'll be her," Borgan said comfortably.

"You were certain of me, then?" came a deep, rich voice. A shadow moved in the darkness at the stern, resolving almost immediately into Nerazi, quite completely naked, save the sealskin thrown over her shoulder.

She's a queenly woman, is Nerazi, her skin brown and smooth, her face round, her eyes large and dark and liquid. Her hair is silver, and worn in a single long braid, much like I've taken to wearing my own black, much shorter hair.

"I thought you might stop by," Borgan said. "Mug o'wine?"

Nerazi dropped her sealskin on the deck somewhat in advance of Borgan's right, from which point she would be able to see both of us and the fireworks, if they ever got going.

"Did Princess Kaederon not instruct you in the proper vessel for wine?"

Back some years ago, a lot of people had called me "Princess Kaederon," now Nerazi's the only one. She might just do it to tweak me, though I doubted it. Nerazi rarely does anything for only one reason. It was possible that she wanted to be sure that I remembered that I'd *been* a princess, once, though all of my House is dead, our servants unmade, and our lands forfeit to the enemy who had destroyed us. Who had then been destroyed himself, by my hand, so it was anybody's guess who held the Sea King's honors now in Sempeki, the Land of the Flowers, since the heir-by-blood—that's me—has no intention of returning.

"Ahzie told me it wasn't nice to give a lady her wine in a coffee mug," Borgan admitted, "and he sold me two wine glasses and a bottle of wine and a contraption to open the bottle with. But, see, I never figured to be entertaining two ladies at the same time, so you caught me short-glassed. Other thing I can do is offer a beer."

"Thank you," Nerazi said drily. "I will hazard the mug." She settled cross-legged onto her sealskin and met my eyes. Hers showed red in the starshine.

"Good evening, fair Nerazi," I said, showing off my court manners. "I trust that all of your affairs prosper."

"It is seldom that *all* of one's affairs flourish, my lady, but I have no cause for complaint of my treatment at the hands of the universe."

"Does the universe have hands?"

"Thank you," Nerazi said, taking the Bug Light mug from Borgan, and, "Surely it must, for are we not warp and weave of the universe?"

Fortunately, I didn't have to answer that, because Nerazi raised her mug with great seriousness.

"For those present: joy, constancy, and hope."

The air shivered a little as her words struck, which meant that a true and powerful well-wish had just been bestowed upon us by one of the most puissant *trenvay* I know, period. Borgan might be badder than Nerazi, magically speaking, but Borgan has the edge of being a Guardian.

"How fares your grandmother, Princess Kaederon? Her passings up and down this land are sorely missed."

Nerazi and Gran go 'way back. I'm not sure I want to know *how* far back, actually—but at least I didn't have to dance with the truth here, as I'd had to do with Henry.

"She's entered her tree and is taking healing there. It's the opinion of my grandsire that she has taken a wound to her soul. Sempeki is not . . . kind to souls, and especially to those souls rooted in the very heart of the Changing Land. I hope—but cannot know—that she will emerge soon, and hale."

"That must be the hope of all of us who value her," Nerazi said solemnly. "And your lady mother, does she thrive? She also was struck to the soul in Sempeki, was she not?"

The torment my mother had endured had nothing to do with Sempeki. She'd freely given her soul to the man who had murdered our House, in exchange for my safe passage to Gran. The man who had taken my mother's soul and sinned upon it as if it were his own—he was dead now; my mother's soul was returned to her, and she had the . . . courage, I suppose it is, to have forgiven him. To *pity* him, who had laid waste to Houses and bloodlines not only in the Land of the Flowers, but across all of the Six Worlds. We got off light here in the Changing Land, but we really don't have much for an Ozali to want.

"My mother is frail, but improving. Dancing at Midsummer Eve was a tonic for her."

"Excellent. Her many friends hope to see her soon and often among us." Nerazi sipped wine. "Friend Borgan, you may wish to know that the *ronstibles* have again taken up residence in their natural abode."

I sat up straight, my heart cramping in my chest. *Ronstibles* are sea witches, close enough, and not too very long ago, the pair of them tried their very best to kill Borgan—or at least imprison him indefinitely. He'd managed to elude them, but—

"You told me you'd taken care of them!" I blurted.

Borgan threw me a startled glance over his shoulder, then held out a hand.

"It's okay, Kate," he told me.

I put my hand in his.

"How exactly is this okay? If they're on the loose, they can start hunting you again. And if they catch you, they might not stop at just putting you to sleep this time!"

"Well, see, I can't destroy them—I told you that, remember it?

They're the sea's children; I'm the Guardian. They're just exactly how the sea made them." He paused, his fingers warm around mine. "I could've imprisoned them, but that brings a whole 'nother set of problems. Nerazi and I did sort of suggest that they not come back into Saco Bay, but Saco Bay's their home."

"So, if you didn't kill them, or imprison them, what did you do to make yourself safe from them?" I asked, in what I felt was, under the circumstances, a reasonably calm tone of voice.

Borgan glanced at Nerazi.

"We made it so, besides not being able to directly do me harm, which the sea enforces—Nerazi and I, we made it so they can't touch me; can't come within ten feet of me without being repelled. *That's* written in the Gulf now, wave and water."

"It is also," said Nerazi, "written into the *ronstibles'* souls. *I* made sure of that binding, Princess. The *ronstibles* will break themselves before they are able to place one webbed finger upon Borgan's knee." She moved plump shoulders in a shrug.

"The fact that they have returned to the place they have made their home for a very long time, is not . . . surprising. But it was noticed, and Borgan needed to be made aware." Another sip from the Bug Light mug, which she lowered, her head tipped to one side.

"I believe they are about to begin," she said quietly.

And right on cue came the *thump* of a canister being launched, followed by the bright blooming of a red flower directly over our heads.

CHAPTER EIGHT

Wednesday, July 5
High Tide 6:48 A.M. EDT
Sunrise 5:06 A.M.

The day after the Fourth dawned hot and bright.

Considerably after dawn, I climbed Heath Hill from the Kinney Harbor side, thinking that I'd pay a family visit.

At the top of the hill, I paused and looked up, to the height of land, and the big so-called "seaside cottage" defacing it.

The house had been the property of the local drug lord, one Joe Nemeier. The Maine Drug Enforcement Agency, the FBI and the Coast Guard had caught up with him just two weeks ago, and swept him, all his employees as could be located at the time, and for everything I knew, those who had tried to hide, too, into a tidy net and taken them away. That was fine by me—Mr. Nemeier and I had a problem from the start, and it'd never gotten any better. The opposite, in fact, with him first sending a boy with a knife to rearrange my face for me, as a friendly warning to stay out of his business, and, when that didn't work, a girl with a gun to just plain kill me—which hadn't worked, either, though it had cost me a perfectly good coffee mug.

Looking up at the house, and the empty eyes of the windows overlooking the ocean, I wondered what would happen to it. Anything purchased with the proceeds of illegal drug sales was supposed to become the property of the police, or applicable law enforcing agency. The house, I guessed, was evidence, and in the custody of one of the three enforcing agencies.

Unless they mounted a round-the-clock guard, they were going to have trouble keeping people out of it.

Well. I shrugged. Not my problem.

My problem was sleeping inside a tree at the heart of the Wood at my back.

I turned away from the house, and stepped into the shadow of the trees.

The air was noticeably cooler within the perimeter of the Wood; I hoped that was just an artifact of tree shade and not a marker of the Wood's current mood. The last time I'd been inside, I'd damn' near froze my nose off, *that's* how cool it had been. Of course, the Wood had been through some trying times. I hoped its lacerated feelings had healed over the last few days.

"It's Kate," I said, and tucked my hands into the pockets of my jeans, prepared to wait for however long it took.

But apparently the Wood had recovered its equanimity.

"*Welcome, Kate,*" the voice of the trees whispered inside my ears.

Before me, a path opened between the low growth and the saplings. I slipped my hands free and followed it.

My mother, Nessa, was alone in the glade at the center of the Wood when I arrived. She was sitting on the soft, plushy grass, frowning at the cell phone in her hand.

"Good morning," I said.

She looked up and smiled, putting the cell phone on her knee.

"Katie! It's good to see you."

"Good to see you, too." I crossed the glade and sat down on the grass across from her. "New toy?"

She sighed, and held it out: a prepaid flip phone like Gregor sold.

"It seemed like a good idea at the time, but it's seeming less so, now."

"Just takes practice," I said, and glanced around the glade. It was unusual to find her completely alone; if Mr. Ignat' had already left—for errands or to do maintenance on Keltic Knot, down in Fun Country—Arbalyr, his companion, should have still been in evidence among the branches, mounting guard—and a not inconsiderable guard, at that.

"Father had something to do, and his bird went with him," my mother said, correctly reading my glance. "I'm fine, Katie. The Wood protects me."

"It's not that I doubt the Wood's ability, especially after its recent...display. But I'd rather not have to be cleaning up any lifeless corpses." I shook my head. "It's high Season, down there in the town. Lifeless corpses *can't* be good for business."

She laughed, which made me smile. My mother had come back from the Land of the Flowers nothing more than a wraith, a thought of her former self that a careless breeze might shred. Her sojourn in-Wood had been good for her, if she had energy enough to laugh. In fact, I thought, looking at her as she glanced down to fiddle with the phone again—in fact, she looked not just well, but *very* well. Her pale skin glowed with an inner radiance, and her brown hair was lustrous and silky, the curls as heavy as grapes.

"But you didn't come by to watch me fuss at my phone," she said abruptly, putting the gadget facedown on the grass, and raising her head to smile at me again. "What can I do for you?"

"As it happens, I dropped by because people have been asking about Gran, and when they might see her again."

"Which people?"

"Henry. Nerazi. Me. Possibly the Wise, real soon now."

She shook her head, green eyes twinkling.

"Katie, what have you done?"

I sighed.

"Well, it's more along the lines of what I didn't do, if you want the truth. And what I didn't do was stop a strong, old, and very sly Ozali from busting the prisoners out of the carousel. Worse, when I could have closed the Gate and prevented the escape of the Ozali and the surviving prisoners?

"I let them go."

My mother nodded.

"Good. None of them belonged here."

"Well, that's three-quarters of the family happy, and Borgan, too, but I'm not sure the Wise are going to take that view. I'm not even sure *Gran's* going to take that view."

"Mother *hated* what they did to the carousel," Gran's daughter said, heatedly.

I blinked, then shrugged.

"So, okay, the family and Borgan are pleased. The smart money still says the Wise won't be, and I'd really like to talk to Gran before they come down on me like a ton of bricks."

"Have you talked with Father?"

I laughed.

"Not only have I *talked* to him, he stood by as moral support while I set up the decoy that was his idea. He said it might buy us some time. The word *might* here is making me a little nervous."

"Well, but, Katie, Father's idea of the abilities of most Ozali is rather...elevated. So, if what he said was that your decoy has a *chance* of succeeding, what he *meant* to say was that it has an *extremely high chance* of succeeding."

"If these were just any old Ozali, that would be a comfort," I admitted. "But the Wise?" I shook my head. "They must be sharper than your average—or even your average elevated—Ozali."

"There's that," she said, and gazed off into the trees, chewing her bottom lip, apparently deep in thought.

That gave me a good chance to study her. My first impression of a significant, general improvement in her health and well-being had been spot-on. Mother was positively glowing.

"Dancing at Midsummer Eve agrees with you," I said.

She looked into my face, an arrested expression on hers.

"Certainly, it helped," she said slowly. "But Midsummer Eve was only—the beginning." She reached out and took my hand.

"Katie, I'm..." She hesitated and then laughed, shaking her head. "When I was your age, I'd've said that I'm *walking out* with Andy."

I blinked, remembering the *trenvay* guitar player at Midsummer Eve, with his hot eyes, and the intense, low-voiced question: *Are you home now?*

My mother's grip softened, as if she thought I disapproved, but honestly, who was I to disapprove of anything that made her this happy?

"You guys go 'way back, though, right?" I said, putting my free hand over hers.

"Andy and I were good friends, and we might eventually have set up together, but your father arrived on the Beach, and he was..." She shook her head, and through the land I felt old sorrow, wryness, and a sort of wistful amusement.

"Nathan was quite something: complex, moody, mysterious,

exotic—everything Andy wasn't. I must've inherited some of Father's wanderlust, or I was just too young to value simplicity, straightforwardness, and constancy."

She squeezed my hand, and gave me an earnest look.

"I don't want you to think—I loved Nathan; and I loved Andy, too. It was just that...as I thought at the time, I loved Nathan more. Mother did ask me if I was certain, and of course the instant she asked, I was more determined than ever, though not more certain. Andy never asked me to stay, or pressed me..." She smiled.

"So, I married Nathan, and went back with him to the Land of the Flowers where I had adventures enough to last me for the rest of my life, no matter how long it might be. All that in addition to the marvel who is my daughter."

"For whom you bartered your soul," I said, my voice harsh in my own ears.

"It was what I had," Mother said simply, and squeezed my hand again. "I'd do it again, Katie. If it was needful."

There wasn't really anything to say to that, so I glanced aside, a little embarrassed by the brightness of her eyes.

"Are you angry with me, Katie?"

I looked back to her face, startled. "Angry? How could I be *angry*? I was horrified, frightened for you..."

Nessa laughed.

"Not about that!" she said gaily. "I meant about Andy."

I blinked.

"Hell, no, I'm not angry about that, either! I wish you every happiness, Mother, and if Andy can give you that, then I'm all for him."

She laughed again and released my hand.

"Well, he can't give me *every* happiness, but...happiness enough, and sharing—and music, too!"

"Then I can't find any fault with the man," I said stoutly. "He play anywhere else except private gigs and Midsummer Eve?"

"He plays at all the places in town. Tonight, he's playing at Jay's—seven to one."

"Maybe Borgan and I can stop by after the park closes. It's past time for me to find out what kind of music he likes."

"It's going well with Borgan, then?"

"Yes," I said, hearing the conviction in my voice, and feeling it reflected back to me from the land. "I'm pretty sure he's not simple, or straightforward. To hear him tell it, though, he's as constant as the tide."

"He would say so," Mother pointed out. "Do you trust him, Katie?"

"Yes," I said, and the reflected truth of *that* damn' near knocked me backward.

My mother smiled.

"You'll do fine, then."

I smiled back at her.

"That had better be a well-wish."

"Of course it is."

The day had turned into a scorcher, and night hadn't brought much relief. The only thing that made the proximity of the carousel tolerable was the wind generated by the passing of the animals. With the ride locked down for the night, it was stifling under the roof, and when I stepped out to pull the storm walls together, heat rose in waves off of the asphalt and smacked me in the face.

By the time I had the walls in place and the door closed, you could've wrung me out like a dishrag and hung me over the fence to dry.

I'd just slipped the padlock key into the pocket of my jeans, when I felt a...frisson, like something with a lot of cold feet had marched down my spine. Straightening, I reached for the land, sending a query, and almost immediately receiving the impression of *weight*, somewhere in the darkness to the right; in the space between the carousel and Summer's Wheel.

A weight on the land—mundane folk don't often have much, or any, land magic in their makeup. They pass along and over the land as unremarked as dead leaves dancing across the street on a playful breeze.

Trenvay, though...*trenvay* are tied to the land; they *are* magic; and despite what they tell you in novels, magic has weight, though it shouldn't, according to Mr. Ignat', be a *burden*. Others who are not native to this land of which I am Guardian may also have weight. Specifically, those who possess *jikinap*, such as an Ozali from another of the Worlds might—and those would also weigh upon the land. The more powerful the *trenvay* or the Ozali was, the heavier they would stand.

The person skulking nearby, now...I thought they might be *trenvay* of a certain age and service. Respectable; say, middle-aged. *Possibly* Ozali, but if so, an Ozali new to power.

Whoever it was, they were motionless, as if they had crouched down and were hoping to pass undetected. Another reason I was thinking *trenvay*. I still didn't know all of the Archers Beach *trenvay*, though I was working on it. If somebody decided to take action and meet the Guardian, and then been overcome with shyness...

I'm not particularly scary-looking, but some *trenvay* are so timid, rabbits look heroic in comparison.

So, a timid *trenvay*, come to see the Guardian, now trembling at their own temerity. That was how we'd play it.

Again, I reached to the land, projecting calm welcome, and spoke very quietly, trusting that my voice would carry far enough.

"Good evening. My name's Kate. I'd like to meet you; to learn your name and your service. I guarantee your safety. Nothing will happen to you while you are in my care."

I turned slowly, until I faced the narrow passage, which was, of course, dark as pitch, the utility light having burned out again.

Carefully, I turned my hands palms up, showing them empty and unthreatening.

There was a long moment when nothing happened, as if whoever was checking the level in the courage tank. Then, there came an increase in weight. I smiled, letting my approval flow, even as the land registered a second and far more substantial presence upon it.

I smiled, recognizing Borgan—and then bit back a curse.

The sense of the timid *trenvay* had evaporated.

I thrust my awareness into the land, but it was no use. Whoever'd been waiting was gone.

CHAPTER NINE

Wednesday, July 5
High Tide 7:10 P.M. EDT
Sunset 8:26 P.M.

Borgan shook his head with a sigh.

"Sorry 'bout that, Kate."

"You couldn't have known," I told him, then gave up a sigh of my own. "I just wish I'd gotten a fix on who they were, or where they call home."

"Land don't know?"

I shook my head.

"And you're sure they were *trenvay*?"

"Well, no, not that either. The land's . . . ambiguous; it kinda, sorta half-recognized he/she/it. I figured *trenvay* because of the timidity—even a new Ozali is going to have some 'tude. Well." I reached up to put my arm through Borgan's. "They'll be back, after they've gathered their courage again. What say we go up to Jay's, get a beer, listen to some music?"

"Sounds like fun."

"Then let's do it."

Neptune's, on the Pier, is the big tourist bar, and you bet there'd be standing room only at ten-thirty on the night after the Fourth. Jay's is a smaller place, a restaurant with a bar; tables for maybe forty, and another dozen at the bar.

The music was on the verandah, so said the bartender, and I almost opted out in order to stay in the lovely air conditioning.

"Music?" Borgan said in my ear.

"Music sounds good; hot, not so much."

"Who's playin'?" Borgan asked the 'tender.

"Andy LaPierre," she said with a smile. "He's local. You folks'll really like what he does. Goes the whole range from folk, blues, rock, classical."

"Wanna try it, Kate? I'm betting it won't be so hot on the porch."

"Bound to be cooling off by now," the bartender put in.

I doubted it, myself. On the other hand, live music is one of my more benign vices, and Andy's mix sounded interesting. Plus, I wanted another look at the man, in what you'd call *ordinary circumstances*. Curiosity, that was all. What I'd told my mother was true—if he made her happy, I was a fan.

"Sure; let's give it a try," I said, and nodded at the 'tender. "Can we get something to drink?"

"Whatcha like?"

"I'd like a Shipyard Brown Ale, and my friend would like . . . ?" I lifted an eyebrow at Borgan, who shook his head ruefully.

"Make it two."

The verandah was comfortably full, most of the floor space taken up by insecure little wrought-iron tables; the wall on the restaurant side was lined with booths; the outside with somewhat less insecure-looking tables; the whole area roofed in blue canvas. Strings of patio lights in the shape of dragonflies outlined the canvas and hung from the black iron fence that marked the verandah's outside boundary.

Borgan and I claimed one of the outside tables for our own, sitting side by side so we could see the tiny stage area, which was vacant at the moment, save for a stool, a microphone and a couple guitars on stands.

No sooner had we gotten our chairs situated, than a waitress materialized—blonde hair in a ponytail, white polo shirt with *Jay's Eatery* embroidered over the pocket, black shorts, white crew socks and white tennis shoes showing off a tan so deep I suspected she'd started it in January, at one of the tanning salons up on Route 1.

She was *not* a greenie, but a genuine Maine girl, as we heard when she asked what she could get for us.

I lifted my bottle to show her we were taken care of, drinkwise. Borgan threw her a grin.

"Order o'onion rings for my lady and me to share?"

Her face lit like he'd given her a present.

"Comin' right up!"

"I hope I like onion rings," I said, settling my back more closely against the chair.

"I'm thinking you will. 'Specially if you put ketchup on 'em."

"*Ketchup* on onion rings? You're a barbarian."

"Could be. What d'you put on?"

"Nothing," I said loftily. "The breading and the hot grease need no further enhancement."

"Well, now, if I'd known you was a connoisseur..."

I laughed, and raised my bottle. Borgan did the same, and we tapped them, carefully.

It was, I thought, definitely cooler now; a breeze had come up, smelling of salt and ozone, cavorting under the canvas like a puppy dog. Just the sort of breeze you might expect to come in on the rising tide, I thought, raising my bottle for another sip of ale.

I lowered the bottle and looked at Borgan. He looked back, face innocent.

"Nice breeze," I said.

"Is," he agreed.

"Tide's going out."

He pursed his lips and looked up toward the blue ceiling, like he was trying to remember the tide chart, damn him.

"Now, I believe you're right there, Kate," he said, after taking longish counsel. "Tide *is* goin' out. Should see dead low right about one-thirty."

Before I could kick him, our onion rings arrived—and the lights over the little stage area cycled from white to gold.

I leaned forward as Andy stepped into the light—a thin guy with a bony face, the intense, strange eyes I recalled hidden behind a pair of lightly smoked glasses. He wore a pair of jeans so broke in they must've had nap like velvet, biker boots, and a plain white dress shirt, sleeves rolled above his wrists.

The conversation level dropped noticeably, as people turned toward the stage.

Andy plucked one of the guitars up from its stand, settled the shoulder strap, and propped a lean hip against the stool.

"Evenin'," he said, while his fingers fondled the strings, seemingly at random. "My name's Andy LaPierre, an' I'd like to play some music for you." He glanced up, multicolored dragonfly light sliding across the smoked lenses.

"Now, you might know some of these songs. If you do, and you feel like it, you sing right on along. You can only add to the music; you can't hurt it, and you can't break it. So, now—what d'ya think of this one?"

His fingers moved, quick and clean, the notes achingly pure. "Simple Gifts" was the offering—not a song I would have expected from a guy playing guitar at one of Archers Beach's restaurants. The audience sat quiet, as if the music had pierced them, every one—that included the two guys in motorcycle leathers in the booth across from us, and the family group 'round one of the most rickety tables up front.

He played it through, once, then he looked up, and smiled, and began to sing.

"'Tis the gift to be simple, 'tis the gift to be free.

"'Tis the gift to come down where we ought to be..."

One of the leathered guys in the booth across from us stirred, and sang out the next doublet, in a rasping tenor.

"And when we find ourselves in the place just right,

"'Twill be in the valley of love and delight."

The set was forty-five minutes of the sweetest magic I've ever had the privilege to observe or experience. The songs ranged from the very old—like "Simple Gifts"—to newer folk songs, to classic rock, to old folk songs played like classic rock. Some, the audience sang; some Andy sang alone; some were just the guitar and the shape of the music being woven about us.

I don't remember eating the onion rings, or ordering another round of ale; but those things must have happened—though Borgan could've taken care of both without any help from me.

Andy's fingers were just fooling around on the strings again, letting us down nice and slow.

"I'm gonna take a little break for some supper now," he told us, and smiled a little, adding, "maybe have a beer. Be gone about half an hour, then I'll come back and play for you some more. If you gotta leave before I come back, I want to thank you for sharing the music. Remember that you're not alone, ever; that there's always the music, connecting all of us, and the whole world, too."

His fingers had stopped moving at some point, and the notes had faded away. He stood, racked his guitar and walked off the stage; through the door, into the main restaurant.

I took a deep, deep breath.

"Boy's good," Borgan said, as conversations picked up again around us. The motorcycle guys got up, leaving a fifty-dollar bill on the table across the check. The little family up front began to gather their things together, and the servers were moving among the tables, taking reorders and delivering checks.

I looked at him. "You never heard him play before?"

"Midsummer Eve, mostly. Don't get out much."

"Well, we're going to have to change that."

He brought a mournful sigh up from the heels of his boots, and cast me a soulful look from bright black eyes.

"Oh, you're gonna make all kinda changes to me; I can see that."

"It's only fair," I pointed out, reaching for my bottle. "After all, you've made all kinds of changes to me."

The glance this time was speculative.

"Have I now? What would those be, exactly?"

Well, Kate, you've put your foot in it, I told myself kindly. *What're you going to tell the man that's fit to be said in a public restaurant?*

But that was easy, wasn't it? *The* change, that my mother had seen, so clearly.

"I'm ... I rely on you," I said slowly. "Used to be, I didn't depend on anybody but myself—and not so much, there. I—"

A shadow moved, a chair clattered into position across the table, and Andy dropped into it, putting his beer bottle, his glasses, and his elbows on the table. His eyes were orange—bright, jack-o'-lantern orange, the pupils slit like cat eyes.

"Sorry to interrupt," he said, with a quick glance to Borgan. "I got a notion Kate come to talk to me. If that's so, we'd best get it over and done."

Borgan looked at me, eyebrows up. *Have I been set up?* That might've been the question. I shook my head and turned back to Andy.

"Mother did tell me you were playing here this evening. When Borgan asked what I'd like to do, I suggested coming here, because

I thought air conditioning, beer, and good music would make a cool end to a really hot day."

"Scorcher, wasn't it? And they're sayin' more of the same, tomorrow." Andy turned his head to look at Borgan. "Thanks for the breeze, Cap'n."

"No trouble. I promised Kate it'd be cooler on the porch."

Andy grinned briefly, before getting back to me.

"Kate, did Nessa tell you..." Words seemed to fail him.

"Did she tell me that the two of you were walking out, as she had it? Sure she did."

"And you're...okay with that?"

Why I was supposed to *not* be okay with it was, apparently, a puzzle for my old age. I swallowed my sigh and met Andy's strange, brilliant eyes.

"I'm happy that she's happy. You hurt her, then I'll have a complaint."

It came out sounding more like a threat than I'd intended, but Andy actually looked relieved.

"Hell I'd hurt her! She's been hurt enough. How she carried that—well, I know the answer, there, don't I? Strong and stubborn—always was, always will be. But she's got less to carry now I picked up half." He blinked, looked aside, grabbed his bottle and had a nice, long swig of beer.

"Listen, then, Kate—we're thinking...Nessa an' me're thinking we'll be doing gigs together. Soon's we work up some harmonies. She's got a great voice, and we'd usta sometimes, back before... Well, that's under the bridge, except to know we can do it. Back then, she played hammer dulcimer; she's talking about seeing how rusty she is..."

I frowned, doing a quick mental inventory of the house at the top of Dube Street.

"I'm not sure I can lay hands on that dulcimer—"

Andy waved the bottle, cutting me off.

"No fears. I got it. She gave it to me—when she—before she married your dad. To remember her by." He glanced over his shoulder.

"Almost time for the next set. You'll talk to your gran and Nessa's father? Kinda smooth the way?"

"I imagine my mother will do that," I said drily. "Strong and stubborn, remember?"

He laughed, his face reflecting a sort of wry pride.

"You're right, there; that's exactly Nessa." He grabbed his glasses, slid them onto his face, and stood, bringing the beer bottle with him.

"Thanks for talking to me, Kate. Cap'n Borgan, I apologize for monopolizing your lady's conversation. Let me make it up to you—name a song and I'll play it, first off."

Borgan considered him.

"How 'bout 'The Mary Ellen Carter'?"

Andy might have blinked—impossible to tell behind the glasses. He did throw back his head and laugh out loud.

"Oh, yeah; that'll play fine! Shoulda thought of it myself!"

I leaned on the rail of the summer parlor and looked out over the dunes, and the long stretch of dark beach.

Far away, the waves were nothing but smooth rolls, showing a faint greenish glow just beneath the surface. The air had finally and truly cooled, and a little landside breeze patted my face shyly. As far as I could see, my vision enhanced by the land, the beach was empty. It was, I supposed, late. Borgan and I had stayed through Andy's last set before paying the tab and walking the long way back to Dube Street.

The town was quiet—as quiet as it had been since the motor-cycles had opened the Fourth. If I listened hard, I could hear the band cranking down at the Neptune, and the occasional high scream of laughter.

I took a deep breath of damp, salt-flavored air and sighed it out, absolutely content.

Borgan sighed, too, his elbows resting on the rail next to me.

"That's an impressive bit of work the man does," I said, slowly. "I wonder if it does any good, in the long run."

"Good's a changing tide. Prolly, he does mix things around, here and there. Whether they stay mixed or no—I'm thinking that's outside what he can do. And, y'know, if all and everything he *can* do is lay heart-ease for a couple hours—there's good done enough."

"I guess..." I let the sentence drift off, as my brain went off in pursuit of a sudden, shiny thought.

"Borgan, did Andy...he said he'd taken half of Mother's *burden*. Her only *burden* was what Ramendysis had done to her soul. Does that mean he...*took*..."

"Andy's *trenvay*," he pointed out, and leaned his shoulder into mine. "*Trenvay* don't have much to do with souls in the general way of things."

"But—"

"Likely all they did was share their magic."

He said it so casually, like it was a simple, usual—even a plea-surable undertaking. My sharing with Prince Aesgyr had damn' near killed me, though it might, I thought, trying to be fair, have been different, if there had been anything like informed consent, or something approaching assistance. Then, it might have been... not traumatic. I could see that. Pleasurable, though...

I cleared my throat.

"Mother doesn't have any power. I offered her some of my *jikinap*, and she turned it down. Said it would eat her."

"Might be true, given the Big Magic's nature," Borgan conceded. "But she's got her magic, don't she? Just like all *trenvay*?"

I'd never actually thought of that. What *was* the child of the union of an Ozali from the Land of the Flowers and a dryad of the Changing Land? Surely, she was... not mundane. But, unlike every *trenvay*—and Guardian—I knew, Nessa had no service, no one place that rooted and nourished her; the source of her magic; intertwined with and informing her life...

Rather, it seemed she was able to take nourishment from any that offered. It was how she had survived in the Land of the Flowers, after Ramendysis had ravished and all but destroyed her. The plants in the garden of what had been our house—the plants had loved her; they had taken her in, and hidden her; nourished her and kept her alive.

"I'll accept your theory as a theory," I told Borgan. I cleared my throat, remembering my mother's look of radiant health...

"So, she and Andy... merged..." I broke off, shivering in hor-ror, the stink of peaches clogging my nose.

Borgan looked down at me, his eyes glinting in the darkness.

"You not as okay with this as you thought?"

I swallowed, and breathed in, banishing the remembered odor of peach with good sea air.

He's making her happy, I reminded myself. *He eased her pain and brought her closer, if not all the way, to full health.*

"I—It just seems... sudden," I said. "And irrevocable."

"You heard what the boy said. The music's all around and in us, too. You can't break it."

"And you can't escape it," I said, more sharply than I had intended.

I felt Borgan flinch, like I'd dealt him a sharp slap on the ear.

"Most people," he said, after a pause. "Most people, they share magic, it's a good thing. It...enriches both; it increases understanding. There's no wishin' for something like *escape*. Be like trying to run away from yourself."

Which, for the record, I had done. Also? It's a really short-term solution. Still, not getting entangled in the first place seemed the best bet.

"If you say so," I told Borgan, dubiously.

"Listen, Kate..."

His voice faded, and he sat down, suddenly, on the deck.

Fear, abrupt and icy, struck, and I dropped to my knees, my hand over his heart, calling the land, in case—

"Borgan?"

He put his hand over mine and held it where it was. I could feel his heart beating, strong and steady, like the waves. The land reported health, and strength, and a solid, pleasant weight upon it.

"You okay?" I asked, anyway.

"Hope to be." He raised his other hand, and touched my lips, gently, with his fingertips. Then he released me, and settled his back against the spindles. "Come give us a snuggle."

I don't know much about it, from personal experience, but my opinion is that Borgan's a world-class snuggler; I got myself onto his lap, leaned into his chest, and put my arms around his waist.

"That's nice," he said, and I heard his voice rumble under my ear. He sighed, and put his arms around me; resting his chin on the top of my head.

"Listen, Kate. You know I won't hurt you or do anything you wouldn't like?"

"'Course I do."

"And why's that?"

"Because I trust you," I said, starting to feel drowsy. I pressed my head closer against his shoulder.

"All right, then," he murmured. "I trust you, too. Remember that, right? Dream on it."

"I will," I promised, my eyes drifting closed; the comforting sound of his heartbeat filling my head...

...until I fell asleep in his arms.

CHAPTER TEN

Thursday, July 6
High Tide 7:44 A.M. EDT
Sunrise 5:06 A.M.

I was too well rested to even think of going back to sleep after I'd seen Borgan off, so I made a pot of coffee and sat down on the living room floor with my maps and guidebooks to hand. Still zone study, that was—an ongoing project. Granted, High Season probably wasn't the best time to go walking the land, looking for this or that wyrd place, having conversations with odd-looking creatures of possibly questionable sanity.

It is true that most . . . mundane folk can't see *trenvay* at all, unless the *trenvay* push the glamor *hard*, nor feel the wyrd pushing them away from this place or that. That's just their nature and nothing to be done, for or about it. A purely mundane person *might* see me talking to myself in the marsh—but most wouldn't. People are pretty good at editing things that are too strange to bear right out of their lives. Editing them out, real-time, before they even permit themselves to realize that something out of the ordinary is happening.

That's a kind of magic, right there, I guess—a nice, tight protection spell.

The folks who are the danger, say, to a Guardian wanting to get about her business with the *trenvay*—those were the folk who can see, or hear, things and beings that just can't be, and the smaller subset of those who aren't frightened, are more curious than frightened. Or are crazy.

That all being true, it would be wisest for me to wait until the Season ended before resuming any physical scouting. I accepted that.

However, there didn't seem to be anything wrong with studying up at home and noting down a few leads. Pinpointing a particular still zone wasn't the easiest thing in the world—in fact, it was damned frustrating. I held out some hope that practice would make perfect, if I just kept at it long enough.

This morning, though, I kept returning to the map, and the land just where Goosefare Brook entered Saco Bay, right where the trestle for the Dummy Railroad used to be...and couldn't you just see the old pilings still there, after all these years, sticking up out of low tide like a row of broken teeth.

That bit of land right there...that had once—long ago—held the service of a *trenvay*. To hear Felsic tell it, the service of that *trenvay* had been to bring ships in close until they broke up on the sandbar, and that had been too strange and terrible even for the Guardian of the time and other of the *trenvay*, who had banded together to *strip her service from her*.

I looked up from the map on my lap, and frowned hard at the ceiling. Stripping a *trenvay* of his or her service was—not something I had the least idea how to accomplish. Apparently, it took the agreement of the land and the rest of the *trenvay*. I'd have to ask Felsic to elaborate, or make an appeal to Nerazi.

In the meanwhile, there was this bit of land, which had no *trenvay* in service to it—not that every bit of land or chunk of rock *did* hold a *trenvay*, but the other part of Felsic's story was that it had been expected in this case that someone else would take up the service.

And that had never happened.

Which gave rise to all sorts of interesting speculation about what attributes made any certain someplace...worthy of? interesting to?...a proto-*trenvay*.

I sighed and reached for my coffee mug.

Hell of a Guardian you are, I scolded myself. *You don't even know how trenvay arise.* I'd have to ask Nerazi that, too, and take my ribbing like a big—

There came a knock at the door. I'd been so deep in my

speculations that it surprised me, even as the land showed me Peggy standing on the porch, bag in hand.

"It's open!" I called.

The latch snapped and she stepped inside.

"Single woman ought not to leave the door unlocked, even if she is the local equivalent of Oz," Peggy said, shutting same firmly.

"I can lock it from here," I said, and did; the *snap* of the deadbolt going home sounded nice and authoritative.

She shook her head.

"Cute, but not enough, if somebody sneaks up on you while you're sitting on the floor covered in books, and your mug empty."

"Old habits die hard; I'll try to do better," I told her, and only about half the contrition I showed her was bogus. Because she was right, I *should* lock the door, and take ordinary reasonable precautions like I'd learned to do, out Away. It wasn't that Archers Beach was any more dangerous than other places, it was only that it wasn't any *less* dangerous.

"Whatcha got?" I asked, closing my books and setting them aside.

"Breakfast!" she announced triumphantly. "Bob made us grilled blueberry muffins."

"Give the woman a raise," I said, and climbed to my feet, bringing my coffee mug with me.

Peggy was already in the kitchen, opening the cabinet and fetching down the yellow mug painted with delphiniums.

"Coffee?" she asked over her shoulder.

I put my mug beside hers and opened the refrigerator to get the creamer.

Leaving Peggy to pour, I grabbed silverware and napkins and carried them over to the table. The bag was sitting in the place of honor at the center; I unrolled the top and took out two foil-wrapped packages, each one as big as my two fists together.

"Civilized, or barbarian?" I asked.

"Barbarian, for the win!"

She put the mugs down by the silverware and napkins, and pulled out a chair. I handed her a foil package.

I unwrapped my package, breathing in appreciatively. Cinnamon, blueberries, hot butter. Mmmm. Beside me, Peggy gave a little gasp.

"That smells awesome!"

"Tastes even better," I told her, flattening the foil and picking up my fork.

We didn't do much talking for the next while. Not until Peggy leaned back in her chair, and put her fork gently down on the empty foil.

"I think I died and went to heaven."

"If you do that, you can't have another one tomorrow."

"You make a very good point, though I probably shouldn't have another one tomorrow, anyway."

She sighed, picked up her mug, and sipped reverently. I finished the last bite of my muffin, savoring it, then leaned back, mug in hand.

"So what's the occasion?" I asked.

She opened her improbably purple eyes wide.

"You don't think maybe I owe you at least a sort of token repayment for all the times you've fed me breakfast?"

"I don't think it, but if you thinking it means having one of Bob's grilled blueberry muffins, and your company, too, I'm not complaining."

Her pink cheeks flushed a little pinker and I wondered if I'd come off flirtatious. I really was glad of her company, the muffin being a plus.

"So's the committee heard anything back from Arbitrary and Cruel yet?" Peggy asked.

"If there's been an answer, nobody told me about it. I imagine they haven't got 'round to it yet, what with the Fourth."

Peggy lowered her mug, and looked at me, her expression that of a tough woman with a tough job ahead of her.

"Kate, listen..." she began.

From the coffeetable, my cell phone trilled.

"'Scuse me," I said, and dove for it.

Caller ID displayed a number I thought I'd never seen before— and then recalled that I had, once, when we did the test run to make sure the speed-dial on his phone worked.

"Vassily," I said, "good morning."

"Kate Archer, also good morning. I am calling to you on my break at the motel. One of the others will not be in work today; he calls in sick, you see?"

"I see," I said.

"The boss, he says that I must stay and do the work of this

sick one. I explain to him about my other job, with you. He says someone has to make the rooms ready, and if I leave when my shift is done, I will be fired. From this, I call Samuil, who comes to talk for me. Samuil just said to me that I must call you and tell you of this situation. Samuil says also to tell you that he goes now to the Chamber office, where he will speak with Mr. Poirier and seek his influence. It is hoped, by Samuil and myself, that I will be able to come to the carousel on time. But, perhaps this discussion will take time." There was a small pause.

"I am sorry, Kate Archer. I hope you will not fire me."

"No, I'm not going to fire you, though I might have a few words with your boss over there."

"This Samuil does, and perhaps Mr. Poirier. Samuil said to tell you that there may be paperwork you must do for Park Manager Marilyn Michaud."

Right. Samuil was the official speaker-for-greenies, and Dan Poirier, head of the Chamber of Commerce as he was, would be a *lot* more persuasive than I would be.

"I'll take care of the paperwork at the park," I told Vassily. "You do your best, keep your head down and let Samuil and Mr. Poirier handle this. Call me when it's all sorted out and we'll look at what's best to do."

"Yes. Thanking you. Again, I am sorry."

"It's not your fault, and there's nothing to thank me for. I'm sorry you're in this position, okay? Now go eat or whatever you need to do before your break's over."

"Yes," Vassily said, and closed the connection.

Peggy had cleared away the breakfast debris, and refreshed the cups while I'd been on the phone.

I sat down and gave her a grin. "Thanks."

"Hey, it's your coffee. What's up?"

"The contract between the Chamber and the agency that hires the greenies stipulates that each greenie work a particular number of hours a week..." I sipped my coffee, staring across the room at nothing particular. "Sixty hours across seven days, I think it is, for the length of the Season. That means most of 'em work for two or even three employers. Another greenie called in sick, and Vassily's other boss is making him fill in. He apparently thinks he doesn't have to pay attention to the fact that Vassily has another job." I sighed and sipped more coffee.

"Samuil—the guy with the agency—tried to fix it; that didn't work, so he's kicking it upstairs, to the Chamber. That oughta do the trick, but in the meantime, Vassily wanted to let me know he might be late, or even completely MIA, today."

"So, you'll be running the carousel today?"

"It's why I get the big bucks." I finished my coffee and glanced at the clock. "There's also some paperwork I need to fill out, so I guess I'll wander on down and get that out of the way before the excitement starts."

"I'll walk with you," Peggy said, getting up. "Got somebody coming in today to train on the smoothie machine."

"Really? Greenie?"

"A local. Somebody Felsic knows. Ethrane, her name is. Used to fill in around the midway when Jens was managing. I found her on his lists as a will-call, so that's okay." She shook her head. "Have to get her to apply for a Social Security card, so I can pay her. I dread the day that stuff goes to computerized filing only; it's gonna change a lot of things."

"Change is what we do, hereabouts."

"Yeah, and it'd be boring if we didn't. I just wish we could turn the speed back a notch or two."

I slipped my keys, wallet and phone into various pockets of my jeans.

"Hey, Kate?"

There was something...tentative in her husky voice and as a general rule, Peggy didn't do tentative. I turned to face her.

"Yeah?"

"I just want to let you know that...I really value our friendship. It's been swell knowing you, and I wouldn't want anything to, you know, come between us."

She was nervous; she was serious; and she was, I thought, going out on a limb to say what she was saying. I wish I knew what limb, exactly, and what she thought might come between us, but that was for later. For now, putting Peggy at ease was my job, I thought.

So, I gave her a grin.

"Sure; bros forever, Jersey." I raised my fist. "Bump?"

She laughed, we did the fist-bump, and headed out for Fun Country.

❋　　❋　　❋

Marilyn was in her office when I arrived. She was sitting at her desk, with the ledger book open—doing accounts the old-fashioned way, which would have been the way she learned it, back before we had personal computers to do that stuff for us.

"Good morning, Kate," she said, in her usual cool, emotionless voice. "Is there something I can do for you?"

"In fact, I think you can," I said, and told her what Vassily had told me.

"So, I'll be opening the carousel today—that's covered," I finished up. "But Samuil seemed to think there was some paperwork I needed to fill out with you here. Also, I'd like to make sure the kid gets his supper."

Marilyn had moved the ledger and was staring down at a list stuck into the corner of her blotter.

"He knows better than that," she muttered.

I tipped my head.

"Who, Vassily?"

"No, Pete—" She pressed her lips tightly together. "Vassily's other employer." She got up, paced over to the file cabinet on the back wall, and pulled open a drawer.

"There is paperwork; it was good of Samuil to remind you."

I took the form she handed me, and moved over to the ticket counting table to fill it in. Marilyn returned to her ledger and for a few minutes we worked in silence, each at our separate task.

I was just finishing up the reason for Vassily's possible tardiness, coming down heavily on the fact that the kid was blameless, when a high, wavering whistle pierced the air.

I jumped slightly in my chair.

Marilyn sighed the sigh of the unjustly put-upon, muttered, "Stupid fax," not quite under her breath, and got up to retrieve it from the machine sitting on top of the file cabinet.

I went back to my form, adding another sentence to make it perfectly clear that Vassily's morning employer was 'way outta line, signed it, dated it—and realized that I hadn't heard Marilyn move since she'd gotten up to fetch the fax.

She was standing, half turned toward the desk, staring down at the page in her hand; her face was rigid and just as white as that sheet of paper.

I got up slowly, and walked to the desk, putting my report in the middle of her ledger page.

Marilyn still hadn't moved.

"Bad news?" I asked, keeping my voice low and easy.

She jerked slightly, as if I'd startled her, raised dazed eyes to my face, and held the sheet out to me, wordlessly.

I glanced down at the page: Management's letterhead, with the stylized funhouse clown... *Please be advised that Fun Country, Archers Beach, Maine, has been put up for sale. We have received several inquiries from developers of ocean-front properties, and will be making a decision within the next few months. We are committed to keeping the park open through the end of the current Season. Ride operators will be sent instructions for removing their equipment before Labor Day. We will, of course, assist in an orderly shutdown-and-vacate process.*

I swallowed, hard, suddenly regretting the grilled blueberry muffin, and the coffee I had for breakfast.

They're selling the land.

I read it again, just in case I'd been mistaken, then looked up at Marilyn, who was standing behind the desk, staring down at the ledger, her hands gripping the back of the chair so tightly, her knuckles looked like ice.

"Can I make a copy of this?" I asked.

She raised a hand, let it drop.

Right, then.

The photocopier was under the windows. On consideration, I made two copies, folded them and stuck them in my back pocket, and put the original next to the form, on top of the ledger book.

"You okay, Marilyn?" I asked, feeling none too well myself.

She looked at me, her eyes dark, her face tense and lined.

"Yeah," I said, when she didn't say or do anything else. "It's a shock. I'll leave you to work, but, before I do—Vassily gets his supper today, whether he makes the shift at the carousel or not, right? Since it's not his fault?"

Marilyn blinked.

"Of course," she said, her voice perfectly flat. "Good morning, Kate."

"Good morning," I said, and fled.

CHAPTER ELEVEN

Thursday, July 6
Low Tide 1:32 P.M. EDT

"Development companies," Jess looked up from her perusal of the letter. "They're gonna make this all into condos."

"Sounds like that's the plan," I agreed. I had one foot braced on the bottom rail of the safety fence, and my arms crossed on the top. I wasn't feeling anything like good, truth told, and I supposed that Jess felt as sick as I did.

"Well, fuck 'em," she said, and I looked up into a face animated by righteous wrath. "Just... *fuck* 'em, that's all." She took a hard breath. "I'm callin' an emergency meeting of the Fun Country subcommittee tonight after the park closes. Gotta check a couple things, then I'll be callin' everybody. Can you come to a meetin' tonight, Kate?"

"Sure."

"All right, then." Jess took a hard breath and pulled her phone out of the wallet clipped to her belt. "Sorry. Gotta get as much of this settled as I can before the crowds hit."

"You got it. Talk to you later."

She was already dialing, and raised her free hand without looking up. I eased off the rail and headed up Baxter Avenue, toward the carousel.

But when I got there, my feet kept moving, taking me on a

leisurely stroll across Fountain Circle, dancing around tourists with their attendant dogs, toddlers, and strollers.

The dance continued up the midway, 'til I reached The Last Mango. There was a tall, thin woman at the juicer, whipping up something frothy and purple. To my eyes, she had green hair in dreads, a dark brown face that looked like it had, indeed, been carved from wood, and long, thin fingers with extra joints.

"Good morning, Ethrane," I said, when the noise stopped.

"Good morning, Kate," she answered. Her voice was soft and rich, like peat.

"Is Peggy in the office?"

"She is, but I imagine she'll be out in—"

Right on cue, Peggy stepped through the door in the back wall. Seeing me, she paused, nodded, held up a finger, and went to Ethrane's side.

"Lookin' good," she said, cheerfully. "You have a taste, yet?"

"Not yet, no."

"Well, pour us both a dab into some sample cups and we'll compare impressions. You want a sip, Kate?"

"Not just this second, thanks."

"Your loss."

Ethrane offered her a little Dixie cup, and poured a healthy slug of purple smoothie into another cup for herself. Peggy held her cup up; after a moment Ethrane copied the motion; they tapped—"To success!" Peggy said, which sounded slightly . . . strained . . . to me—and the two of them drank.

"Well," Peggy said, lowering her cup. "What do you think?"

"I think it's very pleasant."

"Me, too," Peggy said. "You're a natural, Ethrane. You're hired, if you want the job."

"Felsic said there would be papers," the *trenvay* said. "I . . . have little to do with papers, or with writing."

"Can you sign your name?"

Ethrane tipped her head, as if considering this closely.

"Yes," she said eventually.

"Good. What we're going to do is go into the back; you'll answer the questions I read you off the form, I'll fill in the blanks, you'll sign your name, and it's a done deal. That work for you?"

"Yes." She smiled. Her teeth were like sharpened stakes. Peggy didn't seem to notice.

"Excellent. You go in back and make yourself comfortable at the table. Kate needs to talk to me for a minute, then we'll do this thing."

"Yes," Ethrane said again, and slipped between Peggy and the juicer, disappearing through the door into the back office.

I pulled the second copy of the letter out of my pocket and held it out to her.

She sighed, took it, unfolded it with a flick of her wrist and ran her eye down the page.

"How pissed are you?" she asked, without looking up.

"At Arbitrary and Cruel? Plenty. At you, if that's the question, not at all. If you knew, which I guess you did, you're an employee, and something along the lines of a sale would've been confidential."

Peggy refolded the letter and handed it back to me. Her eyes were shining suspiciously, and she cleared her throat.

"You're too understanding, Archer."

"Software engineer, remember? Dotcom startups had the craziest NDAs *ever*."

"Well, I didn't have to sign a nondisclosure agreement. It's company policy, though: What's confidential in Jersey is *confidential*."

"Understood. I do have a question, and if you can't answer it, just say so."

"Shoot."

"Is the midway up for sale, too?"

Peggy shook her head, her mouth twisting.

"Nah," she said, the bluesy rasp of her voice edged with bitterness. "The midway was sold before it opened this year; new owner's taking possession on September fifth. And, because I like and admire you, I'll give you a freebie: it's condos."

Jess Robald called at 12:30. I was busy passing hopeful riders in through the gate to the carousel and let it go to voice mail. Once the ride was moving, I grabbed it, and learned that there would be a meeting of the Fun Country subcommittee at Tony Lee's, after the park closed tonight. Please come if I could, Jess said; she expected the meeting to be short, but very important.

There wasn't enough room in Tony Lee's for all the members of the subcommittee, though it made sense in terms of location. We could spill out into the service alley if we had to, and I could make sure nobody saw us, if *I* had to.

Vassily called about three with the news that the combined efforts of Samuil and Dan Poirier had barely been sufficient to pry him loose from his other employer's clutches. However, they had all eventually agreed that, even if another worker called in sick, Vassily was not to be prevented from doing his shift at the carousel. Indeed, Katrina was at present working with the invalid and Samuil would be checking in with both of them. If it happened that the sickness lingered, Samuil would work tomorrow's shift himself.

"So, you see, I will work tomorrow. I can work now, if..."

"Nope, you worked enough today, even if you didn't work for me. You get your supper from Anna, just like every day. After that, you go ahead and do whatever you usually do after your shift here."

"I walk on the beach, and then I go to sleep."

"Sounds perfect, do that."

The line petered out right around three-thirty—ride popularity moves in waves during the day, depending on a whole bunch of things: the weather, other events happening in town, how cold the beer is, and foot traffic.

The carousel being situated, as it is, by the entrance gate, our traffic went down when there were more people inside the park than were coming in. Around five, we'd start to get play from the people leaving the park to get dinner; then around eight, we'd get another big influx of people who wanted to ride all the rides before closing time.

Tides, that was all, though not exactly like the ocean.

Thinking about the ocean made me smile, and also reminded me that I'd better call Borgan and tell him I was committed to a meeting.

I dialed, got his voice mail, left a message suggesting that we meet in Fountain Circle after the meeting, say eleven o'clock, and snapped the phone shut.

The land whimpered.

I shoved the phone into my pocket and turned, pulling *jikinap* to my fingertips...

Nancy Vois is a wiry, tough woman; an ace mechanic who used to ride with one of the local motorcycle clubs—she hadn't told me which one, but my private guess was the Saracens.

She's also a shapeshifter. Her other form is a calico cat every bit as wiry and tough as the woman herself.

I'd seen Nancy, in cat form, take on a unicorn, and it hadn't been too much for her.

Today, though, it looked like she might've found something that was.

She limped up to the operator's station and sat herself down on the stool, breathing a little hard before raising her head, and pushing the gimme hat back so I could see it all.

It was something to see: shiner, swollen cheek, cuts on the knuckles of the hand she'd used to push back the cap, and that limp hadn't been faked. Worse, she'd probably been doing her best not to limp at all.

I leaned back against the safety rail and crossed my arms over my chest.

"What's the other guy look like?"

Nancy gave me a grim smile.

"Gonna need a tetanus shot, for sure. Maybe couple stitches."

"Sounds like you gave a good accounting. What happened, if you don't mind my asking?"

She shrugged, grimaced, and shifted on the stool.

"I've got friends down the Camp, is all, so I figured to go see how it was going with the negotiations between the townies an'..."

She paused, cut hands flexing, as if she were grasping for a word.

Or a phrase.

"The nice gentleman from Away?" I suggested.

"Hah. That's him. Well, long story short, somebody'd laid poison around near where the cats are known to be. Old Mister, he'd found the treat by the lean-to an' took steps there. Time I come by, he'd already sent out a buncha the older heads to find was there more, and deal with whatever they found. I shifted and put myself on the committee."

She sighed.

"Ain't making it much shorter, am I?"

"Take your time. You want me to get you a coffee or a soda?"

"I'm okay—really not much more to tell.

"Happens I come across one of the cats—a younger who'd found another stash of poison. She was peeing and covering and I figured she didn't need my help when it turned out she did.

"Guy—not the man himself; one of the locals who sides with 'im—comes out 'round the boat shed, sees what she's about, grabs a hammer up outta the tool-catch and starts walking up real quiet. The little queen, she's concentratin'; she don't hear 'im . . ." She threw me a twisted grin.

"Well, you can see I couldn't let that pass. So, him an' me, we had a discussion. He dropped the hammer right quick. I got my licks in an' he got some in, too. Then the little queen, she wrapped herself 'round his ankle, all claws out, and bitin', too. He yelled, dropped me and the two of us ran like hell and hid 'til Old Mister come to find us and give me the all-clear."

"That? Sounds a lot more strenuous than my morning. You want to go home and sleep it off?"

Nancy looked sheepish.

"Don't mean to impose, but if I go home this way, Ma'll start in with me 'bout brawling." She smiled, wrylike. "She'd be right, too. Woman my age oughta know better." She paused. "So, if you could patch me up, Kate, I'd appreciate it."

I might've blinked. Nancy had never called upon me as Guardian, or even seemed to know I was anything other than a little odd in ways that most people weren't.

Kind of like shape-changing.

"Sure," I said. "I'll be glad to do the honors. Give me your hand."

She held her right out. I sandwiched it between my palms and asked the land for healing.

I felt it pass through me, green and vital. I heard Nancy sigh, and released her.

"Thanks."

"No problem at all. You going home and show your mother a clean face?"

"Hell, no; I'm good to work, now. Didn't you just fix me up?"

"Nancy—"

"There's just one more thing, before you go," she said, overriding me easily.

I eyed her. "What's that?"

"Word's out you're looking to take on a cat."

"I am. Who do you have in mind?"

Nancy gave me an earnest look from ale-colored eyes.

"See, that little queen down to the Camp—the one almost got herself hammered? She's got real distinctive markings, and she needs to get outta there. If they find her in the open, she's a dead cat."

"I see the problem. Is she civilized, or will I need to rig out a witness-protection box near the house?"

"She's nice as you please. Young, but got a good head on 'er. Old Mister, he holds 'er high."

"Does he? Well, that's quite a recommendation. Send her along for an interview." I paused, considering the distance between Camp Ellis and Archers Beach. "Or should I go to her?"

"We'll get 'er to you."

"Deal. What's her name?"

"Not mine to say."

Of course not, I thought. *Honestly, Kate, where are your manners?*

"If we got all that settled, I'll be going home," I said. "After I tell you the other big news of the day."

"What's that?" Nancy asked, sliding to her feet and leaning over to pull out the ticket-catch.

"Fun Country Management's selling the park."

Nancy raised her head to look into my face.

"Fuck."

"Pretty much, yeah." I sighed. "Midway's already been sold. The new owner's picking up the keys right after Labor Day. They're looking to put up condos."

"'Course they are. Ain't one damn' thing the seaside's good for 'cept to make more places for rich people from Away to spend two weeks of their summers. *Damn* it." She took a quick breath. "It's all gonna change, ain't it?"

"Yeah, it is. It's what we do here."

CHAPTER TWELVE

Thursday, July 6
High Tide 7:59 P.M. EDT

"How'd the meetin' go?" Borgan asked.

We were sitting at the concrete picnic table nearest the fountain in Fountain Circle. The underwater lights were on, and the spray was alternating blue, pink, and green.

The tall streetlights were also on, full blare; Fountain Circle gets particularly crowded after dark, and running the lighting bright helps keep things . . . peaceful.

Borgan had provided a truly enormous roast beef sandwich with two pickles on the side, and a couple of tall ice teas. The sandwich was cut into quarters, thank God, and I'd been kind of worrying at one quarter, staring out over the circle, maybe looking like I was people-watching, maybe looking like I was brooding, but, either way, not bringing much—or anything at all—to the conversation.

Since I had in fact been brooding about the meeting, Borgan's question hit home. Which shouldn't, I thought, surprise me.

"The meeting was . . . grim. Everybody's upset. They want to fight, but they don't know how, or who. Donny's view is that we're finished; might just as well pack the car and leave. Couple people wanted to talk about relocating the park. Sylvia Laliberte proposed we look at the lot where the Loon had been. Henry believes that negotiations with the developer who was interested in that spot might've stalled. But, even if it was available, if we could somehow figure out how to buy it, and about a dozen other *ifs*, the place isn't big enough for all of us. Could maybe spot rides around town, but the larger feeling was that hanging together as the Young Tourist's Dream of Amusement is best for all. Synergy. Jess thinks we should just buy the land we're on now, since Management's selling. Henry's supposed to be looking into the asking price."

I shook my head, and lapsed into gloomy silence.

"Sounds like that'd be best," Borgan said. "Keepin' the park right where it is, an' all the rides, too."

"Oh, it's the best solution, okay," I said. "It's just that I'm betting the asking price is more than all of us together have in our piggy banks. Prime oceanfront real estate is worth an arm and leg. So I'm told."

I looked down. The quarter sandwich I'd called for mine was pretty mangled. Well. I wasn't hungry anyway. I had a swallow of ice tea, and shook my head, feeling helpless, and hopeless, and screwed over—familiar feelings from the past, which I didn't at all appreciate revisiting in this particular present.

"What else?" Borgan asked. He'd eaten half the sandwich while I was busy glaring and moping. I pointed at the quarter remaining.

"You'd better have that. I'm not hungry."

"I see that," he said, and picked up the quarter. "But there's something more than this thing with the park bothering you. Care to tell me?"

I shook my head.

"By my calculation, you've put up with enough from me tonight. What say I go home and sleep it off, and we'll try again tomorrow?"

"Now, see, if I just let you wander off alone, you'll brood, you won't sleep, and tomorrow you'll be tired and miserable, too. Then you'll start thinking about how you're not good at relationships and that I deserve better, and that's just a slope I'd rather not start sliding down." He gave me a half-smile, his eyes serious.

"You're getting good at this," I said, between amused and irritable, because he was right. Damn him.

"It's taking study, but I'm willing to put in the work, if you are."

'*Way* too good.

I glared at him. He smiled at me.

Okay, I know when I'm licked.

"Well, then," I said, briskly, "if you really want it, I was wondering how incompetent a Guardian has to be, who can't stop this crap from happening. I'm Guardian, and here's people *selling the land*, and there's not one damned thing I can do to stop it!"

Okay, that'd gotten a little heated. I took a deep breath, and met Borgan's eye.

"Maybe I can contrive a volcano; scare the developers away."

"Be rough on the locals."

"I guess. But so will condos, a buncha townies outta work, and nothing to draw the tourists."

"Kate, you're a Guardian, not a god. You can't dictate what people do. Their lives, their duty, and their magic—that's nothing to do with you. Your life, your duty, your magic—mindin' that's enough, ain't it?"

I bit my lip and met his eye.

"The really tough part is that I'd been starting to think that I—that having a Guardian on the spot had ... begun to turn the town around. New businesses coming in; folks getting together to talk about how to build us back up ..."

"So now it looks like the luck crumpled up and blew away—an' that's your fault?"

"Something like."

He made a soft noise; something like *hmph*, and turned his attention to his sandwich. I finished my ice tea, and tried to think happy thoughts. Instead, I found myself wondering what the batwing horse—pardon me, Leynore, the Opal of Dawn, Princess of Daknowyth, the Land of Midnight—was doing just then.

Honestly, Kate, I thought crankily, *if you miss her that much, maybe you should open the World Gate and go pay her a visit.*

Or maybe not.

"So," Borgan said, gathering up the sandwich wrappings and stuffing them back into the bag. "You wanna go for a swim?"

I blinked at him, for an instant entirely at a loss.

"I'm not such a good swimmer," I said, when I'd finally parsed the sentence. "Tarva taught me, but I haven't had much practice lately."

"You'll do fine," he told me. "'Sides which, you'll be with an expert. I won't let anything bad happen to you."

Of all the stupid, unenforceable things that can be said in any or all of the Six Worlds, *I won't let anything bad happen to you* has got to be among the stupidest and the most unenforceable.

And yet, it's so warming...so *comforting*, to hear it.

"You're on," I said.

We got up from the table, precariously deposited our trash in a receptacle overflowing with pizza boxes, and walked toward the beach. Borgan extended his hand, and I took it, feeling the frisson of contact, and a ripple of desire.

There were people on the beach: couples sitting in the sand, cuddling under shared towels; couples walking, like Borgan and me, hand in hand; a few singletons at the wander; and some few boisterous gaggles of teens. We could hear the band playing at Neptune's with really admirable clarity, shouts and laughter and snatches of conversation. The lights spilling from the Pier cast the nearby beach and the various walkers and snugglers into a sort of twilight, where everything was a silhouette.

Borgan led me on an angle—toward the water line under the Pier, until we stepped from twilight to deep shadow, striped here and there with light escaping from above.

"We'll go in here, so's not to give anybody a start," Borgan said, walking us straight down to the water between the pilings.

"If we're going swimming, I'd better at least leave my shoes on the emergency stairs," I said, pulling back a little on his hand.

He kept on walking. "You'll be fine," he said. I saw his eyes glint—dark inside the darkness. "Trust me."

Well, I did; so I let him lead me to the water and into the surf...

"Deep breath, now."

I obeyed, filling my lungs as Borgan's hand tightened around mine.

A wave broke over my head...

...and I was among the waters.

I'd been in the sea with Borgan twice before.

The first time, he'd knocked me over the so-called safety rail around Neptune's on the Pier, and turned himself into a harbor seal so he could give me a ride into the beach. The situation was a little more complicated than that, and I acquit him of malice, though not of having a sense of humor unbefitting a Guardian.

The second time, I'd just missed dying, was too weak to walk, and Borgan had been in what I later deduced was a towering rage, spending power like it was...well, water.

That time, he'd wrapped me inside his magic, stalked into the water at the Pier, and stalked out, both of us perfectly dry, onto the beach directly in front of my house. The whole journey took longer to tell than accomplish, just a moment when I was cool, bodiless, and fluid, before returning to the solidity of dry land.

This time wasn't like either of those.

I was fully conscious; I was aware of my body, and of holding Borgan's hand. I could see, though not well, because of the amount of sand being roiled by the surf. Though I wasn't swimming, I *was* moving, and the sensation was exactly of being *among* the waters, rather than passing through.

Ribbons of water caressed me, each one distinct—cool, warm, chaste, seductive, dangerous. I thought that I might make sense of them—read them, like I read the land—if I could have a moment of stillness and quiet...

...but apparently stillness and quiet was not what this outing—this *swim*—was about.

Borgan—I assumed that we were traveling via Borgan-power—kept us moving along at a brisk clip. The water was clearer now, which I guessed meant we were beyond the breakers. Sand dollars, kelp leaves, and small fishes went past us—or we, them—and I was abruptly aware of a change in the substance we were passing through; it became warmly curious, even amused.

It...giggled.

And suddenly, Borgan and I weren't alone in our passage through the waters. Other bodies rode the flow with us—beside us, over and under us, surrounding us with goodwill...and song.

It flowed like the waters, that song, but rather than buoying me, it...informed me. Passing weightless through the waters as I had been, still I felt...lighter, brighter, lighter still—and suddenly we were flying, all of us, the ribbons of water shattering as the wind and the sky received me. I took a deep breath, and fell with the rest of us, joyously reunited with the waters.

As one, we turned—and then they fell away, peeling off, leaving behind joy, and laughter, and a lingering sense of lightness. Borgan tugged on my hand, guiding me into sandy waters, from which we rose again into the free air, my ears filled with the memory of a wave breaking against the shore.

⚜

The water moved, rocking her as she dreamed.

As she *remembered*.

She remembered a palace of living coral set within gardens of kelp.

She remembered her lovers, one ebon, one ivory—demons, enforcers of her will, guardians; and the only creatures she had ever trusted.

She remembered the taste, the touch, the feel of the sea that had made her a goddess.

She remembered a...delegation, come to offer sweet lies in a poisoned cup. She'd laughed at them.

She remembered that it had been a mistake to do so. A very serious mistake.

She remembered the coral walls as she had last seen them—shattered and dying, and her ebon lover, screaming as he died in the trap meant for her, while the white one howled and spread himself among the waters.

She remembered her enemies, at whom she had laughed; how their eyes gleamed with appetite; how they defiled her, and stripped her power, painfully, away.

She remembered being bound, the bonds burning cold, the passage between the Worlds, and the Wind that had knotted and torn her hair.

She remembered the woman with her cold face and angry eyes, her power rooted and stern.

And she remembered the hippocampus.

Such was her distress and confusion, she had thought it an actual Dragon of the Sea, and cried out to it to aid her.

She remembered laughter and a punishing shove against the creature's side; she remembered despair, as she understood that the hippocampus was a dead wooden carving...

...and nothing more.

She woke then, weeping, to the gentle rocking of the sea that was not hers. Woke, knowing her true name—and that she was a goddess no longer.

CHAPTER THIRTEEN

Friday, July 7
High Tide 8:48 P.M.
Sunset 8:25 P.M.

Sometime during the night, the skies opened and rain poured out.

The good thing about a downpour on one of the precious High Season days was Borgan didn't go out to fish. We took joyous advantage of that, then napped, and woke a second time to make a late breakfast of coffee and toast spread liberally with Mrs. Kristanos' homemade strawberry jam, while the rain hammered the deck above us.

"Good day to curl up in the bunk an' read," Borgan said, splitting the dregs of the pot between our two mugs. "Play cards, maybe."

I sighed.

"I'm not against either of those, on principle, but I'm going to be needing to relieve Vassily at the carousel in about forty-five minutes. I only hope he hasn't expired of boredom."

"Not gonna be much business today, up at the park, will there?"

"In this?" I waggled a hand over my head, meaning to indicate the weather above us. "People're more likely to drive out to the strip and grab a movie, or stay inside and read. Or play cards." I sipped coffee. "For which I blame them not at all, even if it does mean a loss on the day."

"Marilyn likely to shut down?"

"She might call an early night, if this keeps up. Since there's no way of knowing if it *will* keep up, though, she'll keep us open a while yet."

I finished my coffee and put the mug on the table.

"Well, at least I can go between or whatever; save getting wet."

Borgan gave me a sideways glance. "You figure out how that works, yet?"

"Near as I can figure, it works that I think of somewhere I want to be—and I'm there."

My nerves twittered, and I looked at Borgan harder. "You think it's a trap?"

Damn it...

Borgan reached across the table and put his hand over mine.

"I think it's an artifact, and I think you need to figure out how it works, and what it costs, if anything." He pressed my hand warmly. "I *don't* think it's a trap—not an intentional trap. But—things *change* here."

I took a breath.

"You been through everything you got from that share?"

"Every—" I stared at him, feeling slightly sick as his meaning sunk in. "I—Mr. Ignat' watched while I...while I accessed... Prince Aesgyr's reasons, and what memories he—his power—left with me."

I was feeling more than slightly sick, now.

"And you're having memory-dreams." Borgan wasn't letting go of my hand, and I was glad of it. "Might be what you want to do, Kate, is have the old gentleman, or somebody else you trust, watch while you go through all of it."

Right.

I took a deep breath, and another one. Suddenly, I wanted the land's reassuring touch, familiar and loved—to balance... *whatever* tainted things that had been given me, without my knowledge or consent.

"You up for it?" I asked. Borgan has twice now held my spirit safe while I did something dangerous, not to say foolish. I trusted him to do it a third time, no muss, no fuss.

"Sure," he said. "You wanna pencil that in for tonight? I'll come by the carousel at closing."

"It's a plan." Another deep breath, my topmost feeling relief. I could fix this. Borgan would help. Nothing to worry about—well, not much, anyway.

I smiled, lifted the hand that was over mine and kissed his knuckles.

"I'd better get moving," I said.

"Want me to come with you?"

"No reason for both of us to get soaked."

In fact, I arrived at the carousel dry—by reason of the *jikinap* shield I wrapped myself in—calm—by reason of a nice commune with the land as I walked—and about fifteen minutes before the end of Vassily's shift.

As it turned out, my timing was perfect.

Baxter Avenue was deserted, a flash stream running down the middle. The greenie who tended the lobster toss was wearing a yellow slicker with the hood pulled up, and had let down the tarp on the side of the booth facing the Oriental Funhouse in what was probably a futile attempt to stay dry.

The lights were on at the funhouse, but the giant samurai was silent, looking faintly miserable in the downpour.

Summer's Wheel was lit, too, but Brand was nowhere in sight. Probably back in the utility shed, looking at one of the girlie magazines he kept up on a high shelf. His "rainy day fund," as he called them.

The window was open at Tony Lee's but I didn't see Tony or Anna. Most likely, they were having a cup of coffee in the kitchen.

In all, the rainy day would have been a nice interlude—a gift from the weather gods to busy people who'd earned a break—except for the part where nobody was in the park, and that's not the way ride operators and carryouts make money to tide them over the very long rainy day called off-Season.

The carousel was lit; every light on the sweeps a star, and Vassily had had the native wit to turn on the outside lights. I oughta give that kid a raise, I thought—but that wasn't possible; greenie compensation was set by the contract the agency had with the Chamber.

But, I thought suddenly, snapping my *jikinap* rain shield shut as I came under roof, I might be able to give him a present. That idea had appeal. Of course, I didn't know if it was feasible.

Anna would, though.

The kid in question was not at the operator's station, for which I couldn't blame him, and even if I was inclined to be miffed, he hadn't gone far.

He was, in fact, sitting astride the knight's charger, one hand on the powerful armored neck, as if he soothed a living mount, his long, lean legs dangling beyond the stirrups. His head was turned away from me, as if he was contemplating the mural that hid the center pole and generator from public view.

"Slow day?" I asked, leaning on the safety rail.

He turned his head easily, not at all like I had startled him.

"There has been not one person wishing to ride today. It is very sad, but also very peaceful."

He frowned then, the faintest of wrinkles appearing between high-arching reddish brows.

"It is stopped raining?" he asked, then shook his head with a glance toward the tin roof on which the rain was playing a drum solo. "I am too easily fooled. Of course, it still rains."

I glanced down at myself, more than slightly chagrined. There was no way I could have stayed completely dry in the current downpour, something I had forgotten in my desire not to drown.

Honestly, Kate; try not to blow your cover.

The land gave a sharp bark; I spun 'round, and got some distance from the fence—instinct, and wouldn't Grandfather Aeronymous' arms master have been proud to observe it—and watched Doris Vannerhoff, the operator of the log flume and the single holdout on the letter we'd sent to Fun Country Management—stomp under the carousel's roof.

It was amply obvious that Doris had neither used a magically crafted shield to protect her from the weather, nor provided herself with an umbrella. She was wearing a yellow slicker with the water running off of it in sheets, and she was soaked from the knees down.

She was mad, too. So mad that she started yelling the second she caught sight of me.

"So *that* was a good idea, wasn't it, Archer? Challenge Management, draw a line in the sand because you people up here're afraid of a little honest work! Making expensive demands—well, what the *bloody hell* did you think they were gonna do—you and that fool runs the train set?"

"Afternoon, Doris," I said, and tried to send some calm into her through the land. It bounced.

I was impressed; it's rare you find somebody who puts so much effort into being pissed off.

She stopped within grabbing range. I forced myself to stay right where I was, and tucked my hands into my back pockets.

"If you already talked to Jess, you don't have to do a replay just for me; she'll give me the highlights."

"The famous Archer wit. Well, I'll tell you something—*I ain't laughing*! As for even trying to talk to Jess Robald about anything sensible, I guess I know better'n that. Woman's a fool, always been, an' if there were still state sanitoriums, you'd've never had the chance to use her as a cat's paw! Me, I know where the brains are in this. It's you, just like it always was! I just come up here to ask you how it feels to single-handedly close this place down around our ears? You *feel good* about that, Archer?"

My temper was rising, which is what she intended. Doris *wanted* a fight; a real knock-'em-down brawl. Well, I told myself firmly, I didn't have to accommodate her. I reached to the land, and accepted calmness into myself.

"As it happens, I feel lousy about the park closing down, but you're out, if you think the letter did it. Management's apparently had this in mind for a while. The midway was sold to a condo developer before the Season even started. Guess Maine isn't a profit center anymore." I shrugged. "No reason for *you* to care, is there? You're not a townie."

That last, those were fightin' words, so maybe I wasn't quite as calm as I should've been, even if I was calmer than Doris.

"No, I ain't a townie—you'll know that 'cause I'm not an inbred retard! I'm still gonna hafta move the flume to another park, if I can find one, and that's expense I don't need! You, though— you're gonna make out fine. There's a big market for used and ugly wood carvings, ain't there? Organ's prolly worth something, too. Sure, you'll make out fine—s'long's nobody comes by and burns the whole damn' thing down for you."

I took a deep breath. *Calm, Kate. Just be calm.*

"Doris, you can either leave now, or I'm calling the cops and telling them you threatened violence."

"I'll give you violence, you—"

I saw her shift her weight, saw her cock back for the punch; shifted my own balance, and pulled my hands out of my pockets—

"Let me go!"

I looked up.

Vassily had Doris by the wrist, his face as austere as an angel's.

"There is no fighting in the park," he said, his voice dead even. "You will go now, and you will not come back here."

"I'm not about to be sassed by any damn' greenie—" Doris snarled. She yanked against Vassily's grip, but she didn't manage to free herself. Had to hurt, too, him holding her arm in that position.

"I think the best thing is for me to call Marilyn, get her up here to take the complaint and set Doris a fine," I told Vassily.

"That is procedure," he agreed.

Doris took a hard, noisy breath.

"All right, Greenie, let me go; I'm leaving."

He looked at me over her head. I nodded and he let her go, dropping back and swinging around, so that he stood facing her, half blocking me from a renewed attack, if any.

"Tough guy, are you?" Doris snarled. "I said I'm leaving."

And she did, turning around and stomping out the way she came in. I tried again to send her a little calm—and got another bounce for my trouble. You really had to admire that kind of dedication.

"This place, this park—it is being...sold?"

Vassily sounded worried; looked worried too.

"Park Management—that's down in New Jersey—has decided to sell the land," I said. "Doris is right; the rides will all have to be shut down and either sold, or moved to another place."

He swallowed, looked over his shoulder, then met my eyes. His were shining with what might have been tears.

"The carousel...this beautiful thing...where will it—you—go?"

I took a breath and resisted the urge to pat him on the shoulder and say, "There, there."

"We're working on that," I said instead. "We only just got the news yesterday. Well. I guess Doris might've got it today."

Vassily had turned to look at the carousel, shoulders stiff. I felt a twist of guilt for the destruction of his hard-won peace.

"This...this will mean that I will never come here again to work among these beautiful things. This is now a...special place to me. And you—" He turned suddenly, one hand out, like he was going to touch me—and thought better of it.

"You," he repeated, bowing his head. "You have been special to me, Kate Archer. Thanking you." He swallowed. "*Thanking* you."

"You've still got the rest of the Season here," I said, ignoring the internal voice that added, *Why, that's eight whole weeks!* "We're not going anywhere before then. Hell," I added, more for his distress than because I necessarily believed it, "we might not go at all. Keep the faith, Vassily."

His face lit.

"Yes! I will pray to my angel about this place and about you, Kate Archer; and Anna, and Nancy, and—"

"Whoa, whoa! You're still in touch with your angel?" That was disturbing, if true. On the other hand, he could well *believe* that he was—

Vassily looked at me reproachfully.

"Once a man has an angel, he does not *un*have an angel, ever again. You know this. An angel's touch changes the heart, and the soul, forever."

Well, that was either terrifying or depressing. Possibly both. I forced a smile.

"I'm not going to turn down well-wishes, prayers or miracles. However! It is now past time for you to get out of here and have your supper. Thanks for taking care of Doris—that was done well."

"It was not a problem, and you are welcome." He hesitated. "You should pray, too, Kate Archer," he said diffidently. "You were touched by an angel, also, I know."

Oh, did he? That was just special.

"I'm not much of a hand at praying, but I'll give it a whirl tonight. Now, *git!* Your supper's waiting on you."

"Yes," he said. "Good night, Kate Archer. Thanking you."

CHAPTER FOURTEEN

Friday, July 7
High Tide 8:48 P.M. EDT
Sunset 8:25 P.M.

It never did stop raining.

In fact, around seven o'clock, the downpour actually increased, the sound of the drops striking the carousel enclosure's tin roof like the clatter of artillery.

At eight o'clock, Marilyn closed the park, the air horn blasts barely audible over the din of the rain.

I called Borgan, got his voice mail, explained the situation, and asked him to come right around to the house whenever he had a mind to. Then, I locked up and headed over to the midway, protected from drowning by my handy *jikinap* weather shield.

The midway was dark and deserted, so apparently Peggy had reached the same conclusion Marilyn had, though maybe a little sooner. Still, in the interests of thoroughness, I walked back to the Mango. Peggy sometimes stayed late, to do paperwork, though that might change, if Ethrane worked out.

The lights were out at the Mango, except for a thin vertical strip leaking out of the crack between the office door and the frame. Working late, then. Woman was going to kill herself.

I slipped into the booth, saw a shadow leaning in the far inside corner, felt the weight on the land and nodded.

"Felsic," I said, letting my weather shield evaporate as I leaned into the unoccupied corner.

"Kate," Felsic returned, easily. "Peggy's finishing up."

"You mind if I walk up as far as Dube Street with you?" I asked.

"S'where we're going. Peggy says this is a pizza and beer night. Way I understand it, she got a pizza in the freezer and a suitcase o'beer in the fridge."

"That's what I called prepared," I agreed, leaning closer into my corner. Outside, the rain was coming down in sheets. Every now and then, a single drop would catch a random bit of light, and glow bright and sharp, like a diamond.

I asked the land for better vision, and Felsic came into focus, tucked into the opposite corner, a stocky, androgynous figure in T-shirt and jeans; broad chinless face, flat nose, wide, thin-lipped mouth, dark eyes gleaming from beneath the bill of the gimme hat. She had an umbrella cocked over one shoulder, and was holding it by the point.

"I met Ethrane," I said, by way of making conversation.

Felsic sent me a sharp look.

"Not going to fatch, are you, Kate? She's a bit rugged, but her control's good. There'll be no lapses from that quarter."

Well, that was a mite sharp. If I was paranoid, I might think Felsic was a teensy bit defensive. I wondered if I wanted to know why—and admitted that I probably did, if just for my own information. Felsic certainly wouldn't put Peggy at risk.

I was pretty sure of that, anyway.

"Good to know she's competent," I told Felsic. "I can't judge her glamor."

"You see us all as we are?"

"To the best of my knowledge, I do. It'd be nice to get the full effect, now and then, but my eyes don't seem to focus that way."

"Might be we don't put ourselves out enough for you," Felsic said seriously. "Glamorin' most is easy enough, and no need to waste wattage, if you see m'point. Still, I'm thinkin' there's value for the Guardian to know how we look to others who might maybe come to her with a description. For an instance..."

I felt a tiny alteration through the land, as if Felsic's center of balance had shifted.

Across from me was a solid-built woman in jeans and a T-shirt, umbrella over one shoulder. Her face was round, with a retroussé nose, generous mouth, and a sturdy chin. Eyes the color of seventy-percent dark chocolate considered me with a suggestion of mischief from beneath the gimme hat's bill.

"I'll ask Ethrane to show you next time you're by," she said.

"Thank you; that's very kind."

"Not a glamor-user, yourself?" Felsic inquired.

"What you see is what you get," I answered, just as the light snapped out in the back room and Peggy stepped out to join us.

"Flirting with my girlfriend, Archer?" she demanded, in mock outrage.

Felsic came out of her lean with a grin.

"Just discussin' how Kate could glamor up a bit. Nothin' hurt by keeping Cap'n Borgan on his toes." She looked briefly pensive. "In fact, there's some say he wants a little shakin' around."

Peggy laughed.

"I'd love to dress Kate up!" she said, and looked at me. "You get any urges in that direction, give me a call."

"Deal," I said.

"Well," she said, "time to go, I guess. God, how can it have been raining like this *all day*? We're going to *drown*."

"Nothin' like it," Felsic said, holding up the umbrella. "Got us covered."

"Optimist."

She looked back at me suddenly.

"What about you? You *will* drown, Kate! Don't you even have a—"

"I've got an umbrella," I interrupted, taking my cue from Felsic. "I leaned it in the corner and it fell down, stupid..." I bent into the dark corner, as if groping for my fallen bumbershoot. Concentrating, I gave the *jikinap* I'd used for my weather shield a shape, said, "Here it is!" and stood up straight, brandishing a red umbrella with a wooden hook.

"All right then," Peggy said. "Aqualungs—*on*! Let's go."

And she led the way out into the storm.

We reached the top of Dube Street in good order, jeans soaked to the knee, but basically undrowned, which was, as Peggy said, more than we could reasonably have hoped for.

At the house, she and Felsic went right, toward the door to the studio, and I continued up the stairs to the porch, where the light was fighting a losing battle against the rain-swept shadows.

I fished my key out of my pocket, approached the door—and yelped as my ankle was pierced by a number of sharp needles.

"Hey!"

I leaned back, snapped a brighter light onto my fingertips, and glared down into a pair of glittering amber eyes. The eyes belonged to a bedraggled white cat, which was, yes, currently wrapped around my ankle.

"This is not," I said sternly, "a good way to start a working relationship. I presume Old Mister sent you? *I* was told you had manners."

The amber eyes blinked, consideringly.

"Kate?" Peggy called from her sheltered patio below. "You okay?"

"Just having an exchange of views with a neighbor," I called back, as claws slowly retracted from my tender skin.

The cat rolled free, which gave me a better look at her. Bedraggled wasn't the word.

"My God, you poor thing; you're soaked!"

"Kate?"

Rapid footsteps on the stair behind me. I flicked the light off my fingertips and turned to face Peggy as she gained the porch.

"What neigh—" she began, and looked down, her eye possibly drawn by the brightness of the cat's fur.

"Oh, for—you're so *cute!*" She bent down and offered a finger. The cat turned her head aside and yawned.

"Cute and soaked right through to the bone," I said. "I'm going to take her in and get her dried off, if she'll let me."

"Good idea." Peggy straightened, not noticeably cast down by her rejection. "You got cat things?"

I blinked.

"Litter box? Food? Comfy pillow?"

Right—*cat things*. I'd put them on the shopping list. But unfortunately . . .

"I hadn't been expecting her so soon," I explained.

Peggy nodded.

"Okay, then! Here's how we'll handle it—Kate will dry the kitty so she doesn't catch a cold. Felsic?"

"Here," came the answer from the bottom of the stairs.

"You want to start heating the oven for the pizza? I'm running down to Ahz's Market. Back in a flash."

"Peggy, look, I don't want to interrupt your date—"

"I'm on the pizza," Felsic called. "Peggy, you drive careful in this."

"I will," she said, looking over her shoulder with a smile. "It rains in New Jersey, too, you know."

"You'll have to tell me about it," Felsic said, turning toward the studio's protected patio.

Peggy looked back to me.

"See? Date's still on. I'm just going to grab the basics for her—anything else you need while I'm at Ahz's?"

"Peggy—"

"Was that a *no*?" she asked brightly, and smiled. "All righty, then! Back soon."

And she was gone, leaving me alone with a soaked and justifiably annoyed cat.

I sighed.

"Would you care to come inside? I've got a nice fluffy towel, and if you'll let me, I'll use it to dry you off."

There was a pause. The cat blinked her eyes.

"Okay, then. Right this way."

And I turned to unlock the door.

As it happened, she wasn't a sleek white cat, after all.

Gentle hand-drying with a towel warmed by *jikinap* eventually revealed a moderately fluffy, mostly white cat, with an orange patch over her right eye, a brown patch over the left ear, a black spot halfway down her spine, and an extravagant black-and-orange tail.

"No wonder they couldn't leave you at the Camp," I said. "You sure do stand out in a crowd."

The cat blinked again. She was being remarkably patient with the process of being dried off, and if she wasn't exactly purring, she hadn't tried to kill me either.

Peggy had delivered the "cat basics" to the kitchen table, stopped for a moment in the living room to admire the progress with the towel, and departed, locking the door firmly behind her.

"Okay," I said, when the cat was no more than slightly damp. "Let's get you fed."

A survey of the kitchen floorspace suggested that beneath the wall-mounted kitchen phone would be the best place, since it was space I rarely strayed into. I had already placed the water bowl, and was bending down to put the food bowl beside it when I simultaneously heard the front door open, and the land sigh in contentment.

"Here you go," I said, putting the bowl of kibble down. "Peggy splurged on the sirloin, just so you know you're being properly appreciated."

I backed away, and turned, unsurprised to find Borgan leaning against the wall by the fridge.

"Good evening," I said.

"Evenin'," he answered. "Got yourself a cat, I see."

"Old Mister sent her along, with a recommendation. We're going to see how—or if—it works out. We've had an awkward start. I don't know exactly when she arrived, but she was soaked to the bone, and a teensy bit irritable, by the time I got home."

"She's a fetchin' little thing," Borgan said, adding, "Old Mister don't give his approval easy."

"So I gather."

I glanced over my shoulder. The cat was eating with a kind of dainty intensity that was peculiarly satisfying.

"Sorry I didn't get your voice mail 'til late," Borgan said. "One of the guys was needing a hand on a bilge pump, so I offered mine. Took a little longer than either of us hoped, an' by the time it was all said and done, I figured you'd appreciate it if I had a shower."

I grinned at him.

"Thanks for thinking of me. Get you a glass of wine? Or a beer?"

"Maybe after we take care of you going through what you got from your Varothi?" He grinned. "Might appreciate it more, after."

"He's not my Varothi," I said, just to be contrary. "But I take your point."

I squared my shoulders, and nodded at the couch.

"Best get started, then."

"Not so fast," Borgan said, and came away from the wall, opening his arms. I stepped forward—and stopped, startled by a sound like a furious teakettle.

The cat was hissing at Borgan. Her tail was so voluptuous, it was hard to tell, but I thought it might be, maybe, and just a little, fatter than normal.

"Hold on," I said, and bent down to tap her lightly on the top of her head. She stopped hissing, and blinked up at me.

"I appreciate your concern, and I apologize for not having made the situation clear. This—" I put my hand against his chest, "is Borgan. He's welcome here. The woman who brought you the food and the litter box, and who thinks you're cute, is Peggy. She's welcome here, too, but only when I'm here." I considered that, and added. "Though there's no need to get snooty about it, if she really needs to get in and I'm not here."

The cat appeared to be considering this information. Then she blinked her eyes, and turned away, heading back to the food bowl.

"Now," I said to Borgan, "where were we?"

CHAPTER FIFTEEN

Friday, July 7

"So," Borgan said, settling into the corner of the couch. "Given any thought on how you're gonna handle this?"

"In fact, I have." After all, I'd had *many hours* to stare at the rain and think about how I was going to find all the happy surprises Prince Aesgyr had probably entangled in my power.

I put one knee on the cushion beside Borgan, and propped one hand on the back of the sofa, which gave me an excellent view down at his face—a pleasure I rarely enjoyed.

"I built a template and filter system," I said.

He leaned his head back against the cushion and considered me out of narrowed eyes.

"A template and filter system," he repeated.

"Right. I used to be a software engineer, remember? This is what comes of it." I grinned. "Best you know the worst, right up front."

Even to myself, I sounded cocky. Hell, I *felt* cocky—it was an elegant little widget I'd built, and I had a right to be proud of it.

Just, I'd better not be *too* proud of it, with a side order of, *Remember, Kate, that the hacking metaphor is only a metaphor.* Manipulating *jikinap*—or doing magic, if you like it that way—isn't anything like slinging code.

For one thing, it's a whole lot more dangerous.

Which was why Borgan was sitting on my sofa, patiently waiting for me to tell him what the plan was, and what his part in it would be.

"The plan is that you'll be my anchor and my lifeline while I get up close and personal with my power and run it through the template and filter. The template will kick any nonmatch to the filter, which will isolate the nonmatches."

"And your template is...?"

"My own magical signature."

He frowned slightly, eyes half closed, and I resisted the urge to bend down and kiss him. Business before pleasure and all like that.

"Unless," I said, when it seemed like he'd been thinking a little too long, "there's a tried-and-true method that I should know about, but don't, because I'm a dropout from Ozali University?"

He snorted a soft laugh.

"If there is, it never rose to my attention. It's rare somebody shares power by... accident, let's say."

"Rub it in," I said irritably.

"No intention to. It just seems you specialize in coming at things from a unique angle." He gave me a smile that just about turned my knees to water. "So, I'm guessing that unique problems call for unique solutions. I'm ready when you are."

"Right."

I swallowed, because this was the oh-so-not-easy part, and walked out into the middle of the room. In theory, this was unnecessary. In theory, I could do what I needed to do while stretched out on the couch with my head on Borgan's knee.

...which, delightful as it would be, was *not* the image I needed at the moment.

I closed my eyes, the better to feel the heat of my power, coiled but... *interested*, at the base of my spine.

In the usual way of things, an Ozali *calls* her power, and she maintains control in part by imposing the shape it will take and the area it will fill. On the other hand, since I didn't know how "much" *jikinap* I possessed, I could never be sure of calling all of it, and I wanted to be very, *very* sure that I had filtered every single bit of sparkly magic stuff under my control.

Every single bit.

That meant, in a word, merging with my power.

Okay, Kate, I told myself, *it's going to be easy, just like merging with the land.*

Except I wasn't afraid of the land.

It is, of course, fatal for an Ozali to fear her power. And I didn't *fear* my power, though there was a time not too long past when I'd held it in loathing. With Mr. Ignat's assistance, and also with, I'm guessing, plain old familiarity, I'd moved on to respectful acceptance.

Very respectful acceptance.

I took another deep breath to center myself, focusing on the brightness, and the ferocity of my power.

Another breath. I felt my hand taken in a light grip in the instant before I fell headlong into my fires.

I was at sea, surrounded by sticky warmth. A voice that sounded very like my own was whispering in my ear, but too low for me to make out the words.

Butterscotch. I smelled and tasted butterscotch—and that was good. Butterscotch was my signature. I was in the right place. Go, me.

For a moment, it seemed as if I was shapeless, or possibly invisible.

My environment warmed slightly, and abruptly I could look down, and see a sort of colorless outline of myself, like the start of a pencil sketch. I felt something around my right wrist, raised it, and saw a strand of sea blue braceleting it.

Borgan's anchor.

If smiles were possible in that place where I was a ghost of myself, I smiled.

Then, I got down to cases.

Carefully, I brought to mind the template and filter pair I'd spent all the rainy afternoon and evening building. I received an impression of curious attention from the roiling substance about me, no more substantial than the flick of a fond flame against my cheek. That was possibly unsettling, but this wasn't the place or the time to be unsettled.

In an environment not so much *saturated with* magic, as an environment that *was magic*, it was no challenge at all to bring my little machine into being.

Whereupon—quickly, before I had time to overthink it—I threw it into, over, around and below the seething, curious powers.

Heat blasted, my center rocked, the smell of scorched butterscotch filled my nose, while smoke choked me in an innerscape suddenly black and cold.

I was alone. Empty.

Powerless.

My *jikinap*, capricious and dangerous as it was—had deserted me.

Deserted me *where*?

There was only *I*; in this place devoid of all power; an I who was again shapeless, and growing steadily colder inside a bleak, black emptiness.

I couldn't feel my wrist, much less the anchor line wrapped around it. Swallowing panic, I *reached* into the blackness, seeking Borgan, seeking the land, seeking...

But there was nothing.

In case I had closed them, I tried to open my eyes.

Blackness was the answer. Maybe I no longer had eyes.

Panic tasted like butterscotch, then—

Light flickered. It grew warm.

I had shape, and feeling. For instance, I could feel the anchor cord tight around my wrist; tight enough to hurt even a ghost.

And then I forgot the small hurt as my power flowed back, filling me; buoying me.

Making me whole.

The whole universe tasted of butterscotch; flames embraced me; my voice whispered into my ear.

"The filter worked."

I opened my eyes, saw the mantelpiece crowded with photographs and bric-a-brac. My fingers ached, in a grip so firm it was painful.

And on the floor before the cold fireplace, was a...device of strange design, made from what looked to be feathers and storm clouds, its outline slightly obscured, as if it were either very hot, or very cold.

There was the very faintest scent of peaches in the air.

"Kate?" Borgan's voice was soft, counterpoint to the pressure of his fingers.

"Right here." My voice was ragged, and I cleared my throat to get rid of the lingering taste of smoke. "Looks like the filter worked. The delivery system might need a little tweaking, though."

"A little tweaking," he said, his voice utterly flat.

I noticed he wasn't letting go of my hand, and looked up into his face. His mouth was a hard line, his lips pale.

Borgan was frightened.

That...was not a normal state of affairs.

"How scary was it from this side?" I asked, keeping my voice soft, and not mentioning that he was mangling my fingers.

A sigh shuddered through him, and his grip eased somewhat.

"Well, that's a good question. I'd say—not quite as scary as the time you went all over sparkles and started to spread out on the breeze. I never thought I'd be glad to've seen that, but it stood me in good stead tonight." He took a deliberate breath, the pressure of his fingers momentarily increasing.

"Your fires went out," he said. "You were dead cold. I could see you; I was holding your hand, but the power linking us just... floated free, and you—you were *gone*."

He sighed again, not quite as deep as the first.

"And then," he said, "you were back."

"Pretty much the way it played where I was, too," I said, and squeezed his hand before painfully slipping mine free.

"I think I'd like that glass of wine now; then we can look at what we caught."

We sat on the floor with the device between us. "We" being me, Borgan, and the cat, who was sitting very erect, ears alert; marvelous tail wrapped 'round her toes.

I sipped wine, savoring the fact that there had been only this one thing—this single invader—lodged inside of my magic. Now that it was out here for me to see, I could confess to myself that I'd been afraid that I'd secretly become the repository of dozens of such devices. And, as devices went, this one didn't look so bad; in fact, now that it had stopped...steaming, it was kind of pretty.

Though that might have been relief speaking.

"Well," I said, putting my wineglass on the floor at my side. "Let's see what's under the hood."

I extended just a tiny bit of *jikinap*—say toothpick-sized— meaning to probe for a door, or a keyspell, but at the first touch of my magic, the device unfolded, all its secrets on display.

"You seeing this?" I asked Borgan.

"Mm. Some tight engineering here. Your Varothi knows his spellcraft."

"*My Varothi*, as you continue to insultingly and inaccurately refer to him, is the biggest sneak in Six Worlds, and I include in that population, Mr. Ignat'. Who, by the way, said the prince is brilliant."

"That'll look good on the résumé," Borgan said absently. He was leaning forward, studying the thing closely. "What d'you make of this, Kate?"

A portion of the internal workings flared briefly blue, and I also bent closer.

It looked for all the world like a flywheel, and I said so.

"But where the energy comes from and goes to, that's not clear."

"No, now here's what I'm thinking," said Borgan. "What if that flywheel is just there to speed something up? I'm not smelling any disappears or appears in this, or seeing any burnt-up cinders of power littered about. Damn' clean little working, is what it is. Self-contained."

I blinked down at the device, seeing the flywheel's takeoff feed, which looked like a bit of loosely held string, drooping in the middle, and if the energy produced by the flywheel had to follow that droop, but it wouldn't, would it? It would—

"It would arc," I said, seeing it. I looked at Borgan, excited now. "It *is* a tesseract. The flywheel takes up my energy—my urgency—to be at a certain place *quickly*, increases the speed, kicks it *across* the gap. It uses the same energy I would use, by running; it just accelerates the process."

Borgan was grinning.

"It's so clean because it's not consuming anything, and it's not creating anything. It's zero-sum."

"I agree," he said. "But what about range?"

That was a puzzler. I looked back into the machine, but didn't see anything that...

"Wait, what's this?" I pointed at a small glitter at the boundary of the device—

"Here's another one...and two more," I said.

"At prime points," Borgan added. "If it was me doin' it, I'd limit the range to, say, a place I knew real well. Less chance of running myself into a tree."

"Right." I reached for my glass and sipped wine, my eyes on the device.

"So, the guess is that this one's good inside Archers Beach."

"Be reasonable. Your Varothi seems a reasonable man."

"Hm." I leaned closer, extended a *jikinap* pick and touched the northern boundary mark. It gave a little under my probing.

"Some flex there, so maybe not strictly within town boundaries. Be worth checking out, under controlled conditions. But . . . we can test the base proposition right now!"

Borgan considered me. "Can we?"

"Well, I can." I put my glass down and stood up, still grinning.

"Anchor me?" I asked, holding out my wrist.

"Not until you tell me what's in your mind."

"Sure. I'll use the machine to go to Nerazi's rock, then I'll step across the line to Surfside, and try to use it to come back. If it doesn't work, I'll step back across to the Beach side of the line, and come back."

"And if that don't work?"

"Then I'll do it the old-fashioned way, after I give you a call on the cell so you can walk out to meet me in the pouring-down rain."

Borgan smiled slightly.

"Behind the news. It's not raining."

I blinked, and queried the land. The report came back, pronto: no rain, clear skies; the waxing moon riding high.

"I'll anchor," Borgan said. "Mind if I take a copy of that, before you put it away?"

"Why not?" I asked, waving a hand over the device, and glancing to the cat, who was still sitting at attention. She looked up, as if she felt me look at her, and I nodded.

"You can take a copy, too, if you want one. The more the merrier."

The cat yawned.

"Got it," Borgan murmured, and I felt the anchor cord wrap 'round my wrist again.

I looked down at the device, extended another little pick of *jikinap*, and watched it fold up.

Then, I breathed it in.

It accepted my will with a docility I wished my own magic displayed.

"Back in a sec," I told Borgan—

—and smiled at the boundary stone, quietly glowing in the starlight. It was too early for Nerazi to be present, and there weren't any tourists nearby—probably they'd all gone to bed early while the downpour was still pouring.

The ocean breeze tugged on my braid, the way I liked to tug on Borgan's braid. I smiled, and took three steps forward.

I felt it, when I stepped over the line. Surfside wasn't my land. Though I could feel the intelligence, the *aliveness* of it, I had no power to touch it or befriend it.

I stopped.

And willed myself back to my living room.

The breeze yanked harder on my braid. The stars glittered above the ocean and below the waves.

Nothing else happened.

Bingo.

Smiling, I stepped back across the line, laughing when my own dear land leapt up, barking to welcome me back after our long separation.

Without breaking stride, I willed myself into the living room.

...and threw my arms around Borgan in an exuberant hug.

CHAPTER SIXTEEN

Saturday, July 8
High Tide 9:33 A.M. EDT
Sunrise 5:08 A.M.

"Sisters," she said to the goblins, "I would observe your enemy, the Borgan."

The goblin Daphne looked grave.

"He's very dangerous," she said.

"If there's more you need to know," the goblin Olida added, "we'd be pleased to tell you, just ask. There's no need for you to endanger yourself when everything we have is at your service."

Now that, she thought, was very true, though she doubted the goblin meant it in the way it was heard. Goblins were not a truthful race, and these were too ignorant to fear her. Still, they were useful to her, so she set herself to persuade them.

"Your care for me does you credit," she said, "but see how it is, that all of your observations of the Borgan have not been sufficient to allow you to prevail. You held him, subdued and bound, and still he was able to elude you. He makes a mock of you, the first-made! It is not, as you say, to be borne. I would see you returned to your rightful place, but I think, sisters—I do most sincerely think—that this Borgan must bear some charm, or hold some other magic that he has made invisible to you, but which may be perfectly observable to one who is your guest in these waters. Only take me to him."

There was a small silence before Olida spoke.

"A geas is on us, so we're not able to come near him. We can't guide you or guard you."

A geas? If it had been placed by the Borgan, then he was formidable, indeed. Goblins were...difficult to bind.

"He dared to lay a geas upon you?" she demanded, allowing anger to be seen. "Sisters, this Borgan dares too much!"

"No," said Daphne savagely, "that was Nerazi."

"Who is Nerazi?" she asked.

"Seal Woman," said Olida. "Borgan's ally."

This became very interesting, and what a tangled net the poor goblins sought to weave! Clearly, they had not thought beyond the time when all of their enemies were vanquished—or perhaps they planned to dispose of her, once she had done their work for them. That went beyond impertinence, into treachery. Her temper warmed—but she did not allow it to be seen, nor did she act upon it. The goblins were, for the moment, useful to her. Indeed, they were essential to *her* plans.

"It becomes urgent," she said to the goblins, "that I observe this Borgan. If you are forbidden to go near him, then another guide must be found. If there is no one who will dare it, then I will ask you to take me as near as you might, and I will go forward alone. Also," she said, slowly, "it might be well for me to observe this Nerazi."

In order to learn whether Nerazi, too, would need to be put aside, or if she would yield to a greater power, she thought, but she did not say this to the goblins. It would be best, if as many as possible of this lovely sea's creatures and processes were left undisturbed.

The goblins had traded a glance, from which she gathered that they feared Nerazi nearly as much as they loathed the Borgan.

"Let that float for now," she said, soothingly. "First, I must, myself, see this Borgan. How will it be done?"

The goblins were seen to sigh, then Daphne said, with something less than grace, "We'll find you a guide."

⚓

I woke to the sound of an engine revving, and to the realization that there was something damp stuck inside my ear.

"Hey," I said, reaching up to rub the afflicted body part.

My fingers found fur; the engine noise stuttered, and a weight I hadn't noticed on my head shifted slightly, possibly in protest.

Right, I thought, *I have a cat now.*

Not only did I have a cat, but apparently I had a cat who liked to sleep on my head.

"Sorry," I said. "The last cat I knew intimately was too big to sleep on my pillow. He slept beside me or on my chest."

Actually, he'd slept from my chest to my knees. Bowie'd been a *big* cat, and I'd been a smallish kid.

"I'm not complaining, understand," I said. "I'm just out of practice."

The weight on my head shifted and there was some activity that disturbed the peace of the pillow, followed by a brush of fur along my cheek. Then a white and orange face filled my vision while the cat seated herself on the bed by my left elbow.

Amber eyes seemed slightly puzzled, and I raised my right arm and offered a forefinger to her.

She gave it a polite bump, and settled back.

"So," I said, "it seems to be working out all right on my side. I hope it's working out on yours, but if it's not, you just let it be known. Also, you should know that it's usually plenty quiet around here; fun parties like we had last night are rare. Borgan and I have been trading off every other night, so, unless I hear different, I'll be spending tonight on *Gray Lady.*"

I frowned slightly.

"Might be *too* quiet for your taste."

The cat blinked—either an acknowledgment or a smile; I didn't know her well enough yet to call it.

"So, let's keep the lines of communication open, right?"

Another blink, which I took for "right."

"Super. Now, I'm going to go downstairs and start the coffee brewing."

The cat rose to all four feet, stretched daintily, and jumped over my legs, hitting the floor with an authoritative thump. I could see the flag of her tail as she headed for the door.

I threw back the bedclothes and followed.

An hour later, after a quick shower and breakfast with the cat, I was on my way up Archer Avenue, heading first for Wishes Art Gallery. I'd volunteered to take the news of the midway's sale and Fun Country's imminent demise to the on-the-hill members of Archers Beach Twelve to Twelve, and "get their thoughts." Jess had thought there'd be value in paying personal calls, rather than just phoning. I tended to agree with her, even though it wasn't necessarily the best timing in the world, being, as it was, High Season, and customers coming first.

I'd hoped my early start would at least solve the customer problem, a hope that crashed and burned as I walked through the open front door into Wishes. The place was crowded with customers. Each painting and photograph had at least two people admiring it, and the 3D stuff had even more. I slipped through the crowd, heading for the counter at the back of the shop with no real expectation of finding the owner at liberty.

My expectation was wrong.

Joan Anderson was standing behind the counter, overlooking the crowd, with her hands in the pockets of her jeans. She smiled and nodded when she saw me.

"Kate—welcome! What brings you all the way to the top of the hill?"

"News, and a pop quiz." I turned my head slightly to indicate the masses behind me. "Don't want to take you from your customers, though."

"They're not customers until they want to buy something," she said. "Or at least until they have a question. Come on around."

I stepped behind the counter and looked out over the shop. A teen couple, holding hands, paused on the threshold to gaze up and around with wide eyes, matching grins of delight growing on their faces.

"How's it going?" I asked Joan.

"We still have more lookers than buyers," she said comfortably. "But we do have buyers. I'm pleased with progress." She gave me a half-smile. "Is that what you came to ask me?"

"No, actually. I came to tell you that Fun Country has sold the midway and is closing the park at the end of this Season."

Her mouth tightened, but she didn't say anything. Waiting for the other shoe to drop, I guess.

"The question is kind of a double whammy," I said. "One: What do you think about the news, and two: Can you think of anyplace in town that the rides can relocate to? If you think that having an amusement park is a draw?"

"Of course it's a draw," Joan said promptly. "As to what I think about the news, I see some tender ears out there in the crowd, so if you don't mind, I'll limit myself to saying I think these decisions by Park Management are very shortsighted. Big parcels in town ..." She shrugged. "The only one that springs to mind is the empty lot where the Lonely Loon used to be—but that was sold for condos, wasn't it?"

"There's a rumor the deal fell through, but even if—the parcel's not big enough. I guess we could split the kiddie rides out from the adult, but ..."

A clash of metal, followed by a prolonged silvery tinkle, gave me pause.

"But," Joan said, stepping into the breach, "the rides ought to stay together, for synergy, and what's going to happen to the games?" She sighed sharply. "How much are they asking for the property the park's on now?"

"Henry's looking into it."

She nodded, then stepped up to the counter as the teen couple came forward, the girl holding a beaded bracket from which were suspended six silver butter knives and three silver spoons. The utensils chimed sweetly against each other as she walked.

"We'd like to buy this, please," the boy said.

"Certainly," Joan said, reaching under the counter and pulling out some sheets of tissue paper. "These are real silver, you know."

"Yes," the girl whispered, handing over her prize with visible reluctance. "Is there a special way I should treat them?"

I touched Joan lightly on the shoulder.

"I'll be going," I murmured. "Thanks."

She looked up, her hands still busy with tissue and knives. "Will there be a meeting?" she asked.

"Should there be?"

"I'll call Jess. Thanks, Kate."

"Sure."

I gave the kids a smile, slipped around the counter, and headed out to make call number two of the morning.

By the time I'd worked my way down to the bottom of the hill, it was clear that Twelve to Twelve members were horrified by, as Joan had it, Management's short-sighted decisions. The prevailing opinion was that the town should buy the land and lease it to an operator-owned corporation. Running a close second was the idea that the operators should buy the land.

The idea of a leaseback was intriguing, though I wasn't sure how reasonable it was to suppose that the town would be party to such a thing—or that it had sufficient money in its operating budget. Another job for Henry, I thought, turning right into the pass-through between Ronnie's ice cream stand and Lisa's Pizza.

It was in my mind to go up to Heath Hill, check in with family, and get a little relief from what was turning into another scorching hot day. Archer Avenue was choked with the cars of day-trippers coming in for Saturday at the beach, and I reminded myself that this was a *good* thing.

The pass-through gave onto the alley next to Daddy's, and the courtyard where he and Lisa kept their Dumpsters, maybe not the sweetest smelling shortcut for a hot—

"Stop that!" a voice screamed. It was followed immediately by a hollow *boom*, like somebody had just thrown the Dumpster lid back, and shouts of laughter.

Gaby!

I didn't need the land's confirmation; I recognized her voice. Gaby was one of the more timid of the *trenvay*, utterly harmless, and almost completely defenseless. Which of course made her a prime target for bullying assholes.

I tore around the corner into the courtyard, the land snarling like a wolf, ready to attack; to protect Gaby no matter the cost.

There came another *boom*, followed this time by a yell.

I stopped, and stared. Cans and bottles littered the concrete, rolling free, and making for treacherous footing. At the far end of the courtyard, back to the wall, was Gaby—a small, thin figure in gimme hat and khakis. And coming at her fast was a guy twice her height and maybe three times her mass. He reached—and he was air-borne, hitting the Dumpster's metal side about halfway up, the boom reverberating off the walls and the other Dumpsters, and fell to the concrete next to another guy, who was shaking his head in a dazed sort of way.

"Get outta here!" Gaby screamed.

I could see her shaking from where I stood, and the land fed me the taste of her rage—and something else; something like a racing, ravenous wind. It puzzled me—and then I had it—Gaby was calling on all the power of her service, to protect her.

And *that* was a two-edged sword.

"Gaby!" I snapped, and moved forward, setting myself between her and the two guys, knowing the land would warn me if one of them decided to get cute.

"Gaby, let it go. You've got backup now."

She looked up at me with eyes that showed red, her thin face was...graven, as if it were cut from stone.

"Gaby..."

The land snarled; I spun, dropping into a fighting crouch as the guy who had been shaking his head rushed me—

And became airborne, smashing into the side of the Dumpster with a *boom!*

"Gaby!"

The door in the wall to my left—the back door to Daddy's Dance Club—slammed open, and here came the man himself, striding into the midst of it, grabbing both guys by the collars and yanking them up to their knees. The shirts must've been a little tight to the throat, because neither one struggled, or tried to stand.

"Stand down, the both of you!" he snarled, presumably to Gaby and me. "I got 'em, and they ain't going nowhere. Now, who's gonna tell me what happened?"

He looked at me.

I shrugged, showing him empty hands. "I was cutting through and heard Gaby yell; thought she was in trouble and came in to help."

Daddy nodded and looked at Gaby, whose face now was only drawn and tired, though her eyes were still worryingly crimson.

"Pickin' up the returnables," she said, her voice shaking. "Those two—they come in for a bit o'sport. Pushed me, and spilled all my...all my cans..."

Daddy looked grim.

"Hey, man, she tried to kill us," one of the guys said, hoarsely. "Threw me against the Dumpster."

"You be glad *I* don't throw you *in* the Dumpster," Daddy told him, "*after* I break your worthless neck."

"Us!"

"You! What the hell were you doing? Just having some fun? A little freak-bashing to make yourselves feel good?" He yanked on their collars and the guy on the left actually raised his hand toward his throat.

"Pair of goddamn heroes," Daddy continued, apparently not noticing the guy's discomfort. "You make me sick. Gaby."

"What?" she squeaked, once again the timid *trenvay* I knew.

"You wanna report these guys to the cops or should I handle 'em for you?"

"No cops!" Gaby said, which anybody could've predicted she would.

"Right, then. I'll take care of 'em. You an' Kate clean up here. I'll bring you out a couple beers. All right, you two."

He twisted his hands a little more firmly in their shirts and started walking toward the door. The guys walked, too, on their knees, and I heard a deep chuckle.

Standing in the door was a short, whip-thin guy in motorcycle leathers, the Saracen colors on proud display. "Wouldn't've lasted long in our unit, huh, Dad?"

Daddy snorted. His friend chuckled again, swinging out to grab the arm of the guy on Daddy's left.

"I'll take this one," he said, and yanked him to his feet with a snap.

The guy gasped, but didn't yell, which meant nothing was broken. I hoped.

"C'mon, sonny," the biker said. "Time to sit you and your brother down and explain the facts of life."

He swung his prisoner through the doorway, Daddy following with his guy still walking on his knees.

The door closed.

Gaby had picked up one of her bags and was already busy recapturing the rolling returnables. I grabbed another and bent to the task.

"Little dangerous to call the whole power of your service to hand," I said softly, keeping my head bent and my eyes on the task.

"I didn't want to," Gaby said. "I was just so scared."

"Understood. If you don't mind my asking—what *is* your service?"

"Got a little stand o'wood down near the municipal parkin' lot. Nothin' so big and fine as your gran's Wood, but it's mine an' I love it. Hell of a fight, back when they was buildin'. *Hell* of a fight I had to put up when they was clearin' for the lot. They was gonna just keep on goin' while they had the equipment roused, and my wood nothin' but an auxiliary lot."

She shot me a look from under the gimme hat.

"Took it outta us, but we managed to scare the idea away."

"I'm glad you did," I said. "Is that town land, then? For the maps, I mean."

Gaby nodded. "Been up for sale—prolly still is. Ain't enough for nobody to want it, not at the price they're askin'. Just hope they keep askin' high."

"How much, you know?"

"Three hundred thousand, was." Her mouth twisted. "That's a lotta returnables."

The back door to Daddy's opened, and he came out, carrying two beers in bottles so cold the condensation rained off of them.

"Here you go," he said, handing them off. "On the house."

"Thanks," Gaby said, taking hers with a snatch. "Kind of you."

"Thank you," I said. "Daddy?"

"What's on your mind, doll?"

"Those two guys..."

He laughed.

"Don't you worry 'bout them. Keith'll give 'em bloody damn' hell, and by the time he's done, there's nothing they'll want more in their lives than to make him proud. Seen him do it too many times to count. Lucky he happened by today, or else we would've had the cops, since I wouldn't relish breaking their necks, even if they did deserve it—and they only stay scared so long." He looked aside, his mouth twisting a little. "Gaby."

She looked up, shoulders hunched.

"Next time, go a little easy, right? Trip 'em, or knock 'em cold. You got a cell?"

She shook her head, and he sighed, fishing in his pocket.

"Here," he flipped a coin to her; she snatched it out of the air and looked down.

"A quarter?"

"That's *my* quarter," Daddy said. "You're keeping it *for me*, unless you gotta use it for *this one thing*, and that's to *call me* if you get trouble like this again. You knock 'em out, with as little damage as possible, then you find a phone and you *call me*, no matter what day or time. Otherwise, that quarter stays in your pocket and you'll have it for me, if I ever ask for it back. We got a deal?"

Gaby straightened, and looked him square in the eye.

"Deal."

"Shoulda told me right off—well, hell, no. Guess not." He

sighed. "I'll be getting back inside, see how Keith's doing with our heroes."

"Thanks," I said again, meaning it.

"No trouble."

On that, he left us to it, closing the door firmly behind him.

I took a nice, deep swig of beer, sighing as much for its temperature as its taste, then set the bottle near the wall and went back to gathering empties.

CHAPTER SEVENTEEN

Saturday, July 8

The goblins had not said that the Borgan was beautiful.

She lay in the water with her guide; a *shark*, so Olida had it, a creature that had some resemblance to the *herigana* of her own lost sea—toothy, tough-skinned and murderous. When first she beheld it, she had wondered if the goblins at last understood their peril—but, no. It would appear that Olida was owed some service from the creature and it understood, as *herigana* did, that it was wise to bow before those more ferocious than itself.

So the shark brought her to a boat, and, obedient to Olida's command, remained with her. Whether it would seek to protect her from the Borgan, which had been Olida's further command, she doubted; but in any case, it would not be put to the test.

The love the sea held for the Borgan was plain to her senses.

Poor goblins. For such as they to aspire to something so rarified and perfect... It could never be; even the goblins must know it, in the deepest cave of their hearts. And yet, one could not find it in one's own heart, to scorn them.

No, she thought, for the goblins to desire what the Borgan shared with the sea was, perhaps, an effrontery—pathetic and laughable—nothing more. Neither they nor any of theirs could sully or break the purity of the sea's passion. One could almost pity them.

For a moment, she simply floated, rapt in the reflected glory of the sea's love. Then, with an effort, she focused her attention elsewhere.

The Borgan's power was old and deep: subtle and elegant. There was a constancy to it, and a sweetness somewhat familiar, as if it were—as if it were *exactly* the sweetness of the sea itself, which had so struck her when first she had entered these waters.

His power drew her; she felt that she might gaze upon him always and never wish to gaze elsewhere. He was seducing her, of course; seducing her to the sea. Such would fall well within his honor as the beloved of these waters, to capture random elements and weave them into harmony with the waves. She bore him no ill will for the doing of his duty, but *she* would not be seduced.

She drew back from her meditations, and brought his physical seeming under scrutiny.

The form he manifested was a pleasing echo of his power—strong, supple, and sure. His business upon the boat was a harvest of fishes—a duty she had known well, and often performed, in that time before she had become a goddess. For the doing of the work, he had stripped to the waist, showing a broad, bronzed chest, trim waist, and hard belly. She approved both the form and the use of it. Indeed, she was drawn . . . almost, she—loved.

That, she thought, was the action of the sea upon her. It gave her a new respect for the goblins, that they could continue to hate him against all of the sea's persuasions.

Watching him work his nets, she cast aside her plan to wrest this sea from the Borgan and make it her own. The sea would never love her as it loved him, though it would, because it did, treasure those things that the Borgan treasured.

To succeed, then, the plan must be to become the Borgan's foremost treasure. It must not be a rape, nor a battle—nor, as the goblins hoped for, a murder. No. It must be—it could only be—a marriage. She, who had been solitary in her power, who had shared with no other power, not even with her own, her beloved demons . . .

Yet, if she would have this sea for her own, then . . . she must, at first, *share* in the Borgan's power. Later . . . conditions might favor a reordering.

If she had any hesitation in adopting this change of plan, it was that the sea's passion might overwhelm her own necessity. It was, so she admitted to herself, a risk; however, it was not a very great one. She had been a goddess, and with care and cunning, she would be a goddess once more. For such a reward, she could be patient. And perhaps, she thought, watching the Borgan upon the boat... perhaps it would be *interesting* to love, for a little time, at least, without reservation.

A marriage, then. It was decided.

Obedient to the conditions of its debt, the shark had remained nearby. She called it to her now, and cast the web of her will about it, holding it quiescent while she drank of its energies. Her reserves were yet low, and for this, she required strength. Still, she did not sup the shark entirely, but left it to drift, the spark of life still burning. Perhaps it would make a recovery, if none of its kindred found it soon.

Strengthened by the shark's essence, she placed herself upon the deck of the boat.

The Borgan did not look around from his net, though she was certain he was aware of her. She had chosen to manifest in robes of sea green and aqua, extravagant sleeves lined in white. Her hair was an ebony crown, into which coral, pearl, and shell had been woven. He must see at once that she matched him in beauty, and was in every way worthy of him.

"There you are, then," the Borgan said, swinging the net over the hold, muscles moving, sweetly pleasing, beneath red-brown skin.

"Yes," she said, matching his tone of unsurprised composure. "I am here."

"You kill that shark?"

She raised disdainful eyebrows.

"Must you ask?"

The net emptied, he at last turned to look at her. His eyes were dark, his face austere. The long braid that fell over his shoulder was as black as her own hair, inter-woven with shells, beads, and other small items of power.

"In fact, I don't have to ask. I'm curious about your motivation."

She glanced down, feigning a pretty confusion, and looked back at him with a simulation of shyness.

"I am the guest of the sea. Shall I show my gratitude by murdering her children?"

"So it's manners, is it?"

Her smile was shy, but the robe moved seductively as she stepped toward him.

"I have been well schooled, in manners...and in other skills."

"Stop," he said, and she did, finding that she no longer wished to approach him.

"What's your name?" he asked, and she laughed—a true laugh, for surely he knew better. Perhaps he thought to disarm her, to convince her of his ignorance. Or perhaps, she thought, her amusement fading as she stood, held still and content by his will—perhaps he sought to find the limits of his control over her.

She lifted her chin and glared at him.

There had been a time when her displeasure had the power to kill. The Borgan...only shrugged.

"Is it hard to move in that thing? This is a fishing boat, in case you hadn't noticed. Not much use for silk here."

So, he saw her as foolish, and unequal. That would not do. After all, they shared something very important.

The formal robes flowed and melted until she stood in plain cotton tunic and long pants, her hair rolled out of the way, into a knot at the top of her head.

"This is what I wore," she said, "when I fished on my father's boat."

"Looks a deal more useful."

"I will," she said diffidently, "need to learn what is proper here."

"No need at all. Best thing for you is to go home, deah—back to the Land of Wave and Water. This is no good place for you to settle, and I'm not just talking about this piece of water. You know you're in the Changing Land?"

"Yes," she said, and forbore to explain the myriad reasons why she could not, could never, go home.

"Then you know you need to leave, before you take damage."

She considered him, a noble man, and, as she read it, genuinely concerned for her well-being. It would perhaps be advantageous, now, to tell some bare edge of the truth, and make an appeal to the noble heart.

"I have been here, imprisoned, for how long a time, I do not know. Perhaps I am changed; certainly, I am weakened. I have enemies at home. Please, may I not remain for...a few days more, as a guest, to build my strength?"

The noble heart responded; she saw his hesitation, and hid her elation, standing before him docile and patient. She felt his power brush over her, tender as sea foam.

"All right," he said. "Twenty days more, to build your strength. The sea will nourish you that long, so you don't have to feed on any more of my sharks."

She bowed.

"I am grateful," she said.

"Just mind your manners," he told her, turning back to his nets. "Go on, now; I've got work to do."

There was nothing else to do at this moment but demonstrate obedience. And so, she reentered the sea.

It was cooler under leaf.

As I walked the path the Wood opened for me, I began to hear music. Guitar, and something else—piano? A dozen steps down the path and a woman's voice asked the musical question, "Are you going to Scarborough Fair?" with a man's voice joining in the next line, "Parsley, sage, rosemary, and thyme."

Music and the lyrics grew louder as the path led me onward. Not a piano, I decided. Maybe a harp? Mandolin?

The path ended at the edge of the clearing. I stopped where I was.

Not a harp, Kate, I told myself, *dulcimer—remember?*

My mother's concentration was on her instrument, and she smiled as she sang.

Andy's concentration was on my mother. He'd left his smoked glasses off, and his bright orange gaze never left her face. His expression was—well. I've never actually seen a man sight water after wandering days in the desert, so I'll just say that Andy looked like a man who held his heart's desire...

...and knew all too well how fragile it was.

They sounded good together, I thought, and as far as I could tell, Mother wasn't rusty at all.

I sighed, watching them—and sighed again when Nessa turned her head to meet Andy's eyes and they finished off the last line together, their instruments taking the music through the finishing arabesques while they gazed at each other. I couldn't see my mother's face, but Andy looked like he was about to break into tears.

The last note faded. The musicians were still gazing at each other. My mother put her hammers down on her instrument;

swayed toward Andy—and it occurred to me that I'd better announce myself.

I applauded, and whistled.

Andy jumped, orange eyes flashing as he looked across the clearing. Mother turned more slowly, smiling—but the trees would have told her that I was on my way.

"Katie! What do you think?"

"I think you're ready for the Big Time," I said, moving into the clearing proper. "Here Andy was telling me that you were afraid you'd forgotten how to play. It sounds to me like you never had a day away."

"I'm not as rusty as I thought I'd be," she said, picking up the hammers. She frowned down at them, then threw me a smile. "But I *am* rusty."

"I think we did fine," Andy said. "The finish was a bit ragged, but nothing practice can't cure. We might try something simpler, if you just want to get comfortable again."

"Something simpler?" She threw him a grin, raised her hammers, and brought them down.

I blinked, my ear confused for a moment by the dulcimer's voice, and then I had it, and came in on the line.

"In the jungle, the mighty jungle, the lion sleeps tonight!"

Andy joined in, orange eyes slitted in amusement. He drummed his fingers lightly against the belly of his guitar, for the counterpoint, and my mother wove a bright embroidery of *Weeheeheehee dee heeheeheehee* around the chorus, hammering her dulcimer the while. We sang all three verses, and every damn one of the *wimowehs*, Andy raised his hand, brought it down, and we all stopped at once, the Wood around echoing with our music.

And then with our laughter.

"We gotta bring Kate onboard!" Andy was able to say eventually.

"Kate," I answered, somewhat unsteadily, "is not a musician."

"Nothin' the matter with your voice. If you feel like you gotta have an instrument, we'll just hand you a tambourine, and you rattle it when the mood strikes."

My mother didn't say anything. I noticed that, and I didn't look at her as I shook my head, still grinning.

"I've got enough on my plate right now, but maybe I'll take you up on it, after the park's sold."

"What?" Mother was interested now. I turned to face her.

"New Jersey headquarters has put the land the park rests on up for sale. We're finishing out the current Season, but then all the owner-operators have to shift their rides."

She was staring at me, lips parted and eyes wide. I glanced beyond her, to Andy, who stepped forward to put his hand on her shoulder.

"The midway's already been sold," I told him, completing the unloading of bad news as succinctly as possible. "New owner takes it up on September fifth."

"We should have bought the land," Mother said, "but by the time we realized—it had been bought...by the company—" she threw a glance over her shoulder, to Andy. "The first company—you remember? Before the fire."

"I remember, sure." He smiled at her, his fingers gently kneading her shoulder.

"What's going to happen?" Mother asked me.

"Still working on figuring that out. Twelve to Twelve—the citizen's committee I told you about?"

She nodded.

"We're taking suggestions—that's what I've been doing this morning, in fact. The two best ideas are to have the town buy the parcel and lease it back to the operators at a per-year—or the operators buy the land themselves."

"They're going to be asking two legs and an arm up to the elbow for that land," Andy said. "Condos right on the ocean, every one with a view—" He cast bright orange glance in my direction. "Or are they building a hospital?"

I laughed. Andy shook his head, his smile wry.

"Anyway," I looked back to Mother, "how's Gran?"

"Not out of the woods, yet," she said, and gave me a wan smile. "She'll want to hear this, though."

"No hurry," I pointed out. "There's still eight weeks 'til Season ends."

Mother sighed.

"The thing I never could get used to, in Sempeki," she said slowly, "was the...changelessness. I mean—events would take place—there might be a new Aeronymous, but nothing ever really *changed*. It was eerie."

I nodded, though I'd grown up knowing nothing else.

"So," my mother continued, "I'm grateful for it—for the fact that things progress, here at home. That people can influence new outcomes; that we *change*. I just wish, sometimes..."

"That it didn't happen so fast, or so frequently?" I nodded. "My friend Peggy has the same complaint. She wants to dial the speed back. I don't think we get to say how fast, though."

Mother smiled. "Then I suppose we'd best hold on tight."

She raised her hand and placed it over Andy's, where it rested on her shoulder, her face softening.

Don't wear out your welcome, Kate, I told myself and gave them a collective nod.

"I'd better be on my way—it's errand day. I'll leave you guys to practice."

"We'll tell you when we have our first gig. You and Borgan can come cheer us on."

"Deal," I said, including Andy in my smile.

The Wood opened a path for me and I left them, standing so close that they only threw one shadow.

I was weaving through the vehicles in Gentleman Johnnie's parking lot when my cell phone gave tongue. Fishing it out of my pocket, I flipped it open.

"Hey, Jess."

"Kate—sorry this's gotta be quick. We got a meeting of all the Twelve to Twelvers tomorrow morning at the Garden Cafe, six o'clock sharp. There'll be coffee."

"There'd *better* be coffee," I said, with mock ferocity, but Jess had already hung up.

CHAPTER EIGHTEEN

Saturday, July 8
Low Tide 3:13 P.M. EDT
Sunset 8:25 P.M.

Ethrane was on smoothie duty at the Mango when I stopped by. I knew it was Ethrane because the land told me so. What I saw was a slender woman who stood a little above the Maine average height, brown-skinned, and long-fingered. She'd kept the dreads, but changed the color from green to brown. She turned her head to look at me—and, I thought, to show off the broad, handsome face, in which a pair of subtly angled swamp-green eyes glittered with amusement. She smiled, showing teeth that were neither too white, nor too sharp. The right eyetooth was slightly out of line with its fellows; the effect was adorable.

"Looking good," I told her, and she laughed, deep and rich.

"Felsic said you were curious."

"Worse than a cat," I admitted. "I appreciate the effort, but there's no need to spend extra energy just for me."

"I disagree," she said slowly. "We'd gotten lax, some of us, and depended too much on mundane folks' willful blindness. That's powerful magic, but it's best to depend on yourself, and not leave important things to chance."

"Hadn't thought about it in precisely those terms," I said. "But I agree—depending on someone else is never a good idea."

Ethrane's charmingly crooked smile flashed.

"That wasn't what I said," she murmured.

I heard footsteps behind me.

Ethrane heard them, too. The green eyes lifted over my shoulder. "Customers."

"Customers come first," I said. "Peggy in back?"

"To you, yes."

I slipped into the booth; as I opened the door to the office, I heard Ethrane sing out, "Welcome to The Last Mango, best smoothies in Archers Beach! Today's special is blueberry-banana."

Peggy was sitting at the beat-up metal desk, her attention split between the laptop and the top page of a three-inch stack of tally pages.

I scuffed my sneaker against the concrete floor, so I wouldn't startle her. She turned her head and grinned.

"Archer! What's the news?"

"Well," I said, coming 'round to sit in the rickety wooden visitor's chair, "the fresh news is that there's a meeting of Archers Beach Twelve to Twelve tomorrow morning at the crack of dawn, near enough, at the Garden Cafe. We'll be talking about two ideas for keeping the park, and, I'm reasonably sure, how to form a limited liability corporation. Want to come? The coffee's pretty good."

Peggy leaned back in her chair and shook her head.

"I try to stay away from places where I'm going to be seen as Public Enemy Number One."

I frowned. "Why would anybody think that?"

She laughed. "You're cute when you're stupid. Think a minute, Kate. Arbitrary and Cruel has sold the midway and is going to be selling the land out from under the amusement park, thereby causing a lot of annoyance, not to mention real pain and hardship, too. Who in this room is employed by Arbitrary and Cruel?"

I looked at her, opened my mouth, found I didn't have anything much to say, and closed it again.

"Didn't think of that," I admitted, because of course Peggy still had a job; she was one of the company's fixers. They'd just send her on to the next thing that needed fixing.

"I can see that you hadn't. It's a good thing you've got me around to think of stuff for you."

"That's true," I said, around a sudden lump in my throat. I *hadn't* thought things through, not at all. I mean, I *knew* that Peggy was employed as a fixer by Fun Country Corporate, and I *knew* the Season was exactly twelve weeks long.

I just hadn't connected the dots.

In eight weeks, Peggy would be gone—off to her next assignment. And I'd never see her again.

"Kate? You okay?"

I took a hard breath and gave her my best smile.

"I'm fine. Just took a look ahead, which anybody'll tell you is a stupid idea."

She eyed me. "Anything in particular you're going to do about it?"

"Practice living in the moment. Which reminds me of my *other* reason for coming around. I am blessed with a day off, and I'm going to spend part of it in the grocery store. Anything you need?"

"Anything I *don't* need?" She shook her head. "Thanks, Kate, but I can't ask you to do my shopping for me."

"You didn't," I pointed out. "I offered."

"So you did." Peggy smiled slightly, reached to the right of the computer and pulled a sheet of paper toward her. "It's on your head, then, foolish, foolish woman."

She began to write.

She had no cause to fault this small, sweet sea for its use of her, prior to her exchange with the Borgan. Indeed, its gentle generosity had been one of the first aspects of these waters that she had loved. From the first, this sea had granted her sustenance.

Now, at the Borgan's command . . .

She paused, considering—and at last restructuring—that thought.

The Borgan no more commanded the sea than the sea ruled the Borgan. Rather, they were equals, each complementing the other.

The sea had accepted her from the first, as guest of the goblins. And while the goblins' magic would have hidden her, somewhat, from the Borgan, much as they hid themselves, he must still have been aware of her presence in his waters. Knowing this, he had not sought her out, but left her to the sea.

Because the sea liked her.

His own stated preference was that she should return to Cheobaug, and in keeping with that, he had made no attempt to bind her, or to weave her into the life and the balance of the sea. He had, however, allowed the sea's partiality to guide him, and was, perhaps, more generous than he might otherwise have been.

He granted his support, welcoming her fully as a guest in his waters—and see now what a feast lay before her!

Before, the waters had fed her; *now* they nourished her, and her strength increased with every wave. She lay back, and took what good things the sea brought to her; growing stronger, and making her plans.

It was six o'clock by the time I got back from making my rounds. I'd gone a little overboard on cat things, scoring several fleece throws on final clearance. I could put one on the couch, so she could be nearby when I did my mapwork and answered my infrequent emails. If she had a taste for that kind of thing. And I could put another one at the foot of the bed, which would be welcoming—more welcoming, so I hoped, than my pillow.

I'd also gotten a scratching post and a couple of toys with feathers and bells, and a life-sized mouse that squeaked and flashed blue electronic eyes whenever it was struck.

Hopefully, one or two of these offerings would find approval with . . .

Going upstairs to the front door, I sighed.

Gotta give the cat a call name, Kate. You can't just keep calling her "she."

I juggled the grocery bag in one arm, got my key in the lock with the other, shoved the door open, stepped inside . . .

. . . and stopped dead.

Borgan and the cat were sitting on the couch—correction: Borgan was sitting on the couch, reading a book. The cat was sitting on Borgan. They both looked up and smiled rather sleepily at me.

"I hope I'm not interrupting anything," I said.

"Just getting to know each other," Borgan said. "Any more of those in the car?"

"More than I want to think about."

I dumped the first bag on the kitchen table. Borgan put his book down, scooped the cat from his lap to the couch and stood.

"Mind some help?" he asked.

"Hell, no."

The groceries had been stowed; I had shaken out and folded one of the fluffy fleece blankets into quarters, and placed it in the left corner of the sofa. This particular fluffy blanket featured white elephants in a field of blue—it looked like they were floating, not very comfortably, in a midafternoon sky.

"I think I know why this one didn't sell," I said, turning to look at Borgan.

He was leaning against the mantlepiece, his arms crossed over his chest, watching me with amusement, and maybe a touch of resignation.

"Problem?"

"Probably not. Why didn't that one sell, then?"

"The elephants are definitely disquieting. In fact, I don't think I'm going out on a limb if I say that they look downright drunk. Who wants to snuggle up with a bunch of inebriated flying elephants on a cold winter's night? And it's definitely not the kind of thing you want to put in the baby's crib."

"Never had much to do with elephants."

"Me neither—and I'm here to tell you that blanket isn't making me eager to seek them out."

"So you're hoping the cat won't care?"

"The cat is, of course, far more cosmopolitan and suave than either of us. I'm certain she's dealt with situations far more awkward than flying drunken elephants with grace and aplomb."

"I'm guessing you're right. She doesn't startle easy, from my experience."

I eyed him.

"Have you been mistreating my cat?" I asked, mock-stern.

He grinned, and shook his head.

"When I come in, she'd been sleeping in front of the French door. Opened her eyes as calm as you please, got up, stretched and gave me a couple long strops on the ankles. When I sat down to read, she jumped up to take part."

"That's respectful. I did tell her that you were welcome here."

"So you did, and she's got a wicked good memory." He lifted an eyebrow and used his chin to point at me—no, *past* me.

I looked over my shoulder. The cat was kneading the fluffy blanket; I could hear her purr from where I stood. I looked back to Borgan and gave him a grin and a thumb's up.

"Phase one of Project Make the Cat Comfy is a success."

"Looks that way. Got a name for her, yet?"

"Not yet; I need to get to know her a little better."

He nodded. "While she's whipping the elephants into shape, we could have a glass of wine, if you'd like, and adjourn to the summer parlor so you can tell me why you're here."

"Shouldn't I be here?" he asked.

I moved to the kitchen and opened the refrigerator.

"You're welcome here," I said, which was true. "It gave me a bit of a start to find you when I came in, but after I got over it, I—was pleased. Thank you."

"Nothing to thank," he said, and I heard a clink as he got the wineglasses out of the cabinet.

I worked the cork, and poured us each a glass of wine. The cat was still kneading, eyes slitted in pleasure, when we crossed the room to the summer parlor. I left the doors open, and settled onto the deck next to Borgan.

"I should get the chairs out here, but it never occurs to me until I'm already sitting down."

"No sense getting up now," he said comfortably. "'Specially not for a chair."

"I agree. So, why did you decide to exercise your welcome this afternoon?"

He gave me a sideways glance, black eyes glinting.

"As it happens, I have something I want to talk over with you, and I'd rather have it said on land."

I put my wineglass down, and stared at him.

"Something you don't want the sea to hear?"

That was . . . disquieting.

Correction: It was frightening.

"Easy." Borgan put his hand on my knee. "It's not the sea I care about, but what's in it."

"If that was supposed to reassure me—it didn't."

Borgan sighed. "No, I can see that, all right. Think I'd know by this time to start the story at the beginning. Give me a minute to order myself."

I nodded, took up my glass and had a sip, looking out over the beach. There were a lot of walkers this evening, and a good number of people in their beach chairs, stubbornly determined to get as much summer sun as it was possible to get.

"All right," said Borgan, and I turned my attention to him.

He smiled and extended a hand to touch my cheek gently. I shivered—pleasure mingled with yearning. The man knew his work; not only did I like his touch—I *wanted* it. Left to my own devices, I'd even seek it out.

You're in a sorry state, Kate, I told myself.

"It turns out I was wrong, back a couple weeks ago, when I told you the prisoners who'd lived to escape had likely gone home."

I frowned. "Wrong? But the land didn't find any strangers."

"That'd be because one of them went into Saco Bay," Borgan said.

I stared at him, still not feeling soothed, the *ronstibles* very much in my thoughts.

"When did that happen?"

"I'm guessing it happened within hours of your Varothi's little diversion—but that's a guess. There was a lot of magic in the air that night, if you'll recall it."

"I recall it, all right."

"After . . . I had . . . an itch, call it, like there was something out of harmony, but I couldn't put my finger on it 'til today."

Fourteen days and he hadn't been able to put his finger on something that was out of harmony in the sea he guarded? I shivered, and this time it wasn't pleasure.

"How could you not know?" It was a reasonable question, but I could've done a lot better in the phrasing department.

"Sorry," I said, extending a hand. Borgan took it between both of his and smiled at me.

"I'm thinking you already know the answer—you told me yourself, back when you first come home, that there're bits of land, here and around, that you couldn't hear—just static, I think it was."

I nodded, and waved my free hand in the general direction of the living room, meaning to include the maps and guidebooks.

"Right," Borgan said. "So, it won't surprise you to hear that the sea holds places that are . . . not dead, necessarily, but not easy to pick up, either."

"The *ronstibles*' home is one of those places, isn't it? That was why Nerazi had to tell you they'd moved back."

"That's right."

"So the prisoner—ex-prisoner—went to the *ronstibles*?"

"Might've. There's other places, but if the *ronstibles* found her, they might've seen a chance to make mischief. They're as alert to changes in the sea as I am, and they don't have the High Magic to confuse them."

I thought about how it might've happened—but really, it was easy. The prisoner wouldn't have had much *jikinap*, just whatever she could snatch out of the confusion of energies during the great escape. She'd've been disoriented, and she wouldn't have had access to her memories, but you don't need memories to know enough to run away from a firefight.

So she ran—and found further progress blocked by the Atlantic Ocean. Hell, if she was from Cheobaug, which I was willing to bet she was, then her instincts might've *sent* her to the sea. Whereupon, she'd do the only sensible thing open to her—she'd wade into the nice water, for safety. The *ronstibles*, sensing a disturbance in the force—or, at least, in the balance of the sea—would surface to see what was up...and find a confused and amnesiac stranger, with the taint of *jikinap* on her, whom they would have had no trouble seeing as a weapon.

"So...what changed?" I asked Borgan.

"She came to me, today when I was fishing, and let herself be known."

"Two weeks after the fact?"

"A bit long for politeness, I'll grant. She made a proper manifestation, but she had to feed on a shark, to have enough power for it. That says to me that she went into the ocean weak, and—with or without the *ronstibles* in it—she's been using the time since to recuperate."

"So you talked to her? What's her name?"

Borgan snorted lightly.

"Two minds with one thought, there. I tried to fish it outta her, Kate, but she wasn't so weak as that."

"What did she want, then?"

"Well, that's a puzzle. As I get it from the sea, she wanted to look at me—and she did that for a time, from the waters. Maybe I looked reassuring, or maybe she remembered her manners—in either case, she came up on the deck..."

"After draining a shark," I put in.

He waggled his fingers.

"I won't say I liked it, but I will say that she didn't take all she could've. I asked her why not, and her reason was it would be bad manners to start killing the sea's creatures. We mended the shark, after she'd gone, so all's well."

We being himself and the sea together. I nodded.

"So, she came up on deck, dressed to impress—pretty silk robes all flowing like water, her hair done up like a crown. Hinted that a good time could be had, if I wanted it."

I blinked.

"Sounds like she didn't waste any time." That sounded bitchy, so I added, "What did you do?" Which didn't make it any better.

Borgan laughed softly.

"What I did was told her a working boat's no place for silks. She changed 'em for something more reasonable, then; told me it was what she'd worn when she'd fished her father's boat." He paused, as if considering. "That was true."

"After we got the wardrobe fixed, I told her to go home. She asked for a few days' grace, pretty and polite as you'd please, so she could husband her strength. Claims to have enemies at home. That was true, too."

He paused for a leisurely sip of wine.

"What did you do?"

Obviously, he hadn't asked the Gatekeeper—that was me—to open the World Gate, though I wasn't positively certain that he needed me for that. Still, if he'd opened it, I'd've heard it. Alternatively, he could've sung her back to Cheobaug, and I'd never know anything about it.

"I gave her twenty days and the sea's fullness," he said slowly. "The sea...likes her, and it was plain she likes the sea."

"There's a risk," I pointed out. "If she's working for, or with, the *ronstibles*."

"Sure, there's a risk," he agreed placidly. "Nothing's risk-free."

He lifted his glass again, and drank off what was left, his eyes on the beach. Or the sea.

I finished my wine, studying his profile. I wasn't entirely comfortable with the idea that there was a woman of Cheobaug in the waters of Saco Bay. On the other hand, I couldn't fault Borgan's decision. Whatever quarrel was waiting for her at home in Cheobaug, we—meaning me, Borgan and the whole of the Changing Land—didn't have any skin in the game. And while we'd like to keep it that way, there wasn't any percentage in forcing her to go home while she was too weak to cope.

"So," I said softly, "was that what you didn't want the sea to hear?"

The edge of his mouth curved slightly upward.

"It wasn't the sea I cared about. I didn't want her to hear me tell you." He paused, head tipped slightly to one side for a moment before he turned his head and looked directly into my eyes.

"I didn't want her to know about you." His smile grew somewhat fuller. "Turns out, there's risks I'm not willing to take."

CHAPTER NINETEEN

Sunday, July 9
Low Tide 4:06 A.M. EDT
Sunrise 5:09 A.M.

The Garden Cafe was standing room only. Not only was every member of Archers Beach Twelve to Twelve present, it looked like every nonmember store owner was there, too.

I poured myself a cup of coffee from the pot on the counter, and looked around. Brand caught my eye from his lean against the wall, and shifted over enough so that I could have leaning room, too. I gave him a nod and settled in.

"Where'd all these people come from?" I muttered.

"Apparently Joan called Mrs. Kristanos, and Mrs. Kristanos got her kids busy working a phone tree, calling every business in town, and anybody else they could reach." He paused to sip, gingerly, from his cup. "That guy there, in the white T-shirt? He's one of the owners of the 'change. The woman next to him is the curator of the History House."

"Hmm. Who's the guy in the suit, talking to Michelle and looking uncomfortable?"

"Credit union manager."

"Mr. Poirier coming?"

"Now, I wondered that, too. Seems like it's time to bring him in, but if he's coming, he's late."

Right on cue, came Jess Robald's voice, bold enough to override every other voice in the room.

"Okay, everybody!" She was standing as near to the center of the room as possible, holding her arms over her head, so we could all get a fix on her.

"Thank you all for comin'. I know it's an early hour after a late night, so I'm gonna make this short as I can. There's a lot of stuff, and I'm asking you to save any questions 'til I'm finished laying it out, all right?"

"We're all ears," Brand said from beside me. "Go for it, Jess!"

The land murmured, and I looked away from Jess, just as the door to the restaurant opened and a sturdy woman in jeans and T-shirt entered. She closed the door quietly behind her, turned—and met my eyes across the room. We exchanged a cordial nod, and I gave my attention to Jess, as Felsic drifted forward to stand at the edge of the crowd, nudging the gimme hat up an inch or two with a forefinger.

"For those who are comin' in late, this is what's going on that's got the rest of us all scrambled around," Jess said. She then gave an admirably succinct description of the situation, and outlined the most popular proposed solutions.

"Now, I've got some more information that has a bearing. First, the spot where the Loon used to be, right across from Ahzie's store—that deal went through. The new owners'll be siting condos on it, but what they're waiting for is all the licenses and permits and such that they need from the State before they can start building. That's the first thing.

"Second thing is that Henry's talked to a bunch of people. He found out that the asking price for the park land is two million five."

There was a stir and a mutter at that. Jess nodded, but raised her hand.

"Folks? We're short on time, so let me just go on, okay? Yeah, it's a lot of money, but we've got a couple ideas about that, if you'll hear me out."

The muttering subsided.

"All right, then. Henry . . . Henry's been doing a lot of work on this. Henry talked to Mr. Poirier at the Chamber, and he's willing—the Chamber's willing—to be part of the committee working on putting together a leaseback deal with the town. Mr. Poirier's going to be personally involved in putting the proposal together; he doesn't want there to be any loose ends when we take it to the town manager.

"Also, Janice Wing and Sylvia Laliberte are researching how we can form a limited liability company—we're going to need that, no matter which way this goes—and what a Twelve to Twelve LLC has to have in order to borrow enough money to buy the park's land."

She paused and looked around the room.

"The best outcome would be the leaseback, so that's front burner, and if anybody wants to be on that committee, you give me a call or stop by the ride and tell me so. The backup plan is the bank loan.

"Bottom line. We all of us want the park to stay right exactly where it is, and we all think having an amusement park is important to the town, and to the—to Twelve to Twelve's core goal of making Archers Beach into a year-round town, with a twelve month season!"

Brand came out of his lean, his mug tucked between his elbow and his side, and began to clap, loudly.

The entire room took it up, chairs scraping as people leapt to their feet. Someone whistled, piercing and high.

I clapped with the rest, the land showing me Jess, the center of all this adoration, red-faced, and moving her hands, palms out, like she was trying to push the applause away.

Another high sound cut the air—this one made by a coach's whistle—and Michelle jumped up on a table.

"Folks, I've gotta open this restaurant to the public in ten minutes! If you're staying for breakfast, grab a seat. Everybody else—I love ya, but—clear the decks!"

I moved out with the rest, keeping an eye peeled for Felsic. It was interesting that she'd come to the meeting. I wondered if it was her own idea, or if Peggy'd sent her.

Or both.

Whichever, I missed her in the crush and didn't see her outside. The land, queried, showed me a piece of swamp, which I suspected was just behind the Sand Dollar—Felsic's service.

All righty, then; I could take a hint.

I turned left, and headed for Heath Hill.

Mr. Ignat' was sleeping with his back against Gran's tree, legs drawn up, hands folded over his belt buckle, hat tipped down over his face.

I paused at the edge of the Center, looking about me. Mother was nowhere to be seen, but I did spy Mr. Ignat's companion—or perhaps his partner—Arbalyr, the anti-Phoenix, asleep in the high boughs of a yellow birch.

Unwilling to disturb this scene of domestic peace, I turned to leave. After all, my question wasn't—

"Good morning, Katie."

Mr. Ignat' had raised his head, and pushed his hat back. He was smiling at me.

"Good morning. I'm sorry I woke you."

"It's time for me to be waking up," he said, rolling to his feet, and stretching. "Have you had breakfast?"

"I had an early meeting, instead."

He glanced up, as if he could read the sun through the canopy of the trees. "Early, indeed. What was so urgent?"

"Trying to figure out how to save the amusement park. Got a couple of good ideas, and a bunch of good people working on them."

"And the odds of success?"

I shrugged. "Not so good, is my guess. I wish my luck rating were higher."

"Luck rating, Katie?"

"Yeah. I didn't realize it, but apparently just by being here I've boosted the town's luck. You've seen the new businesses, haven't you? Hell, the push to try to expand the Season—that's part of it, too. Not a responsibility I necessarily want, but if I'm going to have it, then I wish I had more of it."

"Ah," said Mr. Ignat', "let's go down to Bob's for breakfast."

I looked up into the yellow birch. Arbalyr, last seen with his head beneath his wing, looked down at me, gimlet-eyed and very much on the case.

"Sure," I said. "There might even be a table for us."

"I'm confident that our luck will hold," he said seriously, and bowed gently. "After you, Katie."

"Was there a particular reason you came to the Wood this morning, Katie?" he asked as we walked down the side of Heath Hill.

"As a matter of fact, there was. I wanted to let you know that one of the prisoners from the carousel took refuge in Saco Bay. Apparently, she's not very strong, and has enemies at home. She's been laying low until she felt up to introducing herself—which she finally did, yesterday. Borgan gave her twenty days and all the resources of the sea."

"That is Borgan's right, as Guardian," Mr. Ignat' said, after we'd moved a dozen steps further down the hill.

"I know it is," I said. "It's just..."

I turned my head to look at him and met his eyes.

"Mr. Ignat', do you know who the prisoners—were? Jaron the Varothi was imprisoned for political gain by Prince Aesgyr's enemies. Did you—did *Gran*—" That sentence wasn't going even close to where I wanted it to go. I waved my hands and abandoned it.

"Your grandmother knows what the Wise told her about the prisoners," Mr. Ignat' murmured.

Let's be clear here that Mr. Ignat's not exactly the Wise's biggest fan ever. Whether that's because of a general preference for chaos over order, or something more personal, I didn't know. And it occurred to me that I ought to.

"Why don't you like the Wise, Mr. Ignat'?"

"Various reasons," he answered promptly, "most of them having to do with the war with Daknowyth. I also object to their use of your grandmother's carousel, and to their abuse of the Changing Land. This is a beautiful and peculiar Land; it is not the trash heap of the other five."

Personal reasons, then, and well-articulated, too. I considered my next question as we walked across Gentleman Johnnie's parking lot, empty at this hour on a Sunday morning.

"What was the war with Daknowyth about?" I asked.

He laughed.

"So simple a question! Say—simply—that it was about access. To *jikinap*. A very long time ago, power circulated freely through the Six Worlds, so that no world had too much, or too little."

"Did we—did the Changing Land—have *jikinap* then?"

Mr. Ignat' moved his shoulders, as if he didn't quite know how to answer.

"From the beginning, the Changing Land has been unique. Power flowed here from the other Worlds, and of course, it changed. That power then flowed back through the other Worlds, where change was slow, and rare. The flow of changed *jikinap* kept the other five Worlds from stagnating."

I remembered that the first story Borgan had ever told me had been about the creation of the Six Worlds, and how our greatest strength, right here in this World, was...change.

"Sounds like a good system that benefited everybody. What happened?"

Mr. Ignat' sighed.

"People hungry for more power, for an established base from which to rule over and control other people, began to...build dams, to devise ways to attract *jikinap*, and capture it. Other people sought to minimize the effects of the flow from the Changing Land, and moved it, just slightly, out of alignment with the other Five Worlds."

I blinked.

"How long ago was this?"

"Some while back," he said. "Before my time."

Okay, an epoch ago, make that.

"By the time Daknowyth mounted its war, the flow of power had long favored Sempeki. Daknowyth was beginning to die, for lack of sufficient *jikinap*. The Queen had to act, and so she did."

"And lost."

"In fact. But it may be said that the war itself created an imbalance in the systems, and Ramendysis arose as the greatest Ozali Sempeki ever produced."

"By killing every other Ozali in existence, and absorbing their power."

"Yes. And, as you may recall, the Queen of Daknowyth promised him her daughter, the Opal of Dawn."

"Why yes," I said drily, "I do recall something along those lines."

Mr. Ignat' smiled gently.

"The plan had been that Ramendysis, replete with the power of a thousand Ozali, would truly wed the Opal, who would then...release their shared *jikinap* into Daknowyth, reviving and restoring it." He shrugged. "It might have worked, too. But by the time Ramendysis came to claim his bride, it was much, much too dangerous to go forward with the plan." He sighed. "Neither the Queen nor her counselors had expected him to be able to control so...very...much *jikinap*. It was by no means certain that the Opal—that *even* the Opal—could have survived the sharing of their powers."

Which was why the Opal had to be hidden. And the carousel had been the perfect hiding place, because there were already souls bound into it. Who was going to notice one more?

That was more or less where I'd come in, except...

"Wait." I replayed the Queen's plan, and shook my head.

"She was—the Opal was not only going to marry Ramendysis"—a risky, not to say outright dangerous, undertaking of itself—"but she would also have to kill him *and* herself in order to release his—their—*jikinap* into her Land?"

I mean—politics is politics, and the Queen of Daknowyth hadn't exactly invented the marriage of state, but the rest of it—that was just *cold*.

"Not quite," Mr. Ignat' murmured as we crossed Fountain Circle. "In her own Land, the Opal occupies a position quite similar to yours, here in Archers Beach. Daknowyth would not have *let* her die."

So—according to the Queen's original plan—Ramendysis wouldn't have survived his wedding night, but the Opal—and the Midnight Land—would have survived, renewed, and with a future before them.

I liked that plan better. *Much* better.

"So, how's Daknowyth doing now?" I asked slowly. The question was tricky—time isn't exactly synchronized between the Six Worlds—but it was the best North American English could do. I caught my breath and stopped, suddenly realizing, there in the middle of the sidewalk, half a block from Bob's—suddenly realizing what I had done.

Mr. Ignat' stopped, too. I looked at him in horror.

"I spiked her guns," I said. "By killing Ramendysis here—in the Changing Land. Tell me I didn't kill Daknowyth, too."

"Katie..." Mr. Ignat' took my hands in his. His smile was fond, which didn't necessarily mean that I *hadn't* killed Daknowyth.

"The Opal of Dawn is clever and resourceful; she reminds me forcibly of you. Therefore, she did what any clever and resourceful Ozali would do when the ether is on fire with power."

"She took it in," I said, feeling relief punch me, hard, in the stomach.

"Not only did she take it in, but she channeled it to her Land."

I frowned. "How?"

"Remember that she is to Daknowyth what you are to Archers Beach. Her Land lives in her, as she lives in her Land. All she needed to do was to open her heart, and accept the gift the Changing Land so generously gave to her."

He squeezed my fingers.

"Far from killing Daknowyth, you made it possible for much more of Ramendysis' power to flow into it than might otherwise have been harvested. For the moment, the Land of Midnight is not only healthy, it is robust. And that's your doing, Katie."

"They're in a position of strength," I said, as we turned and continued walking toward Bob's. "That's why Prince Aesgyr took Jaron to Daknowyth." I sighed sharply. "The Changing Land's going to become a battlefield."

"I...think not," Mr. Ignat' murmured.

"Any particular reason?"

"I think it has become obvious to all that the enemy is not Sempeki," he said slowly. "Prince Aesgyr's recent actions, in particular, lead me to believe that we will see a tightly controlled strike at a very specific target. Battles are messy; they are impossible to control and difficult to predict. Prince Aesgyr is far too canny to allow this...readjustment...to fall out of his hands."

He reached past my shoulder and pushed the door to Bob's open, gesturing me to proceed him in the racket of voices and the clatter of cutlery.

"Booth at the back!" JoAnn called from across the room, waving the coffeepot she was holding in the general direction of *the back*.

I waved and led the way to the last booth in the main dining room, right next to the kitchen door. A perfect place, really, to hold a conversation about almost any secret thing you can think of.

"Do you think the Changing Land will be...pushed back into alignment?"

"Returned to its original purpose and position?" Mr. Ignat's eyes lit—by which I mean the blue flames at their centers momentarily flared. "It would be difficult, given how long the displacement has been in force. It might be necessary to build a conduit, rather than shift..."

"Mornin', Mr. Ignat', Kate. Coffee?"

"Good morning, JoAnn," Mr. Ignat' said, smiling up at her. "Coffee for both of us, please. Kate likes lots of cream."

"If you run through what's in the saucer, there, holler and I'll bring more." JoAnn filled our cups with brisk efficiency. "You know what you want, or do you need a couple minutes?"

"I'll have a grilled blueberry muffin," Mr. Ignat' and I said in unison.

JoAnn laughed.

"Comin' right up."

She had rested all night in the arms of the sea, which had nourished her and cherished her.

Cherished, soothed, and much improved in strength, she refined her plans, and plotted her moves. Now, in the light of a new day, she tested the Borgan's geas, found it adamantine—and laughed as she lay among the waters.

She had grown vainglorious in her imprisonment. Not even at the height of her powers, when she had been a goddess and a force to fear...Not even then could she have broken a command laid upon her by another god, standing at the center of his power.

So be it, then. The Borgan had given her twenty days' grace, now reduced by a night. As tempting as it was to simply rest with the sea and gather her full strength to her, time pressed. If she could not be strong, she would be cunning. If she could not be invincible, she would seem vulnerable.

In no case would she fail.

It was time to return to the goblins.

CHAPTER TWENTY

Sunday, July 9
High Tide 10:24 A.M. EDT

Mr. Ignat' and I parted ways on the sidewalk in front of Bob's. He was bound for Fun Country, and I was bound for the top of Dube Street, and a probable session with the maps and guidebooks.

The cat was sleeping on the fluffy blanket of inebriated elephants when I let myself in. She immediately opened her eyes, rose into a full Halloween cat stretch, and jumped to the floor. I pushed the door closed and stood still as she jogged across the room and wove around my ankles.

"Hi, there," I said, leaning down to offer a finger. "I'm glad to see you, too, but you didn't have to get up for me."

She bumped my finger politely with her nose, and gave me a squinty-eyed cat smile before strolling off to the kitchen.

"The meeting went well," I said, following her. "Jess Robald is shaping up into quite the leader of people. I hope she can lead them to answers that work, if not exactly to the Promised Land."

I opened the fridge, got out the bottle of cranberry juice, and opened the cabinet for a glass.

"After," I continued, for the cat's edification, "I went up to Heath Hill. Mr. Ignat' was in a forthcoming mood, so I got a history lesson. We stopped at Bob's and had grilled blueberry muffins for breakfast, just like old times."

I shook the juice until it was foamy, filled the glass, and put the bottle back in the fridge. Leaning against the counter, I sipped, gasping a little at the icy tartness.

The cat was at her food dish, crunching kibble with enthusiasm. She flicked an ear, which might equally have been a request to continue the fascinating account of my morning, or an appreciation of my brief silence.

"I figure to do a little still zone research," I said. "You can help, if you want, or you can go back to your nap."

No response from the cat. Well, what did I expect? She was eating.

I finished my juice, rinsed the glass and put it in the sink. Then I crossed to the French doors, opened them and stepped outside for a moment to overlook the beach. It being Sunday morning, there weren't epic crowds overflowing the beach, but there was a nice sampling of fun-seekers about, and a vigorous game of volleyball going on in the high, dry sand near the dune fence.

Nice day, I thought, taking a deep breath of salt air. It was good to be home.

I stood for another minute, just...appreciating the fact that I was home, the land making satisfied music at the back of my head, before I went back inside and opened up my books.

I was flat on my back on the floor, map and guidebooks to hand. One deep breath to center me, and another to clear my mind. Third—

Right then I felt a weight on my stomach, which moved up to my chest, and began pushing. Hard.

I opened my eyes, and lifted my head.

The cat smiled at me.

"I'm trying to concentrate here," I said. Then I remembered that I'd told her she could help, if she wanted to. Obviously, she wanted to.

"For this job," I said, "I need to be able to focus, and not be distracted. Kneading my breast bone is distracting." I paused, and added. "If you want to lie on me, that would be a big help. I'm hunting, but inside my head."

The cat smiled again, folded her front paws neatly under her chest and settled in, chicken-style. I could feel her purr, but I didn't think that would create a problem with my concentration. Bowie's purrs had focused me wonderfully.

I closed my eyes, feeling the comfortable weight on my chest. One deep breath to center; two to clear my mind; three, and I opened myself to the land.

The full riot of life and of living that was Archers Beach opened to my senses...diffidently. We'd both learned something in the course of our search for still zones. The land had learned to moderate itself.

And I had learned to trust that the land wouldn't overwhelm me, and swallow me into itself.

They do say that practice makes perfect.

The music of the land beckoned me. I allowed myself to sink just below the surface, observing with a sense that wasn't really like hearing or sight, but a combination of both. From this level, I could feel the disparate voices that made up the song, like the biggest jigsaw puzzle in the universe.

Every piece fit right where it was best suited; each informing the pieces immediately touching it; connecting, and connecting again, the whole stronger than the parts. At least the parts that were doing their jobs. The parts that had fallen silent, they weakened the whole; they offered nothing for pieces adjacent to them to anchor to, and created an unstable situation.

Buoyed by the land's song, *in* it, but not quite *of* it, I allowed myself to expand, casting my net wide, until suddenly, I heard it—Check that.

I *didn't* hear it.

I narrowed my attention until I had that patch of stillness directly in my sights. Holding it close, I expanded myself very, very slowly, trying to identify the pieces nearby, the voices that were still joined in song.

This was the nerve-wracking part, and, sadly, the part that practice hadn't made anywhere near perfect. Or at least, not yet.

I brought every bit of concentration I possessed to bear, and took...call it a *mental snapshot* of the still zone, and its surrounding pieces.

Then I rose to the top of the song, and higher still, until I was fully back in my own body, lying flat on my back on the living room floor, my face cooled by the breeze from the open doors, and a cat purring on my chest.

I raised my hand, and held it near her face, the backs of my fingers parallel with her cheek; close, but not too close.

She leaned into them, rubbing her cheek down my skin, the purr output increasing.

"Okay," I said softly. "Now what happens is that we look at the map and try to match that snapshot I took to the lay of the land, so to speak."

The cat smiled.

"You're cute, too, but I need to change position to look at the map, so here we go..."

I rolled, slowly. The cat came to her feet and walked against the roll—just like I was a log floating down the river, and she was the log driver—until I was on my stomach and she was standing on my ass. I propped up on my elbows, pulled the map to me, and held my mental snapshot against it. The technique that seemed to work best, when it worked at all, was to focus on both the image and the map and wait for a sign.

In the past, the sign had taken the form of a sudden and overwhelming conviction that *this place right here* on the map was what I was looking for. It was pretty damn' intense when that happened.

Unfortunately, what usually happened was that I would focus until my eyes crossed, the map would blur, the mental snapshot would disintegrate and a line of white pain would sear through my head, leaving me with a sullen headache.

I focused, trying to look *through* the snapshot and *into* the map. Distantly, I was aware of something happening on my back, but didn't really connect it with the cat until I felt whiskers tickle my ear as she hunched on my shoulder to stare down at the map with me.

It was either the whiskers in my ear, or the thought of her studying the map—or both. I laughed, the image and the map wavering in my bilevel vision.

I snatched at my control, fumbled, and saw a flash out of the corner of my mental eye before I lost it all.

"Damn," I said mildly. I leaned my head softly against the cat's head.

"You can't do that, kid. I'm an amateur at this stuff. I need all the concentration I can bring to bear. I appreciate the help, though."

I sighed. At least I didn't have a headache this time.

"I thought I saw something just before it all went to hell," I told the cat. "But it went by so fast that I didn't get it."

The cat stiffened on my shoulder, as if in surprise. I felt her weight shift, and saw one furry paw come down hard on the map.

I blinked, and slowly extended a finger toward the paw, which obligingly lifted away. The force of her blow had left a dent in the map; a claw tip had put a tiny tear in the glossy paper.

I put my finger on the tear, and felt a jolt of certainty.

"Holy moly, kiddo, that's seventh-level shit. You're wasted here."

The cat jumped off my shoulder, using her back legs hard. I hastily reached for a magic marker and drew a circle, noting the place with a touch of astonishment.

"St. Margaret's Church?" I asked, and rolled to my feet.

The cat was sitting on the floor between the living room and the kitchen, staring hard at exactly nothing. Somehow, her pose conveyed affronted dignity.

"Hey." I stretched out on my side on the floor next to, but not touching her.

"Hey," I said again. "Nancy should've told you that I'm an idiot. Always saying the wrong thing. What I meant was—you really helped me out, and I'll go check that spot"—no putting this off until it was safe, I thought; not with hurt feelings in play—"tomorrow. That thing with being wasted? I'm only worried you'll get bored with me and the job and move on. I wouldn't like that."

She turned her head and considered me out of solemn amber eyes. Then stretched her neck out—and nipped me lightly on the chin.

The level of relief I felt was 'way out of proportion with the problem. I smiled and reached out to rub her between her ears.

"Thanks."

She purred.

"So, since it seems you're staying, we ought to figure out a call name for you. Any suggestions?"

The cat yawned.

"Not useful, unless you want to be called Sleepy."

That earned me a glare—also not particularly useful. I stared back.

The cat blinked first.

She sighed, stretched, and tucked up against me where I lay on the floor, her back against my chest. Another sigh and she seemed to go immediately to sleep.

I closed my eyes and cleared my mind.

The darkness behind my eyelids lightened, like I was looking through fog; I heard the familiar crash of waves, the sound of a buoy bell underneath. The fog lightened more, and suddenly I was looking at a rock. It was a biggish rock and unusual, even taking into account that I was probably looking at it from cat-high.

For one thing, the surface glittered, like it was made up of a thousand sharp crystals. For a second thing, the crystals seemed to be rooted in a stem of granite—sort of like a knife bouquet.

I noted the rock even as I tried to keep my mind open. If the cat wanted to show me something else, I'd better be with the program.

But it seemed as if the rock was the thing. Gradually, it faded from my awareness, and I opened my eyes to find I was staring into a pair of serious amber eyes.

"Okay," I said, reaching out to rub her ear. "I got it, now all I have to do is decode it. I don't suppose it's remotely possible that you're wanting to be called Crystal?"

The cat yawned.

"Figured."

I thought about it. Given where she'd come from, it was almost a sure thing that the rock in question had been part of the Camp Ellis jetty, though I was willing to bet that the cat didn't want to be called Jetty, either.

"Well," I said, rolling over onto my back, "I'm not going to call you Rocky. Belle? Foggy?"

Two more yawns.

I sighed, rolled to my feet and went over to the bookshelf, and ran my fingers over the spines of the reference books there until I came to the tatty copy of *Roget's International Thesaurus, Fourth Edition*, published in 1977.

Perfect.

I sat down on the floor, crossed my legs and cracked the book.

The cat came over and put front paws on my knee.

"Half a sec," I told her. "We'll getcha something good."

Here we were—383.11. I cleared my throat.

"Let's see—*lithic, adamantine, flinty, spall...*" I looked up. The cat yawned.

"Right. Hey—*chesil's* kind of pretty."

Another yawn. I sighed.

"*Breccia...*"

Claws pricked my skin lightly through my jeans.

I looked up and met the cat's eyes.

"Breccia," I said, just to be sure.

She squinted her eyes in a cat smile, and I closed the thesaurus.

It was Olida alone she found at the goblin's cavern, and that was fortunate. Improved though she was, she thought that taking both at once was yet beyond her.

Indeed, she suspected that Daphne alone would have been... difficult. Olida—

Olida would present no difficulty.

"Sister, you were gone so long that we became concerned," the goblin said, and indeed, her concern seemed genuine.

But, then, she reminded herself, Olida wished the Borgan dead. Of course she would be concerned if the proposed murder weapon became lost.

"Daphne went out to look for you," Olida continued. "Did you see Borgan? What did you learn?"

"I saw the Borgan, yes," she said, smiling as she rested in the secret currents of the goblins' cave. "I learned that he is very strong, and that the sea loves him above all else. Indeed, I must congratulate you, sister, on your strength of will. How have you remained aloof from the sea's emotion?"

Olida's gaunt face grew gaunter.

"We were the first," she hissed. "We! The waters were fierce, and full, and mighty; we served her passions well. She loved us. Us! Then he came, and she—*changed*. He *calms* the waters. He makes her vulnerable. But, we are the first—and we will protect her." Olida spun in a tight circle, and for a moment bubbles obscured her.

"We've been able to resist Borgan's influence on her, because we love her."

So, the poor goblins loved the sea precisely as the sea loved the Borgan. As firstborn, they would have no choice. They *could not* feel otherwise, even though the temper of the sea had changed. In fact, the sea's new love must constantly pain them—and pain kept their hate alive.

Poor goblin. She sincerely pitied it, burdened so long by hatred and pain.

Soon, now, it would feel neither. Surcease—that must be her gift.

She smiled softly and allowed her diminished aspect to arise. The dark waters began to glow, reflecting the small glory of which she was capable. Olida's hard face softened; her eyes grew misty and wide.

"It saddens me," she murmured, "to say this, sister, but—you cannot prevail against the Borgan."

"No...no, we must!" Olida stammered, but her voice was as soft as her face; her will was breached already. "With you—you to aid us..." She lay limp in the waters, vulnerable, unresisting, and utterly unaware of her danger.

It was her will that the goblin knew neither danger nor fear. There was no need to inflict further pain on a being that had been so wracked and for so long.

Not even were that being a goblin.

"Poor child, you cannot prevail," she said, stroking the currents in a subtle request. "Even I...cannot prevail against the Borgan." She opened her arms. "Come to me now. Give me your anguish."

The current obliged her. Olida, bedazzled and unresisting, flowed into her embrace, and lay in her arms like a child in truth, eyes gazing into her face, as if she peacefully watched the moon, floating in the sky.

"You have been so very brave, for so very long," she crooned, bringing the goblin to her breast. "You have been strong. I honor you and all that you have accomplished." She kissed the pale forehead. "What is your name, sweet child of the sea?"

"Korkilig," Olida whispered.

She smiled and bent her head.

"Korkilig," she murmured, "you are mine."

CHAPTER TWENTY-ONE

Sunday, July 9
Low Tide 4:30 P.M. EDT

"It has been a little slow," Vassily told me, adding, with the air of an old hand, "but it is Sunday. When everyone has checked in, and had their dinners, then it will be quick again."

The kid has four Season Sundays under his belt, Kate, I told myself. *If he's not an old hand, he's not a newbie, either.*

Also, he was right. Early Sunday usually was slow, the reason being that the tourist population changed over on Sundays. The weeklies were all checked out by ten o'clock Sunday morning, and heading back to wherever they called home. The new batch of weeklies started check-in at three o'clock. After that, they'd want to grab a couple of hours on the beach, and get something to eat. The amusement park, open 'til midnight—they'd get to the amusement park when the breeze off the ocean turned cool, and the sun was starting to go down. Seven-thirty, eight o'clock, I'd have more riders than I could manage, all the way to midnight, and past, too; until the summer cops managed to herd everybody out, and Marilyn locked the gate.

Monday would be a little less intense, and Tuesday, again, park attendance sliding off until Friday, when everyone suddenly realized that there was only tonight, and Saturday night, to ride all the rides, and play all the games—and the park would be packed past closing again.

"It's nice to have a crowd," I said, "keeps me out of trouble."

"Yes," Vassily said, and hesitated.

"Something wrong?"

"No...I do not think so." He chewed his lip, looking over my shoulder, possibly at the carousel, or possibly at something only he could see. I waited to see which it was—and it proved to be the latter.

"Kate Archer, I have prayed to my angel in heaven," he said seriously.

"Thank you," I answered, hoping I wasn't going to have to dance around the question of whether I, too, had prayed to the angel in heaven. Or in Varoth. Whatever.

"My angel answers me, and he gave me these words to say to you. They are..."

He drew in a breath, and when he exhaled, his voice was deeper, vibrant; each word as fully formed and weighted as a stone.

"For a second time I abase myself, and I offer an apology. The bouquet and depth of your power led me to believe that I dealt with an Ozali of some age and experience. I was mistaken; thus, what I offered as opportunity became an entrapment.

"Though I regret the manner of it, I cannot regret that we have shared power. I have been enriched in the sharing; indeed, I will say to you that I have been *changed*.

"It is my sincere hope that, in time, you will also come to regard the gifts shared, and the alliance thus created, as one of the unexpected treasures of your existence.

"Peace upon you, Kate Archer. May your powers never cease to delight you."

Vassily bowed, and straightened, blinking rapidly before focusing once more on my face.

"The message, it was clear?"

"Clear as glass," I assured him. "How's your head?"

"My head is fine." Vassily smiled beatifically. "My angel is gentle and good."

I opened my mouth—and closed it again. Vassily's relationship with Prince Aesgyr of Varoth was vastly different from my relationship with that same sly prince. Prince Aesgyr had given Vassily peace, while he had given me...what exactly?

Deep breath, Kate.

"Okay!" I told Vassily. "Honor now being satisfied, you can go get your supper; I'll take it from here."

"Yes. Good night, Kate Archer. Thanking you."

He picked his hoody up from the operator's stool, threw it over one shoulder, and left me.

One of these days, I thought, watching him cross Baxter Avenue to Tony Lee's, I was going to have to find out what, exactly, the kid was thanking me for.

There being nobody in line, and nobody on the grounds who looked like they'd be wanting a ride on the carousel anytime soon after I stepped out to look up and down Baxter Avenue, I walked back under the roof and jumped up onto the decking to do an inspection.

The inspection was busywork, but I was thorough, checking the area first for trash. Nothing really to inspect, there—Vassily was meticulous. No chance-blown bit of paper or plastic, no forgotten drink cup, or ketchup-smeared fries cone eluded him. The carousel deck looked freshly swept, and the animals gleamed, as if they'd been rubbed down with a soft cloth and wax.

Even the temporary fiberglass rooster—temporarily a member of the carousel's company, that was; not temporarily fiberglass—shone as if it had been polished.

I walked the carousel widdershins, looking up into the sweeps. All the lights were shining bright. An outside circuit, again looking up, confirmed that the outline lights were all on duty, too.

If I wanted to be as thorough as possible, I'd inspect the cranking rods next, but that was really a job for when the park was closed, involving, as it did, a ladder.

I jumped back onto the deck, and, purely out of habit, stepped Sideways. The five animals that held—that *had held*—prisoners from the other five Worlds each glowed rosily, the supposed life essences partly obscured by the shadowy ropes of the binding spells. The scent of butterscotch—my magical signature—was thick in the air.

I considered them each minutely, detecting neither stress nor weakening. The binding spells and the life-glow not only looked convincing, they *felt* convincing. In fact, they felt so convincing that I wondered if my subconscious hadn't woven a teensy tiny little truth spell into the binding spell. It was, I supposed, possible. Spellcraft, as Mr. Ignat' was often pleased to tell me, was more art than science. He also swore to me that, as my *jikinap* and I got used to each other and how we operated, I'd find my spells informed by past work, and infused with special fillips that I hadn't specifically called for.

Mr. Ignat', being an old and very experienced Ozali, seemed to think that was a feature. Myself, I was leaning toward bug. I didn't necessarily want my power making independent decisions, even based on a comprehensive database of my previous actions. Consistency isn't exactly my strongest suit.

All of which sort of brought me around to Vassily's angel from heaven, Prince Aesgyr of Varoth, the Land of Air and Sunshine.

Since I'd come to know Prince Aesgyr so well, and through no wish of my own, I knew that he was also an old and very experienced Ozali. He'd taken what I had to assume was a calculated risk in forcing a sharing of power—though maybe that should be instead, a *desperate* risk. Certainly, he'd been desperate to recover his consort, and he'd thought that I knew the location of each prisoner *as an individual.* Gran might have known that, but I never did, so Prince Aesgyr had taken his risk for nothing.

Or not. According to the message he'd given Vassily to deliver, he found value in the sharing of power, memory, and spellcraft. I sort of doubted that, since I was a callow and half-trained youth. Even if my *jikinap* tasted old—which it did, and was, since it had belonged to Mr. Ignat', before he gave it to me.

And yet...he specifically mentioned that he had been *changed*.

That...was disquieting. Had the exchange of powers also included the small homey magics that attached to the Guardian of Archers Beach? Or—

My cell phone warbled. I fished it out of my pocket, grinned at the number on the screen and flipped it open.

"Hey, there," I said.

"Hey," Borgan answered. Usually, hearing Borgan's voice made me feel happy. But that *hey*...

I swallowed, feeling a little lump of dread lodge just under my breastbone.

"What's wrong?"

There was a slight pause.

"Well, now, that's what I don't know. Something's gone off; the balance in the waters, say it...changed, and not in a way I've... ever felt before."

He was worried; *really* worried.

"What can I do to help?"

"Don't know until I have an idea of what's going on. Might take some time, so I thought I'd better let you know I won't be by tonight."

The little lump of dread got bigger.

"Be careful," I said, thinking how the *ronstibles*—Daphne and her, as far as I knew, nameless sister—had come 'way too close to his undoing.

"Take Nerazi," I added, and didn't say, *if you won't take me.*

"I'll be careful as can be," he promised, but he didn't promise to take Nerazi as backup. "If I get this settled quick, I'll come by the house, if that's all right?"

"It's all right. Borgan—"

"And if I find there's something you can help me with," he continued, "I'll call you, Kate. Now, you take care, too. I've gotta go."

He cut the connection. I stood there between the dolphin and the deer, staring down at my cell. Finally, I shook myself, snapped it shut, and shoved it back into my pocket.

The dread—that wasn't as easily put away. Something had upset the balance of the Gulf of Maine, and the Guardian had no idea what it was. That was just...

But, really, Kate, I said to myself, *if something went pear-shaped with the land, would you necessarily know what it was, right off? Think of the still zones and how much work it is to scope them out.*

"You worry too much," I said out loud.

It didn't seem to do anything positive for my state of mind.

Fine, then. Borgan was a grown-up, and if he wasn't as old as Mr. Ignat' nor as accomplished as Prince Aesgyr, he was more than able to take care of himself. He'd be *fine.*

"Merry-go-round!" a shrill voice interrupted these reflections. "I want to ride the merry-go-round!"

I looked up.

A little boy in shorts, flip-flops and a red T-shirt emblazoned with the words *New York Yankees* was pulling his mother's hand, urging her to *hurry.*

I swallowed my dread and my agitated thoughts, and jumped off the decking.

"Good evening!" I called, walking toward the operator's station. "It's a terrific night to ride the carousel!"

❦

The goblin Daphne had been...a challenge, with anger and grief buoying her natural abilities.

A challenge, but in the end a challenge met, though it was well, she reflected, as she reclined in the goblins' former dwelling—it was well that she had supped of Olida/Korkilig first.

The sea moved sluggishly in this secret spot; it nourished, but not at the speed nor the depth provided by the open waters of which she had so recently partaken. She therefore faced a decision: remain here, and remain hidden from the Borgan, as the goblins had been hidden from him. Or return to the open waters, where his eye would be upon her.

She considered the choice, though there was very little to recommend the goblins' lair. If she was to bring the Borgan into her net quickly, she must build her strength. The consumption of the goblins had greatly improved her situation; she must not waste that peculiar blessing.

So, she would go again into the open waters. It was in her mind to seek this Seal Woman, whom the goblins had called Nerazi.

It looked like word had gone out that Fun Country was the place for all the cool kids to be, and the cool kids—with their parents, sibs, and in some cases, their grandparents—had come down to the park to play.

The carousel went 'round, with only the briefest possible pauses to off-load and onload more passengers. At one point, there were fifty people in line; at another . . . more than that. Baxter Avenue was so packed with people that I couldn't see past the press of bodies to Tony Lee's. I took tickets and smiled and chatted, inching off the ride time just a little, while the orchestrion belted out "The Man on the Flying Trapeze," "Daisy, Daisy," "Beer Barrel Polka," "The Sidewalks of New York"—and so on, until it went silent, having run to the end of the roll.

Normally, I'd just wait until there was a break in the crowd to rewind and start the machine again. A glance at the line was enough to convince me that there would never be a break in the line ever again—or until closing time, whichever came first.

Well, I thought, it'll just have to run silent. Wouldn't be the first—

"Mommy," a high voice spoke from the depths of the line, "what happened to the music?"

"The CD got to the end," a woman's voice possibly belonging to Mommy answered. "It'll start up again in a second."

I sighed.

The orchestrion is an antique, and it plays punched paper rolls that are incredibly fragile and somewhat difficult to deal with, even if you've had as much practice as I've had. Not much sense trying to explain that to the little boy or his mom. Easier, and more satisfying, for everybody, to just start the music again.

I thought about that, very carefully, as the carousel spun 'round. And careful thought yielded the conviction that I could pull this off, with no loss of life, and without anyone being the wiser.

Therefore, I raised a tiny bit of the *jikinap* napping at the base of my spine, breathed in and very carefully visualized the steps necessary to rewind the roll and start it again. A little tickle of agreement met this effort; I felt a slight ripple of heat, and tasted just a hint of butterscotch at the back of my tongue. All of which meant that magic was on the case.

I hoped.

I hit the bell twice to signal the end of the ride, and watched the carousel slow down.

"Wait 'til she's stopped before you get off," I called. "Wait 'til the animals stop moving!"

They were good and careful—most were, though you'd get the occasional teenager who wanted the thrill of jumping out of the saddle at the height of his mount's up-cycle.

I watched them dismount, again calling out helpful instructions.

"Exit gate right around to the left! Thank you for riding the Fantasy Menagerie Carousel! Come back again soon!"

They walked around the wheel until they found the exit gate, the inevitable two or three opting for their other left, and getting a little tangled in the crowd of their fellow riders, until somebody got them turned around.

While this was going on, I'd become aware of a tingling in my hands and fingers, and a little flicker of motion behind my eyes, accompanied by the barest taste of butterscotch. The pattern was familiar—could it be feedback from the *jikinap* I'd dispatched to rewind the orchestrion? I'd never felt my power working before, and wondered if I ought to be worried.

Though I really didn't have much time to worry, right now.

"Welcome to the Fantasy Menagerie Carousel," I told the first person in line, a teenage boy with feathery blond hair kissed white by the sun, who was holding hands with a girl wearing a purple shirt with a scoop so daring I could see the tops of her breasts.

I resisted the urge to ask, "Does your mom know what you're wearing?" and instead continued the traditional greeting.

"Two tickets each, please; enjoy your ride!"

The last rider was through the gate when I noticed my hands weren't tingling any more.

I hit the bell, and eased the lever up.

The orchestrion began to play.

What with one thing and another, Marilyn didn't actually sound the closing horn until damn' near one o'clock.

So, I told myself, as I stepped through the door in the storm gate, into the at-last-silent park, *it's a good thing Borgan couldn't make it tonight, anyway.*

Which assumed that Borgan had figured out and fixed whatever was wrong in his waters, and was now comfortably asleep on *Gray Lady*. I hoped that was the case.

But I didn't believe it.

I pulled the door to, and reached for the lock, my attention mostly on wondering if I would seem . . . *clingy* if I just gave him a quick call to see how he was.

Kate, he's a grown man—considerable understatement, there. *He knows his waters and his business. Let him do what he knows—*

I felt it, then, the weight on the land. The same weight, I was certain, that I'd felt before—the timid *trenvay* who had run away from Borgan.

Slowly, I turned toward it—as before, he or she was located in the lightless alley between Summer's Wheel and the carousel's storm wall.

"I'm glad you came back," I said softly, while I sent warm tidings and promises of safety through the land. "Please don't run away. I'm Kate Archer, Guardian of Archers Beach. I'd like to see you, and to get to know you—and serve you, if I may."

As on the previous occasion, the weight shifted on the land. I had the impression that whoever it was had come one or even two cautious steps toward me . . .

Which was approximately the moment that all hell broke loose.

CHAPTER TWENTY-TWO

Monday, July 10
Low Tide 4:54 A.M. EDT
Moonset 3:59 A.M.

The noise almost knocked me flat; every *trenvay* and Ozali within the bounds of Archers Beach had to have heard it—and the half-sighted mundane population, too. Hell, Gran'd probably heard it, inside her tree.

Loud as it was, it wasn't the sound of the World Gate being opened, which would have relieved me, if I hadn't noticed right then that the reason the shock hadn't knocked me flat was because my *jikinap* had risen straight up my backbone, holding me up, like—no.

My *jikinap* was being drawn.

Memory flickered, and I was a kid again, in the garden of Aeronymous House. I was helping to gather flowers for the dinner table, a delicate task that taught fine use of one's *jiki-nap*. My tutor was with me, and we had decided that a single crimson blossom would be the finishing touch for the arrangement that I would build from the mound of creamy flowers in the gathering basket.

We had turned, and suddenly the air...altered. Now, I would say that it felt like a storm coming, with ozone fizzing along nerve endings. Then, I only knew that I'd never felt anything like it before. I'd been well trained; in any unusual situation the first thing I was to do was to lock my meager store of power.

I managed to do it just an instant before the air contracted in a sudden sharp snap.

My tutor fell at my feet, pale flowers spilling over the path-stones. I dropped to my knees beside him, touching his face to verify what I could plainly see. His power had been wrenched from him. He was dead.

He'd misted into nothing under my fingertips, leaving them faintly damp.

Back in Archers Beach in the Changing Land, I snatched at my store of *jikinap* too late, exerting all of my will to slam it down to the base of my spine.

The drawing force was too strong for me. Despite my best, and most desperate, efforts, my power was moving up my spine. If I didn't do . . . something . . . the Ozali who had arrived inside of that mind-numbing *bang* was going to drain me of power—and probably my life.

Kate, I told myself, *let it GO.*

But my *jikinap* had been merged, however briefly, with Prince Aesgyr's *jikinap*. And I was willing to bet that the Ozali behind the wall was no friend of Aesgyr's.

Impossibly, the draw increased; I felt my power begin to fragment, cracking like paint that had been baked under the summer sun, tiny chips floating away. There was only one way that this could end. I'd lose my power, my life—*and* Aesgyr's secrets, too.

No. That was not going to happen. I remembered my father, blasted into mist; my grandfather, refusing to believe what was happening to him, even as he crumbled into dust. No. That was not going to happen again. Not here. Not to me.

I was rigid, drawn up onto my toes by the force of the other's will. Panting, I stubbornly clung to my fragmenting power—and opened myself to the land.

There was a sensation of coolness, as of a vast and welcoming grotto blooming beneath my feet.

"Freely given," I gasped.

My *jikinap* . . . quivered. Condensed.

Then, it quietly drained away, *down* my backbone as if the punishing force that called it didn't exist, flowing out of me, and into the land, absorbed like rainwater into a thirsty flowerbed.

The sensation of an intense, irresistible force trying to pull me in half—was gone, like a string snapped, and I went from on pointe to flat-footed, staggering for an instant before the land steadied me. I shivered, and received the impression that a cold, wet nose had been thrust into my hand. The land had my back, that was.

Good to know. Because, having survived the last half minute or so, now I had to deal with whoever was inside the storm gates. Which was, based on our recent interaction, an Ozali of great power and absolutely no concern for the well-being of others.

Who had chosen *not* to use the World Gate.

This isn't good, Kate, I told myself.

On the other hand, reinforcements ought to be arriving soon. I hoped. Mr. Ignat' *had* to have heard that noise—and Arbalyr. Nerazi. Borgan.

"Right beside you, Kate," a familiar voice said calmly.

"Felsic." I tried to keep the surprise out of my voice. "I'm not sure this one's yours."

"Anything that comes in that loud and that hungry is mine," Felsic said grimly. "That ain't good for the land—and it surely ain't good for Peggy. Felled her like a log."

Panic stitched a bright, hot line through my chest.

"You left her?"

"Vornflee's sitting watch. I made sure she was right an' tight before I come down. That's what took me."

"Just as well; we had some preliminary matters to settle." I took a breath, hesitating, still expecting...

"The other's will've gone to their services," Felsic said softly. "To hold as fast as they can for the Guardian and the land."

...and Felsic had left her service, to be the Guardian's backup. That said...a lot about something. Too bad I didn't have time right now to figure out what.

"All right, then," I said, trying to sound cocky, and probably failing miserably. "Let's get this thing done."

I opened myself fully to the land, feeling the whole strength of Archers Beach rise into me. Not *jikinap*, but power. *Considerable* power, that could never be reft from me.

"That's the way of it," Felsic said approvingly, and I shoved the door open.

I'd turned the lights out when I closed the ride down, but the Ozali waiting for us was more than bright enough to light the space.

She was tall, and exuded cold. The metal storm walls already bore a coating of frost; icicles had formed on the carousel's canopy, and a meadow of ice flowers populated the cement floor, clustering tightest at the hem of her robe.

I shivered, but not because of the cold.

The being before us wasn't just a Master Ozali with no manners. *This* ... was one of the Wise.

The fact that I'd been expecting the Wise to arrive any day now for the past couple weeks had done nothing to prepare me for the arrival of *this* Wise One at *this* time, and in such a manner.

"Quite a ruckus you made, there," I said, by way of a greeting, and lifted my head to meet ice-blue eyes. "Would you like to tell me why?"

"I will speak with the Gatekeeper," the Wise One said, though I didn't see her mouth move.

"You're speaking to the Gatekeeper."

A sudden blast of snowflakes struck my face, stinging.

"You are not Ebony Pepperidge."

I took a deep breath; the cold air helped clear my head.

"That's right. I'm Ebony Pepperidge's granddaughter, and I keep the Gate in my own right. Want me to show you how it works, so you can leave quieter than you came?"

The Wise One stared at me, no expression on her icy face. She didn't seem to be aware of Felsic. I'd seen Felsic use that trick before; interesting that it seemed to work on a Wise One just as good as it worked on the Archers Beach cops. I'd have to ask after the technique, assuming that we, the carousel, and the town managed to survive the next couple minutes.

"What," I asked, with as much patience as the occasion deserved—which is to say, none—"do you want?"

The cold eyes narrowed slightly.

"What I want depends upon the answer to my question. There has been an illicit use of this Gate. Why did the Gatekeeper allow this to occur?"

Fuck. I had expected the Wise, when they arrived, would want to do a head-count of the prisoners. That this one was asking, not about the prisoners, but about Gate usage meant...

Well, it meant that Prince Aesgyr had managed to hide his actions from his enemies at home. Good for Prince Aesgyr, but bad for me, because there was no way I could cover for the Gate opening. The prince's magical signature would have been all over that.

No, wait.

He'd used my information, coated in butterscotch, to open the Gate. Technically, then, the Keeper, or at least, the Keeper's *jikinap*, had opened the Gate; nothing to see here, move on...

I took a careful breath.

"There has been no illicit use of the Gate," I said firmly.

"The Gate was opened."

I shrugged, stalling; hoping to annoy her into giving me a clue regarding her purpose.

"I had a customer."

"Where did you send this...customer?"

I raised my eyebrows.

"Check the logbook, why not?"

Snow and wind struck my cheek, and I realized that the first slap had been on the order of a lovetap. I staggered, keeping my feet only because the land wouldn't let me fall.

"Impertinence will be rewarded appropriately," the Wise One told me.

Right. And as it turned out, she'd done me a favor. The blow had shaken loose a potentially useful thought.

Guilty conscience aside, how did I *know* which Gate opening had caught this particular Wise One's attention? Time runs differently across the Six Worlds, and the way between. And God Himself knows how—or if—it operates wherever it is that the Wise keep household. Frosty here could've gotten her snowflakes in a twist over some piece of business that had happened a hundred local years ago, though the temporal drift wasn't, I thought, quite that extreme.

I did a quick calculation. Gran had been in the Land of the Flowers for six months, Changing Land time. Which had roughly equaled two Sempeki weeks.

When she'd run for home, pursued by demons, I'd opened the Gate to let her through. Eleven weeks ago, that had been.

I took a careful breath.

This particular Wise One...was plenty arrogant, and more than willing to take offense. Still, a request for information wasn't... necessarily...impertinence.

"Look," I said, raising my hands so she could see how defense-less I was. "Look, I need some more information. *When* did this so-called illicit use take place?"

The Wise One drew herself up, and a dozen new ice flowers bloomed on the floor at her hem.

"Okay, that's a tough one. How about location? Where did the Gate open *to*?"

Her long nose wrinkled, as if she'd detected a bad odor, and I thought she was going to take another swing at me.

Instead, and to my considerable surprise, she answered.

"The Gate to Sempeki was opened, illicitly."

"Well, not necessarily. I did open the Gate to Sempeki recently. But I didn't send anybody through; I let a traveler in."

"That is illicit." This time the smack was hard enough I saw stars mixed in with the snowflakes.

I shook my head to clear it, which was a mistake; Frosty had clipped me good and proper. Then I realized that the land had caught me before I'd collapsed; my mouth was tingling with the green effect of healing. I tasted blood, too—which was washed away by a sudden infusion of cool, salty energy. I recognized the signature—Felsic's "home brew."

I took a breath and centered myself, letting the power of the land fold right around me as I met the Wise One's eyes again.

"That use was not illicit," I said, impressed to hear that my voice was steady. "The Gate was opened, properly, by the Gate-keeper, and the traveler passed through in good order."

"That traveler was a criminal."

"Not my job to check warrants. If Sempeki didn't want them to cross, Sempeki should've stopped them."

This time, the smack hit the land's protection; I saw the flare when it bounced. Frosty didn't seem to notice.

"We will not argue semantics," she announced. "Be it heard that you, the Gatekeeper, and this, the World of Change, are put on notice by the InterWorld Council of Wisdom. The World of Change has long been a nexus of irregularity, disorder, and inconvenience. This will no longer be permitted. Should there be any more such irregularities as have been noted in the past, the Gate will be closed, and the World of Change will be allowed to wither and die. This by order and decree of the Wise, and the seal set upon it by Isiborg of the Council."

She moved for the first time, opening her arms, blizzards falling from her jagged fingers.

"It is done."

The light went out.

"Dammit!"

I raised my hand, fingers curled around the little ball of fey-light, strode to the circuit box and threw the switch.

Ordinary electric light flooded the enclosure. I turned first to the carousel, which seemed very little the worse for our visitor's chilly nature. There were no icicles dangling dangerously from the canopy; the animals glowed like new-painted, but appeared to be dry. I looked down. The floor was dry, and innocent of frost flowers.

"What did that mean, about cutting us off?" Felsic asked.

"Well, on a sliding scale from Nothing Much to We're All Gonna Die..." I shook my head. "It depends on who you ask. According to a recent history lesson, it seems to me that cutting us out of the loop is much worse for the rest of the loop than it is for us. Unless I'm missing something. Which is possible. But one thing's for certain..."

I paused, feeling a nagging something in the hindbrain. Something to do with the light...

"What's certain?" Felsic asked, derailing my train of thought.

"Oh. We're definitely going to be taken out of the loop, just as soon as my *next* transgression comes up on the Wise's roster, which—best guess—will be just about Labor Day."

"What did you do?"

"How much do you know about the carousel?"

"I know there's been something wrong about the carousel for a long time," Felsic said, matter-of-factly. "And it wasn't making the Lady happy at all."

"That'll do. As to what *I* did—I made the Lady happy. At least, I made Mr. Ignat' happy; Gran's still in-tree. My assumption is that they're in it—whatever it is—together, though."

"That'd be the safe bet." Felsic looked around. "Anything else to do tonight?"

"No... *hell* no. You better go on and see that Peggy's all right. Thanks for getting my back."

"No worries," Felsic said. "Mind walking up with me?"

"Not at all. Let me get the light."

I snapped off the light and followed Felsic to the door, feylight illuminating our path. It wasn't until I'd pulled it shut that I realized I didn't have the lock.

"Must've dropped it when our visitor blew in," I said, extending a request to the land for its assistance. "Can't have gone far."

"In fact, my liege," a man's voice came out of the dark service alley, "it fell not so far. I have it here, safe."

~⁓∞⁓~

The waters delivered her to the shore, and she rose to her full height. Heeding the lesson learned from the Borgan, her robes were modest, and her hair was loose.

She was not here to overawe, but to call upon a woman of power, as she was herself a woman of power. The goblins had revered Nerazi the Seal Woman as an elder; she would therefore respect an elder, and not assume that role for herself.

The Rock she descried at once, shining silver under the gaze of the moon. She crossed the sand to it as a simple woman might, and came around the leeward side of the Rock.

There, seated on a sealskin, was a queen of a woman, full-bodied and voluptuous. Her face was like the moon, round and a-glow with power. Her eyes were bottomless black pools, rubies glinting in their depths.

"Mother." Quite without meaning to, she bowed, her respect unfeigned. Small wonder the goblins had feared and revered this person. There was power here, and wisdom; knowledge and mercy. She might well have been a goddess—perhaps, by the rules of this strange land, she *was* a goddess.

It was well, then, to be prudent.

"Daughter," Seal Woman said. "It were better done, had you sought me sooner."

"I see this is truth," she admitted. "I can offer nothing in defense of my foolishness, save that I was offered asylum elsewhere, and knew no better than to accept it."

"The customs of a strange land are often confusing, I am told. One may make mistakes of naivety, and be forgiven. Other mistakes, I fear, Daughter, are not so easily forgiven."

Such was the power of this elder that she felt a chill. Had she made so grievous an error as that?

"Sit," Seal Woman said.

Obediently, she sank to her knees in the sand, and sat, straight-backed, over her heels.

"That is well. Now, tell me what you have done with the *ron-stibles*, who named themselves Olida and Daphne."

"Mother, I have taken them," she said baldly. "They sought to use me against the Borgan, and I would not have it."

"You interest me. Why not simply refuse them? You were granted twenty days of the water's full grace."

She must be careful here, and resist the elder's power—not fight it, not that. But, truth must seem to flow naturally from her, parting around her necessities as softly as possible, as water moving around a rock. It was a risk—almost, she laughed, for had she not already accepted risk, by seeking this power out?

"Twenty days of the water's grace," she repeated, softly. "Yes, Mother; I was granted that, most generously. But the rest of the Borgan's geas was that I must, at the end of that time, return to the Land whence I came."

"And that, you did not wish to do? If you remain here, Daughter, you will change. You will perhaps change in ways that will not please you, and which may become dangerous to these waters."

"I am not," she said, with perhaps more bravado than truth, "afraid of change."

"Now, that is courage, indeed. But, tell me, *why not* simply refuse the *ronstibles*? Borgan would have protected you, had it been necessary."

"But I do not want his protection, Mother." She drew herself a little straighter, as might any maiden about to declare anything so bold.

"I want his love."

Nerazi the Seal Woman seemed amused, though she was gracious enough not to smile.

"I see that you have, indeed, been informed by the waters. Once your strength is more fully returned, you will recall that love is between equals."

"Mother, I know that," she said firmly. "It is precisely why I took the goblins—the *ronstibles*. I have less than twenty days to recover myself fully, to learn all of this sea that I may, and show him that I am worthy."

Nerazi said nothing.

"I see clearly," she said, insisting upon her point. "Recall that the goblins hated him."

Seal Woman's face grew thoughtful.

"So they did. Well, perhaps you have chosen a good tonic; I cannot say for certain because it has not, to my knowledge, been done before. However that may be, I fear that this step—this taking of the *ronstibles*—will not further your suit. Indeed, we must suppose it a severe setback for your ambition."

She frowned. "By my measure, I have given him a wedding gift fitting to a god. I have rid him of those who wished him only ill, who posed a constant danger to him and to the performance of his duty; who would never be won over, nor brought into alliance with him. Surely, my position is stronger, for having done this thing that honor would not allow him to do for himself."

"What a strange world must Cheobaug be," Seal Woman mused, then paused, and inclined her head courteously. "Your pardon, Daughter; I perhaps make an unworthy assumption. *Are* you of Cheobaug?"

"The Land of Wave and Water bore me, yes. But I do not understand you, Mother. Surely the art of alliance is not so different, between this Land which I hope to make my own, and that Land which repudiates me."

"Perhaps you are correct. But I believe you have acted without first obtaining full knowledge of your . . . potential ally. I, who have known him intimately for many years, believe that Borgan will consider that he is diminished by this loss you have given him. He did not love the *ronstibles*, but the sea loved them, and for that reason alone, he would have preserved them."

That chilled her, indeed, and for a moment—a moment only!—she allowed herself to wonder if she had made an error, and a grievous one.

The moment passed. Done was done, and the goblins beyond recall. She would continue as she had begun. He would see her as worthy, and accept all that she offered.

He would.

CHAPTER TWENTY-THREE

Monday, July 10

"And just who the hell are you?" I asked, but the land was already reporting the twice-familiar weight upon it, while helpfully augmenting my night-sight.

The man who was down on one knee before me, holding the storm gate's padlock out in a slim hand... was *not trenvay*—no *trenvay* you'll ever meet will admit to having any such thing as a *liege*—nor was he an Ozali. He possessed a dollop of *jikinap*—I could see it glowing at the base of his spine—enough for basic work and defense, but nothing near the level of a serious power-monger.

His head was bent, so I couldn't see his face. His hair was cut so close to his head it looked like he was wearing a brown velvet cap; the bowed neck was brown, and not particularly familiar, but then I don't have a great memory for the backs of necks.

"Name?" I suggested again, making no move to take the lock.

"I am Cael, called the Wolf," he said, promptly. His voice was in the midrange, but with a peculiar growly texture to it.

Well, that was letter of the law. I couldn't fault the man for not volunteering beyond what he was asked, but I *really* wasn't in the mood for Twenty Questions.

"Your affiliation?"

He took a breath deep enough to lift his shoulders, but answered steadily enough.

"House Aeronymous."

I had, I thought, been afraid he was going to say that.

"How came you here, Cael of Aeronymous?"

"I was carried here, my lady, and bound against my will and that of my lord. The arrival and the binding, those things I recall, but nothing else until I was freed into the midst of a storm." He hesitated. "I ran away."

"Good call. Now what you want to do is go back to the Land of the Flowers."

He raised his head, lowering the hand holding the lock. His eyes were golden brown, his nose short and broad, his mouth slightly protuberant.

"I went to Sempeki, and to the House of Aeronymous, whose man I had been all my life," he said, his voice significantly more growly. "The House was empty, and the gate hung broken on its hinges. I searched the grounds, and found Aleun tending the gardens, and Tioli, on the walls. All of the House were dead, they told me, taken by the Ozali Ramendysis." The golden brown eyes sparkled, as if with tears.

"*All* of the House, taken," he repeated, his whisper raw with agony, "save Prince Nathan's child, who was now Aeronymous. It was for her that they kept garden and wall, and a vigilant watch against the return of the Ozali Ramendysis."

Aleun the gardener, I recalled, a stick of a woman with very nearly a dryad's understanding of growing things. Tioli...was a less certain memory. My grandfather had seen his walls patrolled by solid professionals, in addition to the layers of spellcraft meant to hold the House secure. I might have passed Tioli a hundred times and never known her name.

I looked down into tired eyes and shook my head, slowly.

"When I was sent from Sempeki to this land, I took up new duties, with a pledge of my life. I did this knowing, as you know, that the House was broken, all were taken, and there was no hope of recover."

He made a small sound in the back of his throat. I paused, but he didn't make the sound into words.

"The duty I now hold will not marry well with the duties of Aeronymous. I have lain that down, and I will not return."

"You will desert us?" I think he'd meant it to sound harsh, but he only managed exhausted.

"Cael the Wolf, you have yourself seen. What would you have me do?"

He swallowed, and drew a breath; let it out in a long sigh.

"At this moment, in all truth, I would have you take my oath, and allow me to serve you in this new duty. My liege."

It was on the tip of my tongue to tell him that I wanted neither oaths nor subjects, but something in the eyes gave me pause, or maybe an old, all-but-buried memory of my grandfather talking to me about loyalty, and how the loyalty of those Lower kept the House and the High secure. He had even touched, briefly, on the means available to the High, in order to ensure loyalty, before breaking off and promising me that I would be taught those things thoroughly, when I came of an age.

I blinked into Side-Sight, and looked at Cael, called the Wolf, seeing at once the unmistakable shine of *jikinap*, twisted in compact triquetra, and anchored near his—no.

My stomach damn' near flipped over; I swallowed, *hard*.

There was *no geas upon him*, as I might lay an order to avoid me upon an importunate drunk.

Cael the Wolf...the geas was woven into the structure and function of his heart, a vital part of a vital organ. As I watched, the knots of *jikinap* flickered, and paled. I heard the man before me, very softly, groan.

I looked more closely, into the warp and the weft of the working. The geas was dependent upon a living oath to Aeronymous. My grandfather was dead; thus the oath required renewal. In a kinder and gentler Sempeki, where Ramendysis hadn't swallowed us whole, Cael and all of our household would have renewed their oaths with my father, upon grandfather's passing. If the oath was not renewed, the knot would unravel; Cael's heart would stop—or burst.

It served no purpose to ask Cael if he knew this. I was betting he did. And that left the outcome of this squarely in my hands, as the last survivor of our House, Aeronymous by default.

I blinked out of Side-Sight. Cael still knelt before me, so deeply dignified that the eye slid past the tremors in his limbs. Possibly he'd be able to stand, if I ordered him up.

Probably not.

I spared a hard thought for my grandfather.

Then, I met Cael's eyes, and extended my hand.

Cael raised his, the lock still held in his fingers.

"Felsic," I said, without turning my head, "would you please take the lock from this gentleman and finish with the door?"

"Sure thing, Kate."

Felsic slipped past on my left side, received the lock with a nod, and moved immediately to the door.

"Thank you," I said. "Cael—your hand, if you will."

He clasped my hand, and I *felt* him trembling, though his eyes were steady and his gaze firm.

"Understand, that I don't know what will happen, if I take your oath. This is a strange land, and I'm bound to it. The act may kill you. It will surely change you."

"My lady, I have already been much altered," he whispered hoarsely, his eyes never leaving mine. "If this act should kill me, it only hastens the inevitable. I hold you blameless, whatever goes forth. You are my liege, and I am bound to love you."

That was...probably the literal truth, considering the device he carried in his chest. I breathed in, and gripped his hand.

"Whenever you wish," I said, and opened myself to the land, as I do when I prepare for a healing.

The man kneeling before me closed his eyes, his grip on my hand not *quite* painful.

"I, Cael, do swear upon my soul that I will keep faith with Aeronymous and never cause her harm. I will defend her and reverence her and in all things obey her, and stand her man forevermore."

That was quite an oath. It struck the land with a boom, reverberating, and I felt power rise and flow through me, to him, as if it were a healing, indeed. He gasped, his grip painful now. His eyes rolled back in his head and for a moment I feared that I had killed him outright—then he blinked and smiled, and the land executed a joyous ripple of what sounded like piccolo notes inside of my head.

I drew a cautiously optimistic breath.

"Rise Cael, called the Wolf, oath-bound to Aeronymous," I said, and he did, to his full height, which was higher than me, but not nearly as high as Borgan.

He wasn't exactly dressed for the beach in a long-sleeved red shirt banded with gold, a gold sash, and skin-tight red trousers. The bare feet—strong and brown—were the only thing topical about him.

"Who had you been, in the House of Aeronymous?" I asked.

"My lady, I was the master of hounds."

The *master of hounds* was taken, under protest, from Aerony-mous House and bound into the high-security carousel prison? That just didn't make sense. It was on the tip of my tongue to ask him *For what crime?* when I realized that it was late, I was beyond exhausted and the only thing holding me up was the land. Time to ask questions later.

"All right, then," I said. "You'll find things a little different here. For one thing, I don't keep dogs, though I do have a cat."

"Might be that he'll find service with the land," Felsic mur-mured from my side. She held her hand out to Cael. "I'm Felsic. I'll be pleased to show you my service, and to help you with any questions about how we do things here."

More power to him, he didn't even hesitate, but put his hand in hers.

"Thank you. I will want guidance, I think."

"Sure thing. Kate, you're taking him where tonight?"

"Figured my house. He can have the couch, if the cat will share."

"Right then, we'd better get going. It got a lot later than I was expecting. Peggy'll be worried, and Vornflee past distracted."

I laughed. "Let's go then," I said, leading the way down the service alley to the gap in the fence that gave onto the beach. "Cael, this might remind you of home."

❧

Her conversation with Seal Woman had very nearly convinced her that the course of wisdom was to return to the goblins' lair, and meekly await the end of her dwindling time here in these sweet, subtle waters.

Almost convinced her—but in the end, it did not matter what she may have or may have not decided.

Because the Borgan found her.

Scarcely had she entered the waters, after having taken courte-ous leave from Nerazi, than she felt the call upon her. Her first impulse was to resist—which was not ill-done, she assured herself, even as the compulsion grew. Anyone would at first resist; it was important, however, to be careful *how much* she resisted.

Not only would too much resistance be unseemly, it would allow him to measure her strength. It would be very foolish to permit him to know precisely how strong, or how weak, she was.

She therefore allowed herself to be overcome, in perhaps the time it might take a shocked girl to realize who it was that called her.

He was angry; she felt it in the waters she passed through. Chilly waters, that had previously been warm. Gentle currents that had cradled her kindly now snatched, and chivvied her along.

By the time the compulsion released her, she had no need to feign concern.

He had brought her to calm waters, a pool of quiet isolated from the sea's busy currents. The water here was potent, sleek with power, and icy cold. As was the one waiting for her—

He fair glowed in white leathers, a waterfowl for which she had no name attending him, its red eyes bright. If she had thought him beautiful before, now, seeing him in his full power among the biting waters, with his eyes glittering, black and pitiless, and his face carved from stone—oh, *now*, she loved him indeed, and trembled before his displeasure like a child.

"What justification, for murdering the sea's firstborn?"

The question crashed over her, and she fell to her knees, there amid the waters, and stretched her arms out to him.

"I am just now come from Nerazi the Seal Woman, from whom I learned my error," she cried. "Forgive me; I meant it for a gift, to repay your mercy to a stranger in your waters."

"A gift," he repeated flatly.

"I am a fool, Nerazi has shown it to me. But, yes—in my ignorance, in my vanity. They hated you so much, the goblins— *ronstibles*. They were a danger to you; an impediment to all your plans. I thought...he will not remove them, because honor does not allow. But *I*—I, whom they attempted to suborn; I could surely kill them, and the act would liberate him."

"And nourish you," he added, his aspect no warmer.

"Yes, certainly, but that was not first in my mind. They hated so deeply—they hated *so well*—I feared the nourishment might rather be poison. Would that it had been! I would willingly be unmade, rather than displease you."

She stilled, then, her words floating on the deep waters; her words *truly spoken*.

He must have known the truth as she said it; the waters would hold no such secret from him. It seemed to her that the waters were—only a little—less frigid. She dared to meet his eyes; he did not speak.

"Please, forgive me," she whispered. "Nerazi said that you would not. But I must ask, for it was an error made by ignorance and overzealousness. I did not know that the sea would care so much, when she had *you*—"

"They were firstborn," he interrupted, his voice harsh. "The sea is diminished—the sea *is damaged*—by their passing."

Horror shook her. She had expected that the sea would grieve her loss; the goblins were her children, after all, and *this* sea loved her children. But to have visited actual harm upon the waters—that she would no sooner do than she would harm the Borgan. She loved the gentle, sweet sea; despite ingesting the goblin's enmity, she loved the Borgan. Almost, she pledged herself, then and there, but it would not do. Her unplanned cry had softened him, a little, and an avowal of her regard would surely soften him more. It was her pride, that she held back from that. She would not approach him while she was yet diminished; an object of pity, whose vulnerability excited his instinct to protect.

No. She would have far more from him than pity and protection.

And so she bent in obeisance, her hair surrounding her in a black nimbus.

"Forgive me," she whispered. "Oh, please, forgive me. I would never knowingly harm this sea, which has been so generous with me. Tell me what I must do to rectify my error."

Silence met this. The waters warmed no further, but they did not cool. From so little, then, she took courage. Truly, she had no hope of eluding the strike, or surviving it, should the Borgan decide her transgression deserved death. It was a piquant feeling, to know that she might die here. She had died, once, or the girl she had been died, wading into those bitter, storm-lashed seas to calm them, and bring her brothers safely home.

She remembered her death. It had been painful, and she had been frightened, even above the joy of having rescued her beloveds. Terrible, the gasping, and the slow strangulation, as the sea filled her lungs, her belly, her veins—and made her his own.

It was possible that something of that terror made its way through the waters to the Borgan, and it came to her that his black eyes glittered, not with rage, but with pain.

If the goblins' deaths had wounded the sea, then the Borgan was likewise wounded. And that understanding might be the sum of her punishment, for it near cracked her heart, that he should suffer for the deaths of those who had hated him so cordially, and daily worked for his ruin.

"There's no mending it," he said now, "so we'll endure it. In the meanwhile, you'll finish out the days we gave you right here. I'll ask you not to do me any more favors."

"No, of course not," she whispered, but the Borgan was already gone.

It was not until she moved to exit the still, potent pool he had brought her to...that she realized she was trapped.

Breccia the cat didn't like Cael the Wolf.

Despite my insistence that he was a friend, she hissed, blew her ridiculous tail up to three times its normal size, arched her back, and in general enacted the super-economy-sized edition of the Cat Is Pissed Off.

"All right, here's what," I finally said, kneeling between her and Cael. "He's staying, for at least tonight. He'll be sleeping on the couch. If you don't like it, go upstairs and sleep on the bed. Out of sight, out of mind, am I right?"

It would appear that I was right, because, after issuing one more, don't-you-try-anything-fast-buddy hiss in Cael's general direction, she stomped down the hall toward the stairs.

"I have distressed the lady," Cael said.

"Nothing fatal," I said. "She's new here, herself, and she's an overachiever. You hungry?"

"My lady, I am not. I am very tired. The last...days have not been easy, and the lack of an oath to sustain me was...exhausting."

"All right, then, let's get your bed cleared off." I headed—again—for the couch. "I'll just put these books somewhere else..."

"That is not necessary," he said, taking the cat's blanket up from the corner, and shaking it out. If he found the elephants in the least unsettling, he didn't let on.

"I will sleep there," he said pointing to a spot on the floor between the coffee table and the French doors.

"If that'll be comfortable enough for you, go for it," I told him. "You want a pillow?"

"No, my lady; truly, I have everything that I need or want."

Anybody would have supposed that to have been not one-hundred-percent true, but the feedback I got from the land was of a tired, but honorable, man speaking a truth he had never thought to speak again.

"All right then; I'll say good night. Tomorrow, we'll have to talk."

"Yes, my lady. May your dreams be soft and sweet."

"And yours," I answered and left him to it.

Breccia was in the middle of the bed in classic chicken pose when I arrived in the bedroom. She glared at me, and then looked, pointedly, away.

"He actually seems to be a pretty nice guy," I told her, sitting down on the edge of the bed and bending over to untie my sneakers. "And he's not a replacement for Borgan, if that's what's on your mind." I dropped one sneaker on the floor and gave a sharp laugh.

"Good God, one boyfriend's all the tightrope walking I can handle! Not to say that I'm handling it all that—"

My cell phone gave tongue. I fished it out of my pocket, saw Borgan's number, and a knot that I hadn't known was tied tight in the middle of my chest suddenly loosened.

"Hey," I said into the phone, trying to sound cheerful, if not perky.

"Are you all right?" His voice was strained, and the knot in my chest tightened again.

"I'm all right, but—"

"I thought I heard the Gate open, but sea business had me, and—"

"I know; it's okay. You had an emergency; you didn't walk out on me. But it wasn't the Gate opening."

"What was it, then?" Still too short and too terse. I bit my lip, wondering if he was going to find the truth soothing.

Well, I wasn't going to lie to the man, not when he'd heard the arrival, plain as plain.

"One of the Wise paid a call," I said, keeping my voice as even as possible. "She was annoyed that the Gate was opened to let Gran bring my mother home, those weeks ago, and we're currently under threat of being cut off from the other Five Worlds, if one more funny thing happens here that disturbs the Wise's peace."

Silence.

"I figure we've got 'til Labor Day before the Varothi's little bon voyage party catches their attention. How was *your* evening?"

He sighed, deeply.

"Turns out the lady the sea gave asylum to the other day figured she owed me." A heavy pause, and another sigh, this one sounding...pained.

"She killed the *ronstibles*."

I opened my mouth—and closed it again, fast, before anything like *Yay!* escaped it.

"Is there anything I can do for you?"

There was another longish pause—and getting worrisomely longer.

"Borgan?"

"Sorry. I'm—I took a hit, there," he said slowly, and then, more quickly, "nothing that won't heal. But I'm—Finn's fishing for me tomorrow. What say I come find you when I wake up. We can get a cup of coffee and list out all the ways we're doomed. Make up an odds sheet and post it in Bob's."

I grinned, worriedly.

"Sounds great," I said, and made a conscious decision not to mention Cael. Time for that tomorrow.

"You get some sleep. And if there *is* anything I can do..."

"Just—stay safe, Kate. I—I'll see you tomorrow. 'Bye."

"'Bye," I answered, but he'd already hung up.

CHAPTER TWENTY-FOUR

Monday, July 10
High Tide 11:13 A.M. EDT
Sunrise, 5:10 A.M.

"My lady, you should not cook for me," Cael the Wolf objected.

I glanced at him over my shoulder. He'd made use of the shower, and re-dressed in his red-and-gold garments. It seemed to me that those were somewhat less grubby than they had been last night, but they still weren't anything like beachwear. Have to do something about that. Later.

For now, there was breakfast to get ready, and talking to do.

"You want to cook?" I asked.

He narrowed his eyes, apparently considering the question.

"I am not familiar with the process, but I can learn, if my lady has no others to serve her."

Right. I was supposed to have servants to do menial things, so my brain and my powers could be freed to do important work. Like protecting the House and preserving the lives of all my oath-sworn.

"The customs here are different," I said, turning the burner on under the frying pan, and glancing at the clock. Eight-thirty.

"For instance," I said to Cael, "I'm not royalty, here. I guard the land, and keep it safe, and assist the *trenvay.*"

"Felsic obeyed your word," he pointed out, coming into the kitchen on bare feet.

"Felsic obeyed my word because it suited Felsic to help me out,"

I said, cracking eggs into the mixing bowl. "She's not bound to do what I say."

"Is that so, my lady? I saw deference, and loyalty, there. Power, too, but bound to your own."

Fork in one hand, bowl in the other, I blinked.

"You saw that?"

"My lady, I did. It is plain that you do not...require the level of fealty your grandfather felt necessary to secure the House."

"It's more of a co-op than a monarchy," I agreed, and remembered to use the fork to whip the eggs.

"Cutlery is in the drawer to the left of the sink," I said over my shoulder, as I poured the eggs into the pan. "Coffee mugs are in the cabinet over the coffeemaker. The coffeemaker is the thing the pot filled with dark liquid sits in—it's all hot, so be careful. Plates are up with the mugs, and it'd be a big help if you brought two over here, please."

He moved silently, which wasn't particularly creepy since the land was doing a good job of providing eyes in the back of my head. I watched him pull two mugs out of the cabinet and place them carefully beside the coffeemaker before going back to slide two plates out of the stack, and carry them to my side.

"On the counter, please," I said, scrambling for all I was worth. "You like scrambled eggs?"

"My lady, I hope soon to discover that."

Fair enough.

"You'd better start in with calling me Kate—everybody does. Well. If you hear my grandmother call me Kaederon, you'd best get out of town, because that means she's hot and ready to blow."

"I will remember. Will I meet your grandmother soon?"

"Funny; a lot of people have been asking that, lately." I turned the heat off under the pan. "Including me."

I divided the eggs and gave him the plates to ferry over to the table.

"Cream in your coffee?" I asked.

"I will have it as you have it," was the reply—and that wasn't too bad for a dog-boy. No. A master of hounds.

I thought about that as I poured cream and coffee. Grandfather Aeronymous had kept hounds, of course; a man of his station was required to keep hounds, so that he could mount a hunt for the entertainment of visitors, if nothing else. What he hadn't kept, in my lifetime, was a master of hounds. A dog-boy had lived in the kennels to care for the dogs; he slept with them, fed them, exercised them, and trained them. What other duties might fall to a master of hounds, I had no idea, though it was obvious, from Cael the Wolf's demeanor and pattern of speech, that he'd held a court position.

Well, something else to talk about. At this rate, we weren't going to run out of topics anytime soon.

"Here you go," I said, bringing the mugs to the table. "Sit, and eat your breakfast."

"My liege is seated first," he said. A glance up into his face showed it stern. A blink Sideways showed a man in distress, seeking to hold strangeness at bay with the proper application of manners.

I sat down and put my napkin on my knee.

"Sit, Cael the Wolf," I said, trying to sound gentle but firm. "The food's better when it's hot, and I have questions to put, over the meal."

He still didn't like it, but he could scarcely refuse an order from his lady. Which gave him another sort of relief—no matter how strange, he was among civilized folk, if the High still gave orders to those who sat Lower.

"Eat," I said again, and picked up my fork to address my eggs, so he could see the way of it.

He watched for a moment, then copied me—I should say that the utensils in the Land of the Flowers are roughly analogous to *knife, spoon, fork*, but that there are a lot more of them, and very specific rules about which to use on what. Including the big, sharp knife athwart the top of the main tray at each place at every meal, which was technically *not* for stabbing the person next to you when they got too annoying to bear, but which, so history taught, had from time to time been pressed into such service.

"I like scrambled eggs," Cael said eventually. "And I like coffee. Thank you, my . . . Kate."

"You're welcome," I said, putting my plate aside. "More coffee?"

"Please, I will serve you."

"Thank you."

He took the mugs away and quickly brought them back, filled to their brims with coffee and cream. Mine was settled first, then his, before he sat down, put his plate to one side, as I had done, and leaned back, gingerly, into the chair.

I nodded.

"I need to know why you were bound into the carousel as a high-security prisoner," I said, watching his face, and bidding the land pay attention and judge the truthfulness of the answers I got.

"I was bound because my lord so decreed."

I frowned. "*Aeronymous* had you bound?"

Grandfather might've been a bastard, but binding prisoners into the carousel was strictly within the honor of the Wise.

"No, my lady. The Wise bound me."

Okay, I had it now; we were going to play chess.

"For what crime were you bound?" I asked, letting him see that I was being patient.

He raised his hands, showing me empty palms.

"There had been complaint; a scheme to create imbalance between the Worlds had been discovered. The Wise came to Lord Aeronymous and laid claim that one of the saboteurs resided within his court. He protested, but as you are aware, my lady, there is no appeal from the Word of the Wise. Therefore, I was given over to them, and brought to this place to be bound."

He paused, then added, softly, "Before I was bound, the warden— who I heard last night was your grandmother—the warden created a diversion, and bought me time to flee."

He shook his head, his face shuttering like a camera, and picked up his mug.

I drank some coffee, too, and waited until he'd put his mug down to ask the next question.

"What happened?"

"I chose the wrong direction in which to run. It went worse with me, then, and in the end, there was the binding, after all."

"*Were* you trying to sabotage the dance of the Worlds?" I asked softly.

"No!"

And *that* was the truth, said so vehemently that my head rang.

"I think, now, and in the days since I have been given my liberty...I think that it was done to make my lord Aeronymous vulnerable. So much of his power was woven into his people— into our oaths. It was in defense of the House, and we all of the House, but..."

The front door opened, sweet and silent, and Gran stepped through, Mr. Ignat' right behind.

"Good morning, Kate," she said crisply, glancing at the book-cluttered couch and the blue blanket of flying elephants folded neatly on the end—Cael's doing, not mine—and then at Cael himself.

He rose with alacrity, and bowed low. Gran's eyebrows rose.

"Introduce me to your friend," she said.

"Gran, this is Cael the Wolf, liegeman of Aeronymous, once master of hounds."

She nodded, face calm, eyes narrowed.

"Cael, this is my grandmother, Ebony Pepperidge, of whom we were just speaking."

"Lady, my thanks, long behind, for producing a moment when I might have saved myself."

"No thanks required, Cael the Wolf. It was a slim chance—what we call here 'a long shot.' That you saw it and took it—that was brave. It has long grieved me, what came after."

She moved a hand and Mr. Ignat' came forward to stand at her side. He was smiling gently, and looking at Cael as if he was a particularly toothsome sweet.

"I make known to you, Cael the Wolf, my consort, the Ozali Belignatious, out of Sempeki. Bel, I'm sure you'll want a word with a countryman while Kate and I have a chat."

A chat, was it? Dammit, the woman was hardly out of her tree and already I was in hot water!

"It will be a pleasure to speak with Cael," Mr. Ignat' said promptly. His smile grew wider. "Have you seen the view over the sands to the ocean?" he asked. "You really must." He raised his hand, beckoning.

Cael cast me a questioning look; I nodded and he allowed Mr. Ignat' to lead him across the living room and out onto the summer parlor.

I took a breath and stood.

"Hi, Gran; it's good to see you. People have been asking after you."

Her time inside her tree had healed her, I saw. She had been observably frail when she had decided to take the cure. Now, she stood straight, her eye was firm, and her voice strong. There were changes, though. The band of white at the front of her dark hair remained, and she seemed to . . . fill up less of the room than formerly.

"You'll have to tell me who," Gran said, "so that I may pay my social dues. Is there any more coffee?"

"Coming right up."

I rose, cleared the table, except for my coffee, and put the dishes in the sink, before opening the cabinet for a clean mug.

Gran drank her coffee black, straight from the pot. I poured it and brought it, putting it down on the table by her hand before resuming my own seat.

"Sorry 'bout the noise last night," I said, taking a sip of coffee. It was tepid, but I didn't get up to warm the cup.

"I imagine so. One of the Wise, I assume?"

"Isiborg, I guess her name is. You want the long form or the short form?"

"The short form will do."

So I gave her the big outline while she sipped her coffee and watched my face, and didn't interrupt.

"We have a few weeks until the next atrocity reaches their attention," I said, "but that one's a doozy."

"So I heard from Bel. I'm sorry for those who died in Prince Aesgyr's attempt. Is Cael the only one who remained?"

"No, Borgan's got a woman of Cheobaug guesting in Saco Bay. He gave her twenty days to build her strength because, so she says, there are enemies at home."

"I expect that there are. It was generous of Borgan to grant her time. And of you, to give Cael shelter. When will he be returning to Sempeki?"

"He did return, but he found things, as he told me the story, *changed*—the House broken, the Gate useless, the grounds deserted except for a gardener and a guard. You were there; does that jibe with what you found?"

Gran nodded.

"Right. Conditions being what they were, then, he came back here because he needed to swear to Aeronymous or die, and he didn't feel quite like dying."

Gran looked at me over the rim of her mug.

"You took his oath."

"I appear to be the closest thing to Aeronymous left. Yes, I took his oath."

I waited to be told that I'd made a very bad, or at least desperately foolish, decision, but Gran only finished with her coffee and put the mug down.

"Henry," I said, changing the subject by main force, "was

particularly asking after you." I paused, then decided not to tell her he was getting old. Gran has outlived generations of human-folk; she's well aware that they get old, and, eventually, die.

She nodded. "I'll try to see him today."

"Nerazi also has an interest."

Gran half-smiled.

"I'll have some explaining to do there, I don't doubt."

That was...interesting. I'd never actually seen Gran give an account of her actions or defend her reasons to anybody. Of course, if there was anybody on the Beach who came close to deserving such an accommodation, aside from Mr. Ignat', it was Nerazi. Her and Gran go 'way, 'way back.

"You know Mother and Andy—" I began.

"Yes," she said briefly.

Okay, then. I picked up my mug of what would now be stone-cold coffee, and put it back down, without sipping.

"Point of information," I said.

"Yes?"

"When will you be moving back?" I waved my hand at the mess in the living room. "I ought to clean up at least. Also—I have a cat."

"Do you? What's her name?"

"Breccia. She's only been here a couple days. One of the Dummy Cats; comes with Old Mister's personal recommendation."

"You can hardly do better than that," Gran said. "How is Frenchy? I haven't seen her in...a very long time."

"Seems to be doing fine. A little annoyed at the disruption around the cats—did you hear about that?"

"I don't think I have; you'll have to catch me up on it a little later. To answer your question..." Her voice drifted off and she turned her head to look down the hall, a slight smile on her lips.

I followed her gaze, just as Breccia strolled 'round the corner into the kitchen, ridiculous tail held at half-mast.

"Still holding a grudge, are you?" I murmured.

She stopped to glare—and her tail lifted high into an ecstatic, quivering welcome. She rushed to Gran and stropped her ankles.

Gran laughed, and bent down to offer a finger.

"Yes, yes, I'm glad to see you, too. Thank you for coming to take care of my granddaughter."

Breccia bumped the offered finger joyously, not once, but three times. Then, she reluctantly tore herself away from Gran, came past my chair and gave me a casual bump before marching on to her food dish.

"She's a little beauty," Gran said. "You're very lucky."

"I think so," I answered, watching the cat's ears twitch as she followed our conversation.

Gran sighed.

"To answer your question, Kate—I'm not certain that I'll be moving back here."

I felt a slight chill.

"Going to retire to the Wood?"

Gran shook her head. "I'm not certain of that, either. Bel and I need to talk—and I should see Henry."

"Gran, look; you deeded the house to me, but we can undeed it, it—"

"No, let's keep everything as it is for the moment—if you don't mind, Kate?"

"I don't mind; but I also don't want you to think you don't have any right to move back into your own house."

She smiled and patted my hand.

"I don't think that at all. Is there anything I can do for you, now that I've disrupted your morning?"

"No, I don't—yes, there is. Do you have time to take Cael down to Dynamite and buy him something a little more Changing Land to wear? I promised the cat I'd check out a still spot she found for me—*today,* so I should probably get on that."

"I'll be happy to; I haven't seen Mrs. Kristanos in too long, so it will give me a chance to catch up. After you're finished with your business, come to the Wood; I'll keep Cael with me."

"Great; I shouldn't be long."

"Take all the time you need," Gran said, and got up. She held out her arms and I stood into her hug.

"Thank you, Katie," she murmured in my ear. "Thank you for freeing the carousel."

I felt her lips against my cheek, then she released and turned away.

CHAPTER TWENTY-FIVE

Monday, July 10

St. Margaret's Catholic Church sits at the corner of Maine Route 5 and Archer Avenue, right at the top of the hill. It's a big church, for so small a place as Archers Beach, but modest despite its size. You might expect a stone church, given its age, but what stands on the site is a wooden building, demurely whitewashed. The entranceway doubles as the base of the bell tower, and of a design that might make a passing tourist think the whole project had started out as a lighthouse.

St. Margaret's fills up its corner lot—there's no cemetery or churchyard, only a small garden plot cuddled into the curve of the wall facing Route 5. The garden itself is a careful foreground planting of hosta, day lilies, and dwarf hydrangea; a neatly trimmed shrubbery behind. Between the shrubbery and the flowers is a large glazed tile, painted in primitive style, portraying a haloed woman in blue and white robes, holding a similarly haloed, white-swaddled babe in her arms. She's standing on the beach, apparently being adored by a starfish, a sand dollar, a few seagulls and some stones. There's a larger stone behind the woman and the child, just at the edge of the dark line of the sea, which bears a disturbing resemblance to Googin Rock.

Not really much here for a trenvay to get their teeth into, I thought, surveying the tidy little garden from the sidewalk.

Well, you never knew until you asked.

I stepped carefully into the garden, drawing a curtain of light fog between me and the sidewalk. No need to attract attention to myself, or to the *trenvay* of this place.

If any.

I settled on my heels on a patch of mulch to the right of the tile, emptied my mind and opened my land-ears, quiescent and receptive to whatever this bit of land might be willing to say, just between us.

The fog curtain isolated me from traffic noise, and the sound of voices. Overhead, a seagull laughed, possibly a commentary on my efforts, or a general observation on life.

Cautiously, I let myself sink into the land, hoping to hear . . . something; to trigger a memory and waken whoever had watched over this small patch once. I heard nothing, saw nothing, sensed only the living land about me, growing things, and the small lives that thrive in the soil. But nothing that indicated that there was— that there had ever been—a spirit entwined with this place.

And, then, just as I began the slow rise back into my body— "Do not leave me!"

Anguish washed through me, and crazed determination.

"I do not allow it! I will heal—"

I froze where I was, listening with my whole being, but there were no more words. There was a sense of rushing, an outpouring of power, and a scream as the land died—and the *trenvay*, too.

"No!" I threw my will into the land, but I was chasing a ghost; whoever had drained the power from their service, in an attempt to heal . . . someone . . . that had happened a long time ago. Something here remembered it, but it wasn't the *trenvay*, nor the little piece of land she had betrayed.

I rose into my body, and let my focus go, realizing as I did so that my fingers were cramped, squeezing hard against a surface as ungiving as rock.

I opened my eyes, and saw that I was gripping the top edge of the tile. The *tile* remembered?

My eyesight became sharper, though I hadn't consciously made the request of the land. There were words written on the tile's reverse, very nearly invisible, even to my enhanced vision.

In loving memory of Margaret, who tended this place for time uncounted. When I lay dying, she traded her life for mine. I set this marker I have made where she perished, and I pray God we will meet again, at His right hand.   —Gerald McKenna

The tile's memory, yes; from the man who had made it, his grief poignant even now. The man Margaret the *trenvay* had loved so much that she had drained her service, and killed herself, to preserve him.

My vision misted. I shook my head, sharply, and surged to my feet, looking around at the mundane little garden, and the raveling curtain of fog.

I wasn't exactly surprised to find that I was shivering.

It was quiet in the little park that had been the site of the Archer family homestead. I sat on one of the benches, closed my eyes and just... savored being alone. The land murmured inside my head, and gave the impression of mine faithful hound curling at my feet. I slid down, resting the back of my head on the bench, and tipped my face up to the sun.

I might've dozed; it was a good day for dozing with the sun on your face. In fact, I *must have* dozed, because the next thing I knew, the land was jumping up with excited yips, like a puppy welcoming one of his favorite people ever.

Well, we all knew who that was, didn't we?

I opened my eyes, and turned my head, not bothering to lift it from the back of the bench.

Borgan had settled sideways into the corner of the bench, apparently so he could get a good angle on my face as it slowly succumbed to sunburn.

"Didn't mean to wake you," he said.

"Didn't mean to fall asleep. I'm glad you found me."

I skooched up straight, turned on the bench to face him, and felt a thrill of cold alarm.

"*Should* you have found me?" My hand moved on its own, reaching out to grip his shoulder. "Borgan, you look like hell."

"Feeling a little better than that," he said, and his smile was tired. He put his hand over mine, and pressed it. "Took a hit, like I said."

"You also said it'll heal. I can—"

"Sure you can—and I 'preciate it, but let's hold any land-healing in reserve."

It looked to me like healing was needed *right now*, but a man had to be the judge of his own wounds. So I've been told. I took a breath, and touched the land on my own behalf. Cold alarm faded, leaving behind warm concern.

"This is—because of the *ronstibles*? How—"

"The *ronstibles* are—were." He paused, mouth tightening. "Part of the sea. Their natures came from the sea; she made them and she valued them. Losing them...diminishes the sea, and—"

"Diminishes you," I finished, when it seemed like he wouldn't—or couldn't.

"That's right, but it's temporary. A hit, and a hard one, but nothing we won't come back from." He took a careful breath, like maybe there were cracked ribs involved. "Me—the sea didn't make me; she just...accepted me."

A long time ago, the sea had accepted him, and he'd been dealing with the consequences of that acceptance ever since. I wondered how long it had taken him, to come to terms with the duties and existence of the sea's Guardian. It didn't seem like the right time to ask, but there was another question that did want asking.

"The lady from Cheobaug," I said carefully. "Where is she now?"

"Tucked up in quiet water. She'll do fine there for the rest of her grant."

"What happens when her grant runs out? Poof! She spontaneously crosses the World Wall into Cheobaug?"

"The sea will send her; that piece of work's all built and set." He shifted slightly on the seat, and released the hand he had been pressing against his shoulder.

"Kate..."

My chest cramped, for no reason I could say.

"What did you do?" He leaned forward sharply, cupping my cheek against his palm, and looked hard into my eyes.

"Do?"

"Your...fires are gone. Let me..."

I smelled salt, felt a tickle of ozone, and a wash of warmth. Then Borgan let me go and sat back into the corner of the bench.

"What made you decide to give your fires to the land?"

"Truthfully, it was more *scared stubborn* than *decide*. When the Wise One dropped in last night, the very first thing she did was try to pull my *jikinap*—I guess so she could get to know me all up close and personal without actually having to put herself through the aggravation of talking to me. I had to do *some*thing, and I couldn't hold long against her, so I—gave it away."

"To the land."

"Why not?" I shifted irritably. "I never wanted *jikinap*—Mr. Ignat' tricked me into taking it, and then I kept it because I figured I had to, in defense of the Beach. But it makes me vulnerable to other, more experienced Ozali. I really hate to be vulnerable."

"Do you, now?" murmured Borgan, and continued before I could answer. "So all those little tricks you used your fires for—the light, and your Varothi's shortcut spell—that's all gone now?"

"Haven't run a diagnostic, but I imagine so." I sighed; the shortcut had been useful, still . . .

"It's okay; I can walk—or run—and get to where I'm needed soon enough. The Beach isn't *that* big."

Borgan nodded. "How 'bout a race, then?"

I frowned. His color was bad; ashy, rather than rich red-brown; and it was clear he was in pain, be it existential or physical.

"Are you sure a race is a great idea? You really don't look good; I'm not just saying that to be amusing."

"Just a little race, with lunch at the end of it, and no harm in between." He waved a hand in the general, downhill, direction of the sea. "How's this? Last one to the entrance of the Pier buys lunch at Neptune's?"

I opened my mouth, but there was nobody to answer.

Borgan had vanished.

"Shit!"

I came to my feet—and I was standing at the base of the ramp that led up to the Pier entrance. The land nudged me; I turned to my left, and found Borgan leaning easily against the guardrail with his arms crossed over his chest. He was, I thought, looking a little white around the mouth, but he was smiling.

"What just happened?" I asked.

His smile morphed into a grin.

"Maybe the Beach's a little bigger than you remembered?"

"Smartass."

"Been said often enough that I'm beginning to think there's justice in it. Now, let me ask you a question."

He unfolded his arms and leaned forward, so I could look directly into his eyes.

"Kate, where are my fires?"

"You're a Guardian; your power comes from the sea."

"Hm." He leaned back against the rail again. "Now, I've always said your gran was a dab hand with a tricky bit of working. Where's she keep her power?"

I could see where he was going with this—I thought. But old certainties don't go down without a fight.

"Gran gets her power from her tree—no." I closed my eyes, counted to ten, and opened them. "*Yes*, dammit; she's *trenvay*. She draws power from her tree."

Except Gran was a very fine magic worker, and if I'd ever doubted that, it would only have taken the distilling of Mr. Ignat's *jikinap* into butterscotch brandy to make me a believer. And that was before we got to the fact that she had survived, away from her tree, in the World of all the Six which was most hostile to souls.

Her tree could not have supported that.

Not her tree, unaugmented.

I sighed, and looked into Borgan's face. "So, why didn't Mr. Ignat' tell me this?"

But I knew why: Mr. Ignat' was from Sempeki, and there he had been a very powerful Ozali, indeed. In Sempeki, power is its own reward; it's sought after and kept close—and it's always on display.

"You'll have to ask him," Borgan said.

"No need; I figured it out. I think." I took his hand. "So, it looks like lunch is on me. Shall we?"

"Could use a bite, now that you mention it."

He shifted away from the rail, and caught his breath, eyes narrowing. My chest cramped, and I gripped his hand tight.

"Maybe instead, I should take you home and put you to bed. *Seriously*, Borgan—"

He grinned down at me, eyes glinting with mischief.

"Well, now we got the whole day planned. That's nice."

There really wasn't any way to answer that without digging myself in deeper. Besides, he was moving now, walking deliberately up the ramp, keeping pace with the tourists seeking out the heady pleasures of the Pier shops—or maybe just a beer.

It was early for the full lunch crowd at Neptune's, but not too early for music—which was being provided by Nessa and Andy, like it said on the chalkboard.

They were deep into a toe-tapping rendition of "Old Dan Tucker," when Borgan and I came onto the big deck. We found a high table sitting perilously close to the low guardrail, with an unobstructed view down the beach, and out, to Wood Island Light and beyond. I pulled out the tall chair, and Borgan gently lifted me into the seat. I sighed, and leaned against him for a moment, just...happy.

"Problem?" he asked, after I'd straightened.

I watched him get into the chair across and shook my head.

"No problem. I just...feel better—I feel calmer—when you touch me."

His eyebrows twitched.

"Don't know that I like to hear that. When'd it change?"

I picked up the menu.

We caught up the events of the last while over burgers and ale, while Neptune's filled up with lunch customers. The band took a break and came back again, waving as they passed our table, but neither stopping to chat.

"Trouble with your mom?" Borgan asked, sipping his second ale.

I shrugged. "I think she's a little jealous of her new life. It's been a long time since she's had one all to herself."

"Hmm."

He set the bottle aside; up on the stage, the band swung into "The Sloop John B," with the dulcimer taking a strong lead.

"Now, this boy from your grandad's House—what did you do to him?"

"I didn't do anything *to* him, except take his oath."

"Right. But normally, wouldn't that involve a sharing of power? *Jikinap*, I'm talking about."

"I guess it might've; Cael's my first oath-sworn, and while he seems a nice enough guy, I hope he's my last." I had a sip from my bottle, relishing the chocolate notes. "What I did...it felt like we—the land and I—it felt like we did a healing. In a sense—well, no, not in a sense—*in reality*, it *was* a healing. The man was dying. Now, he's not."

"So now he belongs to the land?"

"Felsic seems to think so; I'm not sure I can actually do that."

"You're the Guardian. Somebody comes to you and offers to serve—why shouldn't you be able to accept their service?"

Why, indeed? If a Guardian and the *trenvay* could strip someone of their service, then surely service could be granted....

"I'm not sure how he's going to feel about that," I said slowly.

"Best to ask him, then."

I sighed, and nodded at Borgan's depleted bottle.

"You done? Want another beer?"

"I'm fine. Thanks for lunch."

"You're welcome. Now. Am I taking you to *Gray Lady* or to my place, so you can *get some rest*?"

"Your place, if it won't be too crowded. I don't want you on the sea until my guest's gone."

"You don't need me to be with you, and if the sea—"

"Yes," Borgan interrupted, reaching across the table to catch my hand. "I do."

I blinked at him. "Do what?"

He shook his head, his smile crooked.

"Here you tell me how it comforts you to have me touch you. Is it a surprise that you comfort me?"

Reciprocity, Kate, I told myself. *Try to keep up.*

"It does surprise me, yeah," I said, and pushed past the resistance—the fear of being seen vulnerable, was what it was—to add, "but I'm glad."

⁓ҽ✺ꝰ⁓

This pool into which the Borgan had compelled her...its waters were heady; layered and balanced: bright and dark, astringent and smooth.

These complex waters buoyed her, and strengthened her as even the sweet open sea had not.

Old waters, these, and treacherous. She must not trust them; for here was no faint hint of nobility, or gentle kindness.

It was strange, that the Borgan would have left her here, to grow sleek and fat with such power. Or perhaps, she thought, half sunk in the strange dreams carried upon these waters...perhaps he meant them to enchant her, and bind her; a far more potent trap than the mere misty wall he had placed about the pool.

She should, she thought, cast aside the water's seductive charms, shatter the Borgan's wall and go forth into the open sea, to find him and to claim him.

But...no, she thought sleepily. The Borgan's grant had some days yet to run. She had time...time to soak up strength, to be renewed in power and in beauty. When the pool had given her everything it could, *then* she would deal with the misty wall, and seek him out.

He would not then, he *could not* then, withstand her. She would be a bride, indeed, and beloved of the waters.

CHAPTER TWENTY-SIX

Tuesday, July 11
Low Tide, 5:42 A.M. EDT
Sunrise 5:11 A.M.

I called Gran before we left Neptune's, explained that there was a Situation, and asked if she could keep Cael with her. She agreed, then handed the phone to him, so I could give him his orders, which I did as gently as possible.

"This liege thing's getting old," I told Borgan, snapping the phone shut and slipping it away.

I stood up and held my hand out to him. He took it, and rose. Which would've been more comforting if I hadn't received the definite impression that he was grateful for the assist.

At Tupelo House, he was made known to the cat by her call name. That essential courtesy performed, we all went upstairs, where Borgan immediately fell into a profound sleep.

Breccia and I disposed ourselves for our own comfort—me, with my head tucked on his shoulder, the cat curled into a pleased, purring circle on his chest—and the three of us slept straight through until seven o'clock.

I woke to soft nibblings along my earlobe, and a warm hand on my breast. We made slow, leisurely love, drowsed, and finally rose, in no hurry about it, to shower together, and mosey out to the kitchen to see what might be for supper.

The fridge yielded leftover fried chicken, the potato salad I'd made yesterday, and a bottle of wine, which we carried out to the summer parlor and ate as we overlooked the sand and the surf. Twilight slowly obscured the sky, and the stars peered shyly down. The cat came out to join us, draped herself across both of our laps, and purred herself to sleep.

When the wine was gone, Borgan put Breccia on his shoulder, where she snuggled under his ear without quite waking up, and we carried the remains of our picnic inside. Dishes deposited in the sink, and cat on the blanket, we went upstairs again to bed.

"Go back to sleep," he murmured, but he didn't add the little nudge of sea-magic like he usually did, to reinforce the suggestion.

It shouldn't have mattered; I was comfortable enough to drift back into dreamland for a few hours all on my own.

But the lack of that nudge—that *did* matter. Borgan, my waking brain reminded me, had taken a wound. Yesterday's day of mostly rest should have, in my fond hopes, put him on the road to mending.

But if he was husbanding small bits of magic...

...then he was hurt worse than he'd let me nag him into admitting...And it also meant that I was an idiot, keeping him on land when he should have been healing, in the sea.

I opened my eyes, stretched and rolled out of bed.

"How long do you think I—*even* I—can sleep? I'm wide awake. I'll walk you down to the water, then go collect Cael."

Borgan was pulling on his T-shirt. I snagged my jeans and skinned into them, and looked up into his face.

I couldn't say he looked worse than he had yesterday.

But he surely looked no better.

I opened a bureau drawer, pulled out a bra and a T-shirt at random, and finished dressing inside of an absolute silence.

"Kate," Borgan said.

I pulled my shirt down, and turned to face him.

"How bad?" I blurted. "How bad are you hurt, and how long until you're healed? And, while I'm at it—special bonus question, since you didn't want the land healing you—shouldn't you be letting the sea do just that?"

He sat down on the edge of the bed, and held out his hands.

"Kate," he said, and, when I just looked at him, "I'd like a hug, if you got one."

I sighed.

"I don't think I'm out, yet."

I sat across his knees, facing him. He put his arms loosely around my hips; I wrapped my fingers around his braid, and looked at it. Shells, shaped glass, beads. There was a new one, I thought—blue and green swirls, like water. I sighed again, reluctantly let the braid go and put my hands on his shoulders, looking straight into his eyes.

He nodded.

"Those are good questions you're asking. I don't want you thinking that you did me harm by keeping me on land. First thing is, you didn't keep me, except that I wanted to be here, with you. Second thing is, you did me good, not harm. Heart's ease, if not land-healing, and that's not to be discounted.

"Why I can't let the waters heal me..." He sighed, his arms tightening around me. "Kate, it was *the sea* took harm from the *ronstibles'* death. That's where the wound is." Another sigh, and he bent his head until it rested against mine. "It's me that has to heal her."

I took a breath, tasting salt and ozone.

"Isn't there anything I can do to help you?"

He snorted a soft laugh.

"Let me study on it." Deep breath. "And, now, I got to get moving. Hum's boat won't fish itself."

"I'll go with you," I said, "to the sea's edge."

"Sure. Be glad of the company."

Mr. Ignat' was asleep with his back against Gran's tree, which I supposed she had reentered for the night. Cael was curled in soft grasses nearby, Arbalyr on a branch above his head.

Neither the bird nor Mr. Ignat' woke when I stepped into the clearing, but Cael raised his head, nose leading, as if he was in fact a wolf, testing the morning air.

He rolled smoothly to his feet, began to bow, and stopped himself.

"My—Kate. Good morn to you."

"Good morn to you," I answered, considering him.

Gran had done her job well; Cael wore the latest in Archers Beach chic: multipocket khaki shorts and a red T-shirt with an abstract gold design splashed on the front. His feet were, as before, bare.

"Do the clothes please you?"

He glanced down at himself.

"If it pleases my lady that I *blend in*, then the clothes can do naught else but please me," he said.

Bless the lad, he was full of politic answers.

"Would you care to come home with me?"

"Yes," he said simply, and reached behind the tree Arbalyr was sleeping in to pull out a tote bag with DYNAMITE! exploding in orange and yellow across the front.

"I have several changes of clothing, as your lady grandmother advised. She also advised shoes, but, those are not possible."

"You might change your mind, come winter, but for now, bare feet totally blend in."

I waved him forward and turned to follow the path the Wood opened before me.

"I do not think that I like bagels so much as scrambled eggs," he said some while later, "though I think I could become very fond of cream cheese."

"The reason bagels exist is as a carrier for cream cheese," I assured him. "Also peanut butter. And occasionally jam." I took a bite of my own bagel—onion, garlic, and poppy seed, for the curious—and chewed for the amount of time required to chew a bagel, before cleaning my palate with coffee.

"The coffee's good," I said, which it was. Cael'd made it under my direction, though not my supervision. I'd been too busy sawing bagels in half to do anything more than outline the basic technique for him.

"Thank you," he said. "I wonder..." He stopped.

I looked up into his face.

"Don't be shy."

"Yes, my lady. It is only that I wonder—what...has become of the *jikinap* I had held in trust from my liege? The former lord... had considered it prudent to see his oath-sworn capable of their own defense—and of protecting those higher in the House."

Right.

"I need to talk to you about that. My apologies for the delay."

"I've not been...discommoded, my lady. I had only become aware of the absence, and wondered if I had earned your displeasure."

"You haven't displeased me, but you might find yourself displeased with me." I sipped coffee and looked him straight in the eyes.

"On the night I took your oath—just previous to that event—I gave my *jikinap* to the land of which I am Guardian. I did this to keep certain events from the attention of the Wise One."

"Yes," Cael said, as if this was perfectly reasonable. Of course, Cael wasn't a fan of the Wise either, was he?

"Having committed this act, I thought I had done with *jikinap*. When I accepted your oath, it was as Guardian of this land, and through the power inherent in the land." I hesitated, wondering if I ought to go into the healing aspect, or if that would just confuse the narrative.

"So I have become part of this land, through you, its Guardian," Cael said slowly. "With me, the land accepted my power. Thus far, I understand. But what I do not understand, my lady, is what weapon I have been given in return, so that I may stand my liege's man and protect her and her interests, which include myself."

"We're going to have to figure that out," I said. "I should let you know what you've gotten yourself into. I'm a new Ozali, and untrained. Though I'm easier with the powers attending my Guardianship, I'm still learning those, too. I make errors—of ignorance, mostly, but that doesn't matter if my ignorance results in harm."

I bit my lip.

"I learned yesterday—quite a number of things. But the thing which may help us answer your question is that I found my full powers, poor as they are, available to me through my connection with the land. If you reach, as you would, for something typical to your power..."

His eyes blazed. He snapped to his feet and retreated to the living room, dropped into a crouch and thrust his arm up and out, as if about to receive—

A spear.

To be precise, a warrior's short spear, used for close-in fighting, and a very tricky weapon it was.

Oh, any half-trained oaf—I include myself among that number, as my weapons instructor had done—could poke at an opponent with the thing, and even do damage, but to master it required dedication and a certain capacity for focused violence.

I was, let's say, impressed.

Cael straightened, the spear spinning a complicated arabesque between his long, dark fingers. He dropped to one knee, head bowed, the spear held steady in his hand, haft aligned with the inside of his forearm, butt end caught between elbow and body.

I applauded.

His head jerked up, startled, then he grinned, his delight illuminating the already sun-filled room.

"I have lost nothing!" he declared springing to his feet. "It has merely been stored in a different trunk."

Which was actually a pretty good way to look at it.

"Excellent," I said, grinning myself. "However, if the spear has no immediate task—"

It was gone before I could finish the sentence, tucked back into whatever trunk it now lived in, and held against need.

I reached for my coffee just as the cell phone trilled. The number on the screen wasn't familiar. I hit the answer button.

"Is that Kate?" a woman shouted into my ear before I could say *hello?* "Frenchy, here. I need some help down here at the Camp. Fella's come in with dogs; says he's been hired to clean out some wild cats. He ain't listening to reason, and I can't hold him much longer."

"I'm there," I told her.

"Hey!" her voice came strongly out of the speaker. "You can't fire a gun inside o'town, you damn' fool!"

I ended the call. It sounded like Frenchy was going to need her line real soon now, to call the cops.

"I will come, also," Cael said.

I looked at him over my shoulder.

"I don't—"

"I know about dogs," he said firmly.

Well, yeah; I guess he did.

"All right, then, come on."

I reached out, grabbed his arm, thought about the town dock at Camp Ellis...

"I'm here to exterminate vermin," a man's voice said, loud enough to be heard in Portland. "If I was you, I'd just go back inside my shed there, pour another shot o'Allens into the coffee, and let a man get to work. It's gonna get done, with or without your screechin'."

I headed toward the black pickup truck in the middle of the lot. Frenchy was standing between the shouting man and the

Dummy Railroad shed, legs braced, and a wary distance between her and the dog.

The dog was a monster—black and tan, with a big square head and a big square jaw. He was muzzled and there was a business-like leash attached to his harness, but somehow these things only drew attention to the fact that this dog was a hunter, and quite possibly a killer.

Another dog sat, harness-free and unmuzzled, just behind the man's left leg; some kind of hound, I thought. It looked like it had started out white, then been spattered with black paint. It was watching the altercation between his boss and Frenchy with interest, his head tipped to one side.

"Frenchy!" I called, reaching for the power at the base of my spine—which wasn't there.

Because I was standing on another Guardian's land—and I'd given my land all my power.

Maybe not so smart, after all, Kate.

Well, at least I could create a diversion; help Frenchy keep the guy talking until the sheriff arrived.

"Kate, thanks for coming."

"She ain't the sheriff," the guy said. "Step outta the way, girls."

"Jim Robins, you cussid dub," Frenchy snarled, settling herself where she stood. "You ain't settin' them dogs on cats inside this village. Fine thing it'll be, that Howie o'yours takin' a kitten in somebody's dooryard, with the kids lookin' on through the window!"

"Got a contract, paid for. If them cats is smart as Walt Spinney has 'em, they'll run away an' hide, now won't they?"

He whistled, sharp and high.

The leashed dog tensed, his ears pricking.

"Gonna do the job I was paid for," he said, and rapped out, "Oscar! Find!"

"He has left you," said a voice that had lately become familiar. "His oath to you was not strong, and he has accepted mine."

I turned, carefully, and there, indeed, was Cael, standing some eight feet away, the black-spattered dog sitting at his side, the line of his body expressing one long smile. His tail drummed the tarmac twice, and stopped.

"Oscar!" the man said sternly. "Heel!"

The dog raised his head to look adoringly up at Cael, who smiled down at him and said something I almost understood in a guttural tongue I'd never heard before. The dog's tongue lolled in what might have been a doggy laugh.

"You stealing my dog?" the guy asked menacingly.

"No," Cael said. He used his chin to point at the muzzled dog. "You would do well to take that one and leave. There is nothing for him, or for you, to hunt here, in the heart of the village."

The guy jerked on the leash and started forward, the big black-and-tan keeping pace, head low and menacing.

I felt a ripple under my feet; saw the tarmac flow over the guy's boots and harden. Perforce, he stopped walking, but like he'd chosen to do so—and he cast not one single curious look downward.

Magic-blind, this one; the wyrd just didn't exist for him.

"You like dogs? How about I send Howie here over to you?"

"If you loose that dog on me, I will have to kill him," Cael said, as calm as if he was discussing the weather. "His oath is strong, and it does him credit. I would not like to kill him. Be warned, and go."

"Stupid flatlander." One smooth move removed the muzzle and the leash. The dog sat where he had been, and the sense of menace grew stronger.

"Last chance," Robins said. "Gimme back my dog and go."

"No."

"Howie. Take him!"

The dog went from zero to sixty in a heartbeat, launching himself with a snarl. Cael leapt to meet him, caught him by the throat—and held on.

The dog roared, back feet scrabbling, lips peeled back from wicked teeth, inches from Cael's face—and Cael held him, apparently without effort, looking directly into the dog's eyes, his face growing sadder as the dog's efforts faltered, and the big body slumped. He took the weight of it down to the ground, kneeling, his hands still on the massive throat, easing the body down until it was lying on its side, and then it was over: a shuddering breath, and nothing more.

Robins yelled, snatched at his gun, and brought it up. I heard the snap when he took the safety off and there was no time to think it through.

I flung my will out like a whip, even as I felt the Words rise to my lips.

"To me."

Robins squeezed the trigger. Nothing happened.

"What the hell—?"

"It's not loaded," I heard someone say, belatedly recognizing the voice as mine.

I lifted my left hand, and watched with interest as I slowly opened the curled fingers, to reveal—

Six bullets.

Damn, Kate.

Jim Robins stared at the bullets, more in disbelief than awe, snapped the gun open, and checked the chamber.

I saw a very faint quiver of unease pass over his face before he holstered the piece, and looked beyond me, his shoulders sagging.

Cael was still kneeling beside the dead dog. He stroked the big square head, ran his hands down the still body, speaking in that language I could almost hear. Finally, he rose, his face wet with tears, and faced the man held in Frenchy's thrall.

"You are a very cruel man, Jim Robins," he said, and his voice was not quite steady. "You are not worthy of dogs, and they will know that now." He took a breath, and I saw the briefest flicker of power crackle 'round him.

"Dogs are your enemies now. All dogs, everywhere."

Behind him, the obedient black-spattered hound growled where he sat. His former owner started, and stared beyond Cael.

"Oscar?" He took—he tried to take—a step forward, but Frenchy's binding held.

The growl increased. Cael turned his head slightly and spoke; the dog quieted, and Cael looked back to Robins.

"You should leave now. Go where there are no dogs."

"I'm not going without Oscar."

"Would you end it now and here? But, no. He has a large heart, and regarded you well. I will not require your death of him." Cael leaned forward and I felt the power building, like a static charge that released in a single word.

"Go!"

Robins jumped. Frenchy pulled the land's grip away so fast that he staggered and almost fell as he ran for the truck. He scrambled the door open, climbed inside; the engine started with a roar.

He peeled rubber, getting out of the lot.

Cael turned away, back to the body of the big dog, knelt, and murmured. Oscar, apparently freed from the command that had held him quiet during the excitement, trotted over, nuzzled his former pack mate, then licked Cael's cheek.

"He died a noble death," Cael said, "in service of his oath." He raised his head and looked to me, his hand fondling Oscar's ear.

"This death, you understand, it was necessary because he could not deny his oath. He served that man; he loved him. There was no other way."

"Cael." I knelt on the other side of the dog—Howie. Cael raised his eyes to mine.

"That last bit—about all dogs being his enemies, now. Was that just for dramatic effect?"

"No, my—Kate. It was a true curse." Frenchy made a funny noise in her throat. I didn't blame her.

"That means he won't live out the day."

Cael said nothing.

"Ain't murder if a dog turns on 'im," Frenchy pointed out. She knelt next to me.

"Cael?"

He looked at her; she held out her hand.

"I'm Frenchy, Guardian of this piece of land here, Camp Ellis, and everything in and on it. I'm pleased to meet you, and I want to thank you for your service to my land."

He took her hand and bowed his head over it.

"I am pleased to meet you, Frenchy, and pleased to be of service."

"That's fine. Now, I'm wondering about Howie. Best if he ain't here, if the cops I called show up, or if Robins comes back with his own. I can let the land take him, right here, unless there's some other little thing you'd like done."

"You are kind. Yes, let the land have what remains. His spirit runs already with the Great Hunt."

"Right you are."

The tarmac under Howie's body softened and sank. We watched as the big dog slowly disappeared below the surface, until he was gone, and the tarmac hardened again over the place.

"It is done," said Cael, and took a breath.

"Cael," I said, "there's a problem with that curse."

He looked at me. "It is a strong curse, Kate; it will not fail."

"That's what I'm afraid of. See, if a dog kills that man, the law in this land says the dog will be put down. Killed. I don't know if you want that outcome."

There was a longish silence.

"This is a cruel world," Cael said finally.

"Not the world, but, sometimes, the men of it. In this case, the operating force is ignorance. There's very little *jikinap* in this world, and almost no Ozali. The village peacekeepers wouldn't be able to detect the presence of the curse. They'd assume the dog had gone bad—that it was a 'man-killer'—and must be prevented from killing again."

"I will not have any dog suffer for that man."

"Maybe we can do something else. But this curse that you've laid on him—can you call it back?"

He rubbed Oscar's head, and the hound sighed in doggy ecstasy.

"I cannot call it back." He narrowed his eyes, staring at the blameless section of asphalt where Howie's body had been. "I can set . . . a blessing upon him, however."

Frenchy snorted.

"A blessing?" I asked. "What will that do, exactly?"

He smiled.

"My blessing will hold him from harm. No dog will be able to savage him. But they will fear him, and hate him. They will cringe away from him and they will not heed him."

I bit my lip . . .

"That's fair," Frenchy said. "Them dogs was Jim Robins' living—his handling of them, is what I'm sayin'. If he don't have the dogs, he don't have a job." She paused. "Other thing is, he's not well-liked, himself. Mostly tolerated 'cause the dogs got results."

I nodded and looked to Cael.

"Do it."

He closed his eyes briefly. I felt a flicker, like heat lightning. Cael opened his eyes.

"It is done."

"Thank you."

"And now we need to—"

"Wait," said Frenchy, staring over Cael's shoulder. "Here comes somebody."

I looked, and here, indeed, came Old Mister, escorted by—

My fluffy, ridiculous cat.

I came to my feet, as did Frenchy. Cael rose and spoke a word to Oscar, who sat, leaning happily against his leg.

Old Mister paused before Cael, looking up at him with a

measuring stare. Breccia continued on, stropping against his ankle, and then weaving 'round mine.

I bent down and picked her up.

"How in God's name did you *get* here?" I demanded, and abruptly recalled the night that Borgan and the cat and I had unpacked and studied Prince Aesgyr's shortcut. Borgan had asked if he could make a copy, and I had told him sure, and then told the cat that she could make a copy, too.

Gotta watch that, Kate.

"It was the duty of my station," Cael was saying, apparently to Old Mister. "I am master of hounds. That I could serve you is my pleasure, but, if you will take my advice, you must look to better protections for your folk." He tipped his head as if listening. "For that, you must apply to your own Guardian. If she does not have the way of it, perhaps my liege will teach her."

"Sounds like we're in for some work," Frenchy muttered.

"If it'll keep the cats safe, it's worth it, right?" I asked, bending down to pick Breccia up and tuck her over my shoulder.

"Right you are."

"Then, if you got a second right now, we can step into your shed and I'll share with you—and Old Mister, too—a working that'll let you move from here to there without going in between."

"Sounds too damn' useful not to have in hand," Frenchy said. She jerked her head toward the shed. "Best get it done now, though; lot'll start fillin' up soon."

CHAPTER TWENTY-SEVEN

Tuesday, July 11

There's one thing to be said for getting up at four o'clock in the morning: you can sure get a lot done before the workday starts. On the other hand, if you've been that busy, you do need to have a second breakfast.

We were just sitting down to fresh coffee—courtesy of Cael—and grilled sharp cheese with strawberry jam sandwiches, which was what occurred to me as a good idea.

The dog sniffed at the cat food, sneezed, and had a drink from what had, until now, been *the cat's bowl.*

"We're going to have to get him some dog food," I said, looking in the fridge. "There's nothing here that I'd be comfortable feeding him—leftover fried chicken is right out."

"Yes," Cael said, carrying mugs to the table. "After we are done here, I will take him out to hunt."

I closed the fridge and looked at him.

"Maybe you'd better ask what he's used to eating on a regular basis."

"That is well thought," Cael said, and turned to address Oscar.

I went back to the stove and flipped the sandwiches. The cheese was nice and melty and the bread was deeply golden brown. Perfect. I slid them off the griddle and onto plates.

"Food's up."

Cael took the plates away, and carried them to the table. I made sure the burner was off, followed him—and kept going, prompted by the land.

I pulled the door open just as Artie's finger hit the bell. He blinked at me in clear consternation, apparently having forgotten what he was going to say.

"Hey, Artie."

"Kate." He swallowed and held up a manila envelope. "You got a Cael Wolfe living here?"

"Just until he finds his own place," I said, eying the envelope with trepidation.

"This just come in," Artie said, interrupting my thoughts, "*express*, Kate. Ain't nothin' comes in express."

"Well…" I started, but Artie was cruising on.

"All his papers're in here. Born outta the country—place called Sri Lanka—so we got those records, and the ones saying he's a naturalized citizen; got a passport, licenses, Social Security card." He thrust the envelope at me; I grabbed it before it hit my nose.

"You want to meet him?" I asked, and before he could answer, I called over my shoulder. "Cael? There's somebody here you should know."

He arrived silently, Oscar at his knee. I stepped back, so Artie could get a good look.

"Cael, this is Artie; he holds service to the entity called the Enterprise, up the hill. Artie, this is Cael the Wolf, Master of Hounds."

Artie blinked.

"How's he *trenvay*?" he demanded, then shook his head and looked at Cael. "Sorry. Ain't often a new *trenvay* rises, but it's no reason to lose my manners. Pleased to meetcha." He held out a hand.

Cael met it and they shook.

"I am pleased to meet you, Artie. As to how I am *trenvay*, when I gave my oath to my lady, the land accepted me, through her."

Artie's eyes narrowed.

"So you really *ain't* from around here."

"I am, now, from around here," Cael said, and nodded at the envelope in my hand. "My thanks, for delivering my certifications to my lady. They will also say, for those others, that I am now from around here, is that so?"

"That's so, brother."

"Then all is well."

"Anything else we can do for you today, Artie?" I asked.

"Naw; gotta get back up to the Enterprise. I don't like to leave it so early, but I figured with an *express*. Well, like the man says, everything's fine. Good day to the both of you—and Kate, you let me know when I can pick that rooster up."

"Just as soon as the new horse is in, I'll give you a call."

"Right, then."

He bent at the waist in what he might've intended to be a bow, and went down the stairs, his steps heavy. I closed the door, and handed the envelope to Cael.

"Something for you to study. Did you get a wallet, yesterday?"

He tucked the envelope under his arm. "Yes. Your lady grandmother said that I would need one, soon, and to keep it with my extra clothes."

"Everybody's prescient but me," I complained and sat down to address my cooling sandwich.

Oscar had apparently confessed to Cael a partiality for Iams dog food, so we walked down to Ahz's Market to take care of that detail.

Early though it still was, the sidewalks were starting to fill up with tourists. A family group towing a wagon full of beach stuff created a temporary traffic jam until they pulled over to the inside of the walk, so those in more of a hurry—or less burdened—could stream by them. Lots of people had their dogs with them, all respectably leashed. I looked worriedly at Oscar, who was *not* leashed, ambling along unconcernedly at Cael's knee, despite the noise and the darting children, and of course the provocation of other dogs.

Which escalated unexpectedly as we crossed Fountain Circle.

First a beagle barked. A shih tzu whirled around and began pulling against its leash. A brown shorthaired dog did the same. A German shepherd gave a puppylike yip, ears on alert. And a poodle started in our direction, dragging its hapless owner behind it.

Cael froze, his hand dropping first to Oscar's head, then slipping fingers under his collar.

Right, I thought, *the downside to being master of hounds*. I reached for the land, without any clear idea about how I was going to divert the oncoming wave of dogs, when, abruptly—they just stopped. A few shook their heads as if they'd heard an annoying noise. The beagle and the brown dog stuck their noses in the air, as if questing after a scent. The German shepherd's ears drooped slightly, and the poodle allowed itself to be called to heel.

Beside me, Cael sighed, very quietly.

"How long can you hold that?" I asked.

"As long as needed, but Oscar will be distressed, that I am diminished."

"Well, with all these dogs around, maybe we ought to consider getting him a—"

"Hey, buddy!"

A summer cop pulled his bike alongside us, and put out a foot to brace it. He was looking at Cael.

Cael turned to look at the cop.

"Yes?"

"You gotta have that dog on a leash."

"He is on a leash," Cael said promptly.

"Don't get funny. He looks like a nice dog, but you don't want him to get into an argument with a German shepherd, do you? Or a car? So, obey the rules and put him on a leash."

"He is on a leash," Cael repeated, softly. "Look again."

"I—" The cop leaned forward, then settled back, breathing an embarrassed laugh. "Well, I'll be damned. You're right, he is leashed. I gotta remember to get my eyes checked. All right, then. Sorry to have bothered you folks."

"Let us go," Cael said. "Will Ahz's Market also have a leash?"

"If not a leash, then a length of rope, for sure."

Ahz's did have leashes on offer; I bought one and took it to Cael, who was waiting outside with Oscar. He snapped it onto Oscar's collar before hunkering down and draping an arm over the dog's neck.

I went back inside the market, to take on dog food, and a couple of dog bowls. Breccia hadn't seemed to mind sharing her water with Oscar, but why tempt fate? By the time I came out again, Cael was reading the community bulletin board on the outside wall, Oscar's leash held negligently in one hand.

"Any good bake sales coming up?" I asked.

He turned and took the bag from me, tucking it easily into the crook of his arm.

"There is a bake sale coming up on Saturday, July eight," he told me.

"Missed that one. Today's Tuesday, July eleventh."

"I will need to learn the calendar," Cael said. "And—very many other things."

"You will, but you're a quick study."

"How will I know what I need to learn?"

"Trial and error, I'm guessing. The best thing is to bear in mind that this place isn't anything like Sempeki. We do a lot by hand and sweat of brow."

"Because there is little *jikinap* and few Ozali," he said, repeating what I'd told him this morning.

"That's right."

"Then that is why there is a need for an 'Animal Control Officer, must have good rapport with a wide range of animals, good communication skills, and task oriented.' The Houses here do not control their own animals?"

"There aren't any Houses here," I said, leaning in to look at the board. "You looking for a job?"

"I would like to be of use," he said. "I would like to be *of service*. You have taken my oath, and this land has also taken my oath." There was a small pause. "I have been idle, I think, for a very long time."

"I think so, too." I tore the ad off the board and tucked it into my pocket. No harm in calling and seeing what they wanted in the way of references and such.

"Let's go home."

⚜

These waters held happy memories, as beguiling as dreams and might-have-beens.

She recalled her first waking in the palace of living coral, astonishment and delight filling her heart. She rose naked from her couch, and looked out over the gardens, the kelp waving in the currents, and schools of fishes, dainty and bright as flowers, dancing among the moving fronds.

A pale green cephalopod had entered her chamber while her attention was thus engaged, and drew her away to dress her in the blue and green and white robes of her office, to braid her hair with coral and shell, and lead her to the main hall.

There she had first met them, her demons. In dream-memory, she loved them at once, but she remembered, in some portion of her mind uncaught by the pool's enchantment, that she had in truth been a little afraid of them, upon that first meeting.

That had been before she fully knew what had befallen her; that the sea she had defied for the love of her brothers and father—that the sea had taken her and created from her a goddess.

It had been a savage sea: its love won by boldness and cruelty, or by acts of doomed courage. She remembered the sea's savagery, how it had borne her along; how she had delighted in smashing and destroying.

She remembered, also, the day she had risen atop the waves to smite a fishing boat, anticipating the heady pleasure that would come from its destruction. She raised her hand...

...and one of the boys in the boat raised his eyes.

...raised his eyes, *saw her*...

...and did not look away.

For a long time, they contemplated each other, the goddess and the doomed boy. An eternity, perhaps, though such things matter not to a goddess—before she lowered her hands, and calmed the waves, commanding the currents to bear the little boat to its home port, only sinking below the waters herself when she had seen them safe on the rocky landing, with wives and sisters throwing themselves upon their necks with loud cries of joy.

From that moment forward, she had resisted the sea's baser nature, and over time it became—not gentle, never sweet, like the Borgan's noble waters, but...less thirsty for blood and desirous of mayhem.

And her demons, she came to love them, and they her. She took them both to her bed, for was she not a goddess? They were fearsome, but to her they became beautiful, and if she loved the ebon demon for his laugh, did she not love the white demon equally well, for his skill upon the harp?

But, hold! Did she not hear the white demon's harp? Notes rose from the deeps to bear her up in these new waters, while the arms of the ebon demon came 'round her waist.

She sighed, and surrendered herself to their skill and her desires, their ardor warming even these frigid waters.

CHAPTER TWENTY-EIGHT

Tuesday, July 11
Low Tide 5:43 P.M. EDT

I cruised past The Last Mango on my way to the carousel. Peggy and Ethrane were each riding a smoothie-making machine, and the air was fragrant with the scent of oranges and papaya and banana. I waved without much hope of being seen over the crowd, and moved on.

Once past the crowd at the Mango, traffic on the midway seemed light. Well, it was another hot one, and the beach beckoned.

A second wave at Felsic, who was leaning on the front counter of the baseball pitch, apparently watching the empty midway, earned me a casual come-on-over. I obliged.

"Afternoon, Felsic."

"Kate. Just thought I'd ask after Cael, and if there's anything we can do to help him find his feet."

"I think he's doing all right, though it turns out that master of hounds is a lot more complicated than I'd thought, at first."

"That a fact?" Felsic's lips twitched suspiciously.

"Think I'd learn, right? Just this morning, he laid a curse and a blessing, and took the oath of a dog named Oscar. Oh, and he's thinking about applying with the town for Animal Control Officer."

Felsic considered that briefly.

"Need papers to apply with the town."

"Right. Artie brought 'em down this morning."

"That's fast."

"Come in express, Artie said."

Another brief pause.

"Didn't know Artie did express," Felsic said carefully.

"Neither did he. Back to Cael: I don't know his habits, if he's solitary or wants people around him."

"Wolf, that could go both ways. Tell him, if he wants it, we got some who're eager to make his acquaintance. Been talk about having a welcome party—*trenvay* don't arise every day, after all—but I'm not seeing that 'til the Season gets done."

"At which point nobody'll feel like partying," I said gloomily.

Felsic shrugged.

"Could be so, could be no. Might be worthwhile to party for the good times that were, and the rising of a new one, which is a promise of good things to come."

"You need to write poetry, Felsic; I mean that."

"Might try my hand, over the winter. What're the chances of that deal with the town going through?"

I followed the transition without any trouble, but couldn't do anything other than shrug.

"I put it at forty percent, with the Chamber's support behind it. The town doesn't have the kind of money Fun Country's asking for the land."

"Peggy says that towns have better opportunities to raise money," Felsic said. "A bond issue, or applying to the state or federal governments for an assist. 'Specially, if they're applying to preserve a historic area or to promote economic growth." Felsic made owl eyes. "Understand, she was on a tear by then, and I don't think I took it all in. Still, though, Kate, it seemed she was calling above evens."

"I'm the first to admit that Peggy knows more about this stuff than I do. So, what I'm going to do is remain cautiously pessimistic and hope she's right." I straightened. "Time for Vassily to get his supper," I said. "I'll pass your message to Cael."

"'Preciate it. See you later, Kate."

Fountain Circle was as thin of company as the midway, and Baxter Avenue wasn't looking much fatter.

There were five people in line at Tony Lee's for a late dinner or an early supper, and a kid in purple shorts at the lobster toss, pitching rubber crustaceans like they were softballs. Summer's Wheel was running, but the gondolas were empty; no line at the Oriental Fun-house, but I heard faint screams and howls of laughter from inside.

No line for the carousel, either; it sat motionless, the animals probably sweating under the storm roof. I spared a brief moment of regret for the Wise One's frosty flowers as I walked up to the operator's station.

Gran was sitting on the stool; Vassily had a hip braced against the safety rail, his face turned toward hers, hands moving with animation.

"Afternoon," I said, ducking under the rail. "Sorry I'm late, Vassily."

"Good afternoon, Kate Archer. I have not noticed the time as I listened to your grandmother." He turned a beatific smile on me. "I thought you would not mind, if I talked with her while I was working."

"I don't, but that's only because she'd make sure you did work, if there were customers coming in. She taught me how to operate this ride; she tell you that?"

"She did! She said you were—"

Gran cleared her throat, Vassily shot a dancing glance in her direction, and looked back to me.

"She said you were clever, and learned, so very quickly."

"I just bet she did say that. Since you're not paying attention to time, I'll let you know that your shift's done, and Anna's ready to serve up your supper."

"Yes. Good night, Kate Archer. Thanking you." He came out of his lean, took Gran's hand, raised it and kissed her knuckles. "Good night, Babushka. Thanking you."

He vaulted over the rail and walked toward Baxter Avenue, whistling.

"I don't think I've heard him do that before," I commented, looking back to Gran. "You made a conquest."

"He's a nice boy," Gran said comfortably.

In point of fact, Vassily was not a nice boy—at least, he'd done things most "nice boys" didn't, but there was no real reason to share that with Gran, who probably used a whole different mea-suring stick for "nice," anyway.

"He's got a proper feeling for the carousel and the animals," I said, spinning around on a heel. "Been this busy all day?"

"There was a line when I got here, about two, but it's thinned out since. It's really too warm to walk around on tarmac, even with the breeze. Things'll pick up this evening."

"Just my luck." I sighed and lifted myself to the top rung of the safety rail, more or less where Vassily had been leaning. "To what do I owe the pleasure? Nostalgia?"

"Partly, yes. I wanted to see the carousel, and... I thought you'd like an explanation."

"I'm always in favor of an explanation," I said. "Do you want to tour the carousel first, or has Vassily done the honors?"

"I told him I wanted to wait for you. He understood completely. We talked about the Ukraine and what he found different here. I may have told him a few stories about you."

"I hope he laughed in the right places." I slid to my feet. "You won't notice much different. I think. Except for the batwing being gone. I—well, you'll see."

I opened the gate and swept my hand out.

"After you."

It was a slow walk around the wheel, Gran wanted to touch every animal, and when she came to the unicorn, which had, the last time she'd seen it, held an imprisoned soul, she paused, and put both hands on its gilt saddle.

"If the Wise are going to discover what Aesgyr's done in another few weeks, no matter what," she said slowly, "do you think this subterfuge is necessary?"

"Mr. Ignat' seemed to think so. 'Course that was before the Wise served warning on us."

Gran tipped her head, apparently regarding the decoy bindings, and the bogus soul-light.

"Perhaps..." she said, then shook her head. "No, leave them. It won't be that much longer, and we don't want to spike Aesgyr's guns."

"You know the prince?" I asked, as we continued the tour.

"No, but Bel—oh, ridiculous bird!" She stopped with her hands on her hips, shaking her head at the rooster, in either reproof or regret. "Kate, I can't believe..."

"Yes, you can; he's right there. Go put your hand on him if you don't believe it."

She sighed, but to my surprise, she did walk forward and laid a hand on the saddle.

"Fiberglass." She shook her head again.

"Hey, I was desperate. But here's the good news—we ought to have the new, carved horse here just in time to close for the Season."

"What sort of horse did you order? I don't think you ever said."

"Couldn't say; you'd gone in-tree. I ordered in a batwing horse—gray, black mane, white socks. This new one won't have fangs."

"Probably just as well."

"No sense scaring the small fry," I agreed.

We did the rest of the tour in silence, with me not repeating my question about Prince Aesgyr as obviously as possible.

Gran ignored me—or she might just have been so caught up in revisiting that she didn't notice.

We stepped off the wheel across from the operator's station. There were no customers yet, I noticed, but under the circumstances I wasn't going to be too depressed about it.

Gran settled again onto the operator's stool—and no one with any more right to it. I skinned back onto the top rail, and sat there, pitched a little forward, arms straight, hands gripping the rail, head bent so I could watch my feet swing.

"All right, Katie, what's your point?"

I looked up. "My point is that any sentence starting off with, *No, but Bel*—really needs to be finished, so I don't have nightmares."

Gran looked at me seriously.

"I'm afraid that you'll have nightmares, even if I do finish it," she said. "I've had my share of them, since we started down this path. But, even so—even now—I can't see what else we could have done, and it was certain that we had to do something."

"Now you're just having fun with me," I said.

Gran glared—then laughed.

"You're right. If I'm going to tell it, I ought to tell it properly, from the beginning."

"Which is when certain parties interested in achieving great power nudged the Changing Land out of true with the rest of the Six Worlds, so the Wind Between couldn't deliver *jikinap* equally to all?"

"No, after that by a considerable amount of...time. Ramendysis had gone to Daknowyth, bearing the Victor's Terms to Mergine, and come back to plead clemency. Since Ramendysis had argued so urgently for punitive terms, your grandfather wondered what had happened to change his mind..."

"So he paid a social call on Queen Mergine and asked her."

"That's right. Mergine and Bel were long known to each other, and she had no hesitation in speaking with him frankly. She told him that she had promised her daughter Princess Leynore to Ramendysis in true and full marriage, in order to gain clemency and, perhaps something more, for Daknowyth."

She paused, frowning, as if deciding how to explain the next bit.

"Mr. Ignat' told me some of this, in between dodging questions about other things. Ramendysis had to collect a certain amount of *jikinap* in order to be a worthy bridegroom. If he managed to make it to his wedding night, he had very little chance of surviving that true and full marriage, because the Opal's the Guardian of Daknowyth, and she would have just funneled his power straight into her land."

"Yes, that's right. But, at that juncture, Mergine wasn't particularly worried about Ramendysis. As far as she was concerned, Ramendysis was, if not a non-problem, an insignificant one that would eventually solve itself. What frightened her—and Bel assures me that there is very little in all of the Six Worlds that had the power to *frighten* Mergine of Daknowyth—

"What frightened her was that she had received a visit from two of the Wise, who put her on notice that there was a Worlds-spanning conspiracy afoot, to disturb the flow of humors and energies between the Six Worlds. The Wise had already apprehended some of the ringleaders of this conspiracy, and they asked her cooperation, in aiding their search."

"Wait," I said. "I thought that the reason Daknowyth took a war into Sempeki was because the flow of humors and energies between the Worlds had *already* been disrupted, and Daknowyth was dying."

"So Bel tells me, and I know it for the truth, since I hold his soul in safety."

"So...*the Wise* are trying to choke off the Six Worlds? That doesn't make any sense."

"Doesn't it? The Wise may well find that a closed system of power suits their purposes very well. *Jikinap* seeks *jikinap*, and the Wise are Wise because they've figured out how to survive the terrible costs of controlling that much power. *But* we don't need to tease ourselves with what might be. Bel investigated. He found nothing...conclusive, but much that was disturbing.

"The Flaming Land had been subverted. The prisoner that the Wise had placed into the carousel, and forced me to bind—she had been, so Bel found, high in the House of the Supreme Flame. In Cheobaug, he found news of a sea-god who had destroyed himself, his people and his sea—no one knew why. It was thought that his waters had been poisoned, but how, or what poison might touch a god, wasn't known."

"But the woman from Cheobaug—"

"That was after," Gran interrupted. "They'd already brought me your Wolf, who lived up to his name, but was bound at the last."

"No one could have thought that holding his master of hounds hostage would stop Aeronymous, if he felt the need to act," I said.

Gran smiled. "But the Wise thought they had your father. Aeronymous was never a fool, as I've heard it told. When the Wise came with their accusations, Aeronymous produced, as his son Nathan, Cael the Wolf, who stood to do his lord's bidding, holding *jikinap* that stank of the House's power."

"So grandfather wasn't as bound as they thought he was, to do what they wanted him to do." I turned my hands out. "What did they want him to do?"

"They may have only wanted to weaken the House, so Ramendysis wouldn't have any trouble. That's Bel's theory: that the Wise's plan in Sempeki was to allow Ramendysis to absorb as much *jikinap* as possible..."

"...and then pick up Ramendysis."

Gran nodded. "So, getting back to the main tale, Mergine was afraid, for both her daughter and her land. She sent Leynore to her long-time ally in Varoth, Prince Aesgyr, and employed various subterfuges to make it seem that her daughter was still at Daknowyth. Bel and I came to believe that we must become involved..."

"So he brought the Opal here, you bound her into the carousel, and then he led the merry chase of Ozali who wanted his head, and subsequently bound him into Googin Rock, *they thought*, while Queen Mergine kept up the fiction that the Opal was minding her own knitting at home, so he couldn't have had anything to do with her going missing."

"Exactly so."

"Well, as an explanation, it hangs together pretty well," I said, slipping off the rail and onto my feet.

"That wasn't quite what I wanted to explain," Gran said.

I stood in front of her and looked down into her face; there were lines around her eyes and her mouth; she'd aged—as she would, of course. Trees age and die, after all. My head knew that, but my stomach didn't want to have anything to do with it.

"What did you want to explain then?" I asked gently.

"I wanted to explain why I put... everything, really, into such terrible danger. And it's because... the Worlds are interconnected. If one falls, we all fall. It's why Aesgyr is... doing—or is about to do—what he's... decided to do. If it doesn't work, I don't expect we'll notice his failure. The world—our world, the whole globe—will slowly succumb to entropy. If Aesgyr is successful... I don't suppose we'll notice much difference then, either."

She smiled, palely.

"We might miss the slow slide into chaos, but only a handful of us will ever know that was an option. So that's why." She took a breath and met my eyes firmly. "I wanted you to know."

It occurred me then that she wanted me to say something: that this had been a burden she'd been carrying for a long time, a burden that had frightened her, and Gran scares even less easily than Mergine of Daknowyth.

"I'd've done exactly the same thing," I said, and leaned over to give her a hug.

"How's your relationship with Borgan?" Gran asked, after I'd gone over to Tony Lee's and gotten us both an ice tea. It was hot enough to melt the tin roof over the carousel, and while there was a brisk breeze going on, it wasn't by any means cool.

"My relationship with Borgan is, I think, a little one-sided."

"You don't care for him?"

"I care for him a lot." *I might even love him* leapt unbidden and startling to the front of my mind. I wondered how I would know...

"You're not giving up on him, then?"

That, I thought, was being more than a little probing. I sipped ice tea through a straw, and raised my head to meet her eyes.

"Gran?"

"Yes, Katie?"

"This thing with Borgan—did you set it up?"

Have you paid your respects to the sea? I heard her ask, in memory. One of the very first things I'd learned about my new home, once I was well enough to walk up and down the land, was to pay my respects to the sea. There'd been no mention of a Sea Guardian, but there'd been no need; I was a kid, my oath to the land shiny new, and my understanding of my duties... slim at best.

Plenty of time for Sea Guardians when I was grown up, and the scars of childhood had faded.

And bearing in mind that Gran had kind of, sort of, manipulated me into taking up my ancestral duty as Guardian of the Land...

It's not that Gran's cold-blooded—not at all. It's just that she's damn' near five hundred years old and can probably be forgiven for believing that she knows better than a twelve-year-old kid.

Gran sighed.

"Set it up?" she said softly, like she was tasting the words. She shook her head slightly.

"I've known Borgan since I was a sapling, Katie; he's a friend, and he's always been a good one. He early took a decision not to... *become* his duty; to remain, as much as possible, human. The sea's love is a powerful force, and not easy to resist. Human love—mundane folk have such short lives. There comes a time when even a very powerful man just can't bear to have his heart broken one more time."

"So I was going to save him with my love?" That came out with considerably more snark than I'd intended, and I remembered the girl—the Guardian of Surfside, had she only known it—who'd never had any harm in her...

"I had hoped that you might... comfort him with your friendship. You're young, more human than not—and the land's love isn't as *strange* as the sea's. It will be... a very long time before you need to worry about losing yourself to your duty."

And he'd wanted to keep the sea familiar with humans, to keep it calm and well disposed toward the land, wasn't that it?

Well. The man knew how to set himself some goals, didn't he?

"I am his friend," I said now, to my grandmother's quiet and not-*quite*-human eyes. "At least that."

CHAPTER TWENTY-NINE

Tuesday, July 11

The crowd started building right around six, and kept on 'til Marilyn hit the closing horn at ten sharp. I leaned over and shot the bolt on the entry gate, smiling regretfully at the pair of girls standing first in line. They were maybe nine, ten—with turquoise polish on short nails; matching turquoise tank tops over flat chests, and bright yellow short-shorts.

"Sorry, ladies; I'm not allowed to start any new rides after the bell. Come back and see me tomorrow, okay?"

"But we thought the park was open 'til midnight!" the blonde one said.

"Ten o'clock on weeknights. We want to make sure you get your beauty sleep."

"We better go find Andrew in the arcade," the brunette said to her friend or sister. She gave me a solemn nod. "Thank you very much. We'll be back tomorrow."

"Looking forward," I said and hit the bell twice to signal the end of the ride.

"Ladies and gents, exit gate's around to your left!" I called out for the dismounting riders, then turned to address the modest line.

"That loud noise we just heard is the boss' way of telling us that the park's closing for the night! No new rides start after the bell, and we all heard it. *So* we'll play by the rules. Come back tomorrow, please! And bring a friend!"

"And earplugs!" shouted a wag from the end of the line. A smattering of laughter greeted this sally, and the line began to break up.

I felt a shiver of delight run my spine, and smiled as I followed the last of the riders out to Baxter Avenue, then walked to the back, grabbed the edge of the storm wall and hauled it around. It rumbled and boomed, like it did, and I was grinning like a damn' fool by the time I'd gotten to the middle, and met Borgan and the other half there.

The walls joined with a clash and a clatter, and I looked up at him with a grin.

"Hey, there."

"Hey, there, yourself."

He put his arms around me and pulled me into a hug. I went with it, arms around his waist and head resting against his chest. He sighed, deeply, and...just kept on holding me.

"Rough day?" I murmured.

Another sigh, and he stepped back, letting me go, which wasn't *necessarily* what I'd wanted, though I stood back, too, and let my arms fall to my sides.

"You could say it that way—a rough day." He extended a hand, fingertips just brushing my cheek. "It's good to see you, Kate."

"It's good to see you, too," I said, which wasn't a lie, though it did ignore the fact that he looked bone weary.

"Let me finish shutting down."

"Sure." He followed me inside the walls, and leaned on the operator's station, arms crossed carefully atop the board.

I pointed at the orchestrion as I passed, and the paper began to gently reroll itself as I crossed the decking to the door hidden in the center mural. Ducking inside, I turned the generator off, threw the switch for the sweeps lights, and exited, closing the door softly behind me.

The Violano paper was still being rerolled, with all due care, as if I were actually doing the job myself, instead of assigning a doppelganger to the task. I crossed the decking and jumped to the floor, calling my ball of feylight to hand before flipping the switch that killed the inside light.

"Good to go," I said, meeting Borgan at the gate.

"That's a neat trick," he said, following me outside, and pulling the door to behind him.

"Which?" I snapped the lock through the loops and shook the light out.

"Rerolling the paper from across the room."

"It is, isn't it? Realizing that it was possible was a breakthrough."

"I can see that it must've been." He reached out and took my hand, weaving our fingers together. "So, what's it like, using your magic through the land?"

"It's good—natural. I don't feel like I have to keep my eyes open every second to make sure my power's not doing something I'll live to regret. If I'm lucky. And I don't get attitude, either, when I want to do something; I just . . . think about it, and the tool comes to hand—familiar and easy."

"So, you're thinking world domination?" he murmured.

"Who wants to do all that work?"

He led the way down the alley between the carousel and Summer's Wheel, his fingers still linked with mine, and a minute later we were on the beach. Tide was coming in, but the breeze was subdued. In fact, I realized as we came to the water's edge, the *water* was subdued, the waves low and sluggish.

"The ocean's still . . . in pain?" I asked.

"Still . . . yeah," Borgan said. "It . . . *hurt*, moving among the waters today. The sea's never hurt me, even . . ." He took a hard breath. "The first time, when she accepted me as hers, I managed to work myself up into quite a lather until I realized that I didn't *need* to breathe, there below; that the waters would sustain me. But that wasn't her, it was me. This . . . the whole ocean's grieving. I'm not sure how to right it, or if it's best left to run its course . . ."

I slipped under his arm. He cuddled me closer against his side, unconsciously, I thought.

"Aren't the other seafolk able to help?" I asked, thinking of Felsic, running toward the considerable racket of the Wise One's arrival; of Gaby, answering my whispered plea to the land, for help . . . "Surely there's somebody . . ."

He sighed.

"Called in some aid today, but the seafolk are all . . . infected by the sea's sadness. They want to float low, if you take me. I can understand it; they live in the sea, she's their whole world. 'Course they're going to take her mood. The only reason I'm doing so well is I'm an adopted son—and I can separate myself from her, physically. The seafolk don't have that."

His arm tightened briefly, before he shifted to face me, his hands on my shoulders.

"Which kinda brings me around to what I came to tell you. Got a problem down the Vineyard—yearling whale beached himself. The local seafolk, and landfolk, too, are doing what they can, but—I'm needed, is the short of it."

He looked down into my face, mouth wry.

"Sorry I won't be with you—shouldn't be gone more'n three, four days. Less, 'cept there's somebody I need to talk to, down that way, and he's not always easy to net. Give my apologies to Breccia; hate to disappoint that lady."

"I'm considering being jealous," I told him.

"No need for that." He cupped my cheek, and I shivered with mingled pleasure and longing.

"Give you a present?" he asked.

I blinked up at him, and it probably says a lot of unfortunate things about my relationship with Borgan that the first thing I thought *wasn't* that it's a really bad idea to accept a gift from a *trenvay*.

"I don't have a present for you," I said.

"That's okay; you give me one later." He ran his thumb gently over my skin, which was just dirty pool. I took a breath, and went one step back, out from under his hands.

He tipped his head, and waited.

"You're getting a little warm for a man who's leaving right now," I said.

"Guess I wish I wasn't. Leaving, that is." He paused, then said again, "Give you a present?"

Twice now, with the present, I thought. It was important, then.

"All right," I said.

Relief passed over his face, perfectly plain in the moonlight.

"I guess I should've asked what it is," I said ruefully.

Borgan smiled. "Well, see, you get to pick. Put your hand 'round my braid, high as you can reach."

I stepped up close and did as I was told. He put his hand over mine.

"Now, just run your hand down."

I did that, too, loving the feel of his hair against my skin, the various beads and shells lightly grazing my palm. Then I'd reached the end of the braid, and he turned my hand up, so I could see the blue-and-green-swirled bead resting in the palm of my hand.

"There we are then," Borgan said. "Turn around."

I felt his fingers, undoing my own shorter and much less interesting braid, felt him finger-comb the loose strands and rebraid a thinner bit of hair. He may have been humming, deep in his chest; I thought I heard it, but...

"That'll do it."

I turned, and he held the thin braid up, with the single bead gleaming among black strands.

"I'll be afraid of losing it."

"You won't lose it; that bead'll take care of itself."

I took the braid out of his hand, and fingered the bead. It was warm from having been in Borgan's hair, and, as far as I could tell, inert, no tingle of glamor or power about it. An ornament, then.

Something to remember him by.

"Thank you."

"No thank yous," he said, and pulled me into an embrace. His kiss was fierce and sweet and sad, and I returned it as best I could.

He gripped my shoulders when we parted, and looked down into my face, his almost stern.

"You stay safe, Kate." The glimmer of a smile broke the sternness. "I know that's a tall order."

I think I managed to smile back. "I'll give it my best shot."

"Can't ask for more than that."

He moved his hands and stepped away.

"Time I was leaving."

"Right." I cleared my throat. "See you in...a couple days."

I tucked my hands in my pockets, then, and watched him walk away, into the sea.

A wave broke over his head and he was gone.

Cael had been busy while I'd been gone. The dishes had been washed and put away; my research books were neatly stacked on the coffee table. The rug looked like it had been thoroughly vacuumed—did Cael even know what a vacuum cleaner was?—and the windows sparkled.

The man himself was seated cross-legged on the floor, reading a book, Oscar's head on his thigh. Breccia was curled on the inebriated elephant blanket at the end of the couch.

"My lady."

Cael rose in one smooth uncurling, finger marking his place in the book. Oscar got up, too, and stood at his knee.

"At ease," I said, and bowed slightly. "Thank you for cleaning up."

"I was pleased to have occupation, and to be of use to my—to you. Oscar and Breccia advised me." He glanced to the sleeping cat. "She is not at ease with the dirt-eating machine."

"Cats aren't usually in favor of vacuum cleaners," I agreed. "How'd Oscar take it?"

"He showed fitting courage, as did the Lady Breccia. She merely retired abovestairs while I worked down here. When I ascended, she removed herself to this level."

"Sounds like a sensible arrangement."

I sighed and looked around me. Seemed like I didn't exactly know what to do with a free night.

What had I done when all I had were free nights? I thought.

Worked, mostly, I answered myself. Read; watched television. Cleaned the house; did laundry.

Slept.

Well. Maybe Cael would like to play Scrabble? Or...

He cleared his throat, and ducked his head when I focused on him.

"Kate, may your loyal liegeman ask your intentions toward Aleun and Tioli?"

I blinked. Tioli and— Right...Aleun was the gardener, and Tioli was on the wall. The last two survivors of House Aeronymous.

"I don't have any intentions toward them," I said. "They can go home, or stay where they are, whatever they like." I gave him a sharp look. "I'm not going to bring them across to the Changing Land; I don't need...any more servants."

"Your establishment here is modest," Cael agreed, and glanced at Oscar, as if taking counsel.

"It is possible, in the rush of events that night, that I failed to convey that both Aleun and Tioli...are bound."

I felt cold in the pit of my stomach.

"*Bound* bound?" I asked, but I already knew the answer.

Cael met my eyes firmly.

"Aleun is bound to the garden, and Tioli—to the walls."

Goddammit, Grandfather.

Cael cleared his throat.

"While it is...almost certain that, released, Aleun will choose to remain with the plants, the return to her of *a choice* will be a worthy liege-gift. Tioli..."

He hesitated and reached down to tug lightly on Oscar's ear.

"Tioli had been from the village, my lady. The walls are cold and lonely."

...and wet, and treacherous, and all her comrades were dead, and I was going to have to go to Sempeki to undo this. Or I was going to leave two people nailed to a dead House, their futures forfeit because my grandfather had been a control freak to end all control freaks.

I didn't want to go to Sempeki. Never, ever, ever again did I want to set foot inside Aeronymous House. I was ice cold, just thinking about it.

This has nothing to do with me, I thought, but I knew better than that.

"My lady?"

"Opening the World Gate at this time isn't a good idea."

It was a blatant stall, and it didn't stop Cael for more than thirty seconds. Give the man credit, though; he didn't argue with me. He bowed slightly, and murmured.

"You may travel safely with me, your faithful wolf. I will take you as I myself went, and bring you to the House's very gate."

It wasn't exactly a surprise that Cael had sung himself across the World Wall, though I remained skeptical of his ability to bring us both across in good order. But that didn't really matter, because...

"The time," I began—and that *was* a real concern; I couldn't vanish for six months. However, Cael was ahead of me there, too.

"My lady's tie to this land will provide a check. We need be at Aeronymous House only a very short time, as it is counted in this World or that." He looked at me, golden-brown eyes sad. "I serve you, my lady. Will you sully our honor?"

Dammit, Kate. This is what you get from accepting the fealty of strange men.

...and I was still, as I'd told Gran, the closest thing to Aeronymous left. If I didn't right this, it would stay wrong.

And I wouldn't be able to live with myself.

I sighed.

"I'm going to regret this."

"Kate, you will not," Cael told me earnestly, his eyes bright now. Oscar was wagging his tail enthusiastically. Breccia raised her head from her paws and gave me a level look.

"Spot us," I told her, and felt a slight tingle up my spine, almost like *jikinap* rising. The cat squinted a smile at me. I took that as a promise.

I sighed again, and bowed to Cael the Wolf.

"Whenever you're ready," I said.

He extended a hand and took mine.

"Oscar," he said, "stay."

The room went dark, as if someone had thrown a switch; the temperature plummeted, and I lost the feel and taste of the air.

A wolf howled, leaving utter silence in its wake.

CHAPTER THIRTY

Aeronymous House
in Sempeki, the Land of the Flowers

Silence shattered around me.

The first thing I heard was the nerve-wracking jangle of merrybells.

The first thing I tasted was honeyed air.

I opened my eyes...

...and beheld the mighty silver gate that had guarded the estate of Aeronymous, blasted and burned, hanging crazily by one hinge. The blackened metal was sagging and torn, twisted in a half-melted knot around the Great Wave, the sign of our House.

Beyond the ruined gate, and down a wide courtyard, Aeronymous House stood, to all senses, unharmed. To the right of the house, the gardens bloomed plentifully. To the left was a table of rock, falling sharply away. The back wall overlooked sheer cliff, and the sea.

House Aeronymous is—was—aligned with the sea. Back home in the Changing Land, that would've meant that the House owned trade ships, and fisher fleets.

Here in the Land of the Flowers, it meant that those of the House have a certain inborn affinity for water. All Sempeki Houses are aligned with a Sempeki element. One of my grandfather's great cronies, Ozali Eredith, had been aligned with stone. Mr. Ignat', so he'd let slip, came from a House aligned with fire.

Ramendysis...had been aligned with the storm winds.

Which probably explained...everything.

Tears started to my eyes. I swallowed, and realized that I was still gripping Cael's hand.

I turned to look at him, and saw that his face was wet.

"You'd been here before," I said, my voice raspy with the tears I refused to shed.

"Yes," he agreed, and took a hard breath. "And I was here when the Gate was fashioned. Souls were bound into it, and the life-forces of our most ferocious hounds. *Jikinap* from every one of the House, and every one of the village, too. No power should have been able to destroy that Gate, my lady. And yet..."

And yet, it had been destroyed; the first defense of the House, charred and bent and broken; the power bound into it consumed by the enemy of the House; increasing the strength that he brought against us.

"It did well," I said, maybe trying to comfort him. "No one and nothing could have withstood Ozali Ramendysis by the time he came to us."

"I ask that you tell me the tale," he said, his fingers warm around mine. "When you may."

Because Cael had been in prison when Aeronymous House had fallen. It occurred to me to be grateful for that.

"I'll gladly tell you the history, to the extent that I know it myself," I told him. "But first, let's do what we came to do."

"Yes," he said, and stepped past the blasted gate, whereupon he turned right, toward the gardens.

He was still holding my hand, and I made no attempt to pull away. It was comforting in this place, to have that living contact.

Just about then, it occurred to me that Borgan probably wouldn't rate this excursion as *safe*.

"My liege."

Aleun was precisely as I remembered her: wiry and brown, leaf-green hair tousled into elf-locks around her ears. Her face was sharp and her eyes were a shade lighter than her hair.

She bowed with great deliberation.

"Gardener," I said, with what poor dignity I could muster. "I am come at the word of Cael the Wolf, to release you, if that is your desire, from the duty to which you have been bound."

"No one wishes to be compelled, my lady; especially when one would gladly serve, for love."

"Will you stay with the garden then, bound or free?"

"Made free to choose, and free to act, I would remain with the garden, my lady. My love and my sustenance lies with these plants, which your grandsire knew. His binding profaned my service." Her mouth tightened. "Your pardon, Lady. The old lord was a hard man; it wasn't in him, to believe in any ties save those he built and set into place."

That was all true, and if our places had been reversed and I had the saying of it, I wouldn't have been nearly so kind. However, it was Aleun's right to set the bar of courtesy wherever it seemed right to her, she being the wronged party.

"My grandfather was not a gentle man," I agreed—which might win understatement of the year, if I remembered to enter the contest. "As little as it may be, I propose to return choice to you. Also, I offer my apology, that this should have been forced upon you, and your service tainted by it."

"You had no hand in this, Lady. Return me fully to myself, and you will have done all you might, and shown yourself a fair liege, and true."

She extended a brown hand, her eyes piercing mine. I met and held that gaze, at last releasing Cael, so that I might take Aleun's wiry member between my two palms, as if I were about to perform a healing.

I took one breath, and another, and opened my eyes into Side-Sight.

The binding was immediately obvious—a simple thing, though brutal in its simplicity. Grandfather Aeronymous had merely driven thick ropes of *jikinap* through the woman's heart, burying them in the living soil of the garden. If she had tried to leave, she would have very quickly been in pain. If she had persevered, the ropes would have torn her living heart asunder.

There was no healing needed here, only release.

No sooner had I made my judgment than power flowed, cool and potent in my veins. I thought about shears—and the binding parted, *jikinap* melting into the soil, to the benefit, I hoped, of the garden.

"Ah!" cried Aleun.

Her eyes lost focus; her hand softened. I held her as green healing flowed through me, to her.

Only a moment passed before she smiled, strength returning to her hand. She closed her eyes and opened them, her lashes wet, and her cheeks, too.

I released her.

Aleun sighed, and stepped away from me. She bent over to pluck one of the blue-and-gold flowers from the bed she had been tending—and bowed, offering it to me across the palms of her two hands, as if it were a blade.

"Thank you, my lady."

Tioli stood like a wraith in the mist that rose from the waves crashing below.

It was cold here on the wall, in the mist, the footing uncertain and the wind ungiving. I shivered, but if the lone sentinel experienced any discomfort at her post, she didn't show it. Merely, she faced out to the sea, her posture alert; scanning, I supposed, for enemies.

Having led me this far, Cael now put his back against the wall, and called ahead.

"Tioli, it is Cael. I have brought our Lady Aeronymous."

"The Lady Aeronymous may approach," came the answer, as thin and chill as the voice of the wind itself.

Cael looked to me and nodded. Apparently, I was to go on alone. Great.

I thrust the flower Aleun had given me into his hand.

"Keep that safe," I snapped. His eyes widened, but I didn't have time to wonder what it was I'd done *now*. I inched carefully past him, the wind making sport of my braid, and swirling in cunning little by-drafts that might send an unwary walker down to the far-below sea.

Finally, breathing hard, I came to the sentinel's watch.

"My liege," Tioli said.

I was close enough to touch her, yet I could scarcely hear her; her voice was as insubstantial as the mist. She did not turn her head nor offer me any courtesy such as Aleun had done.

"You come to me late," she said, which might have been criticism, but there was no heat in her voice.

"The fault is mine," I said. "I had thought all our House consumed by Ozali Ramendysis, and have only lately learned that you and Aleun survived."

Her lips parted, and I heard a faint *huff-huff* that might have been laughter.

Well, at least she'd kept her sense of humor.

"I would release you," I continued, doggedly, "if you wish it so."

"Above all things, my lady, I wish release."

"Then you shall have it."

She did not raise her hand from the hilt of her weapon, nor yet did she look at me.

All right, then.

I extended my hand, meaning to lay it on her shoulder.

But my fingers passed right through her, ice immediately forming on each digit.

I withdrew. If she noticed my intrusion, she gave no sign.

"Tioli, are you—" My throat closed, and I thought, suddenly, that I knew what she'd found so amusing.

"Am I dead, my lady? Yes. Did Cael not tell you?"

"Cael said you were bound to the wall."

"Why, and so I am, as you can see."

I could indeed see, in Side-Sight—a heavy staple of *jikinap* driven as deeply into her heart and thin Sempeki soul, as into the thick wall at her back. Tioli herself was a shredding shadow, a patchwork thing animated only by the spill from the working that bound her.

"I beg you," Tioli whispered, "finish what is begun. I will love you for it, as I never loved your grandsire." Her lips drew back in a mirthless smile. "Though you will perhaps not find the love of the dead comforting."

"Few enough love me. I'll not refuse the gift, freely given," I said, the glitter of *jikinap* all but blinding me, in Side-Sight.

With an effort, I focused, and once again deployed my will to bite into the binding.

There was a moment of resistance before the staple broke, and the heavy power rained down, and over, the wall.

Tioli—

Tioli shredded in the mocking wind, patchwork bits flowing over me and up, riding the restless air into the flawless Sempeki sky.

I heard a sharp *crack*. The wall shook beneath my feet.

Pebbles rained slowly down around me.

"Kate!" shouted Cael. "Quickly! The house is breaking!"

I ran, heedless of the slick underfoot, grabbed his outstretched hand—and we both ran.

The rain of pebbles and grit became a deluge. I raised my free hand in an effort to protect my eyes, and ran as I've never run in my life, Cael's hand hot in mine, We had almost reached the turret—and who knew what kind of shape the steps would be in, if the steps still existed?—when the section of wall beneath our feet disintegrated into silver sand, and I knew in that moment that I was going to die here, like all the rest of my House—

The wind gusted hard, lifting us, up and beyond the destruction—and down, until it settled softly on our feet, inside the shadow of the melted gate.

"Thank you, my lady," I heard Tioli say, and felt a cold, damp kiss pressed upon my hand.

Behind us, with a groan and a roar, Aeronymous House collapsed, sending clouds of silver sand high into the air.

"Are you all right?" I asked, some minutes later, after the worst of my own shaking had subsided.

Cael bowed. "Your wolf stands ready to serve, my lady."

"I'm glad to hear it. Do you plan on doing this kind of thing often?"

He gazed at me somberly.

"As your liegeman, it is my duty to see your honor pure."

"And you served my grandfather?"

"Yes, my lady."

"Well?"

"Perhaps not so well as I might have done, my lady. I swear to do better, for you."

I stared at him. He didn't avert his gaze, and after a minute I sighed and shook my head, wordless.

The pile of rubble that had been Aeronymous House was already melting back into the silver soil. At the rate it was going, by morning, the only thing that would mark the site would be the blasted gate, and the formal gardens.

"You're completely fine?" I asked Cael. "I don't want bravado; I want the truth."

"I am able, my lady. Nor would I ever lie to you."

Except, maybe, the occasional insignificant sin of omission, I thought, remembering Tioli's ghost, stapled to the walls. I nodded.

"Please take us home."

"Immediately, my lady."

He handed me the blue-and-gold flower. I slid it behind my right ear, and felt the stem seat firmly. I extended my hand, and Cael received it, gently, and one might say, with reverence.

I closed my eyes, waiting for the feeling of being forcibly wrapped inside a thick, cold, soundproof blanket.

I waited somewhat longer.

Finally, I opened my eyes.

Cael shook his head; his face betraying unease.

"There is something—a disturbance. Say, rather, a turbulence. I cannot scent the path to your—to our—lands." He took a breath and met my eyes. "Perhaps if we wait, and try again, when this storm wind has passed . . ."

"Let me see."

"Yes."

His grip on my hand tightened. There was a change in . . . pressure, as if a window had been opened in a slightly stuffy room.

"You will want to take the half step beyond, my lady," Cael murmured.

I stepped Sideways, and was immediately assaulted by the turbulence he described—a hurricane wind, heavy with scents: cinnamon, hot stone, pine tar, kerosene . . .

Peaches.

"Fuck." I shook myself fully back into Sempeki. "The wind is Ozali-made. Prince Aesgyr's starting his move, whatever it is."

"Are we caught here?" Cael asked. "Perhaps we might go to another of your allies . . ."

To Daknowyth, for instance?

No. No, if the prince intended to shift the connections between the Worlds, I might never find my way home again. We had to move, and we had to move *now*, back to the house on Dube Street, where Oscar and Breccia waited—

Breccia.

We were still holding hands. I grabbed Cael's other wrist and thought about Breccia, with the rakish orange patch over one eye, and the brown patch over the opposite ear. About her quick intelligence, and the power of her purrs. I felt a tingle of *jikinap*, caught a whiff of dead fish and peppermint, felt power flare up my spine, feral and on the hunt . . .

"My lady, we are returned!" Cael's voice was exuberant, which gave me some idea of how worried he had been.

Slowly, I shook my head, blinking at the familiar room around me. Oscar was standing on his back feet, front paws on Cael's shoulders. Breccia stretched high in a Halloween arc, toes indenting the soft blanket. She leapt to the floor and strolled over to rub against my knee.

"Thank you," I said. "You did good."

She gave me one more long stroke, then headed for the kitchen, and, presumably, her food dish.

Well—and why not? Reeling people in from Sempeki was hungry work.

In fact, I was feeling a little peckish myself, now that I thought about it. And I could definitely use a glass of wine.

I turned, took one step toward the kitchen . . .

. . . and crashed to my knees.

The lights flickered crazily—and went out.

CHAPTER THIRTY-ONE

Wednesday, July 12
Low Tide, 6:29 A.M. EDT
Sunrise, 5:11 A.M.

I woke to the gentle clink of china on china, and the strong impression that there was a boulder on my stomach.

A deep breath failed to dislodge said boulder, which could be worrisome. On the other hand, I *could* breathe, which I decided was a hopeful sign.

I heard the distinctive squeak of the kitchen cold-water faucet being turned on, the sound of running water, soft steps, and the click of nails against linoleum.

So, it wasn't a dream, that we'd managed to get home after freeing a ghost and a gardener and reducing Aeronymous House to rubble. That was good.

And if it wasn't a dream that Cael and I had won home, that meant he was making coffee, ably assisted by Oscar, while I . . . napped on the couch, beneath Breccia, who, like all cats, weighed twenty pounds more asleep than awake.

I heard water being poured, deduced that it was going from the carafe into the coffeemaker, and opened my eyes.

Breccia was staring into my face, amber eyes pensive—or so I thought. When she saw I was awake, she rose onto feet that weighed approximately eight hundred pounds each, bent her head to butt my chin, and jumped off my chest, onto the floor.

"Oof!"

I sat up, peeling drunken elephants off my torso, letting them pool on my lap. I was fully dressed, absent my shoes. Cael hadn't tried to schlepp me upstairs; he'd just gotten me to the couch. Smart man, Cael. Compassionate, too. I'd've just thrown the blanket over me where I'd crashed.

"Good morning, Kate," he said. I heard a short snap, which was probably the lid being pushed into place over the coffee-maker's reservoir.

God, we'd *actually gone* to the Land of the Flowers.

"What's the date?" I demanded, hoping it was only a couple days missing...

"The day is Wednesday, the twelfth day in July. The year is numbered two thousand six."

I sat back, staring at him.

"We did all that in one night, our time?"

"Your bond with this land is strong," Cael said, moving toward the couch. "Also, Breccia was watching.... Are you well again, this morning?"

"I'm well, but hungry," I said, bundling the elephants up and tossing them to the end of the couch. "Thanks for taking care of me. Didn't mean to get silly."

"No."

I put sock feet flat on the floor, and looked up as Cael perched on the couch's wide arm.

"No?" I asked.

His face was serious.

"What I mean to say is that you were not silly. Such matters as you attended to are expensive of power. And it was well done, if you will allow a liegeman to say it, to bring down the House entire. The last duties of the last Aeronymous have been completed; House Aeronymous is no more." He paused, eyes shadowed, then offered a half-smile.

"All of us are released, now, and free of old chains."

Really? I blinked.

"What is the state of your oath, Cael the Wolf?" I asked, carefully.

"My oath lives, my lady, to you, and through you, to this land." Damn'.

"I'm sorry," I told him.

The smile this time was quizzical.

"Is my service so poor? I will strive to amend my ways."

"Your ways—absent an apparent fondness for social engineering—are everything I could ask in a liegeman. What saddens me is that you remain bound. Surely, you would also prefer your freedom."

"The choice before me was life or death. It speaks to my character that I chose life, knowing full well the condition under which I would live." He moved his shoulders, nothing so inelegant as a shrug.

"As you said, I served your grandfather. If liege-bound I must be, I would far rather it were you—a fair lady and true, who does not regard the honor of others as a weapon to her hand." He bowed his head.

"I am content, my lady, in my choice and in my service. And *you* will not think it an impertinence that I say so."

I blinked again, this time to clear my eyes. The boy was eloquent, give him that. Well, we were both bound by Grandfather's geas—at least for the moment. I'd ask Mr. Ignat' if there was a way to break the damn' thing, while still keeping Cael—and me—alive.

"I thought that today," he said, rising from his perch on the arm of the sofa, "I might find Felsic and speak with her."

"Felsic's liable to be busy with the baseball toss today, but it can't hurt for you to wander by and set up a date. She was eager to be of help to you."

"Then I *will* today see Felsic and set up a date," Cael said with decision. "For this moment, my lady, I suggest that I will make breakfast—scrambled eggs—while you make yourself ready for the day."

By which I guessed he meant that I should take a shower and get presentable.

"*That* sounds like a deal," I said, and stood.

By long habit, I checked the pockets of my jeans. Cell phone, wallet, keys went onto the coffee table—which should've been it.

But it wasn't.

My fingers found a small soft lump at the bottom of the right front pocket, like a wadded-up handkerchief. Frowning, I pulled it out, vaguely aware that both Cael and Breccia were watching me.

It was, in fact, a scrap of fabric, sea-green, like Tioli's uniform, all balled up, and...rather heavier than a balled-up scrap of fabric ought to be.

"What the hell?"

If something had attached to me from the house, I wasn't sure I wanted it—no, scratch that; I was damn' sure I *didn't* want it.

It was in my mind to just throw the little bundle away, take my shower, eat my breakfast, and get on with my day.

Tempting, but not possible. Things from Sempeki...couldn't be trusted to play nice with the realities of the Changing Land.

I took hold of the ragged fabric and pulled it away from its surprise.

A flash of silver is what I saw, in the instant before the amulet hit my naked palm and lightning flashed along every nerve in my body.

I think I blacked out for an instant. Being struck by approximately seven hundred megawatts of *jikinap* is reason enough to black out.

I was on my knees, and Cael's face was the first thing I saw. He didn't look particularly worried, which I took as a good sign. He was, however, propping me up, his hands braced against my shoulders, like he was afraid I was going to take a nose dive.

I sat back on my heels. Cael did the same, his hands resting on his thighs.

Time passed while I did inventory. Aside from the initial shock, it didn't seem that I'd suffered any harm at all. The taste of what might've been sea wrack lingered on my tongue.

"Kate?"

"I'm fine," I said, slightly surprised to find it so. I looked down, saw my right hand fisted on my knee, raised it and opened my fingers, so we both could see.

"Ah." A murmured recognition, that was, from Cael.

Well, and why wouldn't he recognize it? The silver spiral—or the Great Wave, as we of House Aeronymous styled our House sign. It had been my grandfather's mark of office. I'd thought it destroyed with him, but obviously he'd had time to infuse it with *jikinap*—and hide it well enough that Ramendysis had never found it.

"Did you put this in my pocket?" I asked. My voice was really very calm.

Cael shook his head. "No, my lady." He glanced about, found the scrap of fabric on the floor between us, and raised it to his nose.

"Tioli," he murmured, and looked up to meet my eyes. "The old lord must have given it to her. For safekeeping."

And Tioli, naturally, would have passed this item, so precious to the House, and which she had guarded with her life and beyond—to the new Aeronymous.

I took a breath, and did another quick self-inspection, verifying that I was all right and tight. The stored *jikinap* had accepted me as Aeronymous—witness the fact that it hadn't fried me—and, apparently, it had flowed through my new, improved connection to the land, pooling with my other accumulated power, waiting for me to draw on it.

Later, I'd think about how that made me feel. For the moment, though—no harm, no foul.

"Well." I rose, feeling...buoyant, which might be an artifact of my new acquisition, or might just be relief.

Cael also came to his feet.

"Will you still wish breakfast?" he asked.

"More than ever. I'll take a quick shower."

The scrambled eggs were a little tough—Cael had made the beginner's error of cooking them fast over high heat, rather than nice and slow over medium heat.

"I will try again tomorrow."

"Might want to have bagels tomorrow."

He wrinkled his nose.

"Still got cream cheese," I said, sipping my coffee.

His expression softened into pensiveness.

"I could mix the cream cheese into the eggs," he said.

I laughed.

"You could do that, but it would melt. The eggs would taste good, but not as...*cream cheesy* as having it on a bagel."

Cael finished his toast and reached for his coffee. "I will experiment."

"Fair enough. Get good and you can hire out as a cook—or set up your own restaurant, like Michelle."

"This...would be a...service?"

"Don't see why not. Bob feeds the town."

"Bob is...*trenvay?*"

"Sure is—"

My cell trilled.

"Excuse me," I said, fishing it out of my pocket.

The number on the screen wasn't familiar.

"Hello?"

"Kate, it's Dad Davis. Got your number from Anna. Listen, something's...come up...about Gaby, and I—" A sound like wind rushing, which was probably Daddy snorting in frustration.

"Is Gaby all right?" I demanded.

"Far's I know, she's fine. It's me between sixes and sevens. Listen—can you come down to the club? This is gonna go better, face to face. An' I got something to show you."

I raised my eyebrows.

"I'd come to you," he said, like he'd seen me, "but I got a delivery due in."

"I'll come down," I said.

"'Preciate it."

He hung up, and I folded the cell, holding it in my hand and looking at the blue and gold flower in the water glass Cael had given it for a vase.

I liked Daddy, and I didn't think he meant me any harm. But the man had been rattled enough to give me his name—at least, his last name. Which wasn't a state secret, after all—it'd be on the liquor license hanging behind the bar—but I really didn't want to meet whatever it was that could shake Daddy up.

"You will not go alone to treat with this person," Cael said— not a question.

"Actually, I won't," I said, slipping the cell back into my pocket. "You'll come with me, and after we're through with Daddy, we'll go over to the baseball toss so you can make your arrangements with Felsic. That sound good?"

"Yes," said Cael, and got up to clear the table.

The delivery was in progress by the time Cael, Oscar, and I strolled into Daddy's. We waited in the area marked out for the band, Cael squatting on the floor next to Oscar, and me leaning against the wall, watching. I'd never seen the nitty-gritty of a commercial liquor delivery, so I observed it in the spirit of a tutorial, and by the time the delivery man had taken his clipboard and the last box of empties out to the truck, I could say with authority that I didn't want to run a bar. Or a dance club.

"Sorry 'bout that, doll. Thanks for waiting."

Daddy gave Cael and Oscar a glance, then looked back to me, eyebrows up.

"Daddy, this is Cael Wolfe."

"Pleased to meetcha," Daddy said, but he seemed more interested in the dog than the man.

"Is that Jim Robins' Oscar?"

"No longer," Cael said, rising to his feet. "Oscar has accepted my oath."

Daddy gave him a long, level stare, then shrugged.

"Wouldna thought Jim'd let that dog go. Best thing about Jim, the dogs."

Cael just gave him his stare back.

Daddy shrugged again.

"None of my business," he said. "Kate, come over here to the register, willya?"

I followed him across the floor; the land showed me Cael sinking back onto his haunches, his posture—and Oscar's—alert, but not threatening.

"So it was busy last night," Daddy was saying, leading the way behind the bar. "Must've been—hell, twelve-thirty?—Gaby comes in, right up to the bar, and she's looking, I dunno...different. *Steady*, not flinching from the noise, or the lights. She says to me, 'I got your coin safe, Donald Allen Davis; you'll hold mine safe for me.'

"And she hands me this."

He rang out the register's cash drawer, and held up a rectangle of white paper with the Maine State Lottery pine-tree-and-mountain logo at the top.

"A Powerball ticket?" I hadn't known Gaby played. "She a winner?"

Daddy's laugh had an edge to it.

"Is she a winner?" He repeated. "Well, I'll tell you, I figured she might've caught a couple grand—big money for a little freak, right?—so, this morning, I come in early and walked around the corner to the Variety. You know how they put the big winning number up in the front window?"

I nodded.

Daddy shook the ticket at me.

"This number was right there, up in lights. I ducked inside and asked Morris if there was more'n one winner. Just a single, he said—for one and a quarter million bucks."

He shook the ticket again, for emphasis.

"One and a quarter million," he repeated. "And she leaves it with me? It ain't even signed—" He twisted his wrist, showing me the back of the ticket.

"What the *hell*? She can't mean me to have—No, she *don't*

mean me to have it—or not all of it—or she wouldna told me to keep it safe. Thing is, I don't want to be holding this thing any longer than I gotta. And what I don't have is a good way to get hold of her." He gave me a tight grin. "And I figured you might—have a way to get hold of her."

"I can find her," I said, frowning at the lottery ticket. One and a quarter million. That kind of money would change anybody's life—even the life of a *trenvay*.

"How's this?" I said to Daddy. "I'll find Gaby and ask after her intentions. Can you keep the ticket safe until I report back?"

"Can and will. What I don't want is to hold it long." Another grin, slightly wider. "This ain't no quarter, doll."

I laughed.

"There's that. I'll let you know as soon as I've got answers. You'll be here?"

"All day, all night."

"You need to get out more," I told him earnestly, as I went 'round the bar, "see people."

He laughed, sounding a little more natural.

I nodded at Cael and headed for the door.

I left dog and man with Felsic at the baseball toss. I'd expected an argument from Cael, but it turned out that he was on board with the notion that Gaby's service would insure that I was in no danger from her.

Freed to my own recognizance, I queried the land, anticipating a nudge toward downtown, but instead found my feet taking me down Milliken Street, toward Walnut. Just short of the corner, I angled across the municipal parking lot, to the edge of a piece of wild land, its border an unwelcoming tangle of sea rose and saplings, woven together with wild grape vines.

I stopped at the edge of the barrier, and, as if I had been on the edge of Gran's wood, murmured, "It's Kate."

Nothing happened; no welcome whispered inside my ear, nor did I acquire a sudden urge to be elsewhere. Leaves moved on the saplings and the sea roses, but under the same breeze that was teasing strands out of my braid.

I took a breath, and reached to the land as I spoke her name lightly.

"Gaby."

Some more nothing happened, then the bank of the roses directly before me parted like a curtain, and there stood Gaby, looking up at me with calm eyes.

What had Daddy said? That Gaby had seemed *steady* last night, with none of the flinching tentativeness that usually characterized her? I saw what he meant; *felt* what he meant, too, because Gaby had more weight on the land, now.

"Kate," she said. "I was gonna come see you."

"I didn't intend to screw up your timing, but you freaked Daddy out bad. He called me."

Gaby snorted. "That man don't freak."

"In the usual way of things, I'd say you're right. But he's not comfortable holding that ticket. I caught the idea that he doesn't trust himself with that much money, even if you don't have a similar problem."

"I'm holding his coin," she pointed out.

"A lot less worth in that—I'm talking about Daddy's point of view, here. He's mundane, even if he's not blind. A quarter and a million and a quarter—they don't equate with him like they do with us. He's scared he's going to steal from you, and he wants this settled before he cracks. I'll call that a good man—and a man who knows his limits."

She sighed, and nudged the gimme hat back up on her head.

"He's not gonna steal from me. Not so long as I hold his coin." Another sigh. "Shoulda told it better, I guess, but I thought he knew. Safer with him than me, 'til I talked to you."

"I think even Daddy'd agree with that. I'm here, now; if you got time to talk?"

"Sure. C'mon in."

She faded through the rose bank, and I followed her, keeping scrupulously to the path the land showed me—just a couple dozen steps, really, until I stepped out into a tiny clearing; a couple stumps at convenient height for sitting, a carpet of plush green moss, and salt cedars guarding the perimeter.

"Sit an' be comfortable," Gaby told me, and I pulled up a stump.

She sat across from me and took off her cap, running fingers through flattened hair.

"I didn't know you played the lottery," I said, when a couple minutes passed without her doing anything more than resettle the cap.

She sent me a quick, sharp glance, and snorted.

"I don't. But that ticket—it was in the returnables; mine by agreement."

A *trenvay's* agreement is a potent thing, and I really couldn't argue against it. If whoever had thrown the ticket away had been Sighted enough to make an agreement with Gaby, then they were Sighted enough to know they were dealing with somebody...Other.

Or not. It's amazing, how ignorant people are.

Give it your best shot, Kate, I told myself.

"The folks who agreed to let you have the returnables probably weren't thinking in terms of winning lottery tickets," I pointed out, gently.

"Who'd I give it to at the town, then?"

At the town? I frowned, memory providing a clear picture of Gaby rummaging through the beach trash cans. Not an unusual sight, at all. It just hadn't ever occurred to me that she might have *an agreement.*

"You got permission from the town manager?" I asked.

She shook her head.

"One mornin', backaways, a feller in the beach jitney seen me 'bout my business, and asked me what was I doin'. Said I was after the returnables, and anything else useful, just like I done for years. An' *he* said, well then fine, you go ahead and keep doin' that." She nodded once, decisively.

"Said Department of Public Works on his jitney and on his slicker. His shirt said Nathan Quin."

The land volunteered the information that Gaby was telling the truth, though I hadn't doubted her. This put a new complexion on the matter.

Nathan Quin, whoever the heck he was, stipulating that he was alive, much less still employed by Archers Beach Public Works— neither of which was a certain thing, "backaways" being one of those words *trenvay* use when they want to obscure how long ago a particular event had taken place—Nathan Quin was not necessarily the original owner of the winning lottery ticket now in Daddy's uneasy possession. Very likely, it had been accidentally thrown out, along with the soda cans, by a tourist. Who, if they were fortunate, would never miss it.

And if they weren't fortunate, it wasn't really any of Gaby's lookout. The ticket hadn't been signed, which put it squarely in Finders Keepers territory.

"Now, what I was thinkin'," Gaby said, "is for you to take that ticket right down to Mr. Emerson and have him buy the land under the park. Ain't nobody's gotta know where the money come from."

Well, no. Somebody was going to have to pick up the check, and pay the taxes, but that wasn't the first problem with this plan.

"That's generous, Gaby, but, here's the thing—it's not enough money to buy Fun Country's land. They want over two million."

Gaby blinked, and made a recover.

"Down payment, then."

That wasn't a bad idea, either. A million-buck down payment would ease the pressure on the town, if the leaseback went through, and on the proposed limited liability corp., in the far-likelier-in-my-opinion case we were left to our own bootstraps. But there was something else. Something I'd heard...

"Kate?"

"Sorry, thinking," I said, and continued to do so; letting myself sink a little into the easy contentment of this little piece of land. It was a nurturing and patient parcel, mixed wood, here by the parking lot, going to wetland up across from the old condos on Walnut. Ducks used the water there, and the occasional little white egret. There were frogs in abundance, cattails and a few water lilies. The trees sheltered the usual population of small lives and birds.

In sum, it was a pleasant little wild space, that nicely balanced the parking lot next door.

"Town owns this parcel, you said?" I asked Gaby.

She nodded, her eyes narrowing.

"They say charity begins at home," I said. "So here's what I'm thinking. Why don't we—by which I mean *I*—ask Henry Emerson to find out how much the town wants for this land right here? My idea is to buy it and get it designated an in-town wild space— I'm betting that Ms. Wing, the librarian, will be able to put us in touch with the right State agency for that. That's first, so you don't have to lose any more sleep over whether or not they're going to take the notion to plow you under for an auxiliary lot."

Gaby's eyes had widened. She was *trenvay*, and her land came first with her.

I'd kind of been counting on that.

"Will...will Mr. Emerson do that, for me?"

"He'll do it for his fee, like the sane, sensible man he is. After we know how big a dent buying your land'll put in your winnings, you can think about what you want to do with the balance. Might be something to buying up other bits and pieces around town, and setting them up as wild spaces, too. Or you might want to donate toward buying the land under Fun Country, or, hell, setting up a hotel for lost cats. But, that's for later. If you want, I can stop by Henry's office on my way back downtown and ask him to make the call."

"Yes!" Gaby said, her eyes blazing. "Please."

"I'll do that, then. In the meantime, you be thinking about how you want to handle collecting the check from the Lottery Commission. If—"

"You," Gaby interrupted.

I blinked. "What?"

"You collect the money, and keep it safe," Gaby said, rising to her feet, and looking down at me, her face bright and fey. "You're Guardian—makes sense that it's you, 'specially if there's going to be these wild spaces—I like that, Kate. I like that a lot. It'd mean we'd be—we'd have less risk. Lil—you remember Lil?"

"Sure I do."

"If she'd owned her own bit, that guy wouldn't've been able to dump his septic truck and, and poison her, like he did!"

That wasn't certain, by any means, but I didn't interrupt her.

"I'll think on it," she continued. "There's Fun Country, too. Town needs it—the whole town does, and I don't wanna stint."

"No stinting," I said, trying to sound soothing. "Nobody could think that." I rose, and looked around me at the sweet little grove. "Nice place you got here."

Gaby smiled.

"Is, isn't it?"

CHAPTER THIRTY-TWO

Wednesday, July 12
High Tide, 12:50 P.M. EDT

Her ebon lover had sated her; her ivory lover had soothed her. She lay among—almost she lay *within*—the strong waters of the pool, cherished and held close. Half dreaming within that constant embrace, she recalled a past.

The sea was black and stormy; the sounds of fright and horror drew her. Foolish humans to go where they were never meant to go. She rose, grabbed one by his hair and pulled him into her embrace, covering his mouth with hers, and descending, until he let go his paddle; his desire warming the waters.

When they were of a sufficient depth, she took her mouth from his. He gasped, and the sea flowed into his lungs; his eyes grew wide with terror; he reached for her even as the waters entered him, and she laughed to see him die.

To the surface again, passing her sister, tenderly cradling a woman, the babe in its carrier already full of water.

This time when she surfaced, knives met her. She leapt over their foolish craft, and snatched one kneeling at the stern, his bow and his attention focused on the depths. That one fought her on the way down; she tore out his throat and left him for the sharks.

Her sister likewise slashed her next and left the body, drifting.

They looked, each at the other. They looked above them, where the canoes floated.

As one, they drove upward, slamming into the bottom of one with such force that it overturned, spilling all of the prey, screaming, into their arms.

The sharks surged, she grabbed a sweet morsel, opened her mouth—and...the sea changed around them. She and her sister floated, caught inside the sea's fascination. Even the sharks were still; the bloody water scarcely moved.

A voice crashed around them like lightning: pain stitching through a truth so potent she tried to flee back under the waters, until the walls of their abode sheltered her from this voice, this truth, this...passion.

"I bargain for my people! Give them their freedom! Give them their lives! Take me—I come willing, to love you and to serve you, for all of my life!"

The sea...sighed. She—she hung, drained of all power, within waters glorious with love.

Around her, the sea stirred; the sea *gathered*. She felt some part of her flow away, into the gathering wave; she was buoyed when it rushed past her, lifting her into ecstasy.

The wave crashed; the sea swept the man into her embrace.

He was afraid—no, he was terrified, his soul-light flickering. The backwave carried his terror to her and to her sister. It was sweet, and they drank of it, laughing.

But the next ripple carried...a diminishment of fear, and the third was informed not with fear, but with wonder. His soul regained its glow, feeble at first, then more brightly, as the essence of the waters informed him, and he began to know what he had dared to become.

His soul blazed in the currents then, and he gave himself to her, who was their mother. Gave himself as one who loved, as an *equal*; even as the sea accepted and loved him, her equal. They flowed into each other, sharing everything that they were—power to power, and heart to heart.

Held rapt by the sea's adoration, she was forced to witness. She could scarcely think, but she could feel her loss, all too keenly.

Everything she had ever known, everything she had felt, the very certainties upon which her existence was built...

Everything was changing.

She raised her face then...and screamed.

Henry was on the case, promising to make the call that very morning, and let me know just as soon as he had ascertained the asking price for Gaby's little piece of heaven.

From there on, it got harder.

"I'll need to call in a financial expert, Kate. We're fortunate that Beth Ordover's right up in Portland."

"We are?"

"We are," he said firmly. "One of the top two or three in the country at what she does. I'll make that call, too."

So, having put a considerable number of wheels into spinning, I went back to the midway, thoughts half occupied with what I might devise to keep Cael happily occupied. Might need to train him on the carousel, or see if anybody uptown needed a dogsbody. Not that gruntwork was a long-term solution; I was just looking for something to keep the devil from setting up a workshop.

But, as was so often the case, I'd spent perfectly good worries on nothing. Cael was happy to continue to assist Felsic at the baseball toss, and Felsic was happy to have him with her.

"Okay. If either of you need me, you know where to find me," I said, and wove my way through a surprisingly large crowd, given that the day was sunny, and already hot.

"What a disappointment," I heard a woman saying to her escort. "I didn't know jellies came this far north."

"The waves are better in Ocean City," opined a young man to his young brother. "You can bodysurf."

I frowned, and swung left, deviating from my intended course, and followed the wooden walkway over the dunes.

There were some people on the beach, though not as many as the day warranted, and no one at all in the water.

I crossed the beach to the ocean's edge, past the lifeguard tower, flying its red flag—no swimming, that meant. It was usually deployed for storm tides, but today's sea didn't look stormy.

Sort of the opposite, actually.

I stopped at the water line, and looked about me.

Jellies—by which I mean jellyfish—littered the wet sand. There were more in the water, red at the center and trailing hundreds of silvery tentacles. No sharing the water with those; their stings weren't fatal—usually—but they hurt like hell. So that was what the red flag was about.

As for the sea...

The waves were sluggish, at best—definitely not bodysurfing waves, even if the body in question was jellyfish-proof—and the color was a sort of slate green, though the sky was clear and blue. There was a breeze, though not much of one; the air was heavy and carried a faint odor, which was maybe what fried jellyfish smelled like.

I wondered where Borgan was, and if he knew that matters were this bad—but of course he knew. The Gulf of Maine was his service.

And the Gulf of Maine was in mourning.

I frowned, staring out over the turgid water, and reached for the land.

The sense I received was slightly puzzled, and more than a little sorrowful. I understood—there was nothing the land or I could do here, except hope that Borgan's contact—the guy who was "hard to net"—actually had some answers for him.

"Yeah, well, this is fine for a day," Jess was saying, while I leaned against the rail by the operator's station. "Let it go on 'til tomorrow, even, and people'll be takin' their business up Route One to the strip, or the movies, up Freeport, or down to the Kittery stores, and we'll be twiddling our thumbs, wishing for something to do, and wondering how we're gonna live the winter."

I nodded; she wasn't telling me anything I, or any other carny, didn't already know. Not that it made happy hearing.

"We'll just have to hope the sea perks up and the jellyfish go back to wherever they came from."

"Yeah, I'll do that," Jess said, actually sounding cranky. "I'll hope real hard."

❧⚮☙

The memory from the goblins' past—of the Borgan's making—roused her. She came to herself in the subtle, scheming waters, and whirled, her hair snapping around her like ebony whips.

Her thoughts were—not disordered. It was merely that, for a moment, she could not precisely recall, if she was the goddess who had loved two demons, two goblins who had loved a sea, or . . .

. . . a grubby girl scratching out a living on one of the poor stony islands the seas suffered to carry upon their backs. She had mended nets; she wove, and cooked, and gardened; she fished. One of the men of the village had given her father a new boat for her, and she had gone back to his shack with him, where her duties were changed only by so much—the man, her husband, used her for his own satisfaction, and she was no longer permitted to fish.

It was from her husband's house that she had run, when the storm had reached its peak, the winds carrying her brothers' screams to her ears.

Whirling in the clever waters, she came to understand that there was no choice necessary—no choice possible. She was neither girl, nor goddess, nor goblins, but in some way all of those things.

The waters whispered that she was the stronger for it.

It might be so, but she had been lied to, before.

She thought to query the waters, then, as to the number of days which were left to the Borgan's grant of mercy.

The answer came back as a cool whisper inside her ear, and she relaxed again among the waters.

There was time; she had many days yet, to build her strength for the next phase of her plan. These waters were potent; already she was much improved. If she remained here yet another hand of days, she would again hover on the edge of godhood. Then, she would woo the Borgan as an equal, indeed. She would command his love; he would break the geas, and together they would dwell supreme within this sea.

Her thoughts misted into pleasing dreams, and the waters overtook her once more, cradling her as she floated, will-less and content in their embrace.

✌ ❧ ✌

My cell started in as I was on my way back to Daddy's, to fill him in on progress, and survey the state of his nerves. I stopped under the awning of SnowCold Ice Cream, tucking into the corner so as not to take up room needed by a paying customer and answered.

"Hi, Henry."

"Good afternoon, Kate. The asking price for the parcel in question has been lowered to two hundred eighty-nine thousand dollars. Also, the Lottery Commission confirms that winners may elect not to have their names published. The winner, of course, must prove that they are who they say they are."

"Of course," I murmured, wrinkling my nose.

"Our expert in Portland is out of the office today. I left a message and I'll also make a follow-up call tomorrow. Is there anything else I can do for you right now?"

"I—yes, there is. If I bring that...to you, can you lock it up and keep it safe until I talk to the winner?"

"Of course."

"Okay. I'll be down in a few. Thanks, Henry."

"It's entirely my pleasure, Kate. I'll see you in a few minutes."

...and that's pretty much where the rest of my day off went. I relieved Daddy of the ticket, dropped it off with Henry, who gave me a receipt. Then I went in search of Gaby, and helped her harvest returnables while we talked over her options, which at one point meant asking her some very serious questions while the land listened hard, until at last Gaby's temper snapped.

"Is the Guardian gonna steal from the land? You heard what I want, for finding that ticket. I got nothin' more to do with it."

Truth rang like a bell, which was great—for Gaby. For me—well, Henry was going to be drawing up paperwork 'til the middle of next week, and who knew what the financial whiz was going to need. And I was going to have to review and sign it all.

Well, that's why the Guardian got the big bucks.

"You got it," I told Gaby. "The trust will secure your land first."

I expected maybe a handshake, but Gaby only sniffed and returned her attention to the barrel she'd been fishing.

So, I went back to Henry, who got the ticket out of the safe, had me sign it, while he signed a paper that said he'd seen me sign it, and put both together into the safe. Then he gave me another receipt.

"Beth's with a client this morning; I hope to hear from her this afternoon," he said. "In the meantime, this will give you some background on the kinds of trusts available. I've marked the sections." He picked up a book from the top of the pile at the right of his desk. There were maybe a dozen green flags peeking shyly out from the top of the pages.

"Come back to me with questions you may have; we'll stockpile them for Beth."

"Thanks, Henry," I said, and beat it, book clutched to my chest.

At home, I made myself a sandwich, poured a glass of ice tea, and retired, with the book, and Breccia, to the summer parlor.

Which is where Cael found me, some hours later, after the midway had closed. Breccia had gone back inside after the sun went down, doubtless to seek the elephants. I didn't blame her; I'd put the book aside about then, but inertia kept me where I was.

Inertia and a nonsensical hope that, if I stared at the sea long enough, it would start behaving naturally again.

Or that I would see Borgan walking across the sand toward me.

"Good evening, Kate," Cael said, settling to his haunches, so his face was level with mine.

"Good evening. Have fun today?"

"It was pleasant to work with Felsic and to meet those who brought themselves to my attention. Would you like a glass of wine?"

"You know? I would." I shifted, and he put his hand on my shoulder.

"There is no need to rise, unless you wish it. I will bring the glass."

"Thank you," I said, and watched him rise effortlessly and move away. I sighed and wondered how you go about breaking someone who had been a servant for what I suspected was a very long time before he'd been a prisoner, of serving. No, that was wrong—my head was stuffed full of simple, complex, and private trusts, and nonprofit corporations, and whatnot to the point that nothing else could get through. All we needed to do was to identify Cael's service to the land. Though how...

Cael returned bearing two glasses, with Oscar escorting. Two glasses made me a lot happier than one, which he probably knew, so was he being a servant or—

Kate, I told myself, accepting the offered glass with a nod, *you're overthinking it.*

Cael settled cross-legged beside me and raised his glass.

"To the land and the Guardian," he proposed.

"To the land and those who serve," I counterproposed.

We clinked glasses and drank.

"Your day, it was perhaps not so pleasant as mine?"

"I wouldn't call it unpleasant. Things got done, and more things are going to get done—in service of the land, so I was on task, too."

He nodded, and glanced out over the sand to the distant, quiet sea.

"There was much business in the midway, because the sea suffered an affliction of stingers," he said. "Felsic said that Captain Borgan, your leman, does not often permit such things."

"I'm guessing that Felsic knows what she's talking about. As I understand it, this is an...unusual situation. He's gone off down coast to talk to somebody who might advise him."

"A wise lord knows when to ask for advice," Cael said approvingly. He sipped wine, and took a deep breath.

"Felsic says..." He stopped.

I turned my head to meet his gaze.

"Yes?"

Another deep breath.

"Your pardon, my lady. Felsic says that these papers, which are delivered from Artie—she says that papers come only to those whose service... *is wide*. By which she means those who are not tied to only one place or part of the land."

There was an idea. I supposed Felsic knew about that, too. My mother had a packet of papers; Gran definitely had papers. It hadn't occurred to me to wonder how many other *trenvay* had papers. Felsic didn't, nor the overwhelming number of those *trenvay* who worked at the midway. I took a sip of wine, wondering if I should approach Felsic or Artie for more info—and decided on Felsic as generally easier on my nerves.

"Let me think about that," I said, "and... take advice. Not only am I just settling into my Guardianship, you're the first whose service I've accepted for the land."

He nodded, and we sipped in companionable silence for a few minutes, Oscar stretched out between us.

"Felsic also says," Cael murmured, "that tomorrow we ought to have a game night."

I stopped with my glass halfway to my lips.

"She does, does she? Is there a guest list?"

Cael smiled gently, as if he'd known I was going to react badly.

"Felsic said that she and Peggy will bring a game. We—you and I and Breccia and Oscar—we will provide *munchies and beer*. I will tomorrow go to Ahz and purchase munchies and beer..." He hesitated.

"Felsic said that I will need money to do this."

"Right you are." I thought about being annoyed, but what I mostly felt was relief. Game night would take my mind off... things. Especially things related to Borgan.

God, I missed him.

I drank off the rest of my wine, and glanced at Cael.

"I'll give you some money; you get the shopping list from Felsic. In the meantime, you want a sandwich?"

"I do, yes. Shall I make one for you, also?"

"No," I said, coming to my feet somewhat creakily. "Let's go inside and make one for each other."

CHAPTER THIRTY-THREE

Thursday, July 13
Low Tide 7:17 A.M. EDT
Sunrise 5:12 A.M.

The scrambled eggs were much improved, and even tasted cream cheesy. I gave Cael his due, and promised myself to indoctrinate him to the mysteries of cholesterol...soon.

Cael cleared the table while I refilled our coffee mugs and carried them to the table. I'd given him fifty bucks in cash, and part of our breakfast conversation was devoted to his understanding of currency, change, and base ten. Here, it transpired that his day in the booth with Felsic stood him in good stead. I wasn't going to have to worry about him fumbling his change at checkout.

I sat down, and leaned forward to touch the blue-and-gold flower, as fresh now as when Aleun had plucked it for me—had it only been two days ago?

"What kind of flower is this?" I asked, as Cael took his chair.

He blinked, and put his mug down without taking a drink.

"Retorinas, my lady. Should you ever wish to return to...the garden from which it was plucked, all you need do is take it in hand and—ask." He hesitated. "Of course, it is only a flower, and can do no more than find its own bed."

So, it was a one-way ticket to Sempeki, without having to open the World Gate. If it didn't change. If whatever Prince Aesgyr was doing with the Wind Between the Worlds didn't utterly confuse its poor vegetative directional sense. If, if—

Footsteps on the stair—two sets, both heavy. The land showed me an honest-to-God Archers Beach policeman—not a summer cop—and...

Jim Robins.

Oscar had been napping in front of the French doors. He raised his head, and growled softly.

Cael was already out of his chair when the knock came—too loud, and too long. That, I saw through the land's eyes, was Jim Robins' doing. I got out of my chair and strolled into the living room. I opened the French doors, and tried to nudge Oscar out onto the summer parlor—nothing doing. He wasn't rude about it; merely slipped away from my hand and walked over to stand at the knee of the master of hounds.

Cael opened the door.

"That's him!" Jim Robins snapped, lurching forward, like he was going to grab Oscar by the collar. "That's the guy who stole my dog!"

Oscar growled—Cael moved a hand, and he stopped, and sat, head tipped to one side.

The cop grabbed Robins by the arm and hauled him back out onto the porch.

"That your dog, mister—?" the cop asked.

"He is my dog, yes," Cael said composedly. "I am Cael Wolfe."

The cop looked at Jim Robins. Jim Robins said something rude—then pointed, past Cael...

...at me.

"She was in on it!"

The cop looked at me. I came forward to stand at Cael's side in the doorway.

"Good morning, I'm Kate Archer."

"Yes, ma'am," the cop—Cyr, according to his badge—said. "You related to this man?"

"Our families go 'way back," I said. "I'd have to look at one of my grandfather's genealogy charts to give you the exact relationship."

He nodded, and looked back to Cael.

"I don't guess you have any papers for this dog, do you, Mr. Wolfe?"

"Of course I do," Cael said, sounding surprised.

"Liar! That's *my* dog. You got no—" Jim Robins thrust forward again.

Oscar surged to his feet and barked, hard and sharp, like he meant it.

Robins stepped back; I could see the sweat on his face.

"If this man will stop trying to enter Ms. Archer's house, I will bring the license paper. Can this be done?"

"He'll stay right here on the porch," the cop promised.

Cael nodded, and went into the living room, pulling the envelope he'd gotten from Artie off the mantelpiece. He shuffled the papers, chose a yellow quarter-sheet and came back to hand it to the policeman.

Officer Cyr looked down, frowning slightly, like maybe he really ought to look into getting reading glasses.

"Says here, Oscar, German shorthaired pointer, black and white, five years old, last rabies vaccination September of oh-five, all other shots up to date, owner..." He looked at Jim Robins, and said, "Cael Wolfe."

Jim Robins snatched the paper out of the cop's hands, looked down at it—and swayed slightly where he stood, his face going white, then red. I reached for the land, hoping I wasn't going to have to patch up an apoplexy—then he thrust the paper back into the cop's hand, and leaned forward, one hand out slightly, but not over the door frame.

"Oscar," he said, his voice low and pleading. "C'mon, Oscar. You remember Jim."

Oscar snarled, showing teeth.

"Oscar," Cael said mildly, "your manners, sir."

The dog stopped snarling, and sat, reluctantly, to my eye.

Officer Cyr handed the registration back to Cael.

"Thank you, sir. Sorry for the trouble." He looked at Jim Robins.

"Guess you made a mistake. Right, Jim?"

There was a long moment before the man sighed, growing visibly shorter as his anger left him.

"Guess I did," he said, and gave me a nod. "Sorry, ma'am, mister. That dog meant a lot to me. Always a good dog, an' now..." He let it drift off, and turned abruptly away, but not before I'd seen the tears in his eyes.

"Sorry to've bothered you folks," Officer Cyr said. "You have a nice day, now." He followed Jim Robins down the stairs.

Cael closed the door. I put a hand on his shoulder.

"He's suffering," I said, not sure what I wanted.

Cael's mouth thinned.

"He is a cruel and petty man, who brought pain on those who gave him their loyalty and their love." His face softened somewhat. "I admit, it is a harsher punishment than that which I had intended. Had the laws of this land allowed for justice, he would be dead now, and beyond suffering."

There wasn't, I thought, a lot to say to that.

I went back to the kitchen table and picked up my coffee mug.

She was a fool.

The goblins had held the secret of the misty wall surrounding the pool in which she was imprisoned, and she had thought to use their method and thus escape to the wider ocean.

However, the Borgan had altered the working since the goblins had breached it.

Of course he had done so. The Borgan, at least, was not a fool.

She had examined the working and attempted several answers herself, based on her own not-inconsiderable understanding of spellcraft. Nothing served, and it became very quickly obvious that the more power she brought to bear against it, the less power was available to her—and the sturdier the wall became.

Plainly, she could not continue in that current. She would need as much power as she could hold, when the Borgan's grant of mercy expired and his geas returned her to Cheobaug.

Thus, she withdrew to the center of the pool, where the current was coldest and most potent . . . and opened herself to the power of the waters.

There were half a dozen riders on the carousel when I arrived, and maybe three times that many in line. Apparently, yesterday's epic crush had subsided. I wondered if that was good news, or bad.

Vassily answered the question for me.

"There is a sickness upon the ocean," he said, as I joined him at the operator's station. "The waves do not make, there are stinging bladders in the water, and dead fishes, too."

Oh, good. The one thing we'd been missing was dead fish.

"That's too bad," I said, as he rang the bell for the end of the ride. "I was hoping yesterday was a fluke."

He gave me a sideways glance.

"There is nothing that you, yourself, can do for the sad, sick ocean?"

I only stared at him, mouth half open.

Vassily leaned over to open the gate.

"Welcome," he said, smiling at the first person in line—a strapping young man of maybe nine summers. "Two tickets for the fantasy carousel—the best ride in all of Maine!"

He counted off the riders, then closed the gate with a smile for the next in line.

"Next time, you are certain to ride!" he said, then looked back to me.

I shook my head.

"Not my area of expertise," I said, and added, just in case anybody was listening who could make it so, "but I'm sure everything'll be fine in a day or two."

CHAPTER THIRTY-FOUR

Friday, July 28
Low Tide 7:54 a.m EDT
Sunrise 5:26 A.M.

Long story short, everything *wasn't* okay in a day or two. In point of actual, observable fact, everything was going to hell in a handbasket, and nothing any of us—Guardian, *trenvay*, or mundane—could do about it.

Two days after Borgan left for the Vineyard, the stinging jellies and dead fish had been joined by tide after tangled tide of kelp and other weeds that rode in on the backs of the turgid waves, and made heaps on the beach, dry and stinking, a fertile breeding ground for sand fleas and other insects.

The tourists ... well, of course they left in droves. Who's to blame them? You want a nice vacation at the beach, you want to be able to play in the water, lie on the sand, walk up and down the surf line and think about nothing.

If the town had other amusements in addition to the carnival and the midway, or more shopping opportunities than those offered up on Archer Avenue ... well, who was I kidding? We'd've still lost most of the tourists.

"Jane Gilly up the Old Salt says she's getting cancellations for *August*," Jess Robald had said yesterday.

She'd looked ready to break up the place, and I couldn't blame her. If there was one thing that the Archers Beach Twelve to Twelve, and the whole rest of the town, absolutely depended upon, it was that Saco Bay, the Gulf of Maine, and the Atlantic Ocean would play nice, mostly, and not produce plagues of jellyfish during the High Season.

For *fifteen days and counting*, during a High Season that was exactly twelve weeks long from end to end.

"Bound to be done with by August," I said, but my voice even sounded thin to me. Jess only shook her head.

"You don't believe that," she said.

And, actually . . .

I didn't.

Because of all the things that had and hadn't happened during those fifteen days, one notable thing had *not* happened.

Borgan hadn't come back to Archers Beach.

His estimate for return had been four days, depending on when he could hook up with whoever he needed to talk to, and I managed to wait two days beyond that before I cracked, and called his cell.

My call went straight to voice mail.

So did the call I made two days later, after I'd gone down to Kinney Harbor, and onto *Gray Lady* herself. My things were still on the shelf where I'd left them, and there was a thin patina of dust on all the flat surfaces.

I checked the fridge and cleaned out the bad milk and the moldy cheese; there wasn't much else there, save a couple of beers and a bottle of wine. I lay on the bed for a while, fingering the blue-and-green bead he'd braided into my hair. It was cool and soothing against my skin. Eyes closed, I touched it with the tiniest questing bit of power, hoping there might be a connection, after all.

But the bead remained magically inert: a pretty ornament, nothing more.

I made another call, then, but Frenchy couldn't help.

"Old days, there was a Guardian on the Vineyard, Kate, but there ain't been any news o'her since 'fore John Lester gave up his service."

"Is there anybody else, down that way?"

"Not our kind. None I know of." She paused, then continued in a softer tone. "He's tougher'n two sharks, Kate. Been in bad trouble 'fore this and come about. Just needs some time t'work, is all. You live as long as him—or me—time don't seem . . . desperate, like it does to you young folk."

I took a breath, trying to ease the tightness in my belly.

"Thanks, Frenchy. Just...I'm worried."

"Who wouldn't be, lookin' at those seas? Take some ease from your land, Kate, an' carry on with what's yours to do. Things'll change."

"They always do." I cleared my throat. "'Preciate you taking the call," I said. "Sorry to be a bother."

"No bother at all. Call anytime."

We hung up. I lay on the bed, eyes closed, taking nice deep breaths, but my stomach wouldn't settle.

Eventually, I got up, smoothed the covers, and left, feeling sick and unhappy.

Very early on the morning of the ninth day, I visited Nerazi's stone at the border with Pine Point.

But Nerazi didn't come to her stone that morning.

...which was when I lost it, a little.

I dragged Cael out to spot me, telling him what I intended. He didn't even try to talk me out of it.

We stood on the water line, with our backs to Dube Street and Tupelo House, and I raised the power I'd received from my grandfather's amulet, the last treasure of House Aeronymous. It rose quickly, so much power I could feel it sloshing around inside me.

Cael tied a nice stout rope of power about my waist; I waded into the stinking, sluggish water—and dove beneath the waves. It came as no surprise that I could breathe water—maybe it should have, but my attention was elsewhere.

I hadn't expected that the sea would speak to me—and I wasn't disappointed. So far as I could tell, the sea had no awareness that I had entered her waters, despite the noise I made in an effort to attract her attention.

I had hoped—my plan had been to loose a search of my own through the waters, hoping to feel him in the currents, like I could feel him on the land. But that plan needed at least the awareness, if not the active cooperation of the water. *Jikinap* was not the living ocean; it could know only what the ocean allowed it to know.

And that—was nothing.

I hadn't known how much I'd counted on the plan succeeding. Hadn't known until it failed.

Well...what are a few more drops of water, to an ocean?

Cael hauled me back to land about then, and when I protested and would have reentered the water, he picked me up.

"That's enough, my lady. Come home. You do nothing good for your leman nor those others who depend on you, by endangering yourself further."

Still scolding gently, he carried me into the house, sat me down in the kitchen and poured out a glass of wine.

"Drink," he said, handing me the glass.

On consideration, a glass of wine probably wasn't a bad idea. I sipped—and choked.

"That's brandy!"

"It is now, yes. Drink all of it."

He crossed his arms over his chest, frowning. I sighed.

When the glass was empty, Cael sent me upstairs, with Breccia to guard my dreams.

Well.

If it had been possible to ignore the ocean's illness—or if the damned woman from Cheobaug had managed to restrain herself from snacking down the *ronstibles*—if, in a word, the Season was proceeding normally...

Life would've been going along pretty briskly, with some notable events to give it snap, sparkle, and hope.

On Monday the seventeenth, Dan Poirier of the Chamber had given a crack-of-dawn presentation to a standing-room-only crowd of yawning Twelve-to-Twelvers. The upshot of it all, after the dust from the Powerpoint slides had settled, was that he and his committee had crafted a proposal they felt was likely to get the town's attention in a positive way. They had a meeting with the town treasurer on the twenty-eighth, and, if that went well, there'd be a formal presentation to the town council at their meeting on August second.

Continuing in the vein of efficient people being efficient, Henry and his pro in Portland were busy collaborating on the Archers Beach Wilderness Trust, and I'd been cautioned to expect mountains of papers to sign, soon.

And, there'd been yesterday's phone call, asking me when I could accept delivery of one wooden carousel animal, carved and painted in the likeness of a bat-winged horse.

...which is what I was doing opening the carousel's storm

gates at six o'clock in the morning on a day that promised to bring no customers at all.

I'd called Artie, who'd agreed to meet me, and to get the damned fiberglass rooster off of my carousel. I'd called Nancy, too, in case Artie was a no-show—

And here came the woman now, newspaper tucked under one arm and hands in the pockets of her jeans.

"Mornin'," she called. "Artie here yet?"

"Just you and me."

"Good." She pulled the newspaper out from under her arm, snapped it open, and handed it to me.

I took it, glancing down at the *Journal-Trib*'s front page.

SACO MAN COMMITS SUICIDE

I looked at Nancy, who only looked grim, then back to the story.

> Jim Robins, 38, of Saco died Wednesday night at Southern Maine Medical Center, from a self-inflicted gunshot wound to the head. No note was found. Friends say Robins had been increasingly despondent over the last weeks, citing the loss of his dogs. Robins was well known in the area as a dog-handler and hunter. He was sole proprietor of Robins Pest Control, with an office on Spring Street in Saco.
>
> Survivors include a son, Bryan, 8, and estranged wife Elizabeth Robins, both of Biddeford.

I let my breath go in a long sigh, looked up and met Nancy's eyes.

"Is that—" she began, and stopped, her question cut off by Artie's yell.

"Kate! I'm here right like you wanted me! Let's get the job done!"

The new horse arrived within minutes of Artie's departure with the rooster; the trucks probably passed each other crossing Grand Avenue.

We got her installed in record time, and stood back to admire her.

"Looks fine," Nancy said. "Something missing from the old one, though."

"The original had fangs," I reminded her.

"That was it. Good idea, leaving them off."

"Even if this one's not as likely to bite as the original." I sighed, and extended a hand to stroke the painted nose.

"Cap'n Borgan not back yet from his trip down Mass.?" Nancy asked.

I swallowed, and shook my head, not looking at her.

"He's . . . a number of days past when he told me to look for him," I said. I raised my eyes to meet hers and added, "He's not answering the cell. Or collecting voice mail."

Nancy put a gruff hand on my shoulder.

"Business has kept him before, remember."

"Right," I said, and gave her what I hoped bore some passing resemblance to a smile.

She squeezed my shoulder and let me go.

"You hear Marilyn's plans, for when the park closes?" she asked.

It was actually good to hear that Marilyn had plans for after the park closed. She'd worked for Fun Country all her life, going up the ladder from game agent to manager.

"Marilyn doesn't share with me," I said.

"Me, neither. But she was talkin' to Anna."

Of course, she was talking to Anna.

"Turns out that Marilyn's husband retired a couple years back. Wanted her to quit then, and move down to Florida. She wouldn't leave the job. Now there's no job, she's got the house up for sale, and they're planning on wintering this year in the Keys. The husband's pleased, and Marilyn figures she'll look up some work down there, after she has a little vacation."

"Good," I said, and meant it.

"Well." Nancy looked around. "Anything more for me?"

"Not right now. If you've got a sense of adventure, and you don't have to go straight home after closing, I'm told that I'm hosting the second ever Dube Street Game Night tonight. Me, Cael, Felsic, Peggy Marr, Ethrane, a couple others from the midway, maybe. Beer, ale, soda, coffee, munchies."

Nancy looked interested.

"What's the game?"

"God knows. Last time it was something called Munchkin. I have no idea what it'll be this time. Cael's choosing."

"I kinda like Munchkin," Nancy said. "We got my aunt with us while they're fixing the septic at her place. Her and Ma been up every night 'til daylight, talking a streak. They won't miss me if I stop over for a game."

"Be pleased to have you."

"'Kay, then. Best you go home and get some rest, Kate; you're looking worn down."

"I'll do that," I lied, and watched her leave the park before I closed the storm gates, locked the door, and went onto the carousel to sit astride the batwing horse.

CHAPTER THIRTY-FIVE

Friday, July 28
Low Tide 8:01 p.m EDT
Moonset 9:55 P.M.

Three times since the Borgan had bound her to the pool, she had woken; and three times the pool had its way with her.

This time, she woke in the fullness of her power, and she would be trifled with no longer.

It was time—it was well past time—to find the Borgan and compel his love. There was to be no tender wooing such as she had dreamed upon. No. The pool had ruined those plans; there was scarcely time enough to break the wall of mist, find the Borgan and bind him to her. The geas . . . she felt it 'round her throat like a string of pearls, slowly tightening. Now was the time to act—her last opportunity to act! It would not be wasted.

She rose up until the misty wall would allow her to rise no more—and threw the full force of her will against it.

The mists shattered—

And the geas snapped tight around her, the waters flowing away into darkness.

Cael wasn't home when I got back, a little after eleven. Breccia was sitting in the window over the sink, overlooking the alley behind the house. Someone—which is to say, Cael—had helpfully pulled the Venetian blinds up to the top of the window, wound the cord out of the way. Helpful man, Cael.

Too helpful, to my way of thinking. We were going to have to find him some other place to live before he became indispensable.

"Hi, there," I said, waving in Breccia's direction. "Nancy suggests a nap for what ails me. You up for that in, say, an hour?"

She squinted her eyes, which I took for a *yes*. I moved toward the fridge—and altered course when the wall phone rang, loud and tinny.

Setting my feet carefully, so as not to step into a water bowl, or upset the cat's food, I unhooked the receiver.

"Hello?"

"Hello, may I speak to Mr. Wolfe?" The phrasing was business, the accent was Maine.

"Mr. Wolfe isn't here right now. May I take a message?"

"Could you ask him to call the town human resources office? It's about his application. My name is Maureen Pare. The number is..."

She rattled it off, I memorized it, and assured her that I would pass the message to Mr. Wolfe immediately upon his return. She thanked me and we hung up.

"Might be Cael has a job," I said to Breccia, opening up a drawer and pulling out a pen and a notepad. I wrote briefly and left the pad in the middle of the table, under the retorinas, where he'd be sure to see it.

I opened the fridge, but nothing looked appetizing, so I poured myself a glass of cranberry juice and carried it out to the summer parlor.

The beach was deserted, except for the gulls scavenging among the heaps of drying weed. Tide was coming in, but the ocean might as well have been a particularly muddy lake, for all the wave action showing.

If this went on much longer, Archers Beach would be finished as a resort town by the end of the Season. Oh, tourists would come back, eventually, but it would take a good five years before the bravest would give us another chance.

And by that time, Archers Beach would be condos all up and down those seven miles of sand beach the Chamber likes to brag about. The townies, a lot of them, would leave—sell the house for the kind of money rich people from Away might give, and move on someplace inland, to start over.

The *trenvay*...

Well, the *trenvay* would stay, and the Guardian, too.

We didn't have a choice.

Borgan...I reached up to finger the bead in my hair, and tried very hard not to think that I'd never see him again. "Never" was one of those words young folk like me used to make themselves sad, as Frenchy would probably *not* say, unless something had happened to short her temper.

Give the man time to work, Kate, I told myself. It didn't ease my worry any.

I drank juice without really tasting it, staring out over the ugly sea, my fingers caressing the bead in my hair, and I thought...

Why not?

Because, really, if I could use Prince Aesgyr's little toy to travel to places I knew well...why *couldn't* I use it to...travel to people I knew well?

Oh, there was the little matter of the geographical range limit, but did that even come into play if I was focusing on a person, rather than a landmark?

And, as a matter of fact, hadn't I jumped across time and space to Frenchy's side?

...well, no, I hadn't. I'd been thinking Camp Ellis when Cael and I had made that jump—and there was that little bit of flex built into Aesgyr's working—so that was...inconclusive, at best.

What I needed was a test. I sipped juice, eyes squinted against the glare.

Somebody living outside of the Archers Beach/Camp Ellis megaplex, that being what I guessed to be my geographic range, with the flex option *on.* Somebody with whom I shared a close tie...

And that was the sticker. There were very few people with whom I shared a close tie, and all of them, with one notable exception, were right here in Archers Beach.

Well, damn.

No test run today.

And, I told myself firmly, *no just trying to zap yourself to Borgan. You don't know where he is; you don't know what he's doing, and, by extension, what you might fuck up by disturbing him at work. Just—go to bed, Kate.*

That seemed to be sound advice, and the second time I'd heard it, today.

I went inside and did just that.

Something was wrong.

The Borgan's geas lurched, twisted—and began to unravel.

She pushed against the power confining her; felt it give. Exhilarated, she pushed again, opening the flaw wider. Wind whipped through the hole she had made; it slammed her against the spell wall, which was unraveling in earnest now, ragged shreds tangling in her hair. She reached for the wind, but it eluded her will, leaving her choking on the stink of entwined powers—peaches, hot stone, cinnamon, pine tar, vanilla, kerosene.

The spell enclosing her lurched again, and the last threads blew apart.

She was suspended in the maelstrom, unprotected, and without direction.

She might have cried out, but all she heard was the wind rushing in her ears. The wind carried sticks, or stones, or bits of flame; these struck her, and hurt where they struck.

The wind increased, blowing through her, carrying away the power she had gained from the Borgan's sea.

Frightened in earnest, she thrust her will and her self toward Cheobaug. Power rippled against the punishing wind; the particular taste of *her* power tingled on her tongue. She closed her eyes and *pushed.*

But when she opened her eyes again, it was to the storm.

It came to her then, that she was lost between the Worlds.

And she would *die* between the Worlds, her power stripped away like the flesh from her bones, and her soul left to scream in the unending wind.

Horror—but there was no time for horror, or for fear. She must—she would!—act. She was a goddess. She would not perish here.

She cast 'round inside the punishing wind, refusing to be just one more mote driven by its fury. She spun a net of her will and cast it wide. When she pulled it home, she saw that it contained a single, glowing thread, already beginning to fade.

She snatched it to her, and tasted the sweetness of the waters she had lately quit.

Clinging to the fading thread with every ounce of will she possessed, she conjured the image, the taste, and the virtue of the Borgan's sweet, free sea. Laboriously, she built into the conjuration an image of the goblins' humble dwelling.

She poured her will into the little working, informing it with every bit of longing in her heart.

The thread she held took fire; it contracted, snapping her through the abrasive, burning wind; until she lost her sense of self, and everything was black.

Cael was stocking the fridge when Breccia and I came downstairs, a little after six o'clock.

"Good evening," I told his back. "Did you find your message?"

He looked at me over the fridge's door.

"I did find the message and I called Maureen Pare. We have an appointment to meet in her office tomorrow at ten o'clock. I am one of five applicants for Animal Control Officer chosen for personal interviews."

"That's pretty good," I said. "Do you have interview clothes?"

He frowned. "I fear I may not."

"If you want, I'll check out your closet. If there's nothing suitable, I volunteer to go down to Dynamite with you and help pick out clothes. Though, honestly, Mrs. Kristanos' taste is perfect; just tell her what you need."

"Yes," Cael said, which I took as permission to root through his closet.

Gran having stated her intention to remain under leaf for the foreseeable future, Cael had temporary use of her bedroom. I opened the closet and perused the contents. Then I went back to the kitchen to let Cael know that we were going shopping.

CHAPTER THIRTY-SIX

Friday, July 28

In theory, Game Night would be hosted, alternately, by me and by Peggy Marr, whose brainchild it was. The person who provided the place would provide the refreshments; the visitors would bring the game.

It was an equitable plan, but unfortunately not workable, given the setup of Peggy's apartment. So, this time, Cael picked out the game, while Peggy and Felsic funded drinks and munchies.

I'd had more fun than I'd supposed I would at the first Game Night, two days after Borgan left for the Vineyard. I'd expected to have a lot less fun tonight, given one thing and another.

But I was wrong.

Cael's choice was a game called Zoobratic, a lunatic mash-up of Pinochle, Scrabble, and Hazard. A timer was also involved. It was absolutely fatal to lose track of any detail on the board, and before I knew it an hour had passed, the game was over, and I was one of four losers in a field of six, Ethrane and Peggy the two winners.

"*That* . . . was exhausting," Peggy said, bouncing up out of her seat. "Who else needs an ale? Kate?"

"Great, thanks," I said.

Moss was already sweeping the letter squares back into their pouch; I started gathering up cards.

"Got your ale," Peggy said, from my side. "Come out on the deck for a sec?"

Well, why not? I slipped the cards into their box, and followed her outside.

Peggy leaned a hip against the rail, and raised her bottle.

"To change," she said.

I blinked. "You sure of that toast?"

"Sure as I've been about anything in a while. You got a better one?"

"In fact—I don't."

I clinked my bottle against hers.

"To change. May it be quick and merciful."

Peggy chuckled and drank.

I drank, without the benefit of a chuckle.

It was a quiet night. I could hear the band, still cranking down at Neptune's, and the sound of a motorcycle engine, winding out, as it turned into Route 5.

What I didn't hear—what I *still* didn't hear—was the sound of surf, either the crash of incoming waves, or the whisper of those heading out.

My heart cramped.

Give the man time to work, Kate.

"The water's quiet tonight," said Peggy.

"Yeah," I managed. Not much in the way of a conversation starter.

Peggy cleared her throat.

"So, I guess you're wondering why I called you here tonight," she said brightly.

Honestly, Kate; be human. The woman has something she wants to tell you.

"Sorry; I'm a little abstracted. Why *did* you bring me together, Jersey?"

"I'm glad you asked. I want you to be the third to know—I'm first and Felsic's second—that I handed in my resignation at Arbitrary and Cruel, effective the end of this Season."

I blinked. Inside my head, the land tootled a little tune on what sounded like a kazoo.

"You're—that's great, Peg! Better offer somewhere else?"

It came to me that I was having to think about too many things that I didn't want to think about. The continued absence of Borgan, the stagnation of the sea, the end of Archers Beach as a resort community, Peggy leaving at the end of the Season.

"You could say it's a better offer. I do. I'm going to stay in Archers Beach."

I stared at her, torn between relief and disbelief.

"Are you sure?" I blurted, which wasn't probably the best thing to say under the circumstances. Happily, Peggy was used to me by now.

"I'm sure, Felsic's sure, and if you're not, you'll get there. I believe in you."

"You haven't done a winter here. What're you gonna do when you get bored?"

"I don't expect to get bored." She took a swig from her bottle.

Another thought occurred to me.

"I'm not sure the studio's fit for winter living. Might have to put up with work being done around you." I drank some ale. "Since you're not going to be on the big city expense account, we'll readjust the rent..."

"Archer, are you saying you'd let me keep the studio?"

"Why not? You're a good neighbor."

Silence. I could see her fine in the light from inside, and for a second, it looked like she was going to cry.

"That's great of you, Kate. I was thinking, though, that with two of us, the studio's a little snug. We put a down payment on a condo at the Sand Dollar."

That made sense; Felsic's service was the marsh right behind the Dollar.

"Sounds like win-win. Perfect for you and Felsic—and I don't have to deal with the contractors."

She laughed.

I smiled, for lack of having a laugh in me, and leaned forward to touch her hand.

"I'm happy for you, and for Felsic. Congratulations," I said, meaning it.

"Thanks," she said, sounding more serious than Peggy usually sounded. "I'm scared out of my wits, y'know? But—it feels right. Righter'n... anything in my life, ever. So, I'm going with it. Felsic... makes me happy. I make her happy. She says. It's crazy; we only met—what? A month ago? I never—I've always been responsible. All business. But the thought of walking away from Felsic, from this place—makes me want to curl up into a ball and die."

The land had branched out from the kazoo into a complex orchestration, which I had no trouble interpreting as joy and pleasure. It was, unilaterally, happy for Felsic—the land liked Felsic a lot—it was happy for Peggy, it was happy for me...

Cael appeared in the doorway.

"Felsic sends that the second round is beginning. She wonders if Peggy prefers to sit and watch."

"*Hell* I'll sit and watch!" Peggy said, pushing away from the rail.

Cael stepped back to let her through, then stepped forward again. "Kate?"

I straightened, and gave him a smile.

"Sure, I'll play. Why not?"

"Harpy!" yelled Moss. "I need help!"

"How much help?" Peggy asked.

Moss frowned at his card. He fought at a Level Four; the Harpy was a Level Twelve.

"Eight points."

"I can help you out," said Nancy.

Moss looked at her suspiciously. "For what?"

"For all the treasure."

"What? No, I ain't givin' you all the treasure! I'll give you..." Moss paused, staring at his fan of cards. "I'll give you the first treasure," he said decisively.

Nancy shrugged, and casually rearranged the cards in her hand.

"I'll help," Peggy said, smiling brightly at Moss over her cards. "For the first and second treasures."

Moss eyed her, looked back at his cards, and gave a decisive nod. "Done!"

Peggy fought at Level Eight—I was starting to think that Peggy had not only played Munchkin before, but she'd paid off her college tuition by placing genteel little side bets on the outcome. However, Level Eight and Level Four only equaled the monster's strength. In order to kill it, and get into the room to steal whatever treasure it was guarding, Moss and Peggy had to be one point stronger.

"And," she said, "I have this!" She tossed a card faceup on the table.

I craned to see it—

"Cotion of Ponfusion?" Moss read. "Three points! We're over the top!"

Vornflee made a rude noise, while Moss reached out to the second deck to discover what kind of treasure the Hydra had been protecting—

The French doors, which we'd left ajar in case there should ever be a breeze again, banged wide open. I smelled peaches and butterscotch, eelgrass and brine...

I threw my cards down and jumped out of my chair. Cael was already between me and the doors, Oscar at his knee.

"What?" Peggy started to get up; I waved her back, not exactly surprised to find Felsic standing at my left shoulder.

"Stay right there," I murmured, and strolled forward. "Cael, this lady is known to me; please stand away."

He did so, reluctantly. Felsic kept to my side until we actually reached the threshold, which she let me cross alone.

Naked and disheveled, Nerazi stood in the center of the summer parlor. I could see her face clearly with land-sharpened sight, saw lines carven in her forehead and around her mouth, and tears on her round cheeks. Her braid had come loose and her hair floated away from her head, though the air was entirely still.

Nerazi was not entirely still, however.

Nerazi was shaking.

"Cael, bring me a blanket!" I called.

He was beside me almost before I'd spoken, shaking out the cat's blanket. I took it from him and stepped forward to drape it around Nerazi's shoulders, while the land whined inside my head.

I understood the land's distress. Nerazi was the third person I'd met in the Changing Land; she'd helped Gran nurse me back from being elfshot and almost dead. In all the time since, I've seen her at a standstill exactly twice.

And I'd *never* seen her afraid.

Water.

Familiar water, nourishing water; water that knew her, that welcomed her and buoyed her.

She lay back, gasping, and allowed the waters to cradle her until she felt able to look about.

A curtain of sea grass was hung against a rough wall, softening the stone; a couch piled high with pillows awaited her.

She was back—she had returned to the goblins' abode, achingly empty of their presence, yet as much of a home to her as any other waters in this sea.

Once more, she rested, and took stock.

She had lost power to the scouring winds, though not as much as she had feared, and for the moment, she was safe here. For the moment. She dared not suppose that the Borgan would miss her presence in his waters, and this time she must not err.

She must seek him out, immediately, and tell him what had occurred. Certainly, the author of the geas that had removed her from these waters would be able to ascertain the truth of her account for himself.

Truly, she should go to him at once. Her mind knew that, but her pride balked, not wishing him to see her distraught, with the remains of her fear still lodged in her belly, and her power in disarray.

But would not such a state of disarray add verisimilitude to her tale? Would her fear not excite tender concern? It was to her benefit to show herself thusly, for her intention regarding him had not wavered.

Therefore, she left the goblins' humble residence, and entered the larger sea...

To find that the waters were... wrong. Dull. The sweetness lingered, but as an undernote, and the sluggish currents carried a soft keening. She shivered in the sluggard current, grief coating her like oil.

Emptiness ate into her, an emptiness so heavy she thought that her heart would burst under the weight of it. Lethargy gnawed at her soul; she wanted merely to lie among the waters, unmoving, until the pain had hollowed her and she felt nothing at all.

It was terrible, this change in the sweet and joyous sea.

And infinitely more terrible was the knowledge that she had done this.

That part of her soul which she had ceded to the goblins' essence... rejoiced. For surely, *surely* now the Borgan would die, and terribly—for the sea had always loved them best.

But the Borgan... was not dead yet.

She felt him on the sluggish current, recruited her will, and moved through the waters to his side.

CHAPTER THIRTY-SEVEN

Friday, July 28

I put my arm around Nerazi's shoulders, and leaned my head against hers.

"Tell me," I whispered.

She drew a shaking breath.

"I couldn't hold him."

The stars rocked in the sky; a flaming sword sank into my belly. I ground my teeth until the land flowed, soft and green and healing; and melted the scream out of my throat. There could only be one *he* in this. Nerazi was strong, and frequently, as I gathered, covered Borgan's back. If she hadn't been able to hold him...

"He's dead?" I wasn't certain who'd said that, but it was a good question.

"He's with the sea..." Her voice faded out.

"With the sea. All this time, he's been...merged?"

All this time, merged with the sea, and the sea had only gotten...worse?

"No...Your pardon, Princess, I ought tell the tale in order."

I felt her shivering; I felt her guilt and the dull burn of pain. I looked closer, and saw the wound along her soul, raw and oozing. I didn't know what could make such a wound, but I did know what to do about it.

I made the request, and let the land's healing flow from me to Nerazi.

She sighed, and her shivering eased slightly.

"My thanks."

She stirred. I let her shoulders go, and stepped back. The others were crowding the French doors, watching and listening. Peggy stood with Felsic, one step onto the deck; they were holding hands.

"The last thing I had, from Borgan himself," I said, "was that he was headed for Martha's Vineyard, to free a beached whale. There was somebody he wanted to talk to—"

"Turtle," Nerazi murmured. "He wished to ask Old Man Turtle's advice. It was several days, to find Turtle, and when he was found, his advice was...not to Borgan's liking. He wished to avoid a full merging, deeming it not in the sea's best service. That has long been his philosophy and surprises none of us who have known him. When he left Turtle, he traveled to certain...places of power, and attempted..."

Nerazi turned her gaze on the others of her avid audience, then looked back to me, her eyes flaring red.

"He attempted, let us say, various technical adjustments, hoping that an infusion of old waters might divert the larger sea from her loss. In this, he was...partially correct." Nerazi paused.

"But he wasn't correct enough," I said when it seemed like she wasn't going to speak again. "Nerazi, forgive my lapse. Do you require anything? May I offer refreshment?"

"You have already given much, and richly. Only allow me to recruit myself. It was a cunning thrust..."

"Who hurt you?" I asked.

She shook her head.

"In order. Now that my feet have found the path, allow me to say it out in order."

I nodded, and after a moment's further rest, she took up the tale.

"It was as you say, his strategy produced a slight improvement, when what was needed was a dramatic recovery. Understanding that more was required, he returned to Saco Bay, and called upon me to be his lifeline, while he opened himself and merged with the sea." She moved a hand in a gesture that may have meant something to her, but meant nothing to me.

"This was, you understand, Turtle's advice, saving only that Turtle advised a true and complete merging. Such a merging may endure"—a flash of red-lit eyes toward Peggy—"quite a number of years. Borgan accepted that he and the sea must fully merge; her grief was such that there was no other way for him to show her what her pain cost those who are at her mercy, and to alter her course toward reason."

A breath, and Nerazi pulled the blanket close around her shoulders.

"I agreed to be his anchor, and we repaired to...to a place of particular benevolence. The waters there were touched with the sea's grief, though more lightly than elsewhere. I wrapped Borgan in my care; he opened himself to the sea's influence..."

She took a hard breath, and I saw the tears start again.

"She snatched at him, the place we were...the water boiled with her frenzy. I held, she increased her pull upon him. I clasped him tighter..."

"And she struck me, Kate," Nerazi whispered. "Full across the soul. The sea, my mother and my sister...she struck me...and I lost him."

"When?" I heard myself ask. "When did this happen, Nerazi? Just now?"

She shook her head.

"The blow was...it stunned me, and I was parted from my senses for what I believe to be three days."

Three days merged with a desperate and violent sea, with nothing to hold him to...to...the land.

I raised my hand and touched the bead in my braid.

Nerazi drew a sharp breath.

"Tell me," I said again.

"I know only that he said he had cached some small bit of his power...elsewhere. That was everything he said."

And if he had cached a small bit of his power...elsewhere, that meant he could not be fully merged with the sea.

Which, in turn, meant that, maybe, he could be released.

Hope hurt a lot more than despair. I caught my breath on something that sounded horribly like a sob.

"I'll go to him," I said, watching Nerazi's face. "Should I leave—"

"Take it," she interrupted. "It is better to have options, and it is nearly invisible to my eye, and she is all but blind with grief."

I nodded. "I'll need directions."

"Kate!" Cael stepped forward, flanked by Oscar and Breccia.

"You have duties and folk to care for. Will you go into danger, unprotected, with neither plan nor shield?"

I looked at him.

"You're right. I do need to make sure that attention to my duties does not lapse, and that the folk under my care suffer no lack of care."

I offered my proposition to the land, which agreed, reluctantly, but without reservation.

"Felsic," I said.

"Kate?" She sounded startled—who could blame her?—but she stepped up and put her hand on my shoulder. "What's to do?"

"You've been listening close to all of this, and you know the stakes. The *trenvay* and the land need the sea. If we don't somehow fix this mess, and soon, we'll suffer along with the seafolk. Like I just said—and Nerazi agrees that it's the only way, or she wouldn't be shy about telling me stand back... Like I said, I'm going there, under the sea, to try to pull this out."

I grinned, feeling suddenly...buoyant. Centered.

"You know and I know," I said to Felsic, "that it's not impossible that I'll be dead in the next couple hours. Cael's right; I can't leave the Beach without a Guardian. Not now. Not with everything that's going on.

"So...I'm asking you to stand as my heir. If I die, you step into my job and keep everything from going to hell. The land agrees, and will accept you as Guardian." I took a breath, holding her eyes with mine. "Do you agree?"

Her eyes widened, bright and fearful, and I braced myself for a refusal.

She nodded.

The land played a quick *cha-cha-cha!* inside my head. I smiled at Felsic.

"One more formality," I said. "Bear with me."

I didn't know how to do this, not really. But I'd once seen Grandfather Aeronymous transfer a tithe of his power to a new-made paladin of the House. Not precisely the kind of thing we did here in the Changing Land, but it would have to do.

I leaned forward and kissed Felsic on the lips. A flicker of green fire passed from me to her.

She sighed, and I did. We stepped apart.

I looked to Nerazi.

"Kate," Cael said again. "Have me by you."

"Of course," I said. "I trust you to be my anchor."

Relief passed over his face, and he bowed.

"Kate." That was Peggy. I turned to face her.

"Sorry, Jersey." Meaning that even a Sighted person shouldn't have had to witness all that had just passed.

Peggy waved a hand.

"Sorry for what? You do what you've gotta do. But if you die doing it, Archer, I will personally kill you. Got it?"

She surprised a laugh out of me.

"Got it." I looked around at the rest of them, and said, "I solemnly swear that I will do my very best to get back here alive." The land gave the sentence a little jolt of truth, and I saw grim faces relax, a little.

Good.

I extended my hands, one to Nerazi and one to Cael; felt each grip me in turn. I thought about Nerazi's rock, fixed the location in my mind, and took one step forward.

. . .

The night sky stretched overhead, a glorious blanket of stars unreflected in the dark waters of the sea.

Still holding hands, the three of us walked to the water's edge. I paused there, allowing the sea king's power to rise into me.

When I was ready, I murmured, "Cael," and felt his serviceable *jikinap* rope tighten around my waist.

"My lady," he murmured, and loosed my hand.

I looked to Nerazi.

"Directions?" I suggested.

"Yes," she said. I shuddered as the information struck and was absorbed by my *jikinap*.

"Be careful, Kate," Nerazi said, and she, too, loosed my hand.

I closed my eyes, called Nerazi's directions to the front of my mind, took one step forward...

I heard a boom, like wave striking rock.

And the world disappeared.

～⁂～

She entered waters heavy with age, power silking the ponderous current. Such waters might contain the wisdom of the ancestors. Once, such waters might have healed the most desperate of spirits.

But no longer. Anger tainted the waters; roiled the silken currents. It was not so grief-struck nor as angry as the waters near the goblins' residence. Not yet.

Not yet.

Though—she feared it—soon.

Within those wise and angry waters, there the Borgan lay, his will breached, and his power bleeding away. He was beautiful in his doom; clad in white leather, and his braid coiled on his breast, like a funeral wreathe, the little charms and amulets sparkling with their small stores of power.

She came to his side, and gazed down upon his face. There was some sign of struggle written there—drawn brows, and a deep frown. He fought the sea's dominion, even as the sea strove to absorb him into herself. She could see—so clearly in these admirable waters!—she could see his soul beset, and the ocean battering at the walls of his integrity. He was fighting, the Borgan; fighting the force of his sea's desperate grief and love.

Fighting.

And losing.

Ah, now, the question came.

What ought she to do, with the god of this sea imperiled?

She stroked his face, and felt her heart swell. The two of them . . . perhaps they might win the battle the Borgan had joined, and bring the sea back to its former sweet balance.

However, that plan . . . had always been complex—a compromise made from respect of the sea's immense tenderness for the Borgan.

The sea's love was not so tender, now. And its need, with the goblins lost to her, was very much greater.

She kissed the frowning lips, considering the options open to her. Best, she had always thought, to maintain a single focus for the powers of a sea. Best, perhaps and after all, to return to her original plan.

The geas . . . was broken; the author of the geas under siege. She need fear no sudden importunate returns to Cheobaug.

She need only allow the sea to have its way with the Borgan. When that process was complete—*then* would she float forward and propose herself.

Or, she might consume him now, and declare herself immediately. She was strong, he was weak—and growing weaker. Soon, there would be no more possibility of his resisting her as there was of his ultimately resisting the sea.

To consume him, and mix his power, with all its knowledge of this sea, with her own—that was tempting. He would be, she thought, a feast, and she would savor him as he deserved.

But, no, she decided reluctantly.

No. She dared not risk that course, given what had gone before. She would allow the sea its melding; the feast properly belonged to the waters.

However, as she was present at the table, there was no need to deny herself a taste.

She touched the coiled braid, tenderly straightening it, and ran her hand down the length, slowly, sensuously. The Borgan, caught in the sea's enchantment, moaned softly, stern lips softening in pleasure. In that tiny moment of distraction, she saw a bit of his will break off from the citadel around his soul, and drift off into the waters.

She smiled, and caught the braid again. This time, she ran her hand down its length hard and fast, stripping away all the little charms.

A cry, this time, as he felt the loss even in the depths of his struggle—and another bit of his will floated away.

She surveyed the captured bounty in her palm. He had stored more among the little charms than she had expected, ceding her, if not a feast, then a very satisfying dinner, indeed.

Lips pursed in anticipation, she lifted up one of the captured charms—and absorbed the flow of its power.

I slid into the water like it was a silk robe. It was remarkably clear water, not the murk I'd had to deal with when I went in beyond the breakers, days ago. The general feeling was of age, and peace, and power. You could lie down in these waters a monster of depravity, and rise up as pure as a newborn star.

And there, scarcely an arm's length away, was Borgan, his white leathers gleaming, his braid floating free—and unadorned.

"If you arrive to unbind him," a sweet, high voice said, "you arrive too late."

Apparently, the waters here weren't as clear as I'd initially thought. I had to bring real effort to bear, to see the woman at

Borgan's side; her long black hair moving lazily in the ancient current; her slim figure wrapped in the simplest and softest of creamy robes.

She smiled at me, and it was as if I had looked directly into the eyes of the sun.

I averted my gaze, so as not to be blinded, but before I did, I saw her raise something to her lips, like a piece of candy, and saw the tiny flash of power consumed.

"I thought you'd be home in Cheobaug by now," I said, bringing my best attention to Borgan's situation.

"There is a disturbance; the Wind Between the Worlds has become unbalanced. The geas broke inside the storm, my will was insufficient to bring me to Cheobaug—and thus I return here. It is fortunate, is it not?"

I raised my eyes in time to see her consume another bit of candy.

"Fortunate, how?" I asked. "Unless you're going to help me get Borgan out of this."

This was a complex series of bindings. Picture a kracken holding Borgan in its mighty tentacles, applying slow, even pressure. Eventually, Borgan would open; his power, his will and his soul would flow out and he would become one with the sea.

At the moment, his soul was still bright, his defenses battered, but holding. The price of that . . . was his power, which was bleeding out into the ancient waters at an alarming rate. I wasn't sure what the reasoning was, there, unless there was a threshold of diminishing returns involved. If that was the case, how much power did he have to lose before he went below the sea's radar?

Best not to wait around to find that out.

"You come on a useless errand," the woman from Cheobaug told me. I looked up at her. She was still eating candy. "The sea will prevail. He will be one with her, and I shall be goddess in his stead."

"This is the Changing Land. We don't have much truck with goddesses here. Also . . . if what you did to the *ronstibles* is an example of your work, I think we're better off going with the incumbent. Now, if you'll excuse me, I need to concentrate."

The Borgan's power, which had been stored in the small amulets, was sweet, and unexpectedly potent. Strange passions ran in her veins, altering the flow of her blood, mingling with the power she had absorbed from the treacherous waters wherein he had imprisoned her. Strange passions, indeed, and, even stranger, a sense of restraint.

Her intention had been to embrace the interloper who strove to free the Borgan from his fate; she was rich in power—surprisingly old power, or so it seemed to her questing senses. Such would be useful to her...

But, her hand was stayed, her will diverted, her intention floating away on a current she did not fully understand.

The interloper was the Borgan's lover—so much she knew from his power that she had eaten. There was no need to harm the Borgan's lover; after all, she would soon know grief enough.

It was a young creature, the Borgan's mistress, strong in power; her soul fierce and brilliant in these kindly waters.

She had entered her task with a will, snapping the sea's bindings, seeming to care not for the increased loss of the Borgan's power. Perhaps she did not see it, flowing away upon the waters. Perhaps she did not know that he might die, if he lost too much. The Borgan was old, and his power was his life-force.

Also, the determined young mistress did not seem to notice that these deep and placid waters were beginning to warm, and, somewhat, to roil. Anger was rising in the currents—and yet she worked on, oblivious to her danger.

Well, there was no reason for her to remain, to take the brunt of the sea's anger. She might easily return to the goblins' house and wait inside the deep grotto until the currents brought her news of the Borgan's consumption.

Retreat, indeed, was the course of wisdom. Despite which, she remained, watching the young lover work, feeling the sea's anger rise and the bitter taste of guilt upon her tongue.

The sea was getting mad. Check that. The sea was *getting madder.*

I tried to ignore the unsettled sensation in the waters and the bubbles boiling up from the deep, and kept chopping away at the kracken's tentacles.

Each tentacle I broke meant more of Borgan's energy left him. I tried to ignore that, too. There was only one connection that I had to be sure not to break—the brilliant blue rope that bound Borgan's soul to the sea.

It wasn't easy work; the tentacles were tough; they resisted the bite of my will, and, if I didn't strike hard enough for a clean cut—they grew together again, tougher than ever.

Around me the water was heating fast; it was getting downright choppy. I narrowed my concentration and plied my will like shears, the same technique I'd used to free Aleun and Tioli from their bindings.

"The sea is becoming angry," the woman from Cheobaug said.

"At this point, I've got no sympathy for the sea."

"If she grows angry enough, the sea will kill you. You are nothing to her, but an inconvenience and an irritant. Allow me..." She stopped.

I spared her a half glance. Three more biggish bindings to go. She—the woman from Cheobaug—was frozen in place, staring at Borgan's face, her fingers pressed to her lips.

"I will create a diversion," she said slowly, as if she wasn't quite sure what the words meant.

"I'd appreciate it," I said softly, suddenly understanding what was going on.

She'd taken some of Borgan's power—*taken* it, like I'd taken Prince Aesgyr's power, though it had been too much and too hot for me. Unless I missed my guess, the lady from Cheobaug was finding herself suddenly very concerned with caring for the sea, calming the grieving waters.

...and giving Borgan a chance to get gone.

Well, she wasn't my problem. My problem was chopping the last three of the kracken's tentacles and getting the hell out of here.

I managed one, though it took two strikes—couldn't handle too many more of those; my power was blunting, like I was using physical shears, and I had no idea how to sharpen it, except to bring more of my will to bear.

The next time I had leisure to look up, with one tentacle left to break, the woman from Cheobaug was gone.

It was true that not even a goddess may hide from a sea, and she did not wish to hide. Still, she chose her place carefully: the goblins' abode, which had been theirs since the sea had spawned them. There, supported by waters still bearing something of their taint, she rested for a moment.

She had brought this trouble into the sea—she knew that. And having brought trouble to the sea, it fell to her to bring relief. She was a goddess; it was hers to heal, to comfort, and to bring order out of chaos.

There among the waters, she smiled. The Borgan was a subtle man. Perhaps she *could* have loved him, if...

No, let it be, for this moment, perhaps the last of her own existence— Let it be that she *did* love him, that she had loved him for all of her life, and that the influence of his power was no more than that which she herself had always desired.

She opened herself to the waters.

I offer myself willingly, to serve the sea and mingle with the waters. I bring myself, who loves you and wishes nothing else but to serve you as a child serves her mother. I bring also those whom I have in my ignorance consumed. They can be yours again, through me, and our love will never fail you...

Anger rocked her, and a grief so terrible it might never be assuaged. She felt the goblins move in her soul, as the waters washed through her...

And unraveled her.

CHAPTER THIRTY-EIGHT

Saturday, July 29
High Tide 2:17 A.M. EDT
Sunrise 5:27 A.M.

The last tentacle parted just as the sea went crazy.

Water crashed and boomed, the calm and ancient pool was calm no longer. I felt a tugging, growing quickly stronger, as if the sea was pulling back into a tidal wave, which would come crashing down to flatten Archers Beach, and everything and everyone in it...

I felt Cael's rope of *jikinap* tighten around my waist, threw my arms around Borgan and held on for all I was worth.

We landed soft in dry sand.

I rolled to my feet, spinning. The land ran a tickertape parade through my head, while I craned out to sea...

Tide was in; Nerazi's Rock was half-drowned in sea water. If there was a tsunami building, it wasn't going about it in the usual way.

"Are you well, my lady?" Cael was at my shoulder. "There were strange motions upon the waters, and I felt it best to bring you away."

"You did good. Where'd Nerazi go?"

"Into the waters. She would have it so." There was a small pause before Cael said, softly. "And your leman?"

I felt him on the land, before I turned back to the edge of the dune where we had landed. I *felt him*, but not much of him.

Not nearly *enough* of him.

"Oh, God."

I dropped to my knees beside Borgan.

His feet were bare; his leathers were gone, replaced by a soaked and sand-coated black T-shirt and a well-worn pair of jeans.

His eyes were closed, and God, God, he was so light.

"My lady?"

"He was bleeding power, and the lady from Cheobaug..." I reached out to wrap my fingers around his braid. Not one bead or shell remained...

"The lady from Cheobaug stole his cached power... to her undoing."

And possibly to his.

I put my hand on his chest, feeling his heartbeat—slow, and his skin so cold. The land again gave me his measure, worriedly. How much power had he lost?

How much power *could* he lose and still survive?

"Cael," I said, my voice sounded creaky, as if the ocean had rusted my vocal cords. I cleared my throat and tried again, my eyes on Borgan's face. His eyes were closed, his breathing shallow.

"Cael—how do I share power?"

A charged moment of silence; I'd shocked Cael, who sank slowly to his knees beside me.

I looked at him.

"Tell me."

He bent his head.

"My lady, you only call up your power, and you—give it to whomever you would. If—if he is a true leman, and holds you in his heart, he will return the gift to the balance, powers mingled to... produce a new power between you.

"To share power demonstrates a very great trust. In the village, there was a ritual, and everyone gathered to witness—and after, a feast, with dancing and games. I have heard it said that, among lords, such sharing is done in private, for reasons of state."

"Right."

I breathed in, and called my *jikinap*.

It blazed up my spine, just like old times, and only slightly tempered by the power of House Aeronymous. Pleasure flared with it, like I was greeting an old friend after a long absence—and I remembered Cael's delight in finding that his spear was still available to him, only stored in a different trunk.

I whispered to my power, and it subsided, awaiting my command. I leaned close to Borgan, my lips against his ear.

"Borgan," I whispered, and reached to the land for a quick jolt of healing power.

He stirred beneath my hand. I drew back very slightly, and saw that his eyes were open.

"Kate." His voice was a ragged whisper. He moved his left arm, awkwardly, as if it weighed too much for his strength. When he got his hand up, he wrapped his fingers around my braid, and smiled. A smile so faint, I only saw it because I knew his face so well.

"Love you, Kate," he whispered. "Should've said before now."

I leaned forward, my palm pressing flat on his chest, right over his heart.

"Love you, too, Borgan," I murmured, and kissed him, softly.

I retreated just a little, then, looking directly into his eyes, tapped the power burning along my spine, and said, "I freely give you everything that is mine."

My center rocked, the smell of scorched butterscotch filled my nose. I saw Borgan's eyes widen in the instant that I knew I was empty.

My heart stopped—

And jolted back into action.

Jikinap flowed to me, warm and tasting of salted butterscotch. It was undoubtedly my own *jikinap*, yet it was different—enriched. Smoother, you might say, and infused with what might be humor.

I sighed in what I understood to be perfect contentment, and realized I was lying across Borgan's chest, and his hand was pressing me against him.

Somewhere near at hand, someone cleared his throat.

"Witnessed, lady and lord," Cael said, solemnly. "May great joy and long happiness proceed from this sharing."

"Daughter, will you open your eyes, and tell me your name?"

A seal lay in the water beside her. She knew the voice, knew the taste of that particular power, and knew that this was no simple seal.

"Nerazi?"

"Exactly so. I am pleased that you recall me. You are...?"

"I am...changed," she said, and was not surprised to find it so.

"Indeed, you could hardly be other than changed. But I wonder *who* you are."

"I am...the *lahleri*," she said then, as the knowledge flowed into her. "Matsu, I was, and Korkilig, and Rinzirka. I am all, yet none. The sea has rewoven all of my strands." She paused to consider the knowledge within her, and looked again to the seal.

"Perhaps I misspoke. Perhaps I am not *changed*, but made new."

"That is possible. What will you do?"

"I must...learn my place, and so enrich the sea, that I love and wish only to serve."

"It is well," the seal who was Nerazi told her. "I leave you now to learn your place. When you are sure of that, come to see me. We have much to talk about."

"Yes," she said, and closed her eyes again, as the sea flowed through her soul.

⁓⊱⊰⁓

I'd fallen asleep across Borgan's chest; I woke with the sun in my eyes, and a rumbling boom in my ears. Borgan stirred beneath me.

"Listen," he said.

The waves, the sound of the surf, striking the beach with energy and purpose, and the rattle of beach stones, as the water withdrew.

I let go a breath I didn't know I'd been holding.

"What happened?" I asked.

"Well, that's what I'm going to need to find out, though I've got some guesses, you understand."

"The woman from Cheobaug. She was going to create a diversion."

"Looks like she did that just fine, then." He stirred again. "Help me up, Kate."

I froze, knowing his intent, as if it was my own...

...and exactly as if it were my own intention, knew there was no way I could talk him out of it. Battered as he had been, he was yet the sea's chosen Guardian, and duty to the sea trumped... everything.

I sighed and came to my knees, surprised to find hands under my arms, helping *me* to rise.

"Cael?"

"Yes."

"You didn't have to stay."

"I wanted to stay, my lady. Are you able to stand?"

I tested the proposition and found it sound.

"Perfectly steady."

"Good. Sir?"

He leaned forward and offered Borgan his hand.

I took the opportunity to commune a bit with the land, which was beyond happy to see me, and downright delighted with the sharing. There was something a little different in our bond, but I couldn't get enough space between us to study it. Well, tomorrow, everybody'd be calmer.

I asked again, worried, and got the measure of Borgan's weight upon the land—and chewed my lip in worry.

He weighed more than he had when I'd brought him out of the ocean.

That was the good news.

But if he weighed half as much as he had when I'd first met him...

"But now I'm bearing something else," Borgan said from beside me. He took my hand and smiled down at me. "Something special."

"Flatterer."

"Only for you," he said, and that...sounded serious. Even, the land told me, true. I looked up into his face. The smile this time was more apparent, and only slightly whimsical.

"Walk you home?"

"Cael—"

I looked around.

"He went on ahead. Said you'd be hungry, after all that, and he'd better be scrambling up some eggs."

I laughed.

"Sure. Walk me home."

We walked down the beach, splashing through the retreating breakers.

"No jellies," I said, pointing at the waves.

"I'd gotten that much fixed before it swam backward," he said, sounding rueful. "Gonna get the rest of it patched up soon's I can. It'll still be a couple days, week maybe, to get everything back to normal."

Because he was, of course, going back into the water.

Right now, in fact.

We stood at the water line, holding hands, our backs to Dube Street, and Tupelo House. We weren't saying anything, but not because there wasn't anything more to talk about.

"When were you going to tell me that the bead was a power cache?" I asked him.

He sighed.

"I'd been planning on telling you everything, Kate, but the timing ran bad, and you weren't trusting anything like sharing, so ... I held off. And then, when it had to be now, I couldn't figure how to explain what I was doing without making it seem like I was getting in over my head."

"Which you were," I'd pointed out.

"Well," he wasn't exactly ready to concede the point. "Kinda comes with the surf."

"So, it was dangerous, but not above your pay grade. Got it."

He laughed. "Skin me later?"

"I'll mark it on the calendar."

"Well ..." he said, and moved one step further into the water.

"Wait," I said. "One more thing, before you go."

"Sure."

"Borgan ..." My voice died from sheer cowardice, leaving me looking up into his face.

He raised a hand and touched my chin. "Not breaking up with me, are you?"

I choked.

"Not yet," I managed, and took a breath. "I just wonder ... if we *had* ... shared power *before* ... would you have gotten in over your head?"

He frowned slightly, moved his hand and fingered the bead in my braid.

"No way of telling what *would've* happened; what we have to deal with is what *did* happen. Which is why I'm going back to her, now. It's mine, to make peace, and weave together all the raveled bits, into something that's whole again, and strong. I know you're thinking it's not the smartest thing I could do, having lately been unraveling, myself, and I'm not saying you're wrong. But there's nothing else to do." He tipped his head and gave me a slow grin.

"See, this is hard on you, 'cause you'd never do anything like it."

I laughed.

"Okay; point taken."

"That's right. In the meantime, the sooner I start this, the quicker I'll be done." He ran his hand down my braid, and we both shivered in pleasure.

"You need me, Kate, you call me. All right? Anything at all. I'll come."

I nodded. "All right."

He squeezed my hand, and then let go.

I stood and watched him wade out into the surf—until I didn't see him at all.

CHAPTER THIRTY-NINE

Friday, August 4
High Tide 7:13 P.M. EDT
Moonset 12:02 A.M.

The crowd was light for early August; on the other hand, it was good to have a crowd at all.

I slowed the carousel and rang the bell to signal the end of the ride, then turned to the first in line by the gate.

"Two tickets, please," I said to the gray-haired woman.

"Cheap at half the price," she answered, putting the tickets into my hand.

I grinned. "Be just a sec 'til they clear the field."

"No problem at all," she assured me. "I'm feeling lucky; I practically have the place to myself. I figured there wouldn't be room to move, this late in the summer. I'm glad I took a chance."

"We're glad you did, too," I told her, sincerely.

Once the tides stopped bringing in more, the beach cleaners started making real progress with getting the weeds and the dead fish off the beach. Seaweed and dead fish being prime organic matter, it all got hauled up to Public Works, where, word came down, it was starting in to producing next year's compost.

Once the beach was clean, and the waves returned to duty, the tourists—those who hadn't canceled on hearsay—stayed.

So—bad as it had been, it could've been worse, and if we could stay open for the Extended Season, the carnies might even have enough money to live comfortably through the winter.

The jury was still out on that, though. The town's finance officer had liked the Chamber's proposal and given the green light for a presentation to the town council. The council was still deliberating, though. Dan Poirier's office let out that they were confident, but most of the folks I'd talked to agreed that they were bound to say so, adding that the council was known for dragging its feet.

The Human Resources Department, in stark contrast, had moved at the speed of light, and Cael Wolfe was the town's newest Animal Control Officer, pending completion of training, which he was slated to start next week.

I rang the bell and turned to take tickets from the folks in line.

"Hey," yelled a red-haired boy as he mounted the deck. "I want to ride the horse that has *wings!*"

The whistle blew on the stroke of midnight, and the park was clear not many minutes later.

I pulled the gate closed behind me and slid the lock home, noting the weight of someone on the land almost directly behind me.

"Felsic," I said, easily.

"Kate," she answered. "Got a minute?"

"Sure, what's up?"

"This is."

She handed me a manila envelope.

A chill swept me, and I looked at her closely, the land enhancing my sight.

"Open it," she said, and the strain in her voice matched the strain in her face.

I opened it, handling the papers carefully—Social Security card, drivers license, birth certificate, all made out in the name of Frances Eleanor Sicot. I slipped the papers back into the envelope and handed it back to Felsic.

"Congratulations. I think."

"That's said well. But—why this—why *now*? If making me Guardian-next is the cause, I don't want either. Well," she said, with slightly less heat, "I didn't want Guardian-next before this come in."

I could see her point.

"I don't know what triggers something coming in," I confessed. "But, if we build on the theory you spun Cael, about those who have *wide service* win an envelope, then my guess is one of three things rang this in, now.

"One, the Guardian's heir thing—for which I apologize, but—"

"But, you were short on time, an' I would do, with the land liking me, like it does." She sighed and pushed her hat back on her head. "What's two?"

"Your relationship with Peggy," I said promptly.

I felt the shock of that hit her. She stood frozen for a couple of heartbeats before nodding brusquely.

"And three?"

"You were ready. The land trusts you, the land, as you say, likes you, and you're bloody-minded enough to keep it in line."

"My service..."

"I'm thinking this is in the way of *in addition to*, rather than *instead of.*"

Another long moment of silence, followed by a sigh.

"What'm I gonna tell Peggy?"

"Well, I don't know what you've already told her, but in this instance, I'd suggest the truth. Peggy's tough; she can See—and hear—and she loves you." I hesitated, then added, "If she has any particular questions about the Enterprise, you can refer her to me, if you want."

"Might just do that."

She slipped the envelope down the front of her shirt, and sighed again. "Kate?"

"Yeah?"

"I'm glad you come home to us."

I gave a soft laugh.

"Yeah. Me, too."

I parted from Felsic at Fountain Circle, and walked over the sand to the water line. Neptune's was rocking tonight with two bands, one of which would, by audience acclaim, go on to become a contestant in the Epic Battle of the Bands! scheduled for Friday and Saturday nights. Guitars howled and singers did, too, drowning out the soft sound of the low-tide surf.

There were a goodly number of people on the beach, walking mostly, and talking quietly. Some moved along energetically; some strolled. All walked without fear of stepping on something nasty in the dark.

I stood on the wet sand, the toes of my sneakers on the tide line.

"Miss you," I whispered, and felt the breeze like fingers against my lips.

The waves lapped the sand, and retreated; drums rattled and guitars roared. A couple passed between me and the water, holding hands, and speaking in murmurs.

Nothing else happened.

Well, of course not. I didn't need him—not really.

I just...wanted him.

The land performed its version of sticking a wet nose in my ear and huffling. I half-laughed, and pushed it back, yanking on its ears. Then, the two of us turned and ambled up the beach, under the Pier, on the way to Dube Street.

There weren't many people on the north side of the Pier. To my right and up a block or two, I saw three teenage boys playing with a glow-in-the-dark Frisbee, and, 'way up-beach, what might be a family group walking in a loose gaggle. Between me and them, the beach was empty.

No, not quite empty.

Some blocks away—say, right at the Dube Street intersection, if Dube Street ran all the way down to the sea—stood a tall form, hands in pockets, facing down toward the Pier.

The land gave an excited shout, and pelted ahead.

I was too dignified to shout, but I did run. In fact, I ran so fast, I might possibly have become airborne in those last few moments.

Borgan caught me in mid flight. I wrapped my legs around his waist, caught his face between my hands and kissed him, thoroughly.

He cooperated with enthusiasm, which left us both pretty much breathless, and probably having scandalized the youth of America.

"Hey, there," he said, his voice shaking.

"Hey, there, yourself." My voice wasn't so much shaking as quivering in and out of incompatible ranges. "How are you?"

"You gotta ask that, maybe I should kiss you again."

"That sounds like a good idea. Can you stay?"

"I think I might manage—"

A noise like no noise I had ever heard—a noise that maybe a thousand harpies screaming in unison could have produced—split the sky and the peace of Archers Beach. I screamed in reflex and covered my ears, but that was worse than useless. Borgan slammed to his knees, his face pressed into my chest. I felt him trembling. The land howled, and a vision of the carousel swung crazily inside my head, *jikinap* boiling off of it in streamers of wet colors.

The ungodly racket stopped.

I wilted in Borgan's arms, my head on his shoulder.

"What d'you expect that was?" he asked.

"The carousel." I straightened, his arms tightened. "The Wise— oh, God; the Wise..."

I wrapped my arms around his shoulders.

"Hold tight," I whispered, and we were there, Borgan kneeling on the concrete floor, and the enclosure full of burning *jikinap* and the stink of too much power. I gagged; it was like trying to breathe toxic gas—and suddenly there was a breeze, fresh and damp, shredding the clouds of poison.

I extended my will, snapped open the lock on the gate and thrust the storm walls back.

Fire sparked around us; mustard-colored gas swirled, and through the shredding yellow fog came Mr. Ignat', Arbalyr the not-Phoenix on his shoulder and Gran at his side.

Borgan set me gently on my feet and rose.

"Katie!" Gran grabbed my shoulder. "Are you all right?"

"If we don't count terrified, I'm perfectly fine."

"What happened?"

"The carousel..." She and I turned toward it. I stepped into Side-Sight, but there was nothing to see. By which I mean... there was no spellcraft to see.

Which was wrong. I should at least be seeing the binding spells I'd made to hold the non-prisoners, but—the bindings were gone; the fake soul-glow was quenched.

"The Gate," Gran murmured.

I threw my will out in the way I'd been taught, and triggered the Gate.

Power struck, flared, and rebounded, knocking me off my feet, and back into Borgan. He caught me around the waist and held me gently against him.

"So, news of the latest transgression got to them early," I said.

"What about that war you an' the *lahleri* told me about, happening between the Worlds? That's all they have to know; they're sealing up all the holes they know about."

I wondered what the hell a *lahleri* was, but held to the point.

"Prince Aesgyr and his allies had a head start; to make more and better holes."

"Well reasoned, Pirate Kate," Mr. Ignat' murmured. "Aesgyr will have prepared egress points well ahead of mounting any attack."

The land whined, showing me shadows moving in the night; moving toward the carousel. I shifted and Borgan let me go, to turn and face the *trenvay* of Archers Beach, and a smattering, too, of those others, who heard the music at Midsummer Eve.

Felsic was there, her arm around Peggy's waist, Vornflee and Moss behind them. I saw Joan Anderson, and Daddy; Nancy... and the land reported more coming in, gathering outside the enclosure.

"Kate, what happened?" That was Felsic.

"The Wise have closed the World Gate," I said, willing the land to carry my voice to everyone gathered. "We're cut off from the other Five Worlds."

"We are," Gran cried, from the deck of the carousel itself, her voice carrying effortlessly to every corner of the crowd.

"We are free! We are no longer forced to be jailers! We are no longer subject to the whim of the Wise! It's been a long time coming, my friends, but we're free at last!"

The cheer that greeted this was almost as noisy as the closing of the Gate, and I leaned back into Borgan and sighed in sheer relief.

CHAPTER FORTY

**Tuesday, September 5
High Tide 9:42 P.M. EDT
Sunset 7:12 P.M.**

"Bus'll be here in fifteen minutes," I cautioned, leaning against the operator's station.

I crossed my arms over my chest, and watched Vassily jump to the decking and move between the animals, light-footed and respectful, his fingers trailing along carved haunches, patting this one on the nose, rubbing that one's ears.

"This," he said, his voice echoing off the storm walls, "this I will miss."

"Only for a little while. You're coming back next year, aren't you?"

"Samuil says I have done well, and that he will speak to the company, and tell them that I should have a contract for next year."

He vanished around the curve, and I sighed, realizing that I'd miss Vassily, too, and that winter was the longest season.

The remainder of the summer had passed pretty much without incident, and the Chamber was letting it be known that Archers Beach had just completed its best August in twenty years.

That was good, though it did make the lack of a Late Season this year more poignant. The town council had, after all, acted with expediency, and come through on the leaseback plan. Unfortunately, you can't just turn an amusement park around on a dime. Fun Country, New Jersey, had books to close, and other corporate paperwork to be completed. All of which meant the gates would stay locked until we opened the Super Early Season, last week in April, next year.

Then, though, there'd be no stopping us, especially not with Peggy Marr managing. The woman had already set up a war room in the spare bedroom of the condo she and Felsic had moved into, mid-August. I had a feeling we were all in for some changes.

"This one," Vassily said, draping his arm around the dainty neck of the batwing horse. "This one I like very much, though too short a time to know her. Next year, we will be good friends."

"Not a bad plan," I said, and shifted slightly against the box. "You ready?"

"No," he said, stepping off the deck to the concrete and bending to pick up his duffle bag. "I am not ready, but I will go, so that Samuil can say that I am, oh, so very good, and I will come again, next year."

"Keep that thought uppermost," I said, falling in beside him as he walked toward the door. "Be very good—or as good as you can be."

"I will do this—ah!"

He stopped and turned to face me, eyes bright, and face animated.

"Almost I am forgetting that I have a message for you, Kate Archer, from my angel. He asks that I say to you that there are many paths to his kingdom, and that you have not been forgotten." He smiled. "You see, Kate Archer? Even though you will not pray, the angels in heaven care for you."

Or, one particular non-angel in not-exactly heaven. But why quibble?

"I'm grateful to your angel. Please give him my best, the next time you talk with him."

"I will mention you in my prayers," Vassily agreed, and waited while I locked the gate.

The two of us ducked through the gap in the main gate, and walked across Fountain Circle, to the yellow school bus waiting there.

"Vassily," said the burly fellow waiting by the open door, "almost you are late!"

"Almost is not is," Vassily said with dignity, and turned to offer me his hand.

We shook. Vassily released my hand, and made a small, perfect bow.

"Good-bye until next Season, Kate Archer," he said softly. "Thanking you."

I waved until the bus made the turn at the top of the hill, onto Route 5. When it had passed off the land completely, I walked over the boardwalk to the beach, and turned south, toward Kinney Harbor.

There were a few folks on the beach, walking along the twilit water, and a guy tossing a flying ring for his dog. The dog was an impressive jumper.

Ordinarily, I'd be hearing the band tuning up at Neptune's, but tonight, the band was going to be at the municipal park, where the townies—*all* the townies, mundane and *trenvay* alike—were throwing ourselves a party.

Well, why not? We had a lot to celebrate: the rescue of Fun Country, the triumphant return from the plague of jellyfish, the rising of a new *trenvay*—the end of the Season, and the hope of a better Season, next year.

More than enough reason for a party, any of them. All together?

The town might not stop dancing 'til suppertime tomorrow.

Fun Country was behind me now, and a few minutes later I passed Googin Rock, black and bladed in the gloaming. Ahead was the foot of Heath Hill, with sea roses tangled all around it.

I rounded the foot of the hill and met Borgan coming off the dock.

"Sorry I'm late," he said, taking my hand with a smile. "I was down visiting Frenchy."

"How's she doing?"

"Pretty good," he said, as we turned back toward town. "Turns out that the fella from Away? The one put up all the fuss about the cats?"

"What about him?" I asked darkly.

"No, now, you'll like this. He's putting the summer house up for sale. Gonna look on the Vineyard, s'what Frenchy heard."

"Well." I considered that; decided I was pleased. "I hope there aren't any cats on Martha's Vineyard."

"Bound to be cats," Borgan said seriously. "They do a bit of fishing down there."

"Is there a Guardian?" I asked suddenly.

"Vineyard Guardian?" He frowned, as if considering. "Had been, but she's always been a little funny. Don't care for people, much. *Trenvay*, either. I could find out, if you want, I guess, Kate, but I doubt she's got a cell."

"I do want," I said, decisively. "In this day and age, there's no reason why the Guardians can't have their own listserve too, to keep in touch. Share tips."

"Recipes?" Borgan asked.

"Go ahead, laugh!" I said threateningly, and he showed me his palm in surrender.

"I don't dare."

We'd come abreast Googin Rock again, and both of us turned to look at it. Borgan stopped.

And I did.

The land whined a question.

In the black surface, a black door opened, and a black mist swirled, gaining shape and substance until a lady stood among the rocky blades above us. She was tall and elegant in her dappled robes, her dark skin shone as if she was lit from within.

Improbably, I knew her: the Opal of Dawn, Princess Leynore of Daknowyth.

Her sightless blue eyes turned unerringly upon us.

"I'm happy to see you, Princess Leynore," I said, with complete truth.

"Princess Kaederon," she answered, "I am happy to see you. And you also, Prince Borgan."

"Evenin'," said Borgan easily.

"Mind telling me what you're doing, here in a World on which the Wise have closed the Gate?"

"Ah, in my Land, we say that a Gate never closes, but a door opens," she said, her smile showing dainty fangs. "The war is won, and the Worlds are again in alignment." She curtseyed, irony plain.

"I renew my invitation to both of you to come to me, as your duties allow. We have much to speak of, I think."

"I might take you up on that," I said. "Winter's long, and visiting passes the time."

"Then I await winter, and your visit, with anticipation. Until then."

She curtseyed again, the shadows swirled, and I heard a quiet *snick*, as if a door had, gently, been closed.

"Well," Borgan said, eventually, "there's news."

"Good news?" I asked, as we continued our walk.

"Have to wait and see."

We walked in silence for a bit, the land gamboling around us, then Borgan lifted his head.

"Is that Andy's guitar I hear?"

The land brought me the sound, and I smiled.

"I do believe it is—and Mother's dulcimer, too."

"Gonna be a hell of a party."

"Good. We earned it."